"If Tom Clancy were to write a Christian novel, it might read very much like *Blood Moon Rising*. With weapons savvy adding realism to a gripping plot, this page-turner transcends the many 'prophecy' novels currently flooding the market. Against settings that range from Arizona to Mexico and Iraq, Wiggin's arsenal runs the gamut from syringes of asp venom to the neutron bomb as his busy protagonist couple saves Chicago (and probably the U.S.) from anthrax annihilation. Too exotic for credibility? It's more like too close for comfort!"

Paul L. Maier
Author of *A Skeleton in God's Closet*

ERIC E. WIGGIN

BLOOD MOON RISING

ERIC E. WIGGIN

BLOOD MOON RISING

BROADMAN
&HOLMAN
PUBLISHERS

Nashville, Tennessee

0-8054-2028-2

Published by Broadman & Holman Publishers, Nashville, Tennessee
Editorial Team: Leonard G. Goss and John Landers
Page Design and Typesetting: PerfecType, Nashville, Tennessee

Unless otherwise noted, Scripture quotations
are from the King James Version.
Quotations marked NIV are from the Holy Bible, New International
Version, copyright © 1973, 1978, 1984 by International Bible Society.

Dewey Decimal Classification: 813
Subject Heading: CONTEMPORARY FICTION
Library of Congress Cataloging Number: 99-047794

Library of Congress Cataloging-in-Publication Data

Wiggin, Eric E.
   Blood moon rising / Eric E. Wiggin
   p.   cm.
   ISBN 0-8054-2028-2 (pbk.)
   I. Title
PS3573.I383 B56 2000
813'.54—dc21

                                               99-047794
                                               CIP

1 2 3 4 5 04 03 02 01 00

Contents

PROLOGUE

Though the Waters Overflow

In that day there shall be a highway out of Egypt to Assyria,
and . . . Israel [shall] be the third with Egypt and with Assyria
. . . [and] the LORD of hosts shall . . . [say], "Blessed be . . .
Assyria the work of my hands, and Israel mine inheritance."
—Isaiah, writing during the reign of King Hezekiah

Nineveh, Assyria   **August, 612 B.C.**

Ishtari's slender young fingers shook as she held the silken curtain cord up for Hniqi's inspection. She had tied it into a crude,
yet horribly effective slipknot.

"Please come *now!* We can hang ourselves together and go to
your God Yahweh in the afterlife," the sobbing girl begged. Wide-
eyed, she peered into the young widowed queen's lovely, tear-
stained face. "But you—a Jewish princess—you should not weep to
see the Babylonians destroy our great Assyrian city of Nineveh!"

"I . . . I . . . I'm afraid of the chamberlains, like you. King
Sardanapalus has ordered that we, his wives and family, be put to
death before the Babylonians can reach us," Hniqi added quickly. She
fought her own fright, trying to appear calm. A couple of the royal

1

harem ladies had already strangled themselves, and their warm bodies dangled from cords on tapestry hooks. Other wives and concubines screamed to Asshur or Bel for deliverance. The women were terrified of the bloodthirsty Babylonian warriors as well as the king's heartless chamberlains—sexless eunuchs charged with guarding the house of the women, but now commanded to slay them all.

An infant wailing in the nursery nearby was cut off midcry.

"What can our suicide solve?" Hniqi protested. Queen Hniqi fought to regain her composure as she answered the fourteen-year-old concubine's awful plea. "Think about the others, those wretched thousands being slaughtered outside this palace wall." Hniqi's voice quaked. "We must pray for them now."

Ishtari blubbered on, her face contorted in anguish. "If you still love me, hurry!" she shrieked at the beautiful, bronze-haired Jewess. "We can hold hands and die together before the king's eunuchs get to us with their horrid scimitars!" Ishtari glanced at the rattling gates, then returned her gaze to Hniqi. Searching the young widow's features for an answer, she held up the heavy, gold-braided cord she had fashioned into a deadly noose.

"Would that rope really be easier than letting one of the king's chamberlains slit my throat?" Queen Hniqi quietly queried. "Very soon we shall meet our Lord Yahweh in Abraham's bosom—if you believe in Him."

"Abraham . . . he was your ancestor—dead Hezekiah, the king of Judah, your grandfather, princess. You . . . you speak as though we should expect to meet them today," Ishtari sobbed. "Since the day I made Yahweh my God, I . . . I . . ."

"All must die—even those of us who love Yahweh," Hniqi murmured. The unbridled fear in the young slave-wife's face tore at her loving heart. With so much wretched, horrible death surrounding them, Hniqi had no more time for self-pity. She dried her own tears on her silken sleeve.

Hniqi's blue eyes searched the teen beauty's tear-swollen black ones. She turned away to glance around the large main boudoir of the Assyrian king's harem. *Do these young wives and concubines truly expect to stand before the living God this evening?* Hniqi considered. She listened a moment to the cursing and beating of the armed eunuchs as they bashed through the flimsy barricade of broken furniture with which they had barred the gates. *These women's consciences cried out that they could soon expect to meet their Maker and Judge,* Hniqi believed. *Have any of these girls, except Ishtari, received my witness during my years in this dreadful place?*

Hniqi shuddered even now at the decadence she had seen here. While still a young teen, she had been given away as a bride by her father, Judah's King Manasseh, to cement a political alliance with Ashurbanipal, then the Assyrian emperor.

Hniqi returned her gaze to Ishtari. "We are equals now, you and I. I am no longer the widowed queen of Ashurbanipal's vast realm and the young stepmother of your husband, the spoiled King Sardanapalus. These human relationships exist only for time. But we shall this evening quickly step into eternity.

"Nor does it matter to God that I, granddaughter of King Hezekiah, am a Jewish princess of the House of David," Hniqi added. She fingered the polished, six-pointed golden pendant hanging at her bosom. "Tonight we shall both meet Yahweh, Maker of heaven and earth—He who made us both in His image. All that we were in this life is now vanishing before our eyes like a paper scroll consumed in a brazier of glowing coals."

"Ishtar—she was once my god . . ." Ishtari's voice trailed off.

"Ishtar is only an image carved from stone." Hniqi spoke plainly, yet softly and warmly, to the frightened girl. Hniqi put her arms gently around Ishtari's shoulders, pulling the terrified concubine close, mothering her.

"Hniqi, you once tried to tell me about the blood sacrifice furnished by Yahweh, the God who loves humankind—about His Lamb—from that Hebrew book of prophecy you memorized long ago. But though I heard your words, I would not listen then. Please tell me that beautiful story once again," Ishtari begged, calmer now. "I . . . I *do* wish to believe it."

"The very marble tiles on which we now stand in this beautiful house will run red with the blood of Sardanapalus's wives, your blood and mine mingled in as well, ere the moon rises tonight over the River Tigris," Hniqi prophesied. "Whatever woman of this harem who manages to escape the chamberlain's knives will soon face a far more terrible fate—to be abused without mercy by the Babylonians. But you and I shall die quickly with the other women before this can happen. The eunuchs will be swift with us. My son Daniye'l—he also will be slain by them."

Hniqi, her voice hushed, went on. "The Babylonians will discover our silent corpses in the morning and burn them. They will use the cedar rafters and beams of this building for kindling wood." In her heart, Hniqi wished to be sure Ishtari was finally facing reality. Whether one dies in peace in old age or by violence in youth—one dies. What is important is that one is ready.

"But there is blood *already* shed for us—for *all my* sins." Ishtari cut Hniqi off, recalling Hniqi's teaching. "'Yahweh has caused the sins of us all to be placed on Him . . . . He was led like a lamb to the slaughter,'" Ishtari whispered, remembering. "You have told me these good words, the prophet Isaiah's promise of a coming Savior, many, *many* times!"

"I *do* believe, Hniqi!" Ishtari cried. "I now shall die without fear!" Ishtari smiled, brushing the ebony ringlets from her beautiful, olive-complected face with a jewelled hand. Then she saw it. "The bull—I . . . I didn't know!" she gasped. "But you are Jewish!"

With her perfectly tapered fingers, Hniqi modestly brushed aside her richly brocaded silken gown to afford Ishtari another brief glimpse. Over Hniqi's heart Ishtari plainly saw the neat, black-ink tattoo of a winged bull, symbol of imperial Assyria, until then protector of the ancient world. "Yes," agreed Hniqi, "I am Assyrian—a Chaldean, too, as was Abraham of Ur, father of our Jewish ancestors. I received this sacred symbol years ago when old Ashurbanipal took me as his bride."

"So did I, when I entered his son Sardanapalus's harem," Ishtari exclaimed. "All his women have them."

"Of course." Hniqi smiled. "Symbols—the Star of David, the Bull of Assyria—they no longer matter," she sighed. "We have Yahweh and His love. That is all that really matters."

"Moth-err!" It was Daniye'l, racing from the nursery. The youth clutched a newborn infant in a linen cloth. The still bloody child bawled lustily.

Life and death—how they mingle in war! raced through Hniqi's brain. "My boy! Where is the child's mother?" she cried.

"One of the old women strangled her to stop her moaning while she gave birth," Daniye'l answered evenly, fighting his shock. "They would have killed him, too, but I threatened them." He passed his mother the baby.

"The eunuchs will never castrate *this* boy as they did you." Hniqi spoke bitterly as her mind reeled back, recalling when she herself bore a child. Then a teen like Ishtari, Hniqi was the reigning queen. She gave birth to Ashurbanipal's youngest son, Daniye'l, right after the great king and renowned scholar had died. Hniqi shuddered to remember how she had escaped being entombed with her dead king and husband only because she carried his child, possibly heir to the throne of Assyria.

But headstrong, dissipated Sardanapalus had seized his father's throne the day after the funeral when he heard that Hniqi had given premature birth to a son in her sorrow. His first official act had been to order the execution or neutering of all his half-brothers. Then for fourteen years he had squandered the empire's vast resources on women and wild parties, weakening Assyria until he could no longer raise a strong army.

It shocked Hniqi even now to think that the son she had hoped would be king was, like the harem chamberlains, himself a eunuch. And in the horror now facing her, Hniqi recalled Isaiah's awful prophecy, which seemed to her an ironic curse. Judean King Hezekiah's male descendants, Isaiah had foretold, would become eunuchs in the house of a pagan king. She and Daniye'l—the same age as Ishtari, the teen concubine of Sardanapalus—were Hezekiah's descendants, princess and prince, mother and son.

Hniqi's hopes for Daniye'l returned and grew over the years, however, as she discovered that her son had his father's love of learning. She had taught him all she could—to recite the five books of Moses by rote, to study Samuel, Isaiah, and the Psalms. Daily, he donned his simple linen tunic and left the house of the women to pore over scrolls of Hebrew, Aramaic, or Greek script; or to ponder the cuneiform historical writings on the thousands of clay tablets in Ashurbanipal's vast library. A trio of highly educated slaves, the Assyrian emperor's imported librarians, included a Greek philosopher, a Hebrew rabbi, and a Chaldean seer. These three learned men were the quick-witted youth's willing schoolmasters.

But now even his scholarly education would come to nothing. They were trapped like rats, waiting a sudden end only moments away.

Hniqi turned her attention to the crying newborn Assyrian prince. "Grandma Hniqi loves you," she murmured. Holding the struggling babe to her bosom, Hniqi peered up at Daniye'l. "You say you *threatened* them?"

Daniye'l half smiled and drew open his tunic to display a wickedly sharp, curved, machete-like scimitar strapped to his slender thigh. "I took it from a chamberlain who scaled the wall thinking to unbar the gates to the women's compound."

"*Took* it? Just like that?"

"With the help of a potted palm." Daniye'l smiled grimly. "After I broke the pot over his sorry bald head, one of the women ran him through the belly with a bronze curtain rod. When I last saw the guy, he was cursing in the name of his god and coughing up blood. The girls were stoning him with broken floor tiles."

Daniye'l paused, and his eyes brightened with hope. "Come with me, Mother! Quick!" Daniye'l pointed toward the plastered brick wall that fronted the moat around the royal palace. "I'll boost you and the baby up—Ishtari, too. The two of you can pull me up after you. It's not all that high!"

"Let's try that!" Ishtari pleaded.

Hniqi did not answer. In here, she knew, they'd die quickly. Earlier that afternoon Sardanapalus's favorite women had been bound, then escorted to his bedchamber to be slain along with the king's best Arabian horses. Their bodies were thrown onto the king's funeral pyre while Sardanapalus let himself be roasted alive. She glanced back over the gates, seeing in horror the thick column of the black smoke of death that rose from the royal bedchamber.

Hugging the orphaned infant prince close, Hniqi considered that she could not swim the moat with a baby in her arms. Tears welled in her eyes. She eyed Ishtari, then Daniye'l, remembering the screams of the two girls grabbed by Babylonian soldiers the moment they paddled across the moat just an hour before. The eunuchs, at least, would not rape them.

The gates shook and groaned. The inside bar cracked in half. Armed, whooping eunuchs burst through, pushing the heap of reed mattresses and carved wooden furniture ahead of them. Women shrieked and screamed as two of the chamberlains, flashing scimitars, scrambled over the pile of rubble and began to execute the dead Assyrian emperor's last command.

"My Ashurbanipal would have fought the Babylonian army to the very end," Hniqi murmured in horrified scorn. "Your father, Daniye'l—*he* was no coward!"

"*Mother! Look!*" gasped Daniye'l. He pointed toward the moat wall—or toward where it had been. The murky waters of the rising River Tigris sloshed around their ankles, growing deeper by the second. The sun-baked earthen bricks and lime plaster of the vast and glorious palace erected by the great conqueror Esarhaddon collapsed and dissolved into clay and sand before their eyes. The flooding Tigris River, dammed up by the Babylonians like its tributary the Koser, now spread across Nineveh's central city. Babylonian soldiers in armor raced for high ground as Assyrian peasants grabbed floating boards for flimsy rafts.

Crimson moonbeams tinted with the ochre dust of the battle slanted across the plain, throwing a ghastly blood-red luminescence onto the rushing current. Yet, like the Nile that protected baby

Moses, dry in his basket of reeds, the gurgling waters seemed to whisper, "Trust us to carry you to safety."

Hniqi clasped a stone pillar with her free hand while Ishtari lost her footing in the sudden surge of water and silt from the moat. A eunuch with a knife tore at her lush, dripping, waist-length black tresses, yanking her half upright.

Daniye'l bellowed and bounded—too late! A bronze dagger a full cubit in length, mercifully razor sharp, flashed death in the moonlight, and the girl's quivering heart fell asleep. Ishtari slipped silently into the loving arms of Yahweh her Savior.

The wiry, beardless young man leaped and swung his borrowed crescent blade. Daniye'l arced the scimitar with both hands at the fat neck of the crouching killer. The chamberlain's severed head splashed into the current and vanished in the crimson flow.

Daniye'l abandoned his weapon and bounded aboard a floating mattress of pressed reeds wrapped in camel's hair cloth. "Mother, run!" he screamed. "Bring the baby! Jump on with me!"

☾☾☾

Sumayl, Iraq   **August 11, 1933**

"Into the tunnel, Saul—now!" With one trembling hand, Miriam dad-Y'esho rammed an ancient, wax-sealed vase into her slender boy's reluctant arms as she clutched her swollen belly with the other. Fighting hot tears, she glanced at his older sister, twelve-year-old Rebecca, silently swimming in her own blood where she had collapsed just inside the door.

Until Rebecca was murdered, Miriam had held hope that her husband, Yohannon, marched off a day ago by Iraqi soldiers, was only being conscripted into the army. Yesterday Miriam had recalled hopefully how Yohannon, a Chaldean Christian, once bravely answered Col. Lawrence of Arabia's call to fight for the British and free their Assyrian homeland from Turkish tyranny. In shock, Miriam now realized that the newly formed Iraqi government had more sinister plans for Yohannon and their family.

"Mother, why do the soldiers want to kill us?" Saul sobbed as he lay on the packed-earth floor. His legs were slid into the narrow tunnel under the wall, though he still resisted his mother's anxious command to crawl through and hide. Great with child, she could not follow him, Saul realized in terror.

"Our Jesus—they have no room for him in the new Kingdom of Iraq," Miriam answered softly, though her stomach was knotted in dread. She fought an urgent need to vomit as she continued. "You, Saul—you must get out with this precious vase! Run like you were the last Assyrian alive on earth!"

A heavy vehicle clattered to a halt just beyond the family's plank door. The shouts of soldiers cut short Miriam dad-Y'esho's plea. From down on her elbows peering into her son's face, she raised herself to her knees. Miriam gazed through tears at her dead daughter. She glanced at the door. "Saul, go! To America!" she screamed.

The death-chatter of a Mauser machine gun and the splatter of plaster and sun-dried bricks ended the mother's desperate, final charge to her boy. Like neat stitches from the treadle Singer in the corner of the room, a regular row of .50-caliber bullets riddled the stuccoed wall and plank door. Three lead slugs caught Miriam in the middle of her back, and she collapsed onto the horror-struck child's curly head.

Saul cradled his mother until her struggles ceased. Then dragging the ancient vase that had held its mysterious tale of his family's roots for two and a half millennia, Saul dad-Y'esho wriggled downward, toward the dry wadi below the village.

America. Wherever that might be—would such a far-off land welcome a homeless Assyrian waif?

⟨⟨⟨

Some two million Assyrians now roam the earth as refugees, driven from their native land during the past eighty years because they adhere to one or another of several eastern versions of

Christianity. Nearly half of these descendants of Shem through his son, Asshur, live in the United States, where they are sometimes identified as Chaldeans. Detroit, San Francisco, and Chicago have large colonies of Assyrians. This latter city is home to the Ashurbanipal Library, named for the library of the great King Ashurbanipal.

This library in Nineveh was the world's greatest treasury of knowledge until destroyed by Babylonia, buried in timeless mud until 1847. The armies of mighty conquerors have marched down the centuries over the mud-caked ruins of the world's once greatest library: Nebuchadnezzar's rapacious Median hordes; Xerxes' ruthless Persians; Alexander's dauntless Greeks; Caesar's plume-helmeted legions; Mohammed's Moors on their jihads; and until recent times, the Turks, finally put to flight by Allenby's khakied Brits and Lawrence's turbaned Arabs. Today, archaeologists are still unlocking the cuneiform-graven secrets of the Magi, buried here since 612 B.C.

Among these modern Assyrian refugees are scholars conversant in Hebrew and other ancient languages, as well as their own Syriac, a near kin to the Aramaic spoken by Daniel and Jesus. Like their ancestors, who were Chaldeans kept in slavery to be seers for Nebuchadnezzar, many modern Assyrians value learning highly (see Daniel 1:4; 2:2).

At the close of the First World War, Great Britain was given a mandate by the League of Nations to establish several new countries in the Middle East along ethnic and religious lines, out of the rubble of the old Ottoman (Turkish) Empire. These modern nations include Israel, Iraq, Turkey, and Egypt.

Several other ethnic/religious groups were promised lands of their own by the British—or believe they were so promised. The Assyrians, through their church's patriarch, petitioned the League of Nations to direct Britain to provide them a national homeland.

The Muslim Kurds, too, claim they were promised a homeland to be called Kurdistan. The Kurds' agony at the hands of Iraqi dictator Saddam Hussein has been well documented in the secular media, though the Kurds themselves once persecuted and killed Christian Assyrians. Armenian Christians, also, were slaughtered by the Turks, probably more than a million of them in a holocaust, until outside nations intervened after the Armistice with Germany in 1918. Today there is a nation called Armenia, a part of the Soviet empire until recently.

But the Assyrians, though probably not massacred in as great numbers as the Armenians and Kurds, have been denied a nation. For the most part, they have been ignored by the media and forgotten by evangelical Christians. Yet they claim:

- common ancestry with the Jews (Abraham was a Chaldean from Ur. His ancestor, Arphaxad, was a brother to Asshur, ancestor of the Assyrians. Asshur and Arphaxad were among the five sons of Shem);
- adherence to Eastern Christianity for some 1,700 years;
- hope in Christ's return, and with it the fulfillment of Isaiah's cryptic prophecy that Assyria and Egypt will be one with Israel, the three nations to be connected by a highway (see Isa. 19:23–25);
- to have been from ancient times protector of dispersed Jews in the Middle East (the ancient winged bull is considered a symbol of safety for those carried on its back—displaced Israel).

❰❰❰

The fictional Saul dad-Y'esho (*dad-Y'esho* means "beloved of Jesus/Y'shua") fled Iraq as a child in 1933 with his precious wax-filled vase, which contained an ancient, hidden scroll. The document was penned about 600 B.C. by Saul dad-Y'esho's ancestor, Hniqi. She was a Jewish princess, granddaughter of Hezekiah and widow of the Assyrian scholar-king Ashurbanipal. She was also mother of the prophet Daniel.

For some years, Saul wandered in eastern Europe. He then made his way to England, where he learned English and shortened his name to Saul Yesho. After the Second World War, Saul joined a group of refugee immigrants bound for the U.S.

The years passed. The old vase, a family heirloom, remained stashed in a trunk. Saul could not bring himself to violate this last remembrance of his murdered mother by breaking through the wax preservative to examine what lay within. The vase was pretty much forgotten.

Saul became a civil engineer and an American citizen. He married. But his wife, a sickly woman, bore him no children. She died, leaving Saul a widower.

So Saul left his most precious belongings, stored in a single trunk, with a married cousin in Boston, a Mrs. Art (Rachel) Towns. In 1971, he enlisted in the U.S. Army, and shortly after this he found himself an Army engineer, in charge of airstrip construction projects for the military in South Vietnam.

In Saigon, Saul married again to a young Vietnamese woman, who was converted to Christ by Christian and Missionary Alliance (C & MA) missionaries. He left her for several weeks to travel into the interior on a tour of duty. But Saul was killed in a Vietcong ambush. His pregnant war bride missed the boat as the last of the Americans and South Vietnamese officials evacuated Saigon/Ho Chi Minh City.

The child of this union was the beautiful, intrepid Nicki Towns, who once in America, adopted the married name of her father's cousin.

—Eric E. Wiggin

1

The South Wind

When you see the south wind blow you say,
"It's going to get hot . . ." You hypocrites, you can interpret
the face of the sky . . . How is it that you
cannot interpret this present time?

—Jesus

Nicki Towns was a lovely, lonely lady genius. A bit crazy, but friendly. Chuck Reynolds drummed his Corvette's steering wheel, thinking. Nicki was not the kind of woman he'd guess might trigger World War III—or even a minor international crisis. Or was she?

The judge who had sentenced Julius and Ethel Rosenberg to death for what J. Edgar Hoover called "the crime of the century" had declared that the Rosenbergs' actions began the Korean War, Chuck recalled. His stomach knotted. He considered that he guarded military secrets capable of turning Earth into a keg of gunpowder. *Could Towns, like Julius Rosenberg's minions, really have slipped past our security web far enough to light the powder keg's fuse? Perhaps the Old Man's imagination is working overtime*, Chuck told himself, fighting fear.

This Friday evening the northbound lanes of Interstate 95 had ground to a crawl. Work-stressed weekend vacationers from Boston who planned to unwind on Massachusetts' north shore, the New Hampshire beaches, or the Maine coast jousted for their piece of the American Pie. Horns blared as drivers saw precious moments ripped from their weekend fun.

Chuck ignored these petty confrontations. His mind raced ahead to a confrontation he expected just up the road. He tried to focus on what his boss, the CEO of Salem Electronics North, had told him on the phone about their new engineer, Nicki Towns. Had Towns by herself managed to gather the components of the Vanguard Missile System?

Paul Revere had a horse, Chuck fumed. He slipped his vintage 'Vette ragtop out of drive to keep the antique, big-block 396 engine from overheating. *And old Revere rode out of Boston to save only a couple of kegs of powder and a few guns. That had started the American Revolution. What I'm trying to save—whew!* A line from "Paul Revere's Ride" hassled his harried brain: "The fate of a nation was riding that night."

Just an hour before, Chuck had been panfrying a T-bone when the phone rang. "We've got a security breach. You know what that could mean," Harry Thompkins had growled on the line.

"Yeah, our new lady scientist has started World War III," Chuck joked. The Old Man sometimes got rattled over little things. Chuck figured he'd just settle him down.

There was a long pause. "You're psychic, Chuck," Thompkins breathed at last. "That's much too close to the truth." Harry actually sounded afraid. That was a side of the Old Man Chuck had not seen before.

Chuck's stomach now churned, trying to digest the greasy fried steak he'd been munching while driving. *If Nicki Towns is involved and I've guessed it,* Chuck pondered, *Harry may believe I'm implicated too.*

Chuck had learned some pretty heavy things about both the CIA and the FBI during eight years as head of North Carolina's

Bureau of Investigation. The Department of Defense could monitor any phone or computer communication transmitted via satellite microwaves or fiber-optic lines. Illegal, maybe—but that would have to wait until the next Congressional investigation. With today's satellite technology, they didn't even need to tap a wire. Chuck's status as chief of security at a military contractor's plant gave the Defense Investigative Services (DIS) plenty of reason to monitor his calls—maybe even tape them and analyze them at security meetings in Washington.

There was compounded irony in this whole cloak-and-dagger secrecy, Chuck realized. It was necessary to keep top-secret, classified Armed Forces data out of the hands of other government agencies. But you were monitored by the Defense Investigative Services for precisely this reason—to make sure you were impenetrable. Once the DIS learned what you were up to, you were called in like a kid caught with cigarettes under the mattress. If they broke your web of secrecy, they assumed foreign agents could also.

And he knew what the Old Man meant by "what that could mean." Salem's just-perfected cutting-edge design for the new Vanguard missile's computerized radio guidance system might have to be scrapped. Millions of dollars in defense-fund contracts could go down the drain. This could sink a small contractor like Salem, which had fewer than a thousand employees.

Months earlier, Chuck had been promoted to chief of security for Salem's New England operations in Salem, Massachusetts. He had moved to Boston's frantic Silicon Beltway from a slow-paced life in Winston-Salem, North Carolina, where he had worked at Salem Electronics South. "You put me here, Lord," Chuck prayed. "It's up to You to see me through." The traffic began to move again as Chuck felt the Lord's peace begin to settle his digestion.

As Chuck drove, he reviewed for the thousandth time, at least, the direction his life had taken—from military chaplaincy in Vietnam to top security levels of an important military hardware plant. *If this security job doesn't work out. . . .* Chuck sighed, mopping a moist eye with the back of his hand. Chuck had been a pastor in a country church in North Carolina. Then he'd lost Shelly to cancer. While trying to sort out his priorities as a widowed dad, he had passed little Jennifer over to her grandparents in Maine, only an evening's drive north of suburban Boston. After years in police work, then in private security, could he ever return to the ministry?

That *salem* is a variant spelling of *shalom,* the Hebrew word for "peace," had not escaped Chuck's imagination. Protecting American military interests would help ensure peace in the world. Right now, though, Salem Electronics North hardly seemed synonymous with peace.

The traffic, barely up to 30 mph, ground to a halt again short of the crest of a hill. As Chuck waited, he considered one of Nicki Towns's wild theories about the future, which she had shared during their one date. Nicki, perhaps the most brilliant physicist Chuck had ever met, was also an avid reader of Old Testament Bible prophecy. Though a religious skeptic, she seemed to enjoy bouncing her ideas about the future off of Chuck. *If only I could get that lady interested in New Testament Christianity,* Chuck mused.

Nicki seemed obsessed with her notion that the United States might be the clay-iron feet supporting the prophetic image in Nebuchadnezzar's dream in Daniel chapter two. Democracy, she reasoned, was the human clay that weakened the iron of strong government.

"America is basically a democratic nation," she had reminded Chuck, almost in awe of her own observation. "And doesn't the North Atlantic Treaty Organization—NATO—really make the United States an empire?" Nicki's green eyes had gleamed as she spoke, as if this were the greatest revelation since St. John's apocalyptic visions on Patmos. "Gore Vidal thinks so," she said. She pulled an article from her purse in which the famous author had reached that very conclusion. This seemed to clinch her argument.

Nicki is perceptive, though a mite nutty, Chuck had decided. He knew, of course, that Bible scholars viewed this image of gold, silver, bronze, iron, and clay as a prophecy of the world empires of Babylonia, Persia, Greece, and Rome. The feet were thought by many students of prophecy to represent a revival of the Roman Empire, just before Christ's return. Christ, the Stone, would destroy the image's weak feet of clay and iron at His Second Coming.

Chuck swung the 'Vette to the shoulder and tooled along for several hundred yards, ignoring the glares of stranded motorists as he topped the grade. He could be ticketed, but right now national security was a bigger concern. A bridge abutment ended his holiday from the traffic jam, and he tucked back in. The entire northbound roadway was blocked while a wrecker plucked a minivan from a rear-ender in the inside lane.

Chuck sighed, then reached for his cell phone to call Thompkins. *Oh, no! Wrong jacket! My company ID is in my other coat too.*

He slid the shift lever to park once more and closed his eyes. *That was quite a tale Nicki told about her ancestor who escaped from the Assyrian royal harem in Nineveh just ahead of Nebuchadnezzar's brutal Babylonian soldiers,* Chuck mused. If there was any truth to that, she would be part Jewish—a descendant of King David. Maybe a distant cousin of the prophet Daniel. Chuck recalled her strange story as he tried to imagine what she might have done to upset the Old Man. *Am I really on my way to avert . . . to avert what? A global war?* he considered.

2

Desperate Measures

Things are not what they seem.

—Longfellow

L ook at this." Thompkins passed Chuck a crisply photocopied
document with a "TOP SECRET" designation clearly marked,
top and bottom.

Chuck had made himself thoroughly familiar with the tech-
nological principles of the military designs he was guarding. Even
so, it took him a few moments to realize that he was studying a
miniature, lightweight nuclear reactor designed to create a powerful thrust engine for a jet propulsion system, perhaps for use in an
aircraft. Mach 30 plus, the specs indicated, was the expected flight
speed of a craft powered by this engine. Nearly ten times the speed
of the famed Blackbird intercontinental spy plane. "This . . . this is
unbelievable."

"Turn it over," Thompkins snapped.

Chuck flipped the paper. Here was a photo of a bullet-shaped rocket mounted on a large workbench inside what looked like an aircraft hangar. Distinctly painted on the fuselage of the missile was "Falcon Aviation—Prototype 16-B—VANGUARD." "Falcon of Tucson? *We're* not even supposed to know what the Vanguard will look like!" Something much bigger than a document pilfered from Salem was afoot.

Thompkins nodded and smiled weakly.

"You . . . *we* could go to prison for this. Where did you get it?"

"Not likely for that alone. Perhaps for *this!*" He tapped an inch-thick dossier of papers bound with a spring clip on his desk. "The document you are holding, which our friends at Falcon apparently haven't yet missed, was stuck on the bottom of *these!*" He held them up to make his point.

"May I see them?" Chuck was cold with sweat now. Though the Old Man had made no accusations, somebody may actually have gotten their hands on enough sensitive data to start World War III. The Vanguard was the U.S. Air Force's new ATW—its Advanced Tactical Weapon. It was being designed to carry a nuclear warhead, or, if it fell into the wrong hands, the payload could be a biological weapon—enough anthrax to wipe out the population of Moscow or New York. Except at the Air Force's top-secret White Sands Missile Range in New Mexico, no single team of scientists was supposed to be privy to more than one system of the Vanguard, Chuck realized. Falcon was building the propulsion system, and Salem was building the radio-guidance system. Who the other manufacturers were, Harry Thompkins or even Chuck Reynolds could only guess until now. Exactly what the others were designing—it was out of the question for them to know.

The Old Man passed Chuck the papers, then perched on the edge of his chair, eyeing him warily.

Chuck flipped through the dossier. The knot in his stomach grew tighter as he learned, page by page, that the vital, specialized information was pretty much all there—not only Salem's part of the operation, but documents filched from several other plants as well. "And you found this where?" he asked at last.

"Nicki Towns. We took it from her about an hour after you left work today. We fired her and a guard after a secretary reported that she was photocopying classified documents without authorization. Apparently she sweet-talked her way past the guy—told him she'd left her key card in her office. Towns was told to bring the stuff back or face prosecution."

"Towns?—our whiz-kid lady physicist? You were babbling about her when you phoned me—something about her walking off with enough stuff to start another war."

"Was I? *You* were the one who named the larcenous lady!"

"Hey—she's new here. Her name came to mind because at first I figured you were overreacting. You've done it before." Chuck held up his hands. "Anyway, you were supposed to assign her to designing circuit boards for our contract with Packard Bell's computer division. She doesn't have clearance! She's seen stuff she had no right to see, and for all we know she's made duplicates. She should have been arrested on the spot!" Chuck was sweating. He had eaten lunch in the plant cafeteria with this unusual Asian lady a couple of times, and Harry knew this. Though this had no bearing on the case, Chuck realized he might be implicated.

"We checked the page counter on the photocopier she used," the Old Man spat out, still defensive, though not now accusing Chuck. "We know she made only one copy, and I personally drove to her apartment, with a security guard along, to get the papers. She was just getting out of her car when we drove up, and she gave us everything in her briefcase. Reynolds, she *couldn't* have copied the papers on the way home—no time. I'm sure of it." Thompkins shrugged. It finally had sunk in that he was implicated too.

"Couldn't have copied them!" Chuck exploded. "But did she *read* them? Julius Rosenberg's brother-in-law *memorized* the design for the plutonium bomb in '45—and he hadn't even been to college! Besides, what might she have taken home before?"

"We check the counter on that copy machine against the log *every day*. That counter *can't* be bypassed. There's just no evidence . . ." Harry shook his head. "I've got to call a report in to the Defense Department anyway," he added crossly. "Need to cover our tails. And they've gotta know about the Falcon document and the other papers." Harry reached for the phone on his desk.

"Don't—not yet," Chuck warned. *Harry's really rattled*, Chuck thought. *I've warned him several times there's no way to make our phones secure from government snooping.* The security interests of the people of the United States were at stake. Chuck realized that the Feds trusted nobody.

Uncomfortably he remembered the Soviet Embassy building in Washington, where microwave receptor dishes on the roof monitored the phone calls of U.S. government officials for KGB spies for months until the State Department found an effective means to interfere with the Russians' reception. If the Soviets had not been so brazen and instead had hidden the dishes inside their attic out of sight, American military secrets might still be going to Moscow in the microseconds it took for the messages to travel across Washington.

Chuck knew he now had to take charge, whether the Old Man liked it or not. First, he and Harry had to get a handle on things so they could have a neat package of details to report to Washington if it became necessary to inform the Pentagon or the FBI.

"I think we could both use a break," Chuck sighed. "My treat." They had to get out of the office, he decided, to a place where they could talk, safe from worries about being monitored and second-guessed by Washington bureaucrats who might want to advance their own careers. The Federal government's Defense Investigative Services, Chuck believed, not only monitored defense contractors' phone calls, but sometimes even bugged the offices of their clients.

Cappy's Chowder House, minutes from Salem Electronics North's plant, was right on the waterfront in Marblehead. This late in the evening the place would be virtually deserted, except for late-night boozers at the bar. A far-corner table would afford them privacy without danger from eavesdroppers—electronic or otherwise.

The restaurant had become a favorite with Chuck soon after he'd moved north. Once, Chuck had taken Nicki Towns there for lobster and shrimp. Except for the times they had met in the plant cafeteria, that had been the extent of their relationship. Period. Nicki, an independent soul, had even insisted on paying for her own meal.

Chuck now wondered if she hadn't been setting him up, though they had never discussed Salem's business. But no point in bothering Harry with this information, Chuck decided.

Nicki, Chuck had learned, was more or less religious, though apparently she had no church connections. She seemed to hold to a strange mixture of Jewish and Christian beliefs. Nicki had virtually a fanatical faith in an obscure, almost cryptic prophecy in Isaiah about ancient Assyria. "Chuck," Nicki had said that evening, boring into him with those unfathomable green eyes that turned luminescent when she became excited, "one day, the Assyrians will once again rule the mountain land God gave the children of Shem, Noah's oldest son. They were defeated by Babylonia at Haran in 612 B.C. But a century before this, the prophet declared that Assyria, like Israel, is 'the work of Yahweh's hands.'" In an almost inaudible whisper she'd added, "God cannot lie!"

"You evangelicals," Nicki had chuckled, "believe in a Millennium in which Christ will reign over the whole earth. And so do I." She had then continued with her fantastic tale about how a Jewish princess had escaped the destruction of Nineveh 2,600 years ago. The princess had rescued an infant Assyrian prince. Nicki claimed to be descended somehow from both the princess and the prince—as well as related to Daniel the prophet.

Is Nicki trying to disarm me by agreeing with my beliefs? Chuck had wondered. "What do you believe about Christ, Nicki?" he then pressed.

"I believe," she pursed her lips, thinking. "I believe that Jesus died—and that He rose from the grave three days later to set mankind free to love one another." As if an afterthought, she added, "But the idea that we are all sinners, condemned to hell unless we believe—that's a bit much for an intelligent mind to swallow." Nicki smiled confidently.

Chuck smiled back. "A lot of folks agree with you, I realize."

In the weeks since that conversation, Chuck had had no further chance to chat with Nicki about spiritual matters. Sensing that she was avoiding him, he had kept his distance, dealing with her only as one professional to another.

Cappy's though, had become a habit with Chuck. It was a place where he could reflect on the new directions his life had taken in the past decade. From a corner booth he would from time to time use his cell phone to chat with his teenage daughter, Jennifer, living with Shelly's mother and stepfather in Maine. Here also, he would wrestle with his frustration that the most beautiful and desirable woman he had known in years was caught up in an offbeat belief.

But was everything Nicki believed so crazy? Chuck read Isaiah nineteen and twenty through several times himself, and now her notions didn't seem all that loony.

So, out of habit, with Harry as his passenger, Chuck this evening pointed his old ragtop 'Vette toward the chowder house.

(((

"What do we know about Nicki Towns, our new physicist?" Chuck stared at the top of Harry's balding head, watching him shuck a steamer clam, waiting for the Old Man's answer. Chuck had ordered only coffee for himself. Seeing this native New Englander devour clams "guts and all" left Chuck with little appetite for anything else.

"You've been out with Towns," Harry accused. He raised an eyebrow as if to say Chuck should answer his own question. "Our personnel department turned up some interesting details in Ms. Towns's résumé just yesterday," Harry admitted when Chuck did not answer. "A name change—it doesn't look good."

"I ought to have been told at once." Chuck shook his head. He decided, though, that this was no time to rub it in. Harry might lose his job as Salem's CEO and bring the firm down with him if the board of directors believed he sat on this knowledge even a day too long. Or the Pentagon. Especially the Pentagon.

"I know," Harry answered glumly. "Our Ms. Towns is also Ngo 'Nicki' Thieu, which once may have been her legal name. And I'd guess she has used a couple of aliases along the way, as well." Harry pulled a thick folder marked "Towns" from his briefcase and pushed it at Chuck. "I was about to take this home and review it, but in light of this afternoon's developments, I guess we'd better look at it together tonight."

"All night, if we need it," Chuck sighed. He was not used to seeing his boss at less than his usual self-confident, in-command best. "Wow!" Chuck murmured moments later, glancing over a dozen letters from references. "Seven jobs in four years—and all of them with major military contractors. But how?" Chuck knew the answer, though he goaded his boss with the question. No firm would ever admit publicly that an employee had walked off with sensitive documents. Once word leaked to Congress and the media that a mole had gotten into your system, you were usually through. Billions of dollars in contracts depended on pretense to a high level of security. "So they just quietly asked her to resign whenever they caught up with her." Chuck groaned aloud.

"Seems personnel departments just routinely file reference letters as they come in. Our personnel manager—like those at a lot of industries, I'm sure—waits until there's been time to accumulate a collection. It may take a month or two. By then he's busy interviewing prospects for jobs—graduate engineers and the like. So another month can slip by."

"I've read that the State Department knew about the Rosenberg's membership in the Communist Party USA years before the FBI hauled them in for questioning," Chuck said bitterly. "See here," he whispered, "two years ago she spent four months at Farmall, in Fort Wayne, Indiana." Chuck glared at Harry

Thompkins. "Her file ought to have been on my desk the day I came here!"

"Farmall? I don't get it." Thompkins ignored Chuck's accusation.

"A Farmall is a tractor." Chuck collected his thoughts and forced a laugh. As a boy in North Carolina's Piedmont hills, he'd learned to plow the red clay hillsides with his grandfather's big red Farmall. "They're made by International Harvester."

"Oh. You mean . . ."

"The old Harvester heavy-truck plant in Fort Wayne is where Operation Farmall is underway," Chuck explained. He bit his tongue, for this was classified information a CIA agent had only accidentally let slip one day at Salem South. "Since I'm not supposed to know that, I guess I shouldn't have told you," he sighed.

"You mean . . . that's the Pentagon's HQ for the Vanguard Missile's Systems Integrator?"

"Their SI? Could be." Chuck nodded. "If that's so, then the operation at Farmall is more secretive than NASA's labs at Huntsville, Alabama, or any Air Force project in New Mexico."

"Then . . . then Towns's résumé is a paper trail leading us back to each plant where a component for the Vanguard is being designed or built?" Harry rubbed his balding head. "This . . . this stuff happens . . . but . . . but it's supposed to be the other guy that . . ."

Chuck was silent, thoughtful. His countenance, however, agreed with Harry's conclusion.

Harry shuddered visibly. "I remember hearing that Joe Stalin knew about the Manhattan Project at Los Alamos, New Mexico, as early as March 1945. The head of the Soviet Union knew about the atomic bomb before our own president, Harry Truman!"

"Well, at least we don't have the Russians looking down our necks *this* time." Somehow, though, Chuck could not believe things were that simple. In this business, *someone* was always watching, and he knew it. If the Russians were not watching already, they would try soon enough.

"Do you realize that if Roosevelt hadn't died in April '45, we'd have had a Soviet Japan by the end of the year—and probably for the next forty years?" Harry was off on one of his historical speculations again.

"Is this one of your revisionist theories?" Chuck joked, grasping for a lighter moment. "Do we really need a history lesson right now?"

"Revisionism is the department of Peter Jennings at ABC News," Harry wisecracked sardonically. "The Russians had plans to invade Japan on August 14, 1945, the day after Hirohito and his war lords surrendered to MacArthur," he rambled on, as if trying to drown the present with thoughts of the past. "But I think if it had been Roosevelt with Alger Hiss whispering in his ear, meeting at Potsdam in July '45 with Stalin and Churchill—rather than Truman—Roosevelt would have cracked under Stalin's bluffing. To FDR, Stalin was 'Good old Joe.' Franklin Delano Roosevelt would have told the Russians to go ahead and take Tokyo in the fall like they took Berlin in the spring. But American intelligence figured such a ground forces invasion of Japan would cost maybe a million lives. That's D-Day's Omaha Beach multiplied nearly two hundred times!"

"What does all that mean for us tonight?" Chuck was puzzled, impatient.

"It means—could mean—that like the untimely death of one man, Roosevelt, on April 12, 1945, changed the course of the twentieth century, today's events may change the course of the twenty-first," the Old Man rumbled.

"That's what I like about you, Harry," quipped Chuck. "When things begin to fall apart, you really put them in perspective."

"Well, in twenty-four hours this thing will be behind us. We'll be laughing about the war that almost was." It was Harry's turn to try dry humor.

"Or the world's powers will be huddled at another Potsdam summit while we're rotting in jail." Chuck was not joking now. "I recall that Stalin didn't think President Truman had the guts to use the bomb. But as an old gunnery captain who'd just toured the destruction of Berlin, Truman understood war, and he knew what his options were." Chuck knew his history, too. "So what do we know about what this Nicki Towns is capable of? Our personnel manager may have unloaded on us the biggest mole since Julius and Ethel Rosenberg—is that what you're trying to say?"

"*Doctor* Nicki Towns is an MIT *summa cum laude* with a Ph.D.—graduated first in her class. I checked that by phone myself the day we put her to work," Harry continued. He sighed. "She was Ngo Thieu then."

"Figures," said Chuck. "Legal name change? Been married, maybe?"

Harry shrugged. "MIT's student records have her both ways. Never married, though, apparently. We can't hire engineers fast enough to fill our positions," he added lamely.

"And 'Thieu'?" Chuck pressed.

"The name is Vietnamese—she was born in Vietnam shortly before Nixon pulled our troops out. But she lists herself as an Assyrian of Iraqi ancestry. Apparently her father was a naturalized American. And last year she used her passport to travel to Nairobi, in Kenya, East Africa."

"But not to Iraq?"

"No. And no Communist countries. Not even a visit to Vietnam."

"We can be glad of that, at least." Chuck slumped into his chair and sighed, exhausted by the thoughts troubling him. "I've got to report to the Pentagon in Washington, tomorrow at the latest," he slowly enunciated. "Nothing else will do," he said, finally comprehending the sloppiness of Salem's screening processes. "And let's pray that she doesn't have any ties to Saddam."

"Will you report by person or by phone? Or maybe you need to pray about it first?" Harry's joke was not intended as sarcasm. Though he sometimes teased Chuck about his Christian standards, Harry genuinely appreciated Chuck's high principles.

Chuck smiled, then turned serious again. "If I phone, they'll order me to come in now." He shook his head. "You need to call the FBI tonight yourself. Perhaps Towns can be picked up before she skips the country. I should have let you call from your office."

"Maybe we can try some damage control on our own."

"Wouldn't think of it." *Honor is honor,* thought Chuck. Yet it wrenched his heart to see Harry squirm so. *What would Jesus do?* he asked himself. The odds were that an honest man was about to be ruined financially. Harry might even go to prison merely for trusting a careless personnel manager too much. And Chuck could wind up in jail with him.

"Chuck." Harry's voice was fraught with pathos, pleading. "Towns isn't going to run. She's been getting away with this for too long. She thinks we'll be too embarrassed to call in the Feds, like the others."

"Well—what do you have in mind?" Even then, rattling in the far recesses of his mind was the fear that this Nicki Towns, alias Ngo Thieu, might have gotten away with enough data to let some screwloose, tinhorn dictator in Libya or Iraq or who-knows-where in Africa or the Middle East or South America or Eastern Europe deliver a nuclear or anthrax bomb on Washington or Moscow or Jerusalem or on whomever he happened to be mad at at the moment.

"I want to put you on a flight to Tucson at Logan Airport tonight," Harry insisted. "Take Towns's personnel file with you. I'll phone Falcon Aviation and let them know you're coming. We'll get their CEO or head of security to talk with you tomorrow morning. Let's hope you and their people can come up with a report that will satisfy the FBI. If together we can't stop this Ms. Towns, then I'll take the fall myself. Anyway, if we can show that we've helped nail a crook who's filched documents from perhaps half a dozen other companies and maybe from Operation Farmall, the Justice Department will go that much easier on the both of us."

"I can see myself sitting in the Tucson jail tomorrow while the FBI is deciding what to charge me with." Chuck shook his head in dismay. "You're right, though. Falcon's people could be arrested too—unless we can help each other by setting Towns up for prosecution on espionage charges."

"That's all we *can* do." Harry spread his hands in a gesture of resignation.

"I've got to phone the Pentagon tonight, though," Chuck insisted. "They've *got* to get onto this case at once."

"Suppose this is just a fluke? We'd look pretty stupid, and once it gets back to the Air Force, I'm washed up as a military contractor. Maybe this Towns lady is just a smart chick who collects top secret documents for an ego trip, like those Manhattan Project engineers caught taking atomic bomb parts home for ash trays. We fired an engineer only last year for using a secret military design to wire his home appliances for remote control. What a nerd!"

"A possibility, I suppose. And I've heard that ash tray story. Even Ethel Rosenberg's brother had one. But where there's a body, the first assumption is murder."

"Or a grave robbery."

"Get real, man. I'll make you one concession, though. I'll hold the phone call until I'm on the plane. I think you're right that I should go to Tucson. I'd like to talk to those guys about our Ms. Towns, myself. At any rate, if I were to phone the Air Force brass from here, they'd order me directly to Washington or have the FBI pick me up the moment I got home. Your only chance of getting off the hook would then evaporate. I'll catch the earliest afternoon flight from Tucson to Washington tomorrow. The Pentagon will insist on a debriefing the same day."

"I can live with that," Harry sighed. "Anything beats a congressional investigation and you on C-SPAN for a week." Harry forced a hollow laugh.

"One other thing. I'll need that document from Falcon Aviation. It's the main evidence we have that Towns is a spy, and it's pretty damning. I must insist on taking the *only* copy—no photocopies for Salem's files."

"You'll get it." Harry sounded relieved, almost ebullient, Chuck thought. "I tucked it into my briefcase before I left the office." He pulled the document out and slipped it into the personnel file on the table.

◖◖◖

As the DC-10 circled over Boston Bay to gain altitude for the nonstop, late-night flight to Tucson, Chuck picked up the phone folded into the seat ahead of him. He dialed, punching in first the home phone of retired General Armstrong MacAdams, USAF, in Reston, Virginia, then his own phone credit card number. Chuck fretted, recalling that he last used MacAdams's number two years ago when head of North Carolina criminal investigation. He wondered how the general would receive a call at 1 A.M. from a civilian who had no official connection to a law enforcement agency.

But Chuck needn't have been concerned. MacAdams, who had known Chuck from their days together in Vietnam, treated him like an old friend. After Chuck switched his cell phone to a scrambled security channel, MacAdams even asked permission before turning his recorder on. "We'll see you at dinner tomorrow evening, then," MacAdams cordially concluded after five minutes of listening to Chuck explain matters. "I'll personally deliver my tape of this conversation to the Pentagon at seven in the morning." MacAdams, a special technical adviser to the military, agreed. "I don't believe this one needs a priority call in the middle of the night," he added warmly.

Chuck tipped his first-class reclining chair back as far as it would go and fell asleep at once.

◖◖◖

An extra shirt and toilet articles that he kept in his office closet, along with an old blazer for emergencies, was the extent of Chuck's gear—besides his briefcase and a cellular phone borrowed from Harry—when he stepped off the plane in Tucson. Chuckling at the harried tourists who crowded around the baggage carousel, he hurried to a quiet corner and pulled out the cell phone. Harry had of course phoned already, but Chuck decided it might be a good idea to know in advance just whom he was supposed to meet.

A young, muscular Hispanic in sunglasses and natty pin-stripes lounged against a pillar partway across the lobby. There was nothing particularly suspicious about the guy, Chuck decided. He didn't look like a tourist, though, nor did he seem to be waiting for anybody in particular. Chuck noticed that he had a Mexican street gang tattoo between his thumb and forefinger.

The symbol appeared to be a crescent moon outlined in red, Chuck thought, as the man raised his hand. *Odd. I've seen stars, crosses—never a moon as a gang sign.* And the man's hair was cut unusually close for a Mexican.

Chuck saw something else, though, which did make him uncomfortable. Not quite concealed in the man's palm was a compact canister, like a tiny pepper gas weapon he had seen women carrying on the Boston subways.

Why does he need that? Chuck worried. Suddenly it occurred to him that a weapon effective to ward off muggers might also be used to immobilize a tourist while the mugger made off with his bags. *Perhaps I should notify security,* Chuck considered as the man swaggered away, his fancy rattlesnake-skin riding boots clicking along the corridor tiles.

Chuck soon had a secretary at Falcon on the line. "Yes sir, Mr. Reynolds," she chirped, "Mr. Epperson, our chief of security, is expecting you. And we've sent a limo for you—it should be waiting outside the Delta Airlines entrance right now," she told him warmly.

"*Como esta usted, señor* Reynolds?"

Chuck knew a little Spanish, but this greeting caught him by surprise. *Funny accent—odd,* he mused. *Not Mexican. Colombian, maybe?* Instinctively, Chuck backed against the wall. *If the guy has an accomplice, I won't give him a chance to step behind me,* Chuck determined. "*No habla español.*" Chuck shrugged, feigning ignorance.

The guy grinned, extending his hand. "Your briefcase. I carry it."

Chuck recognized him as the young man whom minutes earlier he'd taken for a slick punk. *But he called me 'Señor Reynolds.' He knows my name. Still. . . .*

"No thanks, driver. Just take me to your car."

Then from the corner of his eye Chuck caught a deft maneuver of the guy's other hand. Action for the next half second seemed to run like a slow-motion replay in TV football, Chuck remembered afterward. The man came at him with the handheld gas bomb. But instead of the expected spray in the face, the assailant tried to get his hand under Chuck's jacket. Oddly, he had slipped a latex glove on while Chuck was on the phone.

Chuck grabbed the guy's knuckles, then with his other hand he wrenched the man's wrist away while kneeing him in the groin. He knew the guy might pull a gun or a knife with his free hand. Chuck's police academy self-defense training flashed into focus.

Something in Chuck's subconscious warned him that this could be a far more lethal hazard than a firearm, and he made a lightning decision. Chuck turned the canister against his attacker's chest, then pressed the guy's thumb—hard. The spray made a damp spot on the man's shirt.

Chuck heard the hiss, but oddly no strangling cloud of vapor or stinging pepper odor assaulted his nostrils.

The thug released the bomb, then collapsed as if he'd been struck behind the head with a lead pipe, his jaw slack, his eyes wide.

Chuck scooped up his briefcase with one hand and the canister with the other, dropping it into his jacket pocket. As Chuck bent over, to his horror he saw that the young assailant lay quiet, not breathing, his eyes dilated in a stare of death.

Before a crowd could gather, Chuck hurried toward a row of taxis waiting just outside the wall of glass. In seconds he could feel his knees turning to jelly. Only by sheer force and prayer did he stagger into the nearest cab. "Hyatt Regency," Chuck gasped, uttering the name of the first hotel that came to mind. *Falcon's limo rides too rough today,* Chuck thought as he drifted into unconsciousness.

3

Divided Loyalties

Who is my neighbor?

—A certain lawyer

*N*ot . . . the . . . Hyatt . . . Regency, thought Chuck. The room turned slowly around his bed. He had an IV line in his left arm, and his head felt like an overripe melon. *I've been hit with something meaner than a pit bull,* he painfully considered. Chuck squinted into the desert sunlight flooding his room, then he passed out again.

How many hours—or days—he'd slept Chuck could only guess. His head seemed clearer now, so he opened his eyes. The clock on his wall read 10:10. At night. Outside he could see only streetlights outlining a distant, palm-shaded parking lot.

Arizona, Chuck recalled. Fear swept over him as the events just before he collapsed into the taxi began to come back.

Thirsty. Chuck spotted a glass of water with a straw on the rolling table that was swung partly across his bed. *Apparently the nurses don't expect me to sit up right away,* he decided. But when he tried to reach the glass with his right hand, Chuck was shocked to find himself handcuffed to the steel bed frame.

His first thought was to ring for a nurse. But his years as head of a state investigative division had taught Chuck Reynolds to act first, ask questions later.

His left arm, he quickly learned, was also tied down, most likely to keep him from pulling the IV out. But the double wrap of surgical tape offered little resistance to a few well-placed, ripping bites. His IV needle, too, came out easily with his teeth.

"Ouch!" A bruise or a wound under his left arm, just behind the armpit, caught Chuck's attention. It seemed to be bandaged, so he lowered his arm, careful not to tear the tape loose.

Chuck left the cuff in place on his right wrist while he considered his options. Only the police, he realized, would cuff a man to the bed. Probably a cop was sleeping in a lounge chair outside his door right now.

Why am I being held? Murder of the man who tried to kill me at the airport? Chuck shuddered, recalling the assailant's vacant death-stare. Taking a human life, even in self-defense, was not something he wanted to deal with. *Maybe the FBI wants to bring me in?* he considered.

Were his arrest and the attempt on his life related? Chuck realized that if they were, he was in a bigger bind than mere allegation of murdering a mugger who'd got his hands on a rather creative deadly weapon. This was high-tech junk used by international assassins, probably quick-acting nerve gas.

And that Latino was no ordinary street punk, Chuck decided. The Spanish phrases and broken English had been a ruse to get him off his guard, he figured. Perhaps the guy was not even a Latino.

Getting out of the hospital undetected suddenly became Chuck's first priority.

Across the room from where he lay, a steel clothes closet and several drawers were set into the wall. *If I'm lucky, my clothes are in there. And my wallet?* he grimly considered. Chuck did not dare think what might have happened to his briefcase.

He checked the clock again. Not quite 10:30. A new shift of nurses would probably come on duty at midnight. *Maybe they won't check on me for a couple of hours.*

And the cop, whom he was certain sat right outside? *Probably asleep—if I'm lucky.*

But the cuff? Chuck grinned grimly as he pinched the IV line with his left hand, then extracted the needle from the plastic line, again using his teeth. *Better'n a paper clip—look at the size of that sucker*, he thought as he fondled the needle that had been in his left arm. *Considerate of them.* He pushed it into the handcuff keyhole. A deft poke on a spring, and the cuff loosened. A second push, and it fell open. Police academy training had its good points, he wryly mused.

Chuck tested his feet on the tile floor, then he stood up. Weak. But not wobbly. Good.

Sure enough, his clothes were all there, along with his shoes. He quickly found his wallet in a drawer. Everything was there—his cash, license, pictures of his late wife and his daughter, Jennifer. Even his credit cards. He was not surprised to find that his cards had been rearranged, however.

And no sign of his briefcase or phone. *That confirms it—I'm not being held for murder.* The local police would have confiscated everything had it been a homicide rap. *Am I even legally under arrest?* Probably not, he decided. This made him even more uncomfortable, since the police had evidently been used to detain him.

But who would order a hit man to kill me, then have me cuffed, but give my clothes and wallet back? Such an order must have come from Washington. Chuck guessed he'd better get off to where he could get his thoughts in order without the likelihood of being killed or tossed into jail.

He dressed quickly, carefully, quietly but not rushing. *Can't go out of here looking like a patient or a bum. Too easy to spot me*, he thought.

Chuck slipped noiselessly into the bathroom. The medicine cabinet held plastic cups, toothpaste and brush, a throwaway razor, lotion, talcum powder. *Better than a lot of motels*, he observed. Chuck drank deeply, brushed his teeth, then he shaved. Two days without a shave—or had it been three? He left his upper lip unshaven. A mustache might prove an asset.

Chuck patted through his shirt at the bandage behind his arm, then turned to look over his shoulder in the mirror. No bulge to speak of. The bandage was still a mystery, though. *If I cut myself when I collapsed, why is there no rip or bloodstain on my shirt? And what could a guy cut himself on in the backseat of a taxi?* But there was no time now—he would have to check the wound later.

He grabbed the talc to cover a couple of nicks. Then he got an idea.

Five minutes' work on his hair with the talcum powder turned it gray. Then a little black grease from the rollers of the cabinet drawer darkened his thin mustache, and a little of the same gave him circles under his already bleary eyes. This aged Chuck more than Rip Van Winkle. Then it dawned on him: *I could be as bald as Yul Brunner, as bearded as the Ayatollah. Nobody in Tucson knows what I look like—not even that cop outside.*

The cop? He did present a bit of a problem. *Unless I choose a violent route,* Chuck thought. But Chuck's conscience dismissed that at once.

He glanced at the mirror again. Tie straight. Even the shirt, wrinkled from the flight from Boston, was quite smooth after hanging in the closet. *Nice of the nurses to hang it up.* Eyeing himself critically, Chuck thought, *Not bad—if I can ever get myself into a crowd.* He dropped the razor, toothbrush, and paste into his blazer pocket. No telling when he'd have a chance to replenish his supply.

One more little detail, thought Chuck, remembering his rabbit-tracking days as a boy in the North Carolina hills. *Give the hounds the wrong scent.*

He tore the sheets from the bed, then quickly knotted them together. Opening the window as wide as it would go, Chuck tied a corner of the connected sheets to the hinge of the casement window, then dropped the makeshift escape rope down. "Good," he breathed, noticing that the two sheets just touched a narrow ledge.

It was wide enough for a mountain climber, perhaps, but far too treacherous to negotiate by a man still weak from lack of food and a near-fatal drugging. What was important, though, was that the police would believe he had gotten out that way. *Lord, You've got to do the rest!* Chuck prayed silently.

As a final touch, Chuck carefully positioned a chair like a step stool beneath the open window. Then he slipped noiselessly to the door.

Chuck eased the lever in slowly, half expecting to find it locked. He cracked it an inch. The cop was snoring loudly in a reclining chair, a can of Coke spilled onto his pants. The only nurse at the ward desk was absorbed in filling out reports.

He opened the door enough to get his head out. Down the long corridor in the other direction a nurse's aide pushed a cart of medical supplies, her back turned.

Chuck slipped out, holding his breath as he closed the door.

The cop stirred. Chuck froze in the hall. The cop shifted in his chair, not seeming to notice that his pants were wet.

Chuck paused, then peered over his shoulder. The aide with the cart, a pretty Mexican girl, was turning into a room. She looked right at him from the shadowy hallway, and Chuck noticed that she wore tinted glasses and too much lipstick and rouge. He smiled, thinking of Jennifer, who would soon be seventeen. She smiled back, apparently not having seen where he came from.

Too late to change my mind, he thought. Quickly, confidently, he strolled toward the desk. Fully clothed and freshly shaven, Chuck apparently didn't look like a patient, for the nurse at the desk only gave him a bored glance.

"I'm new here. What floor is Geriatrics?" he bluffed in his best professional voice.

"Five B, doctor. This is 7B." The nurse glanced him over, then returned to her reports.

"Thanks." Chuck strode purposefully toward the elevators at the far end of the wing. No point in rousing that cop by taking the nearby elevator.

By the time the elevator reached the ground floor, Chuck knew it would be foolhardy to leave the hospital before next morning's rush hour. As soon as the cops decided he'd escaped through the window, they'd scour the neighborhood for him. Every garbage can, every fence, every hedge, every parked car and unlocked basement would be checked. Every cab driver and bus jockey for blocks around would be questioned. And if it is the FBI, Chuck realized, his face would be faxed to every police bulletin in Arizona long before the sun rose.

But a dignified elderly gentleman waiting on an ill relative in the emergency room? Chuck followed the lighted signs through interminable corridors toward the ER. Once there, he helped himself to free coffee, then taking a corner seat, he washed down a stale sweet roll from a coin machine.

"Youse here wid d' wife?" Two seats over, an old fellow with a heavy Brooklyn accent obviously needed someone to talk to.

"I'm not married." Chuck was at once sorry he'd been so terse. A young aide with long, dark ringlets, her face buried in a clipboard, strolled past just then.

"Oh. Didn't mean t' pry." The old gentleman apologized.

"You're not prying," Chuck answered, warmer this time. "You here with yours?"

"My Sadie . . . it may be a stroke dis time. I've been here awul night, and d' docs don't know a t'ing. All intoins, still green b'hind d' ears. You know?"

"Yes, I know," Chuck agreed. "You on a vacation?"

"Yeah. Youse?"

"Business. I'm, uh, waiting for a friend." *Lord, make this the truth*, Chuck prayed silently.

"Yeah. I used t' travel myself. Long-distance trucka. Now me 'n the old lady travel alla time. She wants t' see d' woild. Me, I wanta stay home an' enjoy our new house on Long Island. So we compromise—y' know whadda mean?"

"Sure. I've traveled some myself. Someday I may settle down and find a wife," Chuck chuckled.

"Youse better get at it. Not many goils out dere for old fellers like us."

Uh-oh. Chuck patted his hair. In his nervousness, he'd forgotten about the gray. Some of the talc came off on his fingers, and he wiped it under the seat of his chair. "I've got an, uh, interest," Chuck said, remembering Nicki. *If it hadn't been for her, I wouldn't be in this mess,* he pondered angrily.

"Hey, youse got some time free tomorra?" The old man held up two tour-bus tickets. "Goes t' Tombstone fer d' day. D' famous OK Corral—dat sorta ting. But de're good fer one day only. My old lady, last time she had one o' dese spells I camped for a week in a hospital lounge in Barbados."

"Sure. Thanks!" Chuck took the tickets. *Thank You, Lord.* "Maybe I'll find a dame to go with me," he said, getting into the swing of the old fellow's forced levity. *Then again, maybe I won't,* he thought, wincing as Nicki came to mind. Chuck stood up, stretched, and yawned. "See y'."

"Youse have fun. Dem Arizona dames can be trouble. More desperate widders here in Tucson dan in all of New York," he advised, winking.

Chuck took his time, though the coffee and sweet roll had braced him up considerably. He wound his way through the corridors toward the front lobby. A senior citizens' tour was one way out of Tucson that the police would not likely be checking. "Thank you, Lord," he prayed again, realizing that this escape route was far too original to be coincidental.

Tombstone, the tickets said. Chuck had never been there, but it had a Wild West ring to it, something about a gunslinger's shootout and frontier justice. Marshal Dillon, wasn't it? Chuck smiled as he began to formulate a plan.

A city hospital is a city in itself, Chuck realized. *No better place to hide out—that is, as long as the cops fall for that sheet-out-the-window trick.*

Off the main lobby Chuck spied the cafeteria. The sign said it opened for breakfast at 6:30. Across the hall a well-stocked gift shop opened at 7:30. He peered through the glass wall to size up the place. Next to a rack of sunglasses stood a pile of cheap sombreros. Good. He made a mental note.

"You'll need to wait in the Emergency Room lounge, sir." The security guard who stepped up behind Chuck was polite but firm. "The main lobby is closed until 6:30," he added.

Chuck caught his breath. "I . . . I need a money machine—cash to pay a bill," he managed to stammer.

"Over there." The guard pointed to a machine in an alcove along the far wall. "But you *must* move on as soon as you've made your transaction."

"Thanks." Chuck withdrew his one-day maximum, one thousand dollars, on his bank's debit card. Then with his Visa he took his maximum one-day cash advance—again, one thousand dollars. The receipt with the final transaction said 11:59 P.M. "All right!" Chuck murmured, realizing that in about a minute the date would change and he could withdraw another two thousand dollars.

Chuck heard the door buzzer, and he watched, glued to the floor, as the guard let two blue-coated cops and a detective in through the main entrance. *Uh-oh. I've been reported missing. I hope they're looking for a young man in a hospital gown, not an old guy in business clothes.* Chuck hunkered into an arthritic stoop to accompany his gray hair. Then he casually folded the cash into his wallet, watching the policemen out of the corner of his eye.

Chuck waited until the three officers disappeared into an elevator, then he completed two more one-thousand-dollar transactions. *My paper trail has got to stop here in Tucson,* he thought grimly, considering how fast four thousand dollars would evaporate when a man was on the run. *No knowing when I'll be able to get my hands on more money.*

The cops had gone to the seventh floor, Chuck noticed, for he'd watched the elevator light while waiting for his transactions to process. Maternity was on the fourth floor, Chuck saw, quickly scanning the directory. But he knew better than to take a lobby elevator with a guard watching. All late-night admissions were through the emergency room, Chuck realized.

Fair enough, Chuck thought, as moments later he stepped onto an elevator in the emergency wing. *So I'm entering through ER. For the rest of the night I'm a grandfather-to-be waiting on my daughter to deliver.*

When Chuck awoke at dawn in the maternity ward waiting room, a faint, feminine odor of Obsession cologne told him that a lady was seated next to him. And for the first time in months he decided he didn't like this too-familiar fragrance.

He opened one eye to a slit and, without moving his head, explored the room. A row of chairs along the opposite wall was empty, as it had been when he'd slipped into this small room shortly after midnight. His feet were still propped in the cushioned, straight-backed chair in front of him, and he sat in the only easy chair in the room. *So why did this woman decide to plop down right next to me?*

Chuck felt an uncomfortable warmth across the back of his left hand. He gazed down, then frowned. The female hand resting atop his was dark, Asian, almost olive-complected, and the fingers were delicate, perfectly formed, nicely tapered. And vaguely familiar. The hand moved slightly, and Chuck could discern a certain roughness of texture to the palm, a callousing that subtly reminded him that this woman was no lady of leisure.

Chuck opened his eyes fully now and stared at the lovely hand resting on his. "Nicki?" he whispered, not believing.

"I'm your daughter, Ruby," a familiar voice whispered. "We're in here with my sister Alice, who's having a baby. Remember?"

Chuck now stirred and turned. "Nicki Towns . . . how on earth!?"

She smiled, but her eyes were dead serious, worried. Nicki placed a finger to her lips and shook her head. "Later," she whispered.

"All right . . . it's 'Ruby.' How's Alice?" he said, playing her game.

"She's . . . she's expected to come around to receive company in about an hour—had a C-section last night," Nicki said. She nodded toward a clock on the wall, which read 6:10. "I hope her father and sister *do* show up," Nicki snickered nervously. "Apparently she doesn't have a husband."

"Do I have you to thank for the attempt to knock me off?" Chuck whispered, trying to size up his unwanted neighbor.

A momentary look of terror passed over Nicki's face. Chuck felt pity at once, and he was struck with her seemingly helpless beauty. "Y . . . yes," she stammered. "And no. You see, the Babylonians and the . . . how can I explain?" she pleaded. "Say, why don't we have breakfast together in the cafeteria? We can't be here when Alice's family arrives, you know."

What is this crazy stuff she's spouting? Babylonians, indeed!? But Chuck knew he had no time to ask more questions. So he only shrugged and plopped his feet onto the floor. "Does the prisoner get to order what he wants for his last meal?"

"Stop that!" Nicki commanded him so sharply that Chuck thought for a moment that she really was his captor. "They're look-ing for *me* too," she whispered, her voice tinged with terror. Trembling, Nicki urged Chuck to his feet and pointed toward the elevator.

4

Where Pancho Villa Roamed

Keep thy heart with all diligence.

—Solomon

Nicki Towns paid cash for both breakfasts. Chuck, acting far too spry for a white-haired gentleman nearly eighty, carried their meals to a corner booth. *Nicki perks me up,* Chuck thought as he sat down, peeved at himself for not keeping up the father-daughter charade in the cafeteria.

Nicki waited politely for Chuck to say grace, as she had in the past when they'd lunched together. "I haven't lost my religion," she laughed, her eyes smiling for the first time that morning. "But I've never learned how to say grace. God seems so . . . so distant." Quickly changing the subject, she added, "I guess I've got some explaining to do . . . 'Father.'" Her countenance at once turned dark and so mysterious that Chuck was startled.

"Shoot away . . . 'Ruby.'" He picked lightly at his scrambled eggs.

Nicki opened her purse and pulled out her wallet. She displayed an Arizona driver's license with the name 'Ruby Sanchez' and a Tucson address. The photo was hers. "It's an apartment out near the Air Force base," she said, noting the address. "I get mail there occasionally."

"That figures. And Ngo Thieu?" Chuck decided that if he were to be the unwilling guest of a wanted criminal, he might as well ask a few blunt questions.

"My mother was Vietnamese. I am an orphan. I had to come to America before my eighteenth birthday to claim American citizenship, so I disguised myself as a boy and got a job as a ship's cook."

"When was that?"

"Ten years ago. Mother had begged the MPs to let her on a boat out of Saigon in '75." Nicki bristled. "She had my father's papers, but the American commander wouldn't listen."

"Your father was an American GI—a Vietnam vet?" Chuck guessed.

"A civil engineer. He built airstrips for President Nixon's B-52 bombers, just like those old ones rotting away at the Davis-Monthan Air Force Base just outside Tucson," Nicki explained, her tone softening. "But my daddy had not been a citizen long. He was an Assyrian—a displaced person. He'd spent most of his life wandering across Europe after he watched the new Iraqi government murder his mother just for being a Christian. His cousin in Boston told me all about it. Daddy left my mother in Saigon, pregnant with me, just a few days before he was killed in a Vietcong guerilla attack," Nicki rushed on.

"I'm sorry."

"They were *married*," Nicki answered almost fiercely. "By a French Catholic priest. My daddy was Orthodox, and he didn't understand a word of the French ceremony, mother told me when I was still a very little girl. She had been educated in a French parochial school. Just before the war she was converted by Christian and Missionary Alliance missionaries, who gave her a Bible and also taught her English."

"'Converted'? Do you know what that means, Nicki?"

Nicki forced a smile, avoiding his question. She lowered her voice almost to a whisper.

"Mother was killed when I was nine. I spent the next eight years as a street brat. I kept Mother's Bible and Daddy's papers, which I found inside the covers. Every morning for years I'd wake up planning how to get to America. Mixed-parentage kids are outcasts in Saigon."

"Wow!" Chuck shook his head. "Quite a heritage!" He peered at her earnestly.

"We've talked . . . too much," she answered evasively. "Right now we've both got to get out of Tucson."

"We?"

"Both of our lives are in danger."

"Oh. If I were still a cop, Nicki, I'd shackle your pretty little wrists together, and we'd be on the next plane to Washington."

"It would be unwise for you . . . for *either* of us to try anything silly right now, Father. Those tour-bus tickets will get us safely to Tombstone."

"You know about the tickets?" Chuck was taken aback.

"Yes. I saw the old guy give them to you. I walked right past you, carrying a clipboard."

"How long have you been following me?" Chuck found himself growing uncomfortable with his unwanted guest once again. In his years as a pastor, then in police work, he'd heard plenty of tales of tangled lives. Nicki's story, heartrending and unusual as it was, was little worse than a lot of others he'd heard.

"I . . . I set out to rescue you when I learned from Mr. Thompkins that you didn't show up at Falcon Aviation," Nicki explained. "I called him the next day just to apologize."

"You . . . you phoned Harry Thompkins—just like that!?"

"Sure." Nicki grinned impishly. "I have to stay on top of things in my business. He seemed confident that you were OK, though. Said you gave him quite a talking to, and that he was sure you'd have the Feds on me soon enough. Really read me the riot act."

"So how did you find me? I don't understand."

"Through my . . . my, uh, contact." Nicki held up her hand. "I've told you enough. I caught a plane to Tucson. This just happens to be the closest hospital to the airport, and the Tucson PD had you registered in your own name. So I spiked that cop's Coke with a roofie."

"The policeman guarding my room? You gave him Rohypnol? That's a date rape drug!"

"Sure." She grinned slyly. "It has other uses, you know. He even asked me to get the Coke for him. Thought you should know who your friends are. I even smiled at you in the corridor up there, but you were too busy trying to play doctor for that desk nurse to recognize me in my uniform!" She poked her tongue impishly into her cheek. "I've worked here as a nurse's aide for the past two days—credentials and aliases are my forte." Nicki laughed. "A lady in uniform can get away with . . . with murder."

"Now you see her, now you don't," Chuck said in genuine admiration, recalling the aide he'd seen upon leaving his room. He bit his lip nervously, considering Nicki's last remark. "How long was I in that room?"

"Only a few hours, actually. You spent the first two days in intensive care. The nerve gas the cops found in that pressure can in your pocket would kill a tiger in its tracks."

Chuck could only shake his head in disbelief.

"I've got a rented car in the parking lot outside the emergency room," Nicki volunteered.

"Since you insist," Chuck sighed.

"Excuse me. *Don't* turn around," Nicki whispered. "I'll be right back."

Chuck didn't like being the virtual prisoner of a woman whose intentions were so manifestly criminal. But caution took over, and he obediently worked at swallowing the last of his hash browns as Nicki slipped out the door and crossed to the gift shop.

The reason for her caution became clear when Chuck glanced at the polished stainless steel paneling behind the cafeteria serving line. Plainly reflected, two booths from where he sat, two uniformed Tucson city cops and a detective snacked on coffee and cinnamon rolls. Chuck could not be certain, though, if they were the same threesome who had entered the hospital at midnight when his bed was reported empty. *Has Nicki abandoned me, just as I'm about to be arrested?*

"You left your cane in the lobby, Father!" Nicki scurried up, as cheerful as if he really were her doting daddy. Clearly, she was getting a kick out of treating him like a feeble old coot.

The cane was brand-new from the shop across the hall. Chuck quickly peeled off the price tag and wrapped it in his napkin.

"Just a minute." Nicki patted his hand as Chuck started to rise. She fished a hospital wristband from her purse. "I borrowed this from a patient while you were catching your Zs in the maternity ward," she whispered. "We'll just put it on your wrist, but keep your coat sleeve over it until we're outside."

Chuck shot her a quizzical glance, then slid his left arm out, letting Nicki slip the strap into place.

"Not to worry. He won't need it. Dead—under a sheet," she whispered.

Chuck bit his tongue, deciding not to remark on *this* revelation. He had other questions too. Lots more questions. But they could wait.

《《《

"All right, miss." The cop glanced into the backseat, then waved Nicki on.

The moment he had seen the cops in city squad cars checking cars leaving the parking lot, Chuck slouched and braced himself against the dash with one hand like a feeble old man just discharged from the hospital. He was careful to expose the patient ID bracelet to the trooper's view, and he hung his head over his cane, nodding and drooling, his senile spittle dripping onto the carpet of Nicki's rented Ford Taurus.

But why do they want me, anyway? And who *wants me?* Chuck asked himself, as Nicki eased the car into the flow of traffic heading toward the Cactus Community Center, where the senior citizens' tour bus would soon be loading. *And who, really, is this woman I'm traveling with?* he worried.

❰❰❰

Chuck let himself drift into slumber as the big Saguaro Southwest Tours bus loaded down with senior tourists droned southeast on Interstate 10 out of Tucson. Nicki had offered him little clue as to whom *they*—"the Babylonians"—were who had tried to kill him, and who, apparently, wished to do her in also. Puzzling, too, these "Babylonians"—or perhaps someone else—seemed to have an inside track with the Tucson Police, using them to detain him and steal his briefcase. Chuck turned cold to think what use could be made of the papers in his case.

There had been something of the flavor of an international conspiracy, or at least a terrorist organization, hinted at in Nicki's few cautious remarks. And had she implied there was more than one group? He wanted desperately to check in with an old friend at the CIA the first chance he got to use a phone. But the attempt to rub him out with nerve gas, followed by the police detention in a guarded hospital room, left Chuck a bit apprehensive. Phone calls could be dangerous when you weren't sure who was listening. But Nicki seemed to know the answers. If he stuck with her for a while, he could hope she'd divulge the secret.

They had been tipped off by his phone call from the plane to General MacAdams, Chuck considered. Perhaps the Russians—or whoever?—had tapped the general's phone. Or maybe *they* had access to Chuck's own phone card number. He knew that international spies were busy monitoring microwave and fiber-optic phone transmissions, and many spies could also trace a call by means yet undetectable even by advanced technology. Some had access to expensive, state-of-the-art parabolic microphones, which could monitor conversations from blocks away, even through walls.

Or, perhaps Harry's call to Falcon Aviation's security had been intercepted by a mole inside the Salem Electronics plant in Massachusetts, and *they* had decided to take Chuck out before he learned too much and reported back to the CIA or the Pentagon. That could explain the fake chauffeur who met him at Tucson International Airport with homicidal intentions. Or, maybe Harry's call was intercepted here in Arizona on Falcon's end, even.

A mole in the CIA, maybe? Chuck shuddered, remembering Harry's comments about how the Soviet KGB had penetrated the War Department's security in 1944. Chuck recalled also that former CIA agent Aldrich Ames was currently serving a life sentence for reporting the names of his department's personnel to agents of the Soviet KGB in the 1980s and 1990s—reports that had cost at least a dozen Americans their lives.

And how did Nicki, who evidently had helped steal the plans to the Vanguard Missile System—many of them, anyway—fit into this sinister puzzle? *Why does she want me alive? Should I hate her or pity her? Love her or fear her? Follow her or flee from her?*

In Tombstone, Chuck decided, he'd try to get some solid answers. Nicki would explain things, or they'd go separate ways, he determined. At last he sank into a troubled sleep.

But Nicki quickly took charge once they were off the bus in Tombstone an hour and a half later. He allowed her to help "Father" hobble to a park bench, then listened as she rattled off a list of instructions intended to ensure that *they* and the police had as cold a trail as possible. She made the danger seem so real, so grave, that Chuck was half convinced that only Nicki could keep him alive. Still . . . she might have darker motives for protecting him, he realized.

"You'll need to wash the grey out of your hair, Chuck, and ditch that cane. Do you have a razor? Trim your mustache to a thin line," she commanded in a laughing voice. "And we'll both need Mexican shirts, sunglasses, and straw hats." Nicki gestured toward a row of well-stocked curio shops that looked as though they might have the goods to transform her and Chuck into tourists for a few dollars apiece. "And *don't* make any credit card purchases," she cautioned. "I know you've got enough cash. And no phone calls."

"I used to be a police detective," Chuck reminded her. "I appreciate your advice, but I'm not really your senile old father."

"Sorry. I guess I was just overcome with the seriousness of our predicament." Nicki's voice at once took on the soft gentleness he remembered from their date, months earlier. "Where will we meet?" she asked, permitting Chuck one small decision after she made the important ones.

Chuck surveyed Tombstone's business district, of which the famous OK Corral was still a central feature. Already the laughing crowd of oldsters he and Nicki had ridden with from Tucson were strolling inside or snapping pictures.

"We don't have much time," Nicki worried.

Chuck glared at her. "I get the distinct impression that acting too fast to think is what got you into the soup kettle in the first place," he snapped. "I owe you for helping me shake the Tucson cops, but our little game is over. You're a wanted criminal. *I'm* out of here as soon as I change my clothes."

"Suit yourself." Chuck was uncertain whether her tone said contempt or compassion. "But *they* will have us where they want us if we're not out of Arizona by evening—maybe if we're not out of the United States, even. *They* only used the City of Tucson PD as their tool." Nicki waited for Chuck to consider an organization powerful enough to order police departments to do its bidding, then she patted his hand the way she had in the maternity ward. "Chuck, I *am* a criminal, in the eyes of certain people. But I could vanish where you can't find me. I don't need you—you need me. Yet I *do* need you." Her voice grew pleading now.

"Do I need you? I've had thugs on my tail before!"

"But you knew then who your enemies were. Like the time the Atlanta Mafia thought you were a double agent for the IRS," Nicki quietly answered. She smiled sadly, with no trace of gloating.

"You know *that!?*" Chuck was appalled.

"I make it my business to know whom I'm dealing with. Not like the personnel manager at Salem Electronics North," she teased.

"But who are *'they'*—these people?" Chuck returned to his central concern.

"It's best if I don't tell you. You wouldn't live twenty-four hours if you showed up at the Pentagon knowing what I know. You knocked off their assassin at the airport. He was a hired killer whom *they'*d have eliminated anyway as soon as he finished you off, so *they* won't hold his death against you. So far, you don't know enough to be dangerous to them."

"But they tried to kill me!"

"That was a fluke. Seems somebody jumped the gun. I doubt that it'll happen again. However, if you persist in trying to arrest me, we'll both be killed, and there's not a thing I can do about it. So I suggest you take a few days to relax on the beach at Cancun with me, then go back to your job at Salem and forget all about this horrible mess."

"And you?" Chuck asked, concerned. Oddly, he found himself feeling protective of Nicki. Sure, he'd learned that she was a criminal. But now it seemed as though she was about to disappear once again into the shadowy maelstrom of international espionage. Somehow Chuck wanted their relationship to continue.

Nicki shrugged. "I'm used to running. I can handle myself. It's a way of life."

"You know I can't just let things drop. There are lives at stake—national security. And I'm concerned about *your* safety too."

"World War III just around the corner? Armageddon, maybe?" Nicki became dark and mysterious again. "I've given my life to prevent a nation from being annihilated, an ancient people whom I believe will be a close friend to Israel during the third millennium. And let me tell you something else. I already have blood on my hands. I once helped a man kill himself in a business transaction so I wouldn't have to sleep with him. And because," she quickly added, "I fully expected he'd have me killed." Nicki looked into his eyes, pleading for understanding. "Maybe I've said too much," she murmured.

"No . . . no. But I'm not surprised. I believe you could do anything you set your mind to and not look back." What *did* surprise Chuck was his own ability to accept this sinister confession as fact. He did not press her for details.

"I guess it's a question of loyalty," Nicki ventured. *"My people are being destroyed by a madman,"* she added mysteriously.

"Oh, I do believe you. But your people—who are they?"

"Rest your worries. We are on the same side. We're fighting for the same cause, though we've chosen different means," she said, avoiding a full answer. "I'm quite well read on what evangelical Christians like you believe about how this world will end, and I expect to have a part in this great wrap-up of the ages—on my own terms! If Jesus is who you born-again believers say He is, He'll be happy for my aid," she boasted.

"I . . . I'm happy that you expect to have a part." Chuck wanted to believe that Nicki was seeking the Christ of the Bible. Yet she very obviously had an inadequate opinion of the Maker of the Ages. He realized now, though, that she had something pretty heady in mind. He was shocked, intrigued, fascinated—all at once. Yet their conversation was going nowhere. "See you inside an hour, over there." Chuck nodded toward an old-fashioned drugstore with a soda fountain, where a metal sign indicated that Greyhound Bus service had replaced the Concord stagecoach and six galloping horses as public transportation out of Tombstone.

(((

The Mexican señorita behind the sunglasses in the corner booth was about the snazziest-looking lady Chuck had seen in half a lifetime, he thought as he surveyed the antique soda fountain in search of Nicki. "Whew," he whistled, turning his attention to the hand-laid marble tile floor and the old-fashioned, leather-cushioned stools lined up along a polished mahogany counter. "I'll bet

Marshal Dillon met Doc Holliday here for a root beer after their gunfight," he said under his breath. *Well, maybe this place hasn't been here that long,* Chuck decided.

He glanced again toward the lady in the corner booth, then around the room. Besides the clerk behind the counter, the only other patrons were a harried mother and three complaining kids, probably waiting for the bus home to Mexico.

The good-looking girl in the flowered skirt and straw boater was studying a road map through her sunglasses, Chuck realized, as his eyes adjusted to the shady room. He strode toward her table, his new cowboy boots squeaking across the tiles as he walked.

"Hi, Chuck." Nicki grinned over the map, showing a perfect row of pearly teeth. "Bus for Douglas leaves in half an hour." She shoved two tickets toward him from beside her purse. Seeing his puzzled look, she added, "It's right on the border—about another hour and a half. Better order if you're hungry." She slid her sunglasses up and smiled again, the lines around her eyes crinkling so delightfully that Chuck was at once sorry he'd been cross with her an hour earlier.

€€€

Nicki pulled a sheaf of documents from her purse as they rode in the half-empty Greyhound winding through the mountains on U.S. Highway 80, south of Tombstone. She unfolded half a dozen blank certificates and passed them to Chuck. He noticed at once that each was already embossed with an official-looking county seal from courthouses from Maine to California, and they were all signed by a county registrar of births. "Where do you want to hail from? Take your pick," she laughed.

"Good thing Mexico doesn't require a passport," Chuck ventured, as he selected a certificate embossed with Waldo County, Maine. "But I'm going to need a typewriter."

"Douglas is a large enough town to have a business machine store that rents them by the hour," Nicki remarked. She held up several blank driver's licenses with state seals already embossed.

"If we can find a color copier and a laminating machine, we can lift your photo from your Massachusetts license, and bingo, you have a picture ID to match the birth certificate. I'll make you two—you'll be my husband, Ruben Sanchez, on one and W. F. Fuller on the other."

"Suppose a cop wants to see my license." Chuck knew the answer well enough, but he thought he'd test Nicki's savvy.

"The Mexican police aren't tied into the American police department computer networks, so you're OK, so long as it matches the birth certificate," she pointed out. "In the U.S. you'd need to get a *real* license with that false birth certificate, of course, I'm every name but Minnie Mouse in thirteen different states and three Canadian provinces," she confessed. Nicki patted her heavy, saddle-leather purse. "I've been searched several times, but the documents and extra cash I keep in the false bottom don't make a thick enough layer to arouse suspicion."

"Cash?" Chuck worried. He knew that currency often smells of cocaine from contact with the drug trade. Police dogs could sniff out tainted cash right through a leather purse. Perfectly innocent people, he was aware, had lost large sums of money to overzealous DEA officers during airport searches—often spending a night in jail as well.

"Oh, it's *laundered* money," she snickered. "I wash all my fifties and hundreds with dish detergent and ammonia before I carry them—really fools the DEA's drug hounds at the airports."

◖◖◖

"Let's eat here," Nicki chirped. The handsome, historic old Hotel Gadsen was a tourist attraction on Douglas's Main Street, and Chuck and she, now supplied with their doctored identity papers, had several hours to kill before their next move.

"I'm game." Chuck held the door, then he followed her into the air-conditioned foyer.

"This is the most romantic hotel in America!" Nicki squeezed his arm, then she pointed up a wide, white marble grand staircase that parted at a landing into two branches leading to a broad balcony fronting the second floor. The balcony ran around the four sides of the main-floor ballroom.

"You've been here before?"

"Once. I wasn't being followed then. Those steps. Notice the chips and cracks." Nicki nodded toward the marble steps.

"I'm not surprised. This place looks to be a century old."

"More romance than mere age," Nicki laughed. "The famous Mexican bandito Francisco 'Pancho' Villa once rode his horse right up those stairs. He was the terror of every town from Tombstone to Mexico City."

"Villa had dreams of being the dictator of a Mexican empire." Chuck also knew his history. "He wished to reunite the Southwest with Mexico. But he was assassinated before he could accomplish this."

"I guess dreams of empire building are found in every age, on every continent." Nicki sighed ominously. "Jesus said that 'They who take the sword shall perish with the sword,'" she quoted seriously.

"You *do* know a bit of the New Testament." Chuck smiled, but Nicki quickly changed the subject.

They took seats in the hotel's dining room, and Nicki ordered refried beans and tortillas. Chuck ordered a hamburger and a plate of American fries.

"I thought you liked international cuisine," Nicki teased.

"I did. Until I met you. I guess this'll be my last American meal. Maybe my last meal ever." Chuck paused, nodding in concern toward four middle-aged Mexican men who had just swaggered in. Each wore identical trimmed mustaches, and their hair was cut the same and slicked down with pomade. They wore matching white suits trimmed lavishly with gold braid, and huge sombreros were slung across their shoulders. One carried a violin case like an old-time gangster out to bump off an enemy with a tommy gun. Two carried guitar cases—which relieved Chuck. The fourth lugged a heavy accordion case.

All four of the men wore heavy bandoliers of ammunition across their chests, and they carried wicked-looking, pearl-handled revolvers, which dangled menacingly from hip holsters.

"What is going on?" Chuck whispered to Nicki. She, however, seemed more amused than frightened.

"A wedding reception, *señor*," explained the Mexican-American waiter, who had stepped up to pour more coffee. "They are the entertainment. The guns and bullets, they are fake."

"Oh." Chuck was relieved. "'South of the border, down Mexico way,'" he hummed nervously, stirring his coffee.

"We're on our way there," Nicki agreed in a whisper as the waiter strolled away. "But first we've got some shopping to do."

Three blocks from the Hotel Gadsen they found a secondhand store. Chuck let Nicki do the buying. For him she chose a pair of too-large ragged jeans, thin at the knees, a cheap straw Stetson hat, and a faded red plaid shirt with a frayed collar. "Here, you'll need this." She passed him an old belt, cracked in several places. "Best if they don't fit too well," Nicki whispered. She held up a rather shapeless, faded blue print dress she'd chosen for herself, then pointed Chuck toward a makeshift dressing room.

Chuck could not spot Nicki when he left the men's dressing room with his "new" clothes. But it was her voice, all right, coming from a broad-hipped Latino woman chatting with the cashier. "I'll have the change in pesos, please," Nicki's voice said. "And we'll need a couple of those paper sacks—I'll pay you for them," the voice added.

Chuck stared and stifled a laugh. Here was this obese Mexican peasant woman, her hair tied with a bandanna. But the voice and face were Nicki's. She took the change in Mexican pesos from her American fifty-dollar bill, then smiling, she handed Chuck an old grocery sack. "I paid for your stuff. Put your other clothes in this bag."

"Sure." Chuck agreed and obeyed.

"What's with the pesos?" he asked once outside. "Mexican merchants *prefer* American cash. And why on earth did you stuff those pillows under your dress?"

"Mexican customs inspectors expect to be bribed with pesos from *braceros* returning after a shopping trip north of the border. And *I'll* do the talking. As for the pillows, I did pay for them, you know. We're putting up in a cheap hotel in Agua Prieta—tonight! Get the picture?"

"Agua Prieta?" Chuck wrinkled his nose. "The city of dirty water. I know *that* much Spanish. I'm sure I'd prefer the Hotel Gadsen."

"We've stayed in the United States too long already, so get ready for Third-World reality," Nicki said ominously.

Moments later they hid their shopping cart in an alley behind the Hotel Gadsen. Slipping in the side door with their purchases, they quickly took the elevator to the second-floor balcony. Here they found chairs and seated themselves in the shadows next to a pillar to watch the wedding reception in the first-floor ballroom, directly below them.

"Please . . . please hold my hand," Nicki whispered.

Chuck had become entranced with the romantic music and the dancing of the Mexican party in the dim light downstairs that Arizona evening. "Sure," was all he could bring himself to whisper. He took her hand, then slid his arm across her shoulders, pulling Nicki close. "Why . . . why, you're shaking." *Has this woman—the one who has led me to the Mexican border while refusing to tell me what's going on and who our enemy is—has she at last begun to crack?* he wondered. Yet Chuck felt guilty. He could not bring himself to betray Nicki's momentary vulnerability to try to wrest from her more than she was ready to tell.

"It . . . it just seems that there'll never be any rest for me. Once I have done my duty, my mission, will God not give *me* peace?" she worried.

"I'm sure He will," Chuck answered. "The Lord never abandons His own."

"If I could, I'd tell you who *they* are and what *they* want," she said at last, brushing aside Chuck's reference to the Lord's help. "You just made a mistake and got in their way, you know."

"I figured as much." He peered in both directions along the balcony, which also served as the second-floor hallway. Nobody listened to them from the shadows. Chuck leaned on the rail, silently watching the party in the lobby for some moments. Ladies in seventeenth-century colonial Spanish silk gowns whirled and twirled, their full skirts swishing, their tiaras and mantillas bobbing, as dark-haired gentlemen in swallowtail coats spun them to the strains of stringed instruments. "This is some party! And no charge for a ringside seat!" Chuck murmured.

"I . . . I don't suppose I'll ever find out what it's like—" Nicki squeezed his hand—"for a man to love me like that." Nicki nodded toward the bride, who at the moment was dancing with an older gentleman in a striped formal jacket, an orange blossom pinned to his lapel. He was apparently her father.

Something stirred powerfully within Chuck's soul that he had guarded since he'd buried Shelly long ago in that quiet country churchyard in the Piedmont Hills, something that this evening of all evenings he knew he must continue to guard. He held Nicki's shoulder close to his and kept his peace as the rich strains of "La Paloma" flowed from the violins and accordions, and the guitarists softly crooned words of Latin romance *en español*.

"Time to go." Nicki brought Chuck back to reality, nodding toward the clock across the ballroom. It was ten o'clock.

"Yeah," Chuck agreed. "I know this is crazy, but I can't." He took his arm from Nicki's shoulder and grasped the rail.

"I'm waiting. C'mon."

"I'm staying. I'm checking in to this hotel, right here in Douglas. Tomorrow I plan to fax General MacAdams from that office supply store where we doctored our ID documents."

"Chuck—you . . . you can't!" Genuine terror tinged Nicki's voice as she whispered to him hoarsely. "You don't *know* MacAdams!"

"Oh? I've thought this through, Nicki. If the fax can't be traced back to me, *they*—your Babylonians—won't be able to send an assassin after me, will they? MacAdams's reply fax will go to that store. By the time the goons arrive from Tucson to find me, 'Ruben Sanchez' will be halfway to Texas in a rented car, on his way to Washington."

"Chuck!"

"Nicki, I've a good mind to try a citizen's arrest and turn you over to the local cops until the FBI gets here."

"You . . . you have no grounds. Not even probable cause. *You* haven't yet reported Salem's security leak to the CIA. Remember? MacAdams—he hasn't reported me, either." Nicki peered at Chuck darkly.

"General MacAdams?"

Nicki shot Chuck a defiant look that said it was no use to press that angle further.

"But I'm sure Harry Thompkins . . ."

"Thompkins? As I told you, I talked with the Old Man. He's just like the other CEOs I've worked for. He'll sit on what he knows and just hope my crime catches up with me somewhere else so he won't catch the heat. Harry's conscience flew out the window the minute he learned you had disappeared in Tucson. Only you can turn me in, and *they* have you under surveillance. You're checkmated."

"Catch-22, all right. Also, I'm not Sean Connery." Chuck sighed. "All right," he growled. "Tell me enough about these Babylonians to convince me to go with you to Mexico."

"It was in Nairobi, Kenya, that I first tangled with the Babylonians. I am a patriot with CALF—the Contemporary Assyrian Liberation Front. You may know that the Iraqi government has tried to systematically destroy our Assyrian people since 1933, the year they murdered my grandparents and Daddy's older sister. CALF sent me to Nairobi to deal with General Rahman, Saddam Hussein's chief-of-staff. We have finally concluded that to succeed in establishing a national homeland for Assyria, Iraq—Babylonia, to us—has to be destroyed. Simply getting our hands on American weaponry will leave us as mere terrorists. And CALF is *not* a terrorist group!"

"So you don't take any credit for the bombing of the American Embassy in Nairobi in August 1998? And Assyrians? I thought

Assyria perished when Nebuchadnezzar conquered Nineveh hundreds of years before Christ."

"No . . . and no. We consider the U.S. our friend. And yes, the Assyrian empire *was* defeated by Babylonia. But the Assyrian *people* were not destroyed. There are two million of us wandering the earth this very minute, half of them right here in America."

"But isn't it the Kurds that Saddam Hussein wants to destroy?"

"Among others, of course. But you're getting ahead of my story. Let me tell you what happened to me last year in Nairobi."

5

Jael's Nail

And [Deborah] said, ". . . The LORD *shall sell Sisera into the hand of a woman." . . . "Then Jael . . . took a nail . . . and . . . hammer . . . and smote the nail into his temples [driving] it into the ground . . . So [Sisera] died.*

—from the Book of Judges

Nairobi, Kenya

A good night for the lion to stalk the gazelle, no?" Saddam Hussein's General Rahman inquired, his words as smooth as olive oil. He raised a silk-robed arm to the moon, red as the earth of East Africa in the nighttime haze.

Days earlier, Nicki Towns had seen a bearded old lion gorging himself on a sleek, young female gazelle in Kenya's Royal Tsavo National Park. The victim's ravaged entrails had spilled lusciously onto the thirsty red clay as Nicki watched from her rented Land Rover. *Rahman will use a woman with less conscience than a lion killing a gazelle,* Nicki considered as she fought the naked terror that rose like a horrid spectre in her brain.

Only the memory of Isaiah's promise of Assyria's rising again, coupled with the cryptic predictions of her ancestor, Hniqi the prophetess, gave Nicki courage to continue her awful mission. She focused momentarily on the contents of that ancient, Hebrew-Assyrian scroll her family had kept preserved in beeswax in a jar for many centuries. Prophetess Hniqi had been an eyewitness to perhaps the most awful scene of carnage in human history. Granddaughter to Judah's King Hezekiah and young queen of Assyria's greatest emperor, Ashurbanipal, this Hniqi had watched the Babylonians fall like locusts on her capital city, Nineveh, on an August afternoon in 612 B.C.

Princess Hniqi—whose name sounded like "Nicki"—had seen with her own eyes her glorious city's roofs burn as its mud-brick walls were dissolved by the flooding Tigris and Koser Rivers. Women saw their small babies dashed onto the paving stones of Nineveh. Boys were cruelly made eunuchs to become docile house slaves. Girls, bound into gangs with wooden yokes, were marched off naked to Babylon to be sold like cattle as concubines to Nebuchadnezzar's noblemen.

And was it plausible—probable, even—that Queen Hniqi's son later became, in Babylon, the prince-prophet Daniel, whose visions of rising and falling empires reached down twenty-six centuries to Nicki Towns's own time?

Nicki considered how CALF had been secretly formed to free her Assyrian people from modern Babylonian tyranny, while also helping Daniel's Jewish people find security in the Holy Land. This security had vainly been promised both peoples by the League of Nations and the British, with their Mandate, right after World War I. Had not the dashing English colonel T. E. Lawrence of Arabia made such bold promises when he and his warriors raced on camelback across the Middle East? Nicki bit her lovely lower lip, determined to win her hand in this deadly game of international politics this very evening.

This half-drunk Iraqi general who imagines to use me to spy on the Americans—is he not really the tangible modern representative of ancient

Babylon? Nicki asked herself. *Did not they plunder first my Nineveh, then Jerusalem? Do not they continue even today to harass my ancient people, slaughtering them with gas, mortars, machine guns, and deadly viruses on the mountains given them by our father, Shem?* Unconsciously, Nicki touched the spot on her silk blouse that hid the tattoo of the winged bull over her heart. It was the sacred symbol of ancient imperial Assyria, as well as the modern emblem of CALF's cause.

The powerful Sheikh Rahman commanded Saddam Hussein's Republican Guard. This week he was in Nairobi for the African/Pan-Arabian Convention of Armed Forces Commanders. Yet now he fumbled like a fool, hoping to impress an insignificant American lady, who represented his enemy.

"A good night, indeed," Nicki unhappily agreed with her adversary. She shuddered, glad in this dim Nairobi street lighted only by the moon that he could not see her reaction. *God, are You there?* she silently breathed.

Nicki had no more time to think about her plight. Sheikh Rahman took her elbow, gently easing her toward the Rolls Royce at the curb. Nicki eyed the costly limousine. *How many barrels of oil were stolen from my father's Assyrian people to purchase this?* she wondered. A passage from the book of Judges flitted through her brain, something about Sisera, a Canaanite general whose nine hundred grand iron war chariots galloped into battle against Deborah's lightly armed Israeli foot soldiers. Though not fully a believer in either the religion of the Jews or the Christians, Nicki especially enjoyed pondering Bible passages about God delivering His people from cruel oppression.

Ghupta, Rahman's Goliath-like Pakistani chauffeur and bodyguard, stared, stone-faced, as he opened the door for her. Nicki tried a tentative smile. But Rahman's imposing attendant only returned her warm gaze with a look of impassive inscrutability.

Nicki forced another smile, then slipped onto the limo's posh calf-leather seat, sliding in her designer jeans to the other side. She knew she'd better remember to smile a lot more if she were going to pull this off.

This guy is used to Eastern women in heavy veils, robed according to the rules of Islam, she considered. *Well, tonight, in Westernized English Africa, he's having a fling with a sexy American woman.* Nicki frowned in the darkened interior, musing on what her jeans and open-faced smile might say if she were standing on a dark street in Baghdad.

"Do you have the syringes? Are they already loaded? We're not common street junkies, you know?" Rahman fired the questions as if he, a calloused general, were actually embarrassed to admit he craved such a carnal pleasure. He flipped on an interior light at their knees.

"Yes," she murmured. "Enough to kill a horse." Nicki laughed nervously. *To kill a lion too,* she thought grimly.

"Ah, the heroin." Rahman giggled like a schoolgirl. "Good stuff, no doubt about it. Let's see it." He grinned evilly, gesturing toward Nicki's bag. "The best that Baghdad has to offer these days is a pipe of Persian opium," he grunted, not disguising his scorn for the backwardness of his home city. "These trade embargoes, you know."

Nicki opened her shoulder bag and fished out a small leather case. Praying that the general would not notice her trembling fingers, she passed it to him.

He unfolded the envelope and withdrew the syringes, holding them to the light to view the milky liquid. "The nectar of moonbeams," Rahman murmured, rolling the words over his tongue in evident pleasure. He passed back the case of syringes with one hand while he pinched her bottom with the other. "You Americans know how to have fun. I had an American girlfriend when I was a student at Harvard University in Massachusetts. Perhaps I shall learn from one again tonight, no?"

Nicki winced. *No,* she told herself as she restrained a self-defensive action that under other circumstances might have given her romantic Arab host decisive boundaries.

"You will find that my hands can get very tender, like an African night," Rahman chuckled, sensing her displeasure.

"This is a *business* trip, General. Remember? The heroin is the only pleasure I have agreed to share with you."

"Ah, yes." He sighed aloud and fished a silver cigarette case from an inside pocket. "Smoke?" He flipped the case open, tilting it toward her. "American—Camels."

"No, thanks. I don't smoke." Nicki smiled, pretending to be pleased at his offer.

"A lady must choose her pleasures with care." Rahman chuckled. He took a cigarette, then popped open a gold-plated lighter. In the glow from the blue flame, Nicki could make out the inscription, "American Eagle," just above a soaring, bald-headed bird silhouetted against a Rocky Mountain landscape. Art Towns, husband of Nicki's second cousin, had a nickel Zippo identical to this one, except in finish.

Nicki's stomach knotted in rage. She now recalled that Art's military lighter with its portrayal of American power had been a gift from Nicki's own father shortly before his death. Determined more than ever to complete her deal with Rahman, Nicki fought to remain outwardly serene, pleasant, even.

They rode on, Ghupta threading the big auto through the unlit streets until they reached the lighted city center. Kenyan cities have few streetlights, yet Nicki knew that even an unarmed girl ordinarily can stroll at night through metropolises like Nairobi carrying only a flashlight, with no fear of robbery or rape.

Nicki, however, felt knots of fear tighten in her stomach. She giggled nervously, trying to feign excitement when she felt only terror. Two evenings earlier she had walked this very route at night, planning her escape. She'd need more than her jogging shoes and the equipment in her shoulder bag to get out of this one, she decided. *God. Will He help me?*

"Ready for a good time?" Rahman seemed positively elated as he chatted. The aging sheikh was doing his best tonight to pretend to be a romantic playboy.

"Yes," she agreed. Nicki lifted her voice, trying to seem flattered without sounding giddy. "Did *you* bring what we agreed upon?" she asked. She fought the tension that tightened her throat and nodded toward Rahman's attaché case. Whatever might happen to her that evening—these horrors were trivial compared to the real purpose of her mission, to relieve the sufferings of her ancient people. CALF—Contemporary Assyrian Liberation Front— depended on her success this night for its continued mission.

Nicki considered again the black Assyrian winged bull tattooed over her heart, the symbol of her people's struggle against Rahman's oppressive military. Fear knotted her stomach as she thought about what could happen if this cat-and-mouse game were to progress far enough for Rahman to get a peek at that ancient symbol of her people's international cause.

Nicki wondered how Esther felt, a teen torn from her home in Israel, about to have her precious virginity ripped from her by the proud Xerxes, a pagan Persian potentate whose word was law. Nicki had read the Bible tale of Esther that very morning, seeking to steel herself for the task that the CALF directorate had assigned her. "If I perish, I perish," Esther had said in determination, Nicki recalled. *Like me, Esther was on a mission to save her people.* Nicki's resolve stiffened, and her mind began to focus as she considered this.

"Nervous, eh? Let me assure you it's all there." This part of the transaction, at least, Rahman understood in terms equal to hers. "My agents in America—they assure me that you are making progress on getting the pieces of the Vanguard missile puzzle together, no?" It was a mocking question. Nicki had learned only weeks before that Iraqi espionage agents, believing that Nicki was spying for the Russians, had been keeping tabs on her activities.

Sensing a need to prove his point, Rahman unlocked the case. He withdrew a stiff brown envelope and opened it. "One little plastic disk," he said. "But what it contains may turn the world upside down." Smiling magnanimously, as if he were aware of the apostolic, New Testament origin of his figure of speech, he passed the computer diskette to Nicki.

Nicki gasped, though she had expected this. The key to a free future for her ancient people—in America, Eastern Europe, the

Middle East—was encoded on that floppy disk, she believed. Yet she realized fully that despite what he offered in return, it was not enough to buy back her feminine honor, were she forced to relinquish it. Shame rose in her cheeks in the darkened limousine, and Nicki was glad that this clandestine rendezvous at Nairobi's Ivory Towers Hotel had not been her own doing, but that of a CALF agent working behind the scenes. "How do I know you're not offering me a blank disk?" she asked, her thoughts returning again to her purpose in agreeing to the bargain. She had actually expected a file folder full of documents, which she had planned to memorize, then destroy.

"I can deliver what I agreed upon, don't you think?" The man chuckled nervously. Rahman also had cause to fear were Nicki actually to escape from his hotel room to return to America.

"Yes. Sorry, General."

"I carry a notebook computer with me. When we reach the hotel, you can boot it up and read it right off the screen. Once you have the access code, you can run this in your own PC as easily as an American housewife runs a shopping list," he taunted.

"Thank you. I . . . I'll borrow a neutral computer from the hotel to read your disk, if you don't mind." It occurred to Nicki that Rahman might have had a technician reprogram his computer so only it would read the disk in his attaché case. "Or the deal is off!" Nicki surprised herself with her own ability to insist firmly on suitable, iron-clad terms.

"If that is your wish," he murmured. Rahman understood duplicity, and he made no attempt to get her to change her mind. "I am told that you know more about math and nuclear physics than the great Einstein. I would not hope to fool you, Doctor Towns."

Nicki shuddered in silence. *Rahman knows too much about me,* she decided. Aloud she faked a happy sigh. She had already decided how this grim game would end. Two persons would enter a room on the tenth floor of a hotel in downtown Nairobi. One would walk out tonight. The police coroner would remove the other tomorrow.

Yet Rahman needed her alive to go with him to Baghdad and deliver under drug inducement and torture what secrets she had stolen from the American military plants. There would be time enough then to kill her—strangled, hanged in her cell, no doubt. If, for another hour, she could only keep her wily host from realizing just how deadly she knew him to be!

⟨⟨⟨

The stinging hot water felt good on her skin, and the shower helped settle Nicki's nerves for the death dealing encounter just ahead. Too, Nicki figured that the sound of her bathing would help get the general in the mood—for what? Shaking, she turned cold all over pondering, or rather striving to avoid pondering, her next terrible move.

Nicki toweled dry, then pulled on the velour robe she'd folded into her handbag before leaving her own hotel room across town. No. This would not do. Her modesty, coupled with what Nicki believed to be Rahman's expectations from a woman, dictated otherwise. To appear before the sheikh obviously wearing only a bathrobe might say *cheap*. This operation demanded more.

Nicki grabbed her jeans, pulled them on, and rolled the legs to her knees, careful to make the folds as wide and flat as possible. He might indeed discover that she wore her jeans, but Nicki figured that a few feminine giggles, a few rakes of her slender fingers through his beard, and he would melt like the mighty Xerxes before the virgin charms of Esther.

Nicki shuddered, remembering how in the book of Judges Jael drove the tent peg right through General Sisera's unsuspecting temples with a mallet, pinning him to the ground. Somehow it was not the gory means that Jael had used to do her adversary in that bothered Nicki, it was . . . well, what was it? For days, she had struggled to sort out the moral issues contained in the act she now contemplated. Faced now with no room to retreat, she still wrestled with her conscience.

Her chastity again came to Nicki's mind. *Can I get "the nectar of moonbeams" into his hot veins before I have to go to bed with the old lecher?* With a final, fear-filled glance at the computer disk tucked into her shoulder bag, Nicki left the bathroom.

She found Rahman, still fully clothed, on the bed. She sat herself down, fussing with his shoelaces, pampering him. A nice pair of Gucci oxfords, not loafers, like younger men wore. Good. She took her time, picking at the laces, loosening them slowly, teasing, playfully tickling his arches as she slipped the shoes from his feet. Nicki placed the shoes under the bed, using the hem of her robe to discreetly wipe her fingerprints from the shoes' mirror polish.

"Time for . . . for the moonbeam's nectar?" Nicki murmured. She slid off the bed and strolled across the wide boudoir to where she'd left her purse on the dresser as she emerged from the bathroom. *Stupid,* she told herself, terror clutching her throat. *I ought to have placed it right on the nightstand.*

"Ah, yes." Rahman sat up, placing his stockinged feet on the fine, handcrafted rug at the bedside.

Turning, Nicki noticed the lovely carpet for the first time. She felt the blood rush to her cheeks. Many of these rugs, she knew, were made by Iraqi Assyrians in exile and sold as Persian rugs. The symbolism of this evil man's feet on that emblem of what lay so dear to her nearly caused her to cry out in dismay. Instead, carrying the two syringes, she strolled calmly toward the king-size bed. "You choose." She grinned wickedly. Both were loaded with the very same milky white liquid, but she dared not let Rahman believe she was about to offer him a deadly one.

"Thank you. Did you know that it takes only a couple of drops of the poison of an asp to kill—about so much?" He marked off with his thumbnail a line below the needle, indicating two units along the one-half cubic centimeter syringe.

Nicki turned away, pretending to blow her nose on a tissue. It would not do to let Rahman see the horror that crept across her face. Fear welled within Nicki as she considered, too, that muscle-bound Ghupta waited in the hall, ready to rush in on a prearranged signal to finish her off if she proved difficult. His beefy hands could swiftly snap her slender neck and sever her spinal cord. *Where are you, God?* she wondered.

"So . . . America's prettiest physicist is addicted?" Rahman chortled, noticing her forced sniffle. "So many heroin addicts in America. Plenty of them at Harvard and MIT. America is weak, with clay feet, and her cities are jungles of chaos. Too bad. But I can wait, you see. Heroin—'horse,' I think it's called in the alleys of Boston—dulls the senses for what is about to come." He lay his syringe on the nightstand.

"Oh, but you have never tried *real* pleasure. Just a little before-hand will *enhance* the joy of love. We can take the rest later, after we . . . after we have slept." Nicki held her thumbnail where Rahman's had been, at the two-unit line of the syringe. "The poison of an asp," she mimicked him, fighting her horror at what she was doing.

Again she sat down on the bed, snuggling against him. Bending over, letting her waist-length, perfumed ebony tresses fall lightly across the general's dropsied calves, Nicki picked up Rahman's feet, one at a time, tenderly removing his black silk stockings. Passing him one sock, she slipped her arm out of a sleeve of her robe and wound the other sock around her biceps. "Just a couple of drops," she murmured. "It will help us loosen up." Without more delay, Nicki plunged the needle into her arm, emptying half its contents. Her green eyes twinkled in a luminescent glow of apparent bliss as she held the syringe up for his inspection.

"Anything to please the most beautiful woman I have ever seen." He wound the other sock onto his own arm, then poked the needle in.

Nicki bit her lip, watching Rahman slowly push the plunger. Already she could feel the asp venom attack her own system. *Enough to kill a horse.* The irony of her own joke struck her then, and she laughed aloud.

As Nicki struggled to her feet, she felt her robe being peeled away from her shoulders by the general's shaking fingers. Glad for the protection of her jeans, she turned, watching Rahman through slitted eyes. Disappointment crept across his face as his fast-flagging brain perceived dimly that Nicki was still dressed. "Anything to please a pretty lady," he gasped out, as the powerful venom shut down his life-systems even while he spoke.

For the general the fun and games had ended. He let her robe slide to the floor, then collapsed silently on the bed, drooling into his beard.

Nicki did not so much as pull a sheet over the dead commander's body. It had to look like an accidental overdose or suicide. Dead men don't pull the covers up.

She returned to the bathroom where she slipped her running shoes on, then carefully wiped all surfaces clean of fingerprints. The ceramic floor she wiped too. No sense in letting the police find a woman's footprints on the tiles.

Nicki considered Ghupta for a moment, imagining she heard him breathing just outside the door. He'd wait in a chair in the hall for a couple of hours, at least, before calling the cops—maybe all night, she decided. Would he report that his boss entered the room with an American woman? Nicki figured that Ghupta would soon be dispatched by an assassin if this news got back to Baghdad. Not a chance. The big ox won't open his mouth, Nicki decided.

As for the hotel desk clerk, Ghupta had given him fifty American dollars to let Rahman use a computer in a locked office for several minutes. But Rahman himself hadn't touched the computer, and Nicki had carefully wiped the keys clean when she was through. Ghupta had seen to it that Nicki entered Ivory Towers by an alley door so the clerk would not be aware that the general had entertained a woman in his room.

Nicki shot one more glance at the computer diskette that lay in her handbag next to her half-empty syringe with its remaining "moonbeam nectar." Happy as she was to have these state secrets in hand, right now she had one more hurdle, one more fear to deal with. She had given herself as much venom as that which had killed General Rahman, perhaps more. This was the poison that had taken Cleopatra's life. Nicki shuddered to recall it.

Yet Nicki still must perform an excruciating feat, which she had practiced for several days on the sheer cliffs above Kenya's Great Rift Valley.

Fear or the venom—maybe both—hit Nicki's stomach like a sledgehammer. She fumbled with the buckle on her shoulder bag, desperately trying to concentrate, trying not to think about the corpse on the bed. She retrieved a spool of nylon twine from her bag. It was sturdy utility twine, of a higher grade than used for packages, tested for at least 100 kg or 220 lbs. Nicki had earlier unwound more than a hundred feet, tied a large lead fishing sinker about fifty feet down, then rewound it.

Nicki slipped to the window and quietly slid the bottom sash upward. From her bag she pulled the two pieces of a length of wooden broom handle, carefully sawn diagonally from end to end. She slipped this split dowel into the casement's slotted sides, adjusting the pieces to overlap each other. Nicki then fished out a spool of fine steel wire and wound the dowel's pieces deftly, tightly, as she adjusted its length to the width of the window.

She patted the dowel, dropping it into place. *Good,* she thought to herself. *Loose enough for me to pop it free from the ground with a flip of the lead weight. But it's solid, rigid as a piece of pipe.* "Dear God, help!" she prayed aloud. Nicki's faith was philosophical rather than personal. Yet she believed God *could* help her—*if only He would!*

Nicki fastened her nylon cord to the center of the stiffly wired dowel and dropped the cord outside. She then slipped on a pair of leather gloves. Shoving her shoulder bag behind her back, Nicki stepped into space, fully ten stories above a stony alley in the dark of an African night. She had practiced this descent on mountain-side cliffs a dozen times—yet never before with her veins full of snake venom. The toes of Nicki's running shoes caught the bricks below the window. Knotting the twine around the fingers of one hand to hold herself momentarily suspended, she pulled the window nearly down.

"Clever girl," the devil seemed to whisper into Nicki's ear as she rappelled down.

"Dear God—help!" Nicki breathed again into the enveloping night. In her gathering fear, she felt that any pride, any self-satisfaction might cause God to let her fail at the last moment. Only a thin cord and a flimsy dowel stood between her and plummeting to her death, Nicki realized. *Have I pushed things too far at last?* her heart cried out. Her fingers shook. Her shoulders ached as if they were being pulled apart. Her arms, almost out of control, trembled wildly, and her feet had as much feeling as lead weights. Nicki's stomach knotted tighter as, fighting fear and maddening pain, she tried to concentrate on climbing to the ground.

(((

Nicki Towns dropped two empty syringes into a trash bin at Jomo Kenyatta International Airport, Nairobi, along with her wired dowel and nylon cord. Both the syringes had contained the venom of an asp, enough indeed to kill a horse. Yet she had injected half the contents into her veins. It had only given her tremors and a raging bellyache.

There had been more than a dozen other syringes before these. Nicki smiled wryly. She had purchased them from a medical laboratory in Australia. The serum in the syringes that she had shot herself with daily during a month in East Africa really was made from the blood of horses.

The Australian lab kept horses that were immune to asp venom from having been given regular, small doses of it. These horses donated their blood as serum to save the lives of snake-bite victims the world over. Snake handlers at zoos could also become immune to this, the most deadly natural poison on earth, by taking shots of the serum in advance, Nicki had learned. *This antidote really does work*, she thought, marveling, as she hurried to the departure gate, genuinely surprised to be alive.

))))))

Nicki stirred in her seat in the crowded DC-10 and checked her watch. She slid the plane window shade open and peered out into the night sky. Six miles below, she knew, in the mountains of the upper Tigris, a remnant of her ancient people dwelt in daily terror. But CALF—with God's help—would soon change all of that.

Nicki sighed. This fortuitous route to Brussels had been chosen by the airline because these bloody skies were kept safe, patrolled by American fighter jets on orders from the president in Washington. Hostile Libya or volatile Syria were too dangerous as routes for a passenger airliner bound for free Europe. So the night flights from Nairobi always veered far to the east, above Mount Ararat in Turkey, where Noah and Nicki's ancestor, Shem, first set foot after the Flood. Here, American warplanes kept a tenuous peace from day to day, shooting down any Iraqi airship that dared venture into the no-fly zone north of the thirty-sixth latitude.

Nicki shifted again in her seat. She recalled the old legends, how her ancestor, Shem, had led his family out of these mountains into the fertile plain known to history as "the cradle of civilization." Her people, the descendants of Shem's second-born, Asshur, once had been proud and strong, ruling the Middle East from the Persian Gulf to the Nile River, putting all but Hezekiah's Judeans under the yoke of the Assyrian Empire. These Assyrians in their heyday had made a slave of Hezekiah's wayward son, Manasseh, making him lay bricks until he learned to listen to the voice of Yahweh. Now the Assyrians were the despised and rejected among mankind, the scum of the earth. CALF. *And God . . . did He care?*

"Mount Ararat . . ." The pilot's British-accented voice crackled on the airliner's intercom. "It lies just north of us, to the right of our plane if you look out your window. Superstitious folks claim that even today Noah's ark lies there buried in ice," he added with a chuckle.

Suddenly Nicki sat up. She checked her watch. Since her jetliner was running just ahead of the sunrise across the Middle East and eastern Europe, it would not yet be dawn when they landed in Brussels. Nicki enjoyed night flights ordinarily. But on occasions when her plane landed before daylight she would be uneasy, missing her rest.

Something else was amiss, also. She tried to focus on a tiny detail that seemed to grow larger in the back of her mind, gnawing at her fears. The syringe in General Rahman's arm—Nicki had wiped it clean of all prints, since hers were on it too. Then she had left it sticking there. Whether the police assume that Rahman died of a heroin overdose—or tested the liquid in the syringe and in his veins and discovered the truth—it would still appear to be suicide.

Or, would it? *What will the cops in Kenya make of a suicide syringe with no prints on it whatsoever? What will Baghdad do if—or when— they learn this?* Nicki shuddered at the thought, and the knots returned to her stomach.

❰❰❰

"So these 'Babylonians' you say are following us—actually they're Iraqis?" Chuck asked as Nicki finished her tale. He spoke quietly, fearfully almost.

Nicki nodded. "Saddam's people bribed the Kenyans to return Rahman's body without an autopsy. As you know, Hussein's scientists have developed one of the most sophisticated chemical weapons labs on earth. It didn't take the Iraqis long to discover that the drug in his veins wasn't heroin."

"Asp venom—enough to kill a horse, I'm sure."

"You got that right! A little snooping around Nairobi led them to an address where an American woman had received refrigerated packages from a laboratory in Australia."

"And this American woman?"

"The Babylonians still don't know for sure. But they've done a bit of triangulation. Their investigation seems to point to the talents of only one known American woman." Nicki poked her tongue playfully in an olive-complected cheek.

Chuck caught his breath. "Beneath the flesh and behind the face of the world's most attractive woman lies a mind capable of conceiving such a slick scheme—that of laying her hands on the precise location of Saddam's arsenal of biological and atomic weapons. U.N. Secretary General Kofi Annan and his elite team of inspectors tried to pull this stunt off. They failed. But I'm looking right at the lady genius who succeeded!"

Nicki reddened.

"So, you have managed to put together the pieces to the Vanguard missile? And to poison Saddam's top general with asp venom?" Chuck chuckled grimly. "Fortunately, Harry took the papers from your briefcase. And when the FBI sees them . . ."

"He's already shredded them, I'm sure. As far as Mr. Thompkins is concerned, I never existed. Besides, I still have the software." Nicki's eyes glowed with pleasure.

"You have a disk?"

"No. But I have the data." Nicki tapped her forehead.

"Memorized!? And did you also memorize the contents of Rahman's disk?"

Nicki grimaced. "No," she admitted. "Rahman pulled a fast one on us. He feared I might escape, so he gave me a disk we have not been able to read."

"But you said you read it in Nairobi—on the hotel's computer?"

"I'm sure General Rahman had seen that computer before."

"You mean—like his notebook computer, the hotel's computer had been programmed in advance to read the disk?"

"Exactly. It was evidently preloaded with an encrypted program to translate the disk. But we *will* get it! CALF has the world's best computer hacker working for them now."

"You mean the guy who broke into the Pentagon's computer files? He's in federal prison. He won't see daylight for twenty years."

"Seven to twenty, actually. He's out on parole already—just over three years in jail. The American justice system lacks the nerve even to keep enemies of the state out of circulation."

"So your . . . your CALF organization has hired him!" Chuck was appalled.

Nicki grinned. "Don't act so shocked. We've got the guy on a short leash. If he even looks like he wants to try getting into the Pentagon again, we'll call his parole officer."

"Sounds like you could use his talents in espionage."

"Not that way. The military has so many safety devices on its computer systems now that the chances of an unauthorized individual hacking into them without being detected are almost nil," Nicki explained. "But we have other methods," she added smugly.

"Once your hacker cracks Saddam's code, you'd do the world a favor by turning the data over to the CIA."

"No kidding? Like they'd believe it was genuine! The CIA, the FBI, the Pentagon—any federal agency—none of them will take reports seriously unless they themselves have uncovered it. We're amateurs, you know. We are the wild-eyed crowd who believe that Saddam is about to invade America with flying saucers and little green Martians."

"You're right there. Law enforcement at any level has a problem taking civilian reports seriously." Chuck sighed. "No one believed that the Rosenbergs could walk off with the secrets of the atomic bomb. They used a nonprofessional mole, Ethel Rosenberg's brother, who hadn't even been to college. In 1945 he memorized the formula for the bomb at the Manhattan Project's laboratories in Los Alamos, New Mexico."

"He carried no papers from the lab," Nicki cut in. She had studied the Rosenberg case carefully. Nicki had read about young Ethel Rosenberg and her husband Julius. Ethel was a loving mother with two sons. Yet, for her crime, she had had her head shaved, then she was strapped into the heavy oak chair at Sing Sing Prison in New York. Cruel electrodes were attached, and the executioner pulled the switch to send ten thousand volts crackling through her soft body. Nicki gripped the rail as the music continued below them. The strains of the wedding waltz returned to her consciousness as she finished her tale.

For a moment Chuck could only stare. "America hasn't had an execution for espionage since the Rosenbergs, half a century ago. You could get life in prison, though."

Nicki bit her lip. "It would be worth it all for my people. But now that I've told you this, I may have to kill you."

"I'm sure you could do it."

"I . . . I would never kill an innocent man. You know that." She bit her lip again. "But the Iraqis certainly will kill *me* when they find me."

"You're cute as a bug's ear when you bite your lip like that." Chuck figured a little levity might lighten things

"Stop it! You've no right!" she snapped.

"A moment ago you were threatening to do me in. Sorry." Chuck shrugged.

"Yes, I certainly was." Nicki grew sober, anxious again. She held out a hand, limp at the wrist. "'All the perfumes of Arabia . . .'"

"'Will not sweeten this bloody hand.'" Chuck finished Lady Macbeth's line for Nicki, as she spread her perfectly tapered fingers. "Nicki, I am worried about you. I'll admit that I'm a bit fond of you too. And I *do* have a responsibility for national security." Chuck shook his head in dismay. "But I'll go with you to Mexico. I have no choice that I can see until we shake these . . . these 'Babylonian' killers."

"I'm glad you've agreed, Chuck." Nicki grabbed his arm. "It's really late!" she whispered anxiously. "If the customs inspectors are to believe we're just a couple of *braceros* coming home to Agua Prieta after a shopping foray in the U.S., we've got to be going."

6

A Beach Too Far

He that . . . hardeneth his neck,
shall suddenly be destroyed.

—Solomon

To the border guards, the ragged couple who shuffled out of the shadows at the gate from Douglas, Arizona, to Agua Prieta, Mexico, was only another pair of impoverished Mexican shoppers. The *señor* hunkered over two paper sacks of clothing, and his stout *señora* huffed just behind, her hips jiggling with every step. They were evidently returning from a late-evening excursion north of the border where a peso would stretch further.

Chuck pretended to be mute. Nicki purposely picked a quarrel with a customs inspector, and they argued in animated Spanish over a paltry sixty pesos—two dollars—which was the duty charged on the new, worn-once clothing they had bought that morning in Tombstone. Since they were crossing as Mexicans, they weren't asked for their American ID.

〘〘〘

Mexican moonlight streamed softly across the bed as Nicki stirred for the hundredth time on the lumpy, springless mattress in what Chuck guessed must be Agua Prieta's seediest hotel. Chuck squirmed in the broken-down wicker rocker and adjusted once again the cheap sponge pillows Nicki had stuffed under her dress before they strolled across the border.

He and Nicki had registered in this old rat trap as *Señor* Juan and *Señora* Gloria Lopez, Chuck recalled, and no ID had been asked for. To have taken separate rooms, when obviously so poor, would surely have aroused the innkeeper's suspicion. For her sake, as well as his own, Chuck realized he must do everything in his power not to leave a trail the Iraqis could follow.

Nicki groaned aloud, then she rolled onto her back. Chuck opened one eye a sleepy slit, watching her breathe for a moment.

One well-formed arm lay at Nicki's side. With the other she tugged at the sheet as if aware he watched, then she circled her head with it. Nicki was ravishing in the moonlight as her ebony tresses washed like a dark waterfall across her pillow, her chest rising and falling in innocent rhythm beneath the sheet.

Innocent. *Yet, what dark secrets her heart must hold*, Chuck considered. He shuddered, remembering the terrible tale she'd confessed to him in the Hotel Gadsen's balcony. Chuck broke into a cold sweat as he thought about what she seemed capable of doing to him. And if Saddam's people found her? His heart at last fell at peace when he considered that, unlike Rahman, he had done no evil to this intrepid lady.

Chuck turned over again in the rickety chair. *Ouch*, his lips silently formed, as a sore lump in the flesh behind his left armpit struck the rough wicker arm. He patted it and felt the stitches—the bandage had come off a day earlier.

Odd. Chuck puzzled for the dozenth time how this injury had gotten there. "You probably cut yourself when you fell after that encounter with the assassin at the Tucson Airport," Nicki had suggested earlier. "I'll take the stitches out for you, once it's healed."

Still . . . I got into that cab without falling, I'm sure, Chuck worried. He touched the wound again, deciding to have his own doctor look at it when he got back to Boston, if it hadn't returned to normal.

🌙🌙🌙

Juan and Gloria Lopez stepped off the Mexican Trailways coach at Hermosillo International Airport late the next afternoon. The bus had hit every pothole in the poorly paved road as the half-crazed driver squealed the tires on mountain bends in the Sierra Madre range, then barreled across the narrow bridges that spanned deep arroyos and bottomless canyons, as farmers pulled their burros and oxcarts to the guardrails in terror. The Pan Am flight to Mexico City would now seem like a dream trip.

"You used a credit card to pay for our plane tickets," Chuck worried as he and Nicki ate a late lunch in Hermosillo Airport's only cafe while waiting for their flight to Ciudad Mexico to depart.

"Not to worry." Nicki smiled warmly. "Our concern right now is that whoever found you in Tucson is not able to tail us." She fussed with the collar of her new shirt, rumpled from hours on the bottom of an old shopping bag while she and Chuck were the *braceros* Juan and Gloria.

"True," he agreed flatly. Chuck was not convinced, knowing that modern electronics could transfer credit card transactions at the speed of light, even across international boundaries.

"We're not being followed just yet," Nicki asserted. Though her mouth smiled, Chuck saw only worry in her eyes. "It'll take a couple of days for my Discover card record to get through the system. By then the Babylonians will be looking for me in Beirut or Beijing or wherever I decide to send my trail. We'll then both be back in the U.S. under different aliases."

"Oh?"

"No problemo. That W. F. Fuller alias I gave you hasn't been used before. So neither *they* nor the CIA has it in computer files. You can be plain ol' Chuck Reynolds again, once Saddam's assassins realize we're no longer together."

"Yeah. What a relief," he snapped. The night before in the hotel in Agua, Prieta Chuck had felt himself the protector of this beautiful lady. Suddenly he wished he *could* just walk away.

"Me, I've been a chameleon for so long, I'm not even sure who I am," Nicki concluded sadly. "But who are you, Chuck?"

"Meaning?" Chuck raised an eyebrow.

"I know you basically as a security expert in an electronics plant. A nice guy—friendly and all that. And a widower. But exactly who are you, really? Everyone comes from somewhere, and we all have dreams about the future."

"I've got a daughter, Jennifer," Chuck ventured. "She's almost seventeen."

"And she lives in Maine—Waldo County, I think you once said. Go on."

"Jennifer lives with Shelly's parents—her grandparents—in an eighteenth-century, grey-shingled Cape Cod attached by an ell to a rambling old barn. The farmstead is on a dead-end gravel road. It's a place where you could forget the rest of the world existed. Some days the only sound is a woodpecker hunting beetles in an old beech tree along the stone wall beside the back pasture. It's just outside the village of Freedom."

"'Freedom.' I like that. Happiness and contentment too, it sounds like. I . . . I'd love for you to take me there someday, but I guess that can never be."

"We've got an hour to kill." Chuck glanced at his watch and wished that time would freeze and the moment would linger. How powerfully he found himself urged to help Nicki. Yet there were times when he feared to stay with her another minute.

❰❰❰

"Do you like it? Then let me pay for it," Chuck insisted later in the gift shop just off the café. So far, Nicki had paid for nearly everything out of what she said was her expense account from CALF. Though he knew that the cash he'd withdrawn from the money machine at the hospital in Tucson wouldn't last long once he was on his own, right now he was in a magnanimous spending mood.

Nicki held up the hand-wrought, turquoise-studded silver cross on a heavy chain, also handcrafted. "Feel its weight—not your usual imported Chinese stuff."

Chuck took the necklace. "Coin silver, by the weight of it. *Hecho en Mexico,* I believe," he agreed. Before Nicki could stop him, he handed the cashier two fifty-dollar bills.

"Engrave your name on it, *señora?* Just five dollars, American money." The clerk looked expectantly at Nicki and motioned at the engraving tools behind the counter.

"No thanks . . . wait, *señorita* . . . can you put a bull, with wings like a bird, on the back of the cross?"

"A bull with wings?" The girl frowned at Nicki.

"*El toro,*" explained Nicki. She pointed to a stack of restaurant paper place mats on a tray by the door. "Hand me one of those, please."

"OK, *señora.*"

"*Gracias.*" Nicki spread the mat on the glass jewelry counter. Quickly she sketched a pair of eagle wings on the bull, which was in the mat's center. "Like this."

"OK. I can copy that easy." The girl went to work at once.

Nicki hung the necklace around her neck several minutes later after the cashier had finished engraving the winged bull on the back. Both decided it went well with the denim shirt she'd bought in Tombstone. But then she dropped the cross inside her shirt. "No point in tempting the local sticky fingers crowd looking for American tourists. Besides . . ." Nicki pushed her tongue into her cheek, blushing. "There's a verse about this, Song of Solomon 1:13, as I recall. Read it when you're thinking of me."

"I've sworn to forget you as soon as we're out of Mexico," Chuck laughed.

At the Mexico City International Airport, Nicki purchased tickets to Cancun using the Ruby Sanchez alias, this time charging them to a Visa card in *Señora* Sanchez's name. "We both could use a couple of days at the beach," she said brightly. "Then I'll come back here to Mexico City and give the Babylonians a rabbit trail to follow overseas while I go on to the U.S., but *not* on the same plane with you," she added unhappily.

"Why are you telling me this? I've got to report you to Washington at my first opportunity."

"I know. But Washington is the *least* of my worries. You'll disappoint me if you *don't* tell them all you know about me. But my time is about up—my work is almost done. If I'm lucky, I'll get a chance to report to a congressional committee before I go to prison. And if not . . ." She drew her finger across her throat.

"What will you tell Congress about CALF?"

"Nothing whatsoever. As far as they're concerned, CALF doesn't even exist. I can say I acted as an individual, and that's what got the Russians and Iraqis after me."

"The Russians too?"

"Chuck, don't play dumb. The Russians try to place moles in every military contract plant in America. Otherwise, you'd be out of a job."

"You're right, of course," Chuck admitted. "So you have some firsthand knowledge of the Russian operations?"

"More than I care to think about. I'll fill you in someday."

Chuck and Nicki had passed the security gate at Hermosillo's sleepy airport without ringing the alarm. But Mexico City was a different story. Chuck's stainless steel wristwatch set the alarm off. No problem. He handed his watch to a guard, then stepped through without another beep.

Nicki had already placed her watch and a handful of Mexican copper coins into a basket to pass around the metal detector, and her purse had gone through the X-ray machine behind their paper shopping sacks of clothing. She stepped through.

Beep! Beep! Beep! Beep!

"This way, *señora*." A female guard pointed Nicki to a dressing room.

"That won't be necessary," Nicki said in English. She pulled her chain and silver cross over her head and passed it to the guard. This time there was no alarm.

"You'd have thought I was packing a gun," Nicki wisecracked, as soon as they were out of earshot.

"It's the drug trade. International terrorists too. They can't be too careful," Chuck pointed out.

"I suppose. But I hardly ever carry anything more deadly than pepper gas. Or asp venom," she added, suppressing a snicker. "The way *they* operate, if they get you, they get you."

"Yeah, like at the Tucson Airport." Chuck shuddered.

◖◖◖

The second morning at Cancun's Hotel Atlantico, rested from his run as a fugitive across Arizona and Mexico, Chuck awoke before dawn. He showered and slipped into his swimming trunks. Stepping into a pair of flip-flops and pulling a hotel-supplied bathrobe over his trunks, Chuck took the elevator to the main floor.

I wish I had my Bible with me, Chuck mused, as he crossed the lobby toward where the early shift of wait staff was just setting tables for breakfast. He peered through the glass doors. Across the dining room a long wall of plate glass separated the main restaurant from an outdoor dining deck.

Chuck strolled to a table just inside the windows, which proved to be sliding glass doors. *At least I can sit alone to pray and meditate while the sun rises over the Caribbean,* Chuck decided.

"Breakfast will be ready in an hour, *señor*," advised a busboy, hurrying up.

"Coffee?"

"*Si.* We have a pot ready. Cappuccino, if you'd prefer."

"Sounds great!"

The busboy hurried off.

Chuck amused himself for a moment watching a pelican through the glass, bolder than most of the other shore birds. It had landed near the glass, and it waddled impudently past, expecting to be fed. The fowl flapped its wings, and its cumbersome bulk lifted only a few feet as it skittered across the deck planks. Chuck watched as the bird plopped down beside another early-rising tourist who sat at a table alone on the far side of the deck. The sun burst through the haze in a blaze of fire just then, and the tourist on the deck became a black silhouette against the solar glare.

"Your cappuccino, *señor.*"

"Thanks . . . *gracias,*" Chuck murmured. He glanced outside again, and the tourist seemed to be feeding the pelican, tossing it crumbs, maybe. Chuck watched for just a second longer, then he turned back to the retreating busboy who had served him. "Waiter!" Chuck called.

"*Señor?*" The boy turned.

"May I carry my mug to the patio?"

"Of course, *señor!*"

"Then bring me another one, please."

"Right away, *señor!*" A moment later the busboy returned with the second drink. "The waiters, they get angry when we do their work," he confided.

"And they're not even here yet," Chuck chuckled. He passed the busboy a dollar, then picked up the steaming mugs. "Slide the patio door open for me, please."

((((

"Early riser?" Nicki raised an eyebrow as Chuck placed the glass mugs on her deck table.

"Earlier riser, yourself! May I sit down?"

"Seems you've already claimed your right to a seat. And I do love cappuccino!"

Chuck slid into a chair opposite Nicki. "I was just wishing I'd brought mine." He nodded toward the book she'd been reading in the morning twilight. It was a Bible, a slender pocket edition bound in brown calfskin.

"The only thing I have of my mother's," Nicki answered slowly, almost solemnly. "I carried this with me all those years on the street in Saigon. Mother got it from the missionaries who taught her English. The Elizabethan language is a little old-fashioned. But then it comes easily to a linguist," she laughed.

"Really! I thought you were an engineer."

"That, too." Nicki shrugged. "I got bored with studying just nuclear physics at MIT. So I enrolled in Harvard Divinity School's evening division as a special student. After Greek and Hebrew, I learned Aramaic, as well as Sumerian and Akkadian. My father's cousin and her husband didn't mind paying my tuition, as long as I kept my grades up. Assyrians in exile help one another."

"Akkadian? Never heard of it."

"Few folks have—except experts in ancient cuneiform writings."

"The Babylonians wrote in cuneiform," Chuck recalled from a course he'd once taken in ancient history.

Nicki smiled wryly. "The Babylonians *borrowed* cuneiform from the Assyrians, just as the Romans borrowed the writing system we use today from the Greeks, whom they conquered."

"Let me guess—Akkadian was the language of the ancient Assyrians. But what use does an engineer with a Ph.D. in nuclear physics have for a dead language?" Chuck was puzzled.

"See here." Nicki slid her Bible across the table's glass top. "I never tire of reading this." She tapped her finger on a page in Ezekiel 37, where she had highlighted several verses with a marker: "Thus saith the LORD God unto these bones; Behold, I will cause breath to enter into you, and ye shall live."

"I'm familiar with that verse. He was prophesying that dead Israel would one day be restored as a nation and worship the Lord once again."

"Indeed!" Nicki agreed, her eyes ablaze. "Yet the world's great wise men have always predicted that a nation, once dead, stays dead. Like Longfellow."

"His 'Jewish Cemetery at Newport,'" Chuck recalled. "Nineteenth-century poet Henry W. Longfellow was confident that 'These Hebrews in their graves' would remain there. He was wrong, of course. Israel has been alive and well since 1948."

"Is Israel the only nation spoken of in Old Testament prophecy?" Nicki queried, her eyes now aglow with glee.

"Well . . ." Chuck thought for a moment. "The Lord did send Jonah to preach the word in Nineveh, the capital of Assyria. Jonah was a prophet of sorts."

"And Isaiah?" Nicki bore into Chuck with her intense eyes. The morning sun now played with her tresses, which flowed loose in the south sea breeze, not yet tied back for the day. Chuck gasped. Her beauty? Her obvious intelligence? Or her knowledge of the Bible? He could not tell which struck him the most forcefully. "Isaiah *does* mention Assyria," he agreed. "Something about a highway . . ." His voice trailed off at the realization.

"Chapter nineteen." Nicki sipped her cappuccino in silence, waiting for Chuck to find the passage.

He picked up the old Bible that had belonged to Nicki's Vietnamese mother, turning to Isaiah 19, half expecting to find a reference to Vietnam there. In verses twenty-three and twenty-four, Chuck read, "'In that day there shall be a highway out of Egypt to Assyria, and . . . Israel [shall] be the third with Egypt and with Assyria.' I'm impressed," he admitted. "Apparently Assyria will be restored; its dry bones will be given life like Israel's. Isaiah does seem to say this," Chuck concluded.

"Recall that both Egypt and Israel were nonexistent for hundreds of years, their lands parts of the Ottoman Empire," Nicki noted.

"But Assyria? And where do *you* fit in? I'm not sure . . ."

Nicki took his hand. "My daddy was . . ."

"An Assyrian refugee," Chuck finished for her, remembering.

"Someday, when you're of a mind to do some research, compare the boundaries of the lands inhabited by the Assyrians under the Ottomans with the territory of ancient Assyria. You may be surprised." Nicki stretched. She stood, loosening the tie on her white corduroy robe, identical to the hotel robe Chuck wore. "How about a swim before breakfast—just the two of us," she laughed. "No one else is out this early." She nodded toward the hotel's Olympic-size pool. "C'mon!"

"I like to live dangerously," Chuck laughed. He peeled off his robe, tossing it with hers on a bench.

☾☾☾

I guess she changed her mind, Chuck thought, disappointed, as he strode toward where Nicki relaxed in a chaise lounge. This was the afternoon, out of earshot of others, that Chuck had determined to press Nicki for some facts: Why did this international cause, CALF, so motivate her and drive her to near-superhuman exploits? What plans did CALF have to set up a nation in a territory also claimed by the Kurds? How did CALF expect to succeed in accomplishing what the British Mandate and the League of Nations failed to do between 1919 and 1939? More importantly, was CALF a threat to the United States?

Nicki had gone to her room right after lunch, promising to change into her new swimsuit for a stroll on the Cancun beach with Chuck later that afternoon, then perhaps to take a dip in the tropical breakers if the surf was not too rough. But instead, Nicki now wore the denim shirt and ankle-length, flowered peasant skirt she'd bought at that tourist shop in Tombstone. Though she wore wide sunglasses, she also had her snappy straw boater pushed down onto her forehead to shade her eyes. *Oh well,* Chuck told himself. *She's unpredictable—I guess I'd be too, if I had her troubles.*

It was a long walk across the hotel's broad, Bermuda grass lawn, which swept down toward the waterfront, and Chuck took his time as he strolled toward Nicki on the seaside patio. *Perhaps this isn't the Lord's time for me to press her for the details,* he mused. Chuck had left Boston a week ago, and he was tempted to tell Nicki no more games, then take the next plane to Washington. He figured he'd probably be arrested for his involvement with Nicki, allegedly helping her skip the country, and related charges, whether he went now or later. The Feds nailed you first and asked questions afterward. Given the probable nature of the charges he expected, the bail would be a million dollars, at least. After what Nicki had told him about her phone chat with Harry Thompkins, Chuck hardly expected the Old Man to post bail for him. *Or, was she even telling me the truth?*

So, where am I gonna raise that kind of bread? Chuck worried. He sighed, watching Nicki for a moment, pausing in his stride, considering. It seemed to Chuck that he was trapped in an Edenlike hiatus between a vicious attempt on his life just days ago and probable prosecution for infamous crimes, a few days away. He shook his head. These incredible circumstances nearly overwhelmed him. *Yet God has been good enough to give me a time of relaxation, even in my desperate predicament,* he considered.

Why can't the present go on forever? Chuck pondered. The image of Keats's "Ode to a Grecian Urn" now flashed through Chuck's mind: a forlorn youth chasing a lithe maiden around a glazed vase—the youth frozen in eternal desire, the maiden never to be captured, the chase never to conclude. "The story of *my* life," Chuck muttered half aloud. "Nicki!" he called.

The lady on the chaise lounge tipped her head toward him and smiled beneath her wide, dark glasses.

Chuck hurried on, trying to figure out his best move when he returned to the States. Harry *could* raise the bail, of course, Chuck knew. But he guessed the Old Man would look on him no more kindly than would the U.S. Justice Department, since he'd actually run off to Mexico with Nicki Towns, a wanted criminal. Harry already believed Chuck had a romantic interest in her. Besides, Harry could no doubt serve his own interests best by pretending to be ignorant of the whole mess. Nicki had that figured right.

I've committed myself to stay with her until this is over. One more day after this, she promised, and we'll both head back to the United States, separately.

Odd, Chuck mused. The man in the white linen suit and Panama hat strolling toward the patio from a motor launch drawn up on the beach had appeared from a distance to be just another well-heeled Latin American businessman. But as they both drew near where Nicki sunned herself, the man seemed instead to be an Arab—wiry, athletic, in his early thirties. The guy was perhaps half a dozen steps ahead of Chuck, so he reached Nicki first.

"Excuse me, miss," the man said in British-accented English, "I have a message for Ruby Sanchez."

"I am she." Nicki spoke huskily like a heavy smoker. She adjusted her sunglasses and looked directly at the messenger. Nicki's purse lay across her knees, and she had pushed one hand inside while Chuck hurried up, as if she was about to show him something.

Chuck had not heard this tone of voice from Nicki before. *She's surprised, I guess. Probably a little afraid. No one is supposed to know we're here. She didn't register as "Ruby Sanchez." That Arab? Deja vu!*

Chuck decided in a nanosecond to jump the man, frisk him, let him prove he was unarmed before delivering any message to Nicki. He crossed the remaining yards over the clay tiles in three bounds, tackling the guy in a quarterback dive he hadn't used since college.

Chuck saw Nicki's free hand cover her face in terror just as he dove, and she seemed to struggle to pull her other hand from her purse. "No!" she shrieked.

Her scream was cut short by two blasts from a double-barreled, sawed-off shotgun as Chuck's shoulder impacted the man's hip, sending him sprawling, the discharged gun skittering across the tiles.

Nicki's assailant leaped the low wall onto the beach and raced for his boat. Chuck tried to rise, but the killer had already delivered an expert punch beneath his diaphragm, effectively paralyzing his lungs. His eyes blurred as his brain starved for oxygen, and his last conscious memory was Nicki sprawled on the lounge, her lifeblood spurting onto the tiles from her face and throat—or from where her face had been.

◖◖◖

"Señorita Sanchez's body is a grisly sight, but you can see it if you insist, Mister Fuller." Captain Eduardo Peron of the police department of Quintana Roo State on Mexico's Yucatan Peninsula addressed Chuck by the name he had used on his hotel registration.

"Her face is . . . ?"

"It's gone." Captain Peron finished Chuck's horrified sentence. "Both barrels went off in sequence. The weapon has a single trigger, and when you tackled the killer, it naturally caused his finger to squeeze it all the way." Peron raised an eyebrow. "The second charge of buckshot might have had your name on it, *señor?*"

Chuck shuddered. "Yeah," he sighed, shaking his head. "Thanks," he croaked finally.

"You are free to go, now that we've established that your fingerprints are not those on the shotgun—or on her gun." Peron grinned, fingering the hundred-dollar bill Chuck had kept tucked into his trunks along with his room key. "Our processing fee for quick service," he chuckled. "Fortunately for you, I'm the fingerprint expert as well as captain in this district." Peron smiled broadly.

"*Her* gun?" Chuck was startled.

"Your lady friend carried a gun, *señor*, a 9-millimeter Glock. She was clutching it when she died. It is a fourteen-shot police weapon—the very best!" Peron showed evident envy as he described the fine gun he'd found in Nicki's possession. "A very popular weapon among drug dealers in the States, no?"

"A gun!" Chuck repeated. He was amazed, perplexed. "I'm not used to such . . . such dangerous company." Chuck glanced again at the swimming trunks, his only clothing. "It's five miles in the hot sun back to my hotel. And as I told you, my wallet is in my room. I don't even have cab fare left in my trunks," he protested.

Peron shrugged, then he nodded toward a surly youth in a rumpled uniform smoking a cigarillo, lounging behind the counter. "Drive *Señor* Fuller out to the Hotel Atlantico," he ordered. "And hurry."

"Oh—wait a minute." Peron stepped into a back room and returned seconds later with Nicki's blood-splattered purse. "You might as well take this with you back to the States, Mister Fuller. Give to her mother, maybe? We've photocopied all her papers— we'll notify her family to send for the body."

"Thanks." Chuck was dumbfounded. Shaking, he took her handbag and folded it under his arm.

❮❮❮

Chuck cleaned the blood off Nicki's purse and went through it in his room as soon as he dressed. To his relief he found the secret compartment undisturbed—even her cash was still there. The Quintana Roo police had not bothered to search Nicki's room, he concluded, when he let himself in with the key he found in her purse. The hotel register had no "Ruby Sanchez" listed, Chuck knew. And apparently the police decided that her papers gave them all they needed. *Pistol-packing señoritas evidently aren't a novelty around here,* Chuck figured. It then occurred to him that the papers from Nicki's secret compartment just might get him off the hook with the FBI.

He gathered the few belongings she had purchased since they left Tucson, though he had little idea what he would do with them. *I guess I can probably find her cousin in Boston,* he told himself.

Chuck next noticed Nicki's mother's well-thumbed, leather-bound Bible on the nightstand, held open by the necklace he had bought her. He shook his head, considering the inconsistency—she had lied to him, carried a gun illegally, yet he knew that she was a student of the Word of God.

Chuck picked up the Bible. It had thoughtful notes written in Nicki's hand in the margin of nearly every page—not the kind of notations scribbled by a cultist who takes a few verses out of context here and there to satisfy preconceived notions. He glanced at the passage where she'd used the necklace as a bookmark. Song of Solomon 1:13 was highlighted: "A bundle of myrrh is my well-beloved unto me; he shall lie all night betwixt my breasts."

In the margin Nicki had penned, "Oh that I could have a 'beloved lover' to rest his head on my bosom!" This notation was dated—yesterday!

Trembling, nearly in shock, Chuck dropped the Bible and the necklace into the purse. He sank onto the bed, weeping, sobbing aloud.

After some moments Chuck rose to his feet and struggled into the bathroom to wash his face. Behind the door he found Nicki's new sandals, which he tossed into the center of the bed with the other stuff.

He stared at the pile for a moment. *What haven't I found?—her new black maillot swimsuit,* he realized. He recalled how delightfully, yet modestly, the suit had flattered her femininity. "You look great in that," he had told her only that morning when she'd worn it to the pool after breakfast. Chuck peered into the shower, but the suit wasn't hanging there to drip. He rechecked the drawers and closet. She must have had it on underneath her skirt, he finally concluded, recalling again that Nicki had definitely said she planned to change into her swimsuit.

Back in his own room, Chuck worked quickly to extract himself from the evil web that had caught Nicki, and which, he felt certain, he himself was being drawn into by their association. He found himself baffled and perturbed, not merely so much by her murder, but that she'd obviously been lying to him. Where did she get that gun? A woman who could play him along, while finding a way to slip a heavy automatic pistol through security at one of the world's major airports—right under Chuck's very eyes—had to have been clever and dangerous beyond belief. And she'd killed before, he mused, shuddering. *Had she told me the whole story?* he asked himself.

Chuck quickly phoned the airport, and while waiting for a ticket agent to answer, he made a decision. Rather than fly directly to Washington, he would catch a plane to Los Angeles using his alias, W. F. Fuller. Nicki had assured him that, once they separated, he was safe. But he could no longer trust her promises. Her duplicity had been betrayed even in her death.

Once he got to L.A., Chuck figured he could travel east, often changing aliases and means of transportation, always looking over his shoulder until he was certain he was no longer being tailed. Whether Nicki's murder had been set up by a political conspiracy or international terrorists, these people—*they,* the "Babylonians"—obviously were expert at tracking and destroying their enemies. Uncomfortably, Chuck recalled that he had warned Nicki about twice using a credit card to purchase their tickets.

"We can hold your ticket until one hour before departure at 7:10 A.M., *Señor* Fuller. Or if you wish to use a credit card, we'll hold it until departure time, and your boarding pass will be at the gate."

Chuck stared unhappily at his Visa card, which from habit he'd placed beside the phone. He could simply give the girl the number to hold his seat until 7:10, then arrive early and pay cash. That way Citibank would have no record that he'd used the card. Still . . . there would be a record of the transaction at the ticketing office.

"*Señor* Fuller?"

"Uh . . . I'll arrive early and pay cash," he decided.

"Very well, sir. We'll hold your seat until 6:10 A.M."

Chuck now had to deal with the possibility that Nicki's assassin would return during the night to kill him. He remembered the killer's double-barreled shotgun—*two* shots! His stomach knotted involuntarily.

Chuck quickly stuffed his possessions—and Nicki's, with the purse—into their two shopping bags. He chuckled grimly when he saw the size of his burden, for both their belongings made only enough baggage that he could easily tote on foot for miles, if necessary. The haste with which he'd departed Boston had not left him time to pack. He supposed that in Nicki's venture to rescue him from the Tucson Police Department—and from whomever set him up—she'd likewise left home without packing.

There were hotels and resorts all along this strip of sand fronting the Caribbean. He'd just hike until he found a cheap room and pick an alias out of a hat, so to speak, paying cash. No phone calls and no credit cards. And no cab until he needed a ride to the airport. Who could know who might be asking questions of taxi drivers?

The Ponce de Leon was a third-rate tourist hotel near the center of town, a mile from the beach. The restaurant didn't offer American food except hamburgers, so Chuck ordered a hamburger. The meat was greasy, and the fries tasted of fish.

Chuck paid cash under the name of Walt Smith for a room on the top floor of the old, stuccoed hotel, and he retired upstairs as soon as he finished eating. The door, he discovered, had only a single lock, besides a badly worn bolt and no chain. Homemade security would have to do for tonight, so he pulled the heavy dresser across the doorway. Chuck tipped his room's only chair against the dresser, balancing it so it would crash over with a clatter if the dresser were shoved as little as an inch from the outside. *Too bad that helpful police captain didn't give me Nicki's gun with the rest of her stuff,* he thought grimly.

The window was shuttered on the outside, not barred like the ground-floor windows. Chuck raised the blind, then pushed the shutters apart, sticking his head out. Five stories straight down to the alley. There were no ledges or downspouts nearby that a cat burglar could use. *Good.* From above, Chuck observed, the eaves of the clay tile roof were smooth, with no gutters for a handhold. *Also good.*

He pulled the wooden shutters across the window. Their louvers would barely admit enough air in the closed position to give sufficient circulation, Chuck realized. Digging his rumpled silk necktie from the bottom of a shopping bag, he laced it through the rickety louvers, knotting it on the inside.

Chuck found himself handling Nicki's purse tenderly, like a precious treasure as he laid it on the bed, intent on a closer look at its contents now that he was safe in his room. He had already scrubbed the blood splatters off while at the Hotel Atlantico, using cold water and a scouring pad a maid had left beneath his sink. No sense in attracting needless attention.

The handbag was soft, hand-polished sheepskin. It had been hand-tooled by lepers at a Christian leprosarium in Kenya, Nicki had told him. Though she had not received the Jesus of the gospel, she admired His work of mercy toward the maimed and handicapped. Nicki never missed an opportunity to assist the down-and-out, Chuck had learned.

One highlight of Nicki's trip to Africa had been her visit to this leprosarium, where she had bought this purse and a matching wallet from their store. What a contradictory mixture of compassion and cold-blooded ruthlessness Nicki had been!

Not for a moment did Chuck consider helping himself to the dead woman's money from the secret compartment, which he discovered to be nearly ten thousand dollars. *Nicki might want me to have it*, he thought. But the idea of helping himself to it seemed like robbing a grave. Too, the contents of that hidden compartment might be his ticket to freedom from prosecution, once he got to Washington, Chuck realized. Better let the FBI examine it intact.

He fished her wallet from the purse and examined the contents. Rather sparse. All of Nicki's ID, except the fake driver's license and papers for her Ruby Sanchez alias, she had apparently placed in the bottom compartment of the shoulder purse. No money left in the wallet. The police had gotten their "fee," Chuck indignantly considered, remembering the thick wad of fifties and hundreds she had carried.

Then Chuck came across Nicki's Visa card in the name of Ruby Sanchez. Chuck knew he'd have no way to repay the bank if he were to charge a purchase on this card. That would plainly be theft. Yet a card in the name of an alias has its uses. He could secure a rental car or guarantee a room or a plane ticket with this and his Ruben Sanchez driver's license, even though he would certainly pay cash. This alone he slipped into his own wallet. Tucking everything carefully into her purse, he placed it on the nightstand by his bed.

⦗⦗⦗

Chuck rose at four A.M. and quickly dressed and shaved. He was slipping the cheap razor and toothbrush back into his shopping bag when he happened to glance at the nightstand. His watch was there, along with his wallet and a nail clipper. Nicki's purse, which had held her wallet, her Bible, and the engraved turquoise necklace, was gone!

He checked his own wallet. His money, still nearly three thousand dollars, hadn't been touched. The Visa card with the Ruby Sanchez alias was undisturbed. Both bags of clothing were still there, on the floor where he'd tossed them.

Shaking, Chuck stepped to the window, where the shutters were still closed. He reached for his tie to find that it had been neatly slit from the outside, opposite the knot, then deftly poked back into place.

For nearly an hour Chuck frantically searched the alley and nearby parking lots in the predawn darkness. He checked garbage cans for several blocks in both directions. *Thieves in America usually clean out the purses they steal, then ditch them at the first opportunity. But this is Mexico, and American tourists seldom stick around to press charges.* Chuck chortled grimly, imagining some Mexican woman proudly carrying her black-market, hand-tooled leather handbag for the next several years, never aware that its stiff bottom contained thousands of good American dollars, spendable all over Mexico!

Then Chuck's heart sank as he considered what he'd tell the FBI, with no proof that Nicki Towns, a.k.a. Ruby Sanchez and Ngo Thieu, had ever existed! "God, what are you doing to me?!" he prayed, groaning. Nicki was gone. A thief had stolen her possessions. Now Chuck didn't even have any evidence for the authorities.

Chuck hurried to the lobby and phoned a cab for a ride to the airport, glad now that he'd decided not to fly directly to Washington. "Thank You, Lord, for wisdom," he breathed as his cab pulled up minutes later. Still troubling Chuck, though, was the thought that Nicki had died without trusting Christ as her Savior.

7

The Homecoming

Jacob went on his way,
and the angels of God met him.

—Moses

C are for a drink, *Señor* Fuller?" The flight attendant had just
served first class, and she was working her way back, through
business then tourist class. Chuck had taken a tourist-class seat for
the seven-hour flight from Cancun to L.A., since he had absolutely
no idea when he'd see another paycheck—if Harry still had a job
for him when he got back to Boston.

"Sure." He glanced past the wines and beers and settled his gaze
on a soft drink. "Sprite, please." Glad for a window seat, Chuck sipped
the Sprite and chewed on ice. He changed his position and stared out
the window. The big 747 had already left the Caribbean Sea and the
Yucatan Peninsula behind. Six miles below, the pale blue Gulf of
Mexico stretched to the horizon. To the west only the thin, brown line
of the coast of Mexico showed that they were still in North America.

Chuck slid the window shade closed and tried to sleep. *With Nicki gone, I can return to my job at Salem Electronics*, he decided. There'd likely be a debriefing by the FBI. There could even be an arrest for flight to avoid arrest, but Chuck didn't think so. The attempt on his life in Tucson wasn't government related—not at the federal level, he was certain. Besides, the FBI didn't even know he had left the country, since he and Nicki had crossed the border as Mexican *braceros*.

Still, the terrorists got Nicki, and somebody sure wants me dead too, Chuck considered. *Or maybe they'd prefer to capture me alive to use me—for what? Whoever it was, they apparently hadn't been trying to get to Nicki through me, since I was attacked two days before she came to my rescue. No one would have a reason to link us up before then*, he mused.

Or would they? Chuck remembered uncomfortably that he had once had a date with Nicki, and they had had coffee together a couple of times. Had she been shadowed by international thugs even while she worked at Salem Electronics? The thought worried him.

Then there was the involvement of the Tucson City PD and the police manhunt when he escaped his hospital room. Nicki's dire warnings about foreign agents inside the Pentagon flitted through his fevered brain just now. Chuck had made a number of friends in the Raleigh, North Carolina, office of the FBI during his years as head of the North Carolina Bureau of Investigation. *Maybe I'll ask one of them to nose around in Washington for me*, he thought. The FBI may have simply asked the Tucson PD to detain him.

Sleep would not come. The travel magazines in the seat-back rack held little interest. And didn't these tourist flights ever show anything but corny comedy movies?

Chuck stared for a moment at the folding door leading to first class. *Business reading. All the good mags are in there*, he decided. He struggled from his seat.

Forbes. Fortune. Business Week. Barron's. He found all the current issues in a rack just inside first class. *Great. And here's one with an article on "Keeping Your Industry's Secrets Hidden from Electronic Snooping." I sure could use this*, Chuck decided.

He turned from the rack, gloating, almost, at having discovered something to sink his teeth into. His eye caught an attractive Latin lady two rows back. She wore a pricey linen suit in navy blue, with dark hose and expensive pumps. For reasons not fully formed in his heart, Chuck tried to get a glimpse of the woman's face without her thinking he was staring. But her features, framed in long glossy ebony ringlets, were veiled behind sunglasses. Just then she raised her copy of the *Wall Street Journal*, as if to shield from sun streaming in through her window, completely blocking his view.

Nicki. Chuck was numb as he shuffled back to his seat. *Nicki? No. She's dead.*

Briefly, Chuck remembered how, weeks after he had laid his Shelly to rest in that country churchyard in North Carolina, he had left little Jennifer with Grandma Mae Basford and had driven into Winston-Salem for a job interview. He didn't feel up to continuing in the pastorate, and police work, his second vocation, seemed attractive just then.

Chuck had found himself by habit that day at the door of Old Salem Tavern, an eighteenth-century, romantic Moravian eatery where he had sometimes taken Shelly for a treat. Only then it dawned on him that Shoney's buffet would be more appropriate for a man dining alone. Still, he was there already, so he walked inside and asked the hostess for his accustomed window seat.

Some minutes after he had ordered the broiled fish, giggles from a pair of college girls caught his attention. Or were they college girls? The brunette, whose face he could see, was maybe nineteen, plain, well-scrubbed, pretty, probably a student from the nearby Baptist college. She was the one giggling.

The other, a blonde, had her back to him. She wore a conservative, inexpensive dress with a cardigan sweater, like a schoolteacher or a preacher's wife. Her figure, slightly full, could have been that of his Shelly. And that voice: the lovely, lilting mountain drawl that pronounced two distinct vowels in many monosyllabic words: "yea-iss" for yes, or "they-it" for that. The voice was tender, soft, sweet.

Chuck's imagination ran wild. Had the hospital given the undertaker the wrong body after Shelly died of cancer? Shelly was alive, well, living here in Winston-Salem, an amnesia victim trying to discover her true identity!

It was too much. Chuck had canceled his food order and paid for his iced tea. He strode out of Old Salem Tavern without ever seeing the soft-voiced, blonde mountain woman's face. In the years that followed, Chuck had kicked himself many times over, first for not getting a peek at her face, and again for ever allowing the devil to taunt him with the longing notion that Shelly might still be alive.

Or had it really been the master deceiver? A man's heart can often conjure up visions as lucid as from supernatural sources, Chuck realized now, dismissing his longing glimpse of the Latin beauty in first class.

The sun hung low over the Pacific when the big airship circled to land at Los Angeles International Airport. Chuck checked his papers: birth certificate and driver's license for W. F. Fuller, born in Freedom, Maine—all supplied by Nicki. He considered the irony: he would soon be in rural, backwoods Freedom to visit his teen daughter, Jennifer, where she lived with his wife's mother and stepfather.

Next to his own parents, Mom and Pop Basford were the greatest people on earth, a unique couple. His mother-in-law, Mae Basford, was a North Carolina hillbilly from the Smoky Mountains. Pop, Stan Basford, would never have left the Maine woods where he grew up except that a rare form of bone cancer had sent Stan, a widower, to Boston's Old Bay Hospital for tests. Here, he had met and married Mae, a registered nurse, the widowed mother of a small girl, Rochelle. The couple, with Mae's girl, Shelly, had returned together to Mae's community in the Smokies, where Stan Basford worked in a nearby textile mill until he retired. By that time Mae's daughter, Shelly, had become Chuck's wife and a mother.

After Shelly died, little Jennifer went to live with Stan and Mae, her grandmother, for Chuck knew how badly his daughter needed a mother's love. Then when Jen was a teen, Stan Basford bought an abandoned backwoods farmstead near Freedom, Maine, as a retirement home. He settled there to enjoy a late-life career as a hunting guide, while he and Mae raised Jennifer as if she were their own. Chuck's move from North Carolina to Salem Electronics North, outside Boston, was in part motivated by a need to be near enough to Jennifer to visit her on weekends.

The squawk of the plane's tires at touchdown, followed by the rumble of rubber on asphalt, brought Chuck out of his reverie. As soon as the plane stopped rolling, he grabbed his single bag from the overhead rack. Glad that he did not need to wait with the others at the baggage carousel, he hurried to the nearest men's room.

Chuck did not see the black-haired lady in the sunglasses when she exited the plane. He was relieved that the first-class passengers departed ahead of him. *Feeding a fantasy about ever seeing Nicki alive is wallowing in needless misery,* he decided. Chuck realized he could no longer fill his emptiness with visions of Nicki. The Lord, he trusted, would fill this void in His good time.

Careless, Chuck thought. An expensive alligator briefcase stood just inside a stall door, where a thief could readily hook it with a cane. He had seen such petty crooks—white cane like a blind man, loose trench coat to hold their contraband. *Some guys like to take chances, I guess.* Then he noticed that the briefcase's owner, a tall, powerfully built man in sunglasses, was standing up, silently facing the door.

Odd, Chuck thought.

As he held his hands beneath the electric dryer, Chuck recalled uncomfortably the last instance when he had considered reporting a suspicious character to airport security. He had not done so, and the consequences were the chain reaction that had cost Nicki her life, still reverberating in his own life. *Guess I'm just a bit paranoid,* he decided, as he bent to pick up his own bag.

"Try to run, Mister Reynolds, and I'll blow your head off." It was the man from the toilet stall. "Drop your bag. Stand up slowly."

Chuck obeyed.

"You're going to walk ahead of me to that stall, very carefully. Now move!"

Yeah, right. Aloud, Chuck asked, "Are you going to flush me down, Bozo?"

"I'll kill . . ." the voice behind him hissed. The thug didn't finish his sentence, as Chuck dodged sideways, then brought the full weight of his right shoulder into the man's chest.

A pistol went off behind Chuck, its blast muffled by Chuck's jacket and shirt. A searing pain shot across his left shoulder blade.

The assailant scrambled to his feet as Chuck spun around, but too late to kick. The man was muscular—a swarthy Middle Easterner. Chuck quickly took it all in. His only resource was to follow up on the surprise—and pray. The guy brought his pistol back up, his other arm flailing to regain his balance.

Chuck had one hand on the pistol barrel and the other on the guy's wrist in a flash. He turned the double-barreled derringer's muzzle up under the hitman's chin. The hammer snapped down, the weapon blasted. The thug fell heavily against the door, blocking the entrance, blood flowing out into the hallway.

Chuck rammed the smoking pistol into his jacket pocket and grabbed his bag. As he circled to the other exit, it occurred to him that the men's room, strangely, was empty except for himself and the dead assailant. He stepped into the passageway and glanced around. Yellow and red signs on both doors proclaimed, "Out of Order" in both English and Spanish. A young man in an airport maintenance uniform appeared to be trying frantically to push open the door held by the big thug's body.

That guy was also a Middle Easterner, possibly an Arab, Chuck noticed as he hurried away.

((((

The Palms Motel, on Harbor Boulevard in Costa Mesa, was more than an hour's ride by city bus from the airport. Chuck changed busses half a dozen times, making sure he was not followed, always watching the bus's rear to be sure no one was tailing him in a car.

His injured shoulder posed a minor problem. Though not bleeding heavily, blood had oozed down beneath his shirt into his pants so that they stuck to his buttocks when he sat down. He managed to hide the wound from curious gazes by fishing a rumpled sweatshirt from his bag and tossing it casually over his shoulder, letting it hang down like a draped towel.

The pistol-shaped lump in his coat pocket? Chuck didn't dare look at it.

The motel was next to a shopping mall, and once he got his room key Chuck went straight to a Walgreens for medical supplies. Going to a hospital emergency room to get patched up was out of the question. Gunshot wounds usually involved a felony, and a felony involved cops, and cops asked questions. And they frisked you. Then more questions.

Armed with a hand-held mirror, a package of wide, old-fashioned single-edge razor blades, rubbing alcohol, antibiotic ointment, gauze, and surgical tape, Chuck hurried toward the cash register. He spotted a display of two-pound boxes of fig newtons, and he grabbed a package. He'd been fed well on the long flight from Cancun, but Chuck didn't know when it would be safe to go into a restaurant—if ever.

His room, on the second floor of The Palms, was entered from an inside hallway. The single, large window overlooked a golf course, and it did not open. Chuck had requested an inside room overlooking the palm-shaded pool, since anyone passing into the courtyard had to pass the muster of motel security. But, "Sorry, sir, those rooms are always given to guests with advance reservations," the desk clerk told him.

Chuck's bathroom window was another matter. It was an old-fashioned, wood-sash affair, with only a thin brass catch. Chuck removed the lid from the toilet tank, and, placing it vertically on top of the bottom sash, he jammed it in place. *Good. Quite a racket if that thing tumbles onto the tile floor,* he decided.

Next, he examined the unusual, large-bore pistol with which his intended assassin had accidentally shot himself. *Odd,* he thought. The technology was old and crude, even using rubber bands to snap the hammers onto the firing pins. But it was clever and efficient enough to deliver two lethal shots at close range, and it was possibly effective up to one hundred feet.

But new, high-tech materials had also gone into this weapon. Chuck smiled wryly at the terrorist's ingenuity as he examined the centuries-old, over-and-under design of the neat little derringer. It was carefully sawn and drilled from a solid block of high-tech carbon fiber. *This little jewel will go right through airport security without triggering an alarm*, Chuck noted.

The handgrip and trigger, he quickly discovered, were carved from ebony wood of a beautiful, close-grained variety grown in southern India, which Chuck had seen made into expensive jewelry boxes. The handle was screwed to the barrel with tiny stainless steel screws. *Not enough mass in these screws to set off a metal detector, either.* Chuck recognized at once that the firing pins were the steel pins from ordinary nail clippers. These were slammed into the cartridges by ebony hammers pulled by heavy rubber bands.

The pins might set off an alarm, of course. But if they were not removed from the clippers, and carried in the terrorist's pocket with his keys for sight inspection, they would pass.

Chuck now wished he'd had a chance to examine the sawed-off shotgun that had killed Nicki in Cancun.

He broke the weapon open. Two spent, all-plastic .410 shotgun shells were inside. He slid one out. It had been cut with a knife to about two-thirds its original length and reloaded by hand, apparently. *No doubt the thug that tried to kill me had a pocketful of these babies.*

But the bullets? Bullets could be made of lead, brass, or steel, any of which would set off a metal detector, Chuck knew. *The guy who tried to kill me nailed me in a secure area of the L.A. Airport. Or he followed me from Cancun. Either way, he would've had to pass through a detector.*

Chuck stared at the derringer. He had no ammo for it, so it was of no use to him for self-defense. In fact, it was a liability, given that concealed possession of a firearm would land him in jail most anywhere. He removed the screws with his pocketknife's screwdriver blade, cut the rubber bands off, and flushed the light weapon down the toilet a piece at a time.

With that task completed, Chuck prepared for a much-needed shower. The wound had stopped bleeding and had clotted over, he was gratified to see as he peeled his shirt off. The bullet's path had crossed the scar from the attack in Tucson, Chuck noticed, looking with his hand mirror as he bent over the sink.

That one is still a puzzler, Chuck mused. *I didn't do anything to cut myself in that fight with the guy carrying the nerve gas. Maybe something cut me when I passed out in that cab.* Chuck tried to think what there was in the backseat of a Chevy Caprice taxicab that could cause such a gash. *At any rate, the doctors at the Tucson hospital did a good job sewing me up,* he concluded.

After a good scrub in a hot shower, Chuck braced himself with half a dozen fig bars chased down with chlorinated tap water. Then he went to work. He swung the shower door out toward the sink and plastered his hand mirror onto the door's aluminum frame with surgical tape. *Too far back, but at least I can see my shoulder when I look in the mirror.*

Chuck rinsed the wound with alcohol. He prodded. "Ouch!" There was a good-sized lump at the end of the wound.

He sliced across it with a razor blade, then sterilized his knife and began to dig. *Blood. Tears.* Chuck caught his breath and sliced some more. A huge clot of blood . . . No. He got his forefinger and thumb around the object. Hard. Sharp edges. He fished it out and held it under the faucet. Glass—half a kid's glass marble. That explains why the bullets didn't set off the metal detectors.

More alcohol. "Argh!" He mopped the wound with a towel and reached for the gauze. He let the towel drop, then deftly pinched the wound with his fingers.

What's this? Chuck found a thin, plastic-shielded wire in his wound, and it looped out enough to get his finger under it. *Why would an assassin shoot a wire into me?*

Then the lights went on. Chuck went cold in terror.

He tugged at the wire, and then caught his breath in pain. *No wonder these killers turn up everywhere I go,* he realized as he worked, frantically, feverishly digging and tugging.

Chuck stopped for a moment to peer out the bathroom window, past his toilet lid security brace. A thirty-six-hole professional golf course stretched toward Newport Beach and the Pacific. Several golfers played or waited to tee off. A couple of electric golf carts scooted about.

Atop a distant ridge a cart was parked next to a cabbage palmetto, facing Chuck's room. He could make out two riders, one with long hair. *Female?*

The other was resting his arms on the steering wheel. He was looking toward Chuck's room with binoculars. No doubt about it. *They probably won't strike until well after dark. Meanwhile, I've got work to do.*

Ignoring the wire in his shoulder for a moment, Chuck crossed the room and braced the hall door with a chair. *No reason to let them surprise me,* he decided.

Then he returned to opening the scar from his hospital stay in Tucson. "Mama said big boys don't cry," he muttered, as, inch after inch, he followed the coiled wire back into the fatty tissue behind his armpit.

"Gotcha, you little beast!" he gasped finally. The antenna wire, when uncoiled, was at least a foot and a half long. At its end Chuck found a miniature computer-chip radio transmitter the size of a quarter. "Whoever is following me owns their own satellite," he concluded, aloud again. "These suckers can be tracked only by satellite. Not your run-of-the-mill terrorists. Got to be a government with billions to put into such an operation."

I wonder how many other poor saps are running around with satellite-tuned transmitters under their sorry hides? Did the FBI do this? No, he concluded. *They wouldn't send thugs after me.*

CIA? Either possibility leads back to our own government, and it doesn't add up.

Chuck considered simply flushing the bloody transmitter down. *No. Stupid to let them know I've found their bug. I could maybe just run, while those guys are still on the golf course. But I want a close-up look at those goons.*

He finished bandaging his shoulder. Leaving the tiny transmitter on the bathroom shelf, he relaxed on the bed, exhausted after his self-surgery. *Got to think.*

Chuck lifted the Gideon Bible from the nightstand and turned to Isaiah 40:31, where he read: "But they that wait upon the LORD shall renew their strength; they shall mount up with wings as eagles; they shall run, and not be weary; and they shall walk, and not faint."

Wait for God. Chuck closed the Bible and slept.

"Eleven thirty-five." Chuck stared in the darkness at the lighted digital clock on the motel TV set. He sat up in a cold sweat. His fevered mind began to recollect the events of the afternoon. *They want to kill me, and I've been asleep for hours!*

"You needed the sleep, my son." The voice was not audible, but the message was real. *What else could I have done while I waited for my killers to act?*

Now I need to act. In the dark he yanked on his clothes and packed his few belongings into his bag. Then he made the bed, using his two pillows and the pillows from the vacant bed as a bolster in the shape of a sleeping human body.

He removed the chair from beneath the doorknob and grabbed the only weapon he could lay his hands on—a wooden coat hanger. Chuck slipped into the bathroom, unbraced and opened the window. Adding the toilet tank lid to his arsenal, he sat on the toilet and waited.

Which thug will come here to kill me? Probably the woman. Plenty of desk clerks let women into their motels late at night for a cut of the profits.

The motel used card-keyed electric locks. Chuck patted the one in his pocket just now, considering. *Professional terrorists have access to computerized universal keys that will read the code on any lock made and snap the doors open. Such devices cost several grand, so they aren't available for your back-alley thugs. But then, back-alley punks don't own satellites, either. Not even the Mafia owns a satellite.*

Chuck got up and placed his small mirror on a shelf where he could watch the door from the bathroom. He returned to the bathroom and waited some more.

A low hum. He held his breath. *Click.* Slowly the door opened. A form slipped in. It was the woman—long, dark hair, tall, her figure shrouded in a trench coat. She placed a large purse on the dresser and stared at the sleeper in the bed.

Chuck held his breath.

She reached into her purse and pulled out a pistol. It was a derringer, like the one Chuck had taken from the dead assailant at the airport.

Chuck held the heavy tank lid in one hand and the coat hanger in the other. *Should I bash her with the lid, which would probably kill her? Or . . . ?*

She bent toward the head of the bed.

Chuck laid the lid silently on a towel. He slipped into the room, the hanger his only weapon. He jammed the wooden hanger into her ribs, hard. "Don't move. Now lay the gun down. Straighten up *real slow.* Don't turn around."

"Want me to undress, mister?" she purred.

"Start with your coat. Keep your hands in sight." Chuck dropped the hanger and picked up the woman's derringer. He stepped back a pace. "Toss your coat toward your purse."

The lady complied. "Shall I get naked?" The woman's voice was oily, servile.

"That won't be necessary." Chuck snapped the light on. It was the Latin woman from first class—Chuck recognized the natty, navy blue business outfit. But her face wasn't Latin. This puzzled Chuck, but it began to make some sense. "Lie on the bed, face-down—DO IT NOW!"

"My pimp—he's waiting in the hall." The sweetness was gone, and her protest sounded lame.

"I don't think prostitution is your racket. GET DOWN!" Chuck cocked and uncocked the gun to make his point.

She complied.

Chuck grabbed the woman's coat, patting the pockets. He was not surprised to find a two-way radio in the pocket—turned on. He turned it off. Clamping the light weapon with his teeth, he ripped the trench coat up the center seam. "Get your wrists next to the bedposts." He quickly tied her hands to the bed with the shredded coat.

"Getting ready for an execution?" she sneered.

"Wouldn't want to mess up the bed." He unloaded the handmade pistol and tossed it under the bed.

Grabbing his bag, Chuck dashed for the bathroom and locked the door. He found that he could easily reach the motel's flat roof from the windowsill. Throwing his duffel bag up first, he scrambled out. Angry male yells behind him in the room told him that the "pimp"—or whoever it was—had arrived.

Chuck ran in the direction of Harbor Boulevard, dropping to the office roof. To avoid the bullets that were now whizzing past him, he leaped off the roof into a tall holly bush at the streetside corner of the motel. Soft. Like a pincushion with the points outward.

Still managing to hang on to his duffel bag, he dived into the front seat of a new, four-door rental Buick Regal left parked at the curb, motor idling.

"Thoughtful of them," Chuck chortled. He scrambled under the wheel, yanked the lever into *drive,* and floored the gas.

Two hours later Chuck wheeled into Lost Gulch Phillips 66 Truck Stop, at the intersection of I-40 and I-15, near Barstow, California. Parking the Buick, he strode directly toward a big, chromed semi rig with "Potter Brothers Produce Haulers— Caution, in case of rapture, this truck will be unmanned," stenciled on the trailer. Chuck could see by the fancy trim and extra lettering that this was an independent hauler.

"Going east?" he asked the driver, a lanky, red-bearded man about to climb into the cab. Chuck held out a twenty. "I'm down on my luck—I need a ride," he said truthfully.

"No prob, brother," said the driver. "Jesus wants you to ride with me tonight, if you're not afraid of losing your driver to the upward call. Keep your twenty—you'll need it to eat."

"I'm expecting Christ's return too." Chuck grinned and climbed in. *Thank You, Jesus,* he silently prayed.

"Name's Pete—Peter Potter, from Indianapolis. I own this here rig, so's I don't have to worry about company rules against hitchhikers. Good to have another Christian aboard. Life's rough without Christian fellowship."

"Rougher than you could imagine!" Chuck tried to make himself comfortable, but his heart was astir with the past two days' events. He tried to relax as Pete ran through the gears of the big Autocar Diesel on the entrance ramp to I-15. "What are we hauling?" he asked at last.

"Tomatoes. Bound for Indiana." Pete flipped the interior light on for a glance at a map clipped to a board screwed to the dash. "Route 15 through Vegas, then I-70 the rest of the way east." He snapped the light off. "I'm not stopping at Las Vegas, so I hope you're not a gambling man."

"No sir." *But you gambled with your life when you picked me up.* Chuck decided not to say this aloud.

"Get mugged and robbed?" Pete wanted to get to know his passenger, no doubt about it. "I mean, you look like you've been fighting a tiger."

"Mugged," Chuck admitted. "Not robbed, though. The other guy got the worst of it."

"By the look of you, he must be pretty bad off."

Chuck felt his cheeks. The scratches from the holly bush had left welts and scabs. "Guess I'm thanking the Lord to be alive." Chuck winced, patting his bandaged shoulder. With the tiny transmitter gone, his assailants could no longer trace his steps. What worried him, though, was that they certainly could plant a stakeout wherever he was likely to turn up.

❰❰❰

Indianapolis, two days later, was a welcome sight. Chuck left Pete at Midwest Fruit & Produce and caught a cab to the Greyhound bus terminal. Here, he took a city bus to a complex of shopping centers, restaurants, and motels on the city's north side. He rented a room at a Knights Inn, where he shaved and showered and changed his bandage. With talc, he managed to get his face looking respectable again.

Then, leaving his key in the room, he crossed the street to a Robert Hall's Menswear, where he bought new slacks, a jacket, shirt, tie, and shoes, paying cash. He caught another city bus to the airport, where he rented a car. He signed for it as Reuben Sanchez and paid cash in advance. The agent didn't question Nicki's "Ruby Sanchez" credit card, which he used only as a security deposit.

Next morning Chuck awoke at dawn at Baer Field Inn, Fort Wayne, two hours northeast of Indianapolis. He was actually surprised to still be alive—no one had tried to kill him since leaving California, or even to tail him, so far as he knew. So he hopped a shuttle bus to the airport, where he found a Delta flight to Boston already boarding, with one seat left. His boarding pass was issued to Reuben Sanchez.

❰❰❰

Who wants me dead and why? During the two-hour flight from Fort Wayne to Boston, Chuck repeatedly reviewed the events since Nicki's death.

Nicki's killer, or an accomplice, had tracked him to the seedy Ponce de Leon hotel in downtown Cancun. This had been easy, seeing that his radio transmitter could tell whoever monitored the satellite his location within a two-hundred-yard radius. Then there was the cat burglar who stole Nicki's purse. *Same people, no doubt about it.*

But why did they let me live when they could have killed me in my bed at the Ponce de Leon? Perhaps something they found in Nicki's purse later made them decide to kill me. Or they simply wanted to do me in inside U.S. borders.

Chuck shuddered, remembering the Latin lady in first class on the flight to Los Angeles. With that two-shot gun, she easily could have hijacked the plane, had that been her plan.

Or was it the same woman? He remembered the well-dressed Middle Eastern woman he'd left tied to his bed at The Palms in Costa Mesa. *They were much alike, to be sure. But I didn't really get a glimpse behind the sunglasses of that woman on the plane.*

Who are these guys? Arab terrorists? Saddam Hussein's thugs? If I were the president, I'd understand it—they'd have reason to be mad at me. Chuck recalled that two successive American heads of state had rained terror on Baghdad.

And do they want me for myself—or merely because I was Nicki's companion?

Revenge for killing that thug in Tucson? Chuck didn't think so. *They'd have killed me in the hospital, if that were the case.* In a lot of espionage operations, Chuck knew loyalty was dedicated to the state to such an extent that there was little sense of personal loss when a comrade was killed.

Chuck tightened his seat belt as the plane circled Boston Bay to approach the runway. It was good to come home. But could he ever call this place home again?

ⅭⅭⅭ

"Art and Rachel Towns," said the brass nameplate above the doorbell at 88 Highland Avenue, Somerville, Massachusetts. Chuck had considered finding Arthur Towns at his Volvo dealership in Cambridge and letting him break the news of Nicki's death to his wife himself. *No,* he decided, *I want to meet them both, and Nicki's second cousin will certainly want to meet me.*

"We haven't seen Nicki in several weeks. She had her own apartment, you know." Rachel Towns smoothed her grey hair back and wrinkled her thin brow.

"I know. I've never been there, but her address is Danvers—it's in our personnel files."

"What do you do at Salem Electronics, Mr. Reynolds?" Art Towns bored in on Chuck, almost accusing him. "You said, 'personnel files'?"

"I'm head of security, so I have reason to know what's in our files. Mrs. Towns's cousin has an impressive résumé."

"We are aware of that. But what does this have to do with us? Government men—FBI—they've been nosing around. Now you."

"I assure you, sir, I'm not here to ask questions. But it's my understanding that Nicki had no other family. As next of kin . . ."

"Good heavens . . . not?" Rachel Towns clasped her chest.

"I'm afraid Nicki has been killed. I'm deeply sorry. I was her friend. This has haunted me all the way back from Mexico."

"Murdered, I'm sure. Assassination?" Art's voice was flat, but his face was ashen. "I warned that girl . . ."

"Yes. We don't know who. The police there will furnish you the details."

"You don't know about our people, Mr. Reynolds," Rachel tried to explain. "Nicki's grandmother—my mother's sister—was machine-gunned in Iraq in 1933 in an officially sponsored ethnic cleansing. My father was shot too—most of our family died. Nicki's father was only ten when he fled for his life. There are those who'd still like to get the rest of us."

"That was a long time ago," Chuck observed.

"Before Saddam Hussein, but the struggle continues," Art said. "My wife's family is Assyrian, but the present regime in Iraq consider themselves heirs to Babylonia. As you may know, Nebuchadnezzar's Babylonians overthrew Assyria in 612 B.C."

"Nicki told me some of that. But did she tell you about CALF?" Chuck queried.

Rachel shot a glance of fear at Art.

Art's face contorted in rage. "We don't talk about it."

"Did you tell the FBI about CALF?"

"No. We did tell them that she changes jobs often. But CALF . . . ?" Art shrugged.

"Have I ventured into sacred territory? Nicki has told me a great deal—about her ancestor Hniqi's prophetic scroll, for instance."

"And her wild dream of fancy that the Lord is coming back to restore Assyria to its ancient glory?" Rachel said.

"That's stretching things a bit, I think. But yes, she firmly believed Isaiah's prophecy that Assyria and Egypt will one day, in the millennium, form an economic pact with Israel and be joined by a major highway," Chuck explained.

"We're in the millennium already. Things don't seem to have changed much." Art Towns shot a glance at a wall calendar.

"It's not that simple." Chuck smiled. "The short version is that Christ will reign on David's throne for a thousand years. There's nothing in Bible prophecy to indicate that the millennial reign of Christ will exactly coincide with the third millennium A.D."

"Nicki imagines she's descended both from the Jewish House of David and from Ashurbanipal, the great Assyrian emperor," Art growled.

"I am descended from them, too, if that old scroll is correct." Rachel forced a pinched smile. "You asked about CALF, though. One day when Nicki was a student at MIT, she came home with a tattoo."

"CALF's symbol is a winged bull," Chuck said.

"You've seen it, then?"

"No, ma'am. But she told me about it."

"I've seen it," Rachel said. "It was on her left breast, to symbolize both the nurture of the Assyrian nation and the strength of heart of her people. Nicki believed that this bull was worn by all the king's wives in ancient Assyria, and by the king himself."

"So she told me."

"A symbol of rebellion, to my thinking," Art said. "It cost her her life. We raised her to be a good, loyal American, and we put a quarter of a million dollars into her education."

"I wouldn't ask for one penny of it back, Art." Rachel began
to weep.

(((

Chuck let himself into his apartment with his key. Wishing for
a gun, he gingerly reached inside and switched the light on. There
was no shotgun blast, no assassin hiding inside. So he slipped in.
Five minutes' search satisfied Chuck that no one was waiting for
him.

He popped the cover off the smoke detector in his living
room. A transmitter, a bit larger than the one he'd found beneath
his arm, had been glued just inside. FBI work. *These guys always hide
them in the smoke detector*, Chuck told himself. *You'd think they could
get creative, like the thugs who've been chasing me.* He left the bug in
place, then checked behind an outlet plate in his bathroom. "Might
as well humor them and leave that one too," he sighed. "If they
realize I'm onto them, they'll haul me in for questioning."

Next, with a can of grey fingerprint powder, Chuck dusted for
prints on his computer keyboard. He held a high-intensity reading
lamp over the keys and flipped it on. Whoever had last used his
computer had arched prints. Chuck glanced at his own fingertips.
Looped prints.

*I've got more important things to do with my time, or I'd ask the FBI
to trace these prints,* Chuck thought, frustrated. He imagined the federal agency's embarrassment at finding one of their own agent's
prints after an apparent burglary. "I could even call a news conference, maybe," he said aloud. Chuck, however, was not surprised to
learn that the FBI was trying to shadow him.

*No point in even looking for phone bugs, since there won't be any
wire connection in the house that I can disconnect,* he mused. Nothing
short of a Congressional investigation would stop such antics,
Chuck realized. But that would certainly embarrass the Old Man
and Salem Electronics, probably meaning that Harry Thompkins
would never again get a defense contract.

☾☾☾

"I like your work, Chuck," Harry said over lunch at Cappy's Chowder House the following day. "But I'm nervous about having you around the plant, after all you've told me about your unplanned trip to Mexico. So take your month's vacation—you've got it coming since you transferred so much unused time from Salem South. I'll personally extend it for a second month, if necessary, and continue your pay. We've got to get this Vanguard leak behind us."

"Have the feds been asking questions?"

"Only what I've already told you. They came by and took a statement when I reported that you didn't show up at Falcon Aviation in Tucson. You could visit your family in . . ."

"Don't say it, Harry!" Chuck shushed his boss. "Let's talk about your deep sea fishing. Your golf. Anything."

Harry frowned.

"Reheat your coffee, Mr. Reynolds?" the waitress asked.

"Sure, Susie." Chuck pushed his cup toward her.

"Haven't seen you lately. Been away?"

"For sure!" Chuck smiled. He pointed toward a new speaker cabinet high in a corner across the restaurant. "New sound system?"

"Uh, sorta. Guys came in from Coastal Sound Systems Installers about a week ago and hung it up. We have a contract with them to maintain our system. They claimed our recessed ceiling speakers weren't doing the job. Boss came in the next morning, and he was really miffed. Said he didn't order no speaker, and if he got billed for it, they could just come and yank it out. I don't even think it works."

"Well, well," Chuck laughed, "so the sound didn't improve?"

"Hardly," Susie snorted.

"I'll check it out for you. Do you mind?"

Susie shrugged. "Suit yourself, Mr. Reynolds. You work for an electronics company, so you ought to know."

"Nice someone has confidence in me." He winked at Harry, then strode quickly to the new speaker. Standing on a chair, Chuck unscrewed the grille's four screws with the screwdriver blade on his pocketknife.

"What's wrong with it, Mr. Reynolds?"

"Is that a security camera your boss had installed?" Chuck pointed to a new Toshiba television camera, which was aimed at the corner table where he and Harry had been sitting. In the box with the camera was a small, parabolic directional microphone, which Chuck sincerely prayed Susie mistook for a speaker.

"I . . . I'm sure the boss doesn't know about it."

Chuck reached behind both the mike and the camera, where his fingers found a transmitter wired to both devices. An antenna wire ran from the transmitter into a neatly drilled hole in the wall. With his hand still hidden behind the equipment, Chuck swiftly cut the antenna wire. He then bolted the lid back on.

"I'll tell the boss you fixed it," Susie chirped.

"I'd appreciate that," said Chuck.

"I'll be a monkey's uncle," Harry said.

8

The Killing Field

Their flesh shall dissolve while they stand on their feet,
Their eyes shall dissolve in their sockets.

—Zechariah

Zeke Lewis wanted that paint colt for his granddaughter. Marcie would be twelve next week, and he needed to train the critter for the saddle. He fumed as he rammed the shift-lever of his '72 Ford Ranger 4 x 4 into bulldog gear to crawl up the far side of the dry arroyo. Zeke knew he was on government turf the moment he passed that broken fence at the washout, but "Fool hoss don't know no better, Marcie," he growled. "Guv'mint's gotta allow for that."

Zeke knew very well that government officials wouldn't allow trespassing on the White Sands Missile Range, even to chase a child's horse that had wandered inside. But a gaping hole had been torn in the fence when a sudden rain in the San Andres Mountains last evening had caused the gully bank to cave in. The chain-link-and-barbed-wire security fence separating Bar L Ranch from the missile range had collapsed into the arroyo, along with its clay bank.

Half a century earlier Zeke Lewis had had an experience that convinced him that the Atomic Energy Commission, NASA, the U.S. Army Air Corps, the Army—or whatever military or civilian operation was running the shows at Holloman Air Force Base and the Los Alamos Laboratories—were cold-blooded bullies with no regard for the rights of ordinary citizens. Zeke never could untangle the various confusing branches of the nation's defense team, even after spending a tour of duty with the U S Army Air Corps as a tail gunner on a B-24 engaged in bombing raids over Japan.

The endless fences that had turned sixteen million New Mexico desert acres into a vast no-man's-land were still being erected when Zeke, two years after the bombing of Hiroshima had ended World War II, had seen some strange lights beyond his back range one evening in 1947. He had saddled a horse and, armed with a carbine and a three-cell flashlight, had ridden off to investigate.

Two days later the Roswell Daily News had published a cryptic report about the so-called Roswell flying saucer incident. The crashed plane—what else could Zeke call it?—was a saucer-shaped aluminum and glass aircraft. The pilots—Zeke had seen them close up—were obviously young Japanese, he explained to the reporter. Zeke had seen Japanese prisoners enough in the war, so he figured he ought to know.

Two older men had also ridden over to the crash site. Like Zeke, they arrived just before Air Corps personnel got there to cordon off the area. They also had seen the dead aviators. Small creatures with yellow skin and slit eyes. "These were Martians," the old men told the Roswell News's reporter. A lot like Mexicans, one man said, except that Mexicans, being human, have round eyes. Besides, the aircraft was saucer shaped, and it had no propellers—only jets, like those newfangled planes the Air Corps was experimenting with out of Holloman Air Force Base. It must have come from outer space—no doubt about it, the older men agreed.

Zeke never learned whether it was his opinion that the flyers were Japanese POWs or whether it was because he was a recently discharged veteran shooting his mouth off that he was singled out for abuse. But two MPs had dragged him out of his bed in the ranch house before daylight the morning after the story hit the papers. He was blindfolded, carted off to Holloman (his captors were stupid—Zeke's ears told him he was at an air base), and interrogated. Not your usual debriefing, either. Zeke had been cuffed to a chair with a light in his face for two days. He was alternately threatened by a major, then consoled by a sergeant, who pretended to sympathize. Not allowed to use the bathroom, he messed his pants.

When finally the "brainwashing" (this was a supposedly scientific psychological technique the American Armed Services had borrowed from their Japanese conquests) was completed, Zeke was allowed to shower, eat a meal, and then he was driven—blindfolded again—back to his ranch. Never to this day has Zeke Lewis talked with another news reporter.

But his fears had faded with the years, and the Air Force owed him this one, Zeke decided. He'd just find his horse, bug out of there, and keep his mouth shut. Unless, of course, he got caught. Then he could use the fact that it was a little girl's horse to get the media's sympathy. News stories could cut both ways, Zeke realized. Marcie, he was certain, would not be prosecuted for being a passenger in her grampa's pickup when he drove through the fence.

"Cows, Grampa!" Marcie ignored the old man's disgusted complaints, pointing to several skinny, worn-out critters in a field right ahead. "Dozens of 'em. But something's weird."

Zeke reined the Ford truck in and cut the motor. Something was weird, Marcie was right about that. Maybe four dozen cattle were spread over about three acres. They were not your usual herd of southwestern ranch beef animals: white faces, with a scattering of Charolais and Angus crosses. These were the offscouring of a cattle auctioneer's nightmare: broken-down dairy cows, worn-out bulls, scrubby, crossbred steers—the best would make cheap bologna and poor hides.

Crazier still, they were evenly spaced, laid out like a grid, not bunched up, not all grazing pretty much the same direction like normal cows. Then he saw—each bovine beast was tethered, tied with light rope to a ring in the ground, like a dog on a backyard tether.

"Weird, awright, Marcie." Zeke shook his grizzled head, then tipped the brim of his stained Stetson against the bright southwestern sun of a New Mexico afternoon. "Another nutty guv'mint experiment. Like those . . ."

"Like the Roswell flying saucers, Grampa? Our teacher told us about that when I was in the third grade. She said it was the fiftieth anniversary of the Martians landing near Roswell. Something like that. You must remember that, Grampa."

"Yuh." Zeke was silent for a long moment. "Yuh," he repeated, "I remember." Moments earlier, Zeke had been plain angry, willing to believe he wouldn't have to endure another brainwashing if he got caught inside the missile range again. But driving right up on another experiment unhinged him, even after more than half a century.

"What was it about, Grampa?"

"I . . . I'll tell you one of these days, honey. Now let's look for that crazy hoss and git on home."

"Over there, Grampa, our colt!" Marcie pointed to a tangle of sagebrush near where a rocky hillside rose past the cattle. The paint stood half hidden near a tall jack pine, nibbling on prickly pear cactus.

"Stay in the cussed truck!" Zeke ordered. At once he was sorry he had spoken so roughly to the child. He grabbed his lariat, hoping that Marcie did not notice his hand tremble as he reached for it where it lay next to the gearshift lever. He looped it over his shoulder and climbed out. His head felt light, and his knees trembled. Zeke grasped the open door to steady himself, then turned back. "If one o' them Air Force experimenters comes along, tell 'em y' granddaddy'll explain. Hear?"

"I will, Grampa. Please be careful."

Muttering a curse, old Zeke hobbled in an arthritic hitch toward the colt.

But the colt, which had wandered more than five miles since it escaped the corral behind the paddock, was not about to be easily captured. She raised her head, snuffing like a wild jackass.

"Here, girl! Easy, girl." Zeke paused, trying not to spook her. He realized that if he failed to catch the filly on the first throw, he'd have to give up and ask the Air Force to catch her. He refused even to consider the red tape that would entail.

"C'mon." Zeke made kissing sounds with his lips, then drew a handful of sugar cubes from a pocket of his bib overalls. "Sugar for y'." Zeke eased toward the colt a couple of steps. Then a third. *Snap!* A piece of dry sagebrush cracked beneath his boot.

The colt snuffed, then whinnied and trotted behind the pine. And vanished.

Old Zeke gasped in dismay. He hurried toward the pine. A square hole maybe ten feet across had opened where rotting planks covered with pine needles had collapsed beneath the animal's wayward hooves. Zeke knelt. The sun was high, and the shaft was lighted enough to see to the bottom, perhaps twenty feet. Right where the horizontal shaft of an abandoned silver mine went into the mountain lay the colt, kicking and thrashing, her neck twisted grotesquely.

Zeke considered returning to the truck to fetch his carbine to finish the hapless beast off. But that would only mean upsetting Marcie. He watched another minute, then made a decision. The old mine shaft had iron rungs set into the rock, where a man could climb down. Zeke's knees were arthritic, but his shoulders were still powerful—he regularly beat his teen grandsons at arm wrestling. And if a man can use his arms, he can climb.

The descent was a waste of time and energy. Zeke realized this as soon as his boots struck the gravel bottom. The colt had ceased her breathing, but he bent in the shadows for a closer look.

Zeke's next sensation was that the paint colt seemed to glow, as the brown-and-white hair covering her hide lit so that the white blotches fairly blinded him with their brilliance. The entire pit around him glowed in white light, as if an antiaircraft spotlight had been turned on directly overhead. In a split second Zeke's tired old eyes took in every pebble, every crack, every gunpowder blasting groove cut into the rock walls by the miners a century ago. Then the light went out.

As soon as Zeke's eyes adjusted to the dim shaft of sunlight left for illumination, he found the iron ladder and scrambled for the surface. What met his eyes when he returned to the normal light of day shocked the old rancher more in the twenty-first century than the wrecked flying saucer had upset the young soldier more than half a century earlier.

The pine trees had become toothpicks, tongue suppressors, golf tees, and ice cream spoons in an instant. They weren't perfectly formed, of course, as milling would do. But the jack pine was reduced to splinters. Even its roots had ruptured, so that the ground was ripped apart for several feet in each direction from where it had stood.

A giant saguaro cactus was now only a splayed stump, like a hungry Hercules had shredded it for slaw.

The cattle. They were dead, all right. Every one of them. Bloated, too, their legs stiff and sticking up in protest. Three or four were actually still standing in death. Zeke Lewis had seen dead cows on the range over the years. It takes three or four days for a cow to bloat like that, and by then the vultures would be feasting on it. But only ten minutes ago these poor brutes had been chewing their cuds.

Zeke's old Ford pickup still looked normal enough right where he'd left it, the glass unbroken. But the truck was not his real concern.

Zeke began to run, his arthritis forgotten for the time. He crossed the field and circled the pickup.

Marcie sat on the aluminum running board, the passenger-side door open, chin up, her curly head braced back against the seat. Her arms were stretched out as if welcoming him.

"Marcie," he whispered. Then his knees buckled. Zeke caught himself on the door, fighting total collapse as he knelt down. The run in the sun had left the old man exhausted, and though he felt his heart tighten in pain, he refused to sit down.

Marcie was a scene out of a Stephen King movie: her eyes had simply exploded, leaving their sockets void, skull-like; her flesh, like the cattle, was bloated; her skin, her chest where the sudden swelling had popped open the snaps of her Western shirt, was a mass of red welts.

Marcie had died without even saying, "Good-bye, Grampa."

Zeke tenderly lifted the young body. With her arms and legs splayed and stiff, there was no way he could think of propping his granddaughter on the seat for the ride home. So without putting her down, he managed to drag an old khaki army blanket from behind the seat.

He let Marcie rest on the bare steel of the truck body while he spread out the blanket. He wrapped her young body as decently as possible and closed the tailgate.

Zeke turned the key. Nothing. He had presence of mind not to blow the horn and possibly attract unwanted attention. Instead, he turned the headlamp switch to try the dome light. Dead battery. *Marcie must have run it down by leaving the door open too long,* he thought. He'd known it had a bad cell, but in New Mexico's mild climate you can squeeze a few extra months out of an old battery if the alternator is good and you're careful with the lights.

Zeke's wits were beginning to return. Gingerly he hobbled to the front and reached up to undo the hood latch. Then he stared. Why hadn't he seen it sooner? There was a rectangular hole in the hood directly above the battery. The sheet metal was peeled back like a sardine can. He peered through. As if a stupid, impatient giant had simply popped the battery *through* the hood without bothering to open it, the battery was gone!

"God—Jesus!" This was a prayer, not a curse. The last time Zeke had used the Lord's name except in profanity was in April '45. His Liberator B-24 crew had run into a hornet's nest of Japanese Zeroes during a bombing run over Okinawa. Alone in the tail gunner's turret, Zeke had faced two very determined Jap pilots. Already two of the B-24's four huge engines were ablaze, and the lumbering airship was losing altitude. Many tail gunners, forced to crawl on their hands and knees to the bomb bay door after the rest of the crew had bailed out, had gone down with their ships.

Zeke had prayed then. He readily shot one Zero down; the other had put itself in front of a wing gun in a kamikaze try, and it had been nailed by the copilot. Ten minutes later the crew ditched safely over the East China Sea where they were quickly rescued by an American destroyer.

Now he prayed again. Would the Lord hear an old sinner who had ignored God for most of seventy-eight years?

Calmer now, Zeke examined the motor. The radiator had burst—tubes, tanks, hoses, thermostat housing—he'd never seen anything like it. There ought to have been radiator coolant splashed all over everything, but incredibly, it was bone dry beneath the hood.

He checked the oil. Full. Good.

When Marcie had hollered about the cows, he had hit the brakes. Therefore he was stopped on a slight incline, which pitched back toward the arroyo. Zeke remembered an old trick he hadn't used in years. He shuffled painfully to the cab and climbed in. Reverse, key on, clutch down. The old Ford was coasting into the gully, picking up speed.

Zeke popped the clutch up. The motor coughed, fired, sprang to life. He rammed the gas pedal down and shot up the other side, steering by the mirrors. Back on his own territory, Zeke's confidence waxed, his confusion waned. He was heartsick over Marcie, but he had to get home. It was five miles with a dry motor. In only minutes, he realized, the engine block would be cherry red, and he was sure it would seize and stall.

Zeke prayed that God would help him get close enough to walk the rest of the way to the ranch house.

◖◖◖

Reporter Eddie Chisholm turned up the volume on the police scanner squawking away on the shelf above his computer. He had just two days a week to spend at this rural crossroads west of Roswell, New Mexico, and rarely did he catch anything on the radio worth following up. This was Eddie's first job since receiving his journalism degree at the University of New Mexico. He was hanging on here—two days a week in Perro Prieta and three in Roswell—until he finally got a real break.

The back-and-forth chatter between the highway patrolman and the Socorro County General Hospital gave Chisholm a strange report. An old man had staggered home to the Bar L's ranch house lugging his dead granddaughter, who seemed to be cooked, broiled like meat. He was babbling something about a lot of cows, bloated already, the state trooper said. Yet the old rancher alleged the cattle had been dead only a few minutes. And he alleged there was a dead horse in a mine shaft too.

Some city factory had dumped chemicals illegally again, trucking them into the country to dispose of them in an old silver mine, Eddie concluded. Modern industry was ruining the pristine environment of the beautiful desert countryside of New Mexico, at one time the home of free, nature-respecting Apache and Navajo.

Another Love Canal? Chisholm considered. He smiled. Then he grinned. News audiences love this kind of anti-industry stuff: the press going after the money-grubbing, nature-trashing exploiters— the great abusers of us all. Chisholm had a sudden pipe dream of making the Associated Press at last. Hashish was never so heady.

Eddie Chisholm grabbed his camera and notebook. Ten minutes later he pulled into the broad circle drive of the Bar L Ranch.

9

The Necklace

My son was dead, and is alive again;
he was lost, and is found.

—A certain man

A s head of security at Salem, I have access to every office in this building, Molly."

"You don't belong in there without Mr. Thompkins present, Mr. Reynolds." Molly Olin was a prim spinster with an iron will. "The Old Man's Old Lady" she was called behind her back for the way she managed Salem Electronics North by manipulating Harry Thompkins.

"I'm sorry. I'm on vacation, and I needed to leave some documents on Harry's desk on my way out of town. He's expecting my report."

"You could have left the material with me, Mr. Reynolds!"

Chuck tugged the door shut, making sure it was solidly latched. He had known since coming to Salem that the CEO's office door had exactly two keys. Harry kept one for himself. Chuck had the other, and he had no intention of letting Miss Olin see the papers in Harry's office before Harry got to them. Chuck had considered faxing Harry his ten-page report about his trip to Tucson and the unplanned hiatus in Mexico, ending in Nicki's murder. But since Molly had the executive-office fax machine on her own desk, he decided to hand deliver the papers. She often had free access to Harry's office during business hours, anyway, since Harry frequently strolled around the plant, leaving her to guard his sanctum. Chuck felt that she sometimes used this liberty to look further into company business than she was authorized.

"I'm sorry, Molly," Chuck said. "I'll remember that next time. Do you know something that I don't?" *Was it possible that Harry had shared plans to fire him with Molly?*

"Well, uh . . . ." Molly reddened.

"Go on."

"There were two FBI agents here last week."

"Harry has told me that already. Did they have a warrant for my arrest?"

"No, no, no. Nothing like that. They don't think you can be . . . can be, well counted on to be totally loyal."

"They don't think I can be trusted." Chuck forced a smile. "Did they say that? I assure you, Miss Olin, Harry has not fired me. He hasn't taken my keys. Check the payroll—you'll find my name with the others."

"Well . . . I . . . ."

"Harry!" Harry had arrived for work several minutes earlier than usual that morning

"Chuck? You're supposed to be on vacation!"

"I had to leave you a report—remember? It's on your desk."

"Great. Have a good trip!"

"May I see you in your office?"

"Sure." Harry unlocked the door, motioning Chuck in ahead of him.

"First, Harry, thanks for keeping my destination confidential." As Chuck spoke, he lifted a notepad from Harry's desk. On it he wrote: *May I have the names of the two FBI agents who were here last week? In writing, please.*

Harry read the note, then frowned. "Sure thing, Chuck." He frowned again. "I'd really like to have this place fumigated for bugs. Molly, step in here, please."

Miss Olin stepped just inside the door. "Mr. Thompkins?"

"Please jot down what Mr. Reynolds has requested." Harry passed Chuck's note to Miss Olin.

"Yes, Mr. Thompkins. Let's see, I recall that their names were . . ."

"Molly!?"

"Yes?"

"Just write them down—please!"

"If you insist." She hurried out.

Is there something out of the way about those FBI guys? Harry wrote.

"Hard to say," Chuck answered. "I'll see what I can find out. Meanwhile, you might be careful who you share your thoughts with. And my report, too." Chuck nodded toward Molly's desk.

Molly had written "Jack Arnold and Larry Contradini" on the paper next to Chuck's query.

"Thanks, Molly." Chuck slipped the paper into his wallet as he strode out the door.

Ten minutes later Chuck pulled his vintage 'Vette into the long-term parking lot at Marblehead Municipal Airport. He had had every intention of tooling up to Maine in his favorite sports car. But Harry's remark about "fumigating" for bugs had put Chuck on guard. His recent experience with satellite radio transmitters was one he did not wish to repeat. Not right away.

Chuck rented a new Buick Grand Sport Regal at Top Hat Rent-a-Car. After five minutes' drive toward Interstate 95, he pulled into a Burger King parking lot. Quickly squirreling beneath the dash, he reached up over the glove box and unplugged the factory-installed, theft-tracking system. *What will Arnold and Contradini pull when they find my Corvette in that airport lot?* Chuck wondered.

"Maine—Life the Way It's Supposed to Be" raved the billboard next to I-95 north of Portland. Chuck whistled happily as the wind rushed in the open window. He had cut the air conditioner off miles back, and the salt tang of the sea air lifted his spirits.

(((

"Fuller Road," read the sign at the entrance to the one-lane gravel road leading back to Stan and Mae Basford's country home, outside Freedom Village. South Freedom, Maine, had once been a community with schools, stores, and a post office, Chuck had learned during his visits to the Basford home. The W. F. Fuller homestead—with a rambling barn, country store, orchards, and poultry houses—had once dominated the neighborhood. Now, as he wound the Grand Sport Regal through the narrow lane, only a spreading clump of lilacs shading a vacant cellar hole showed where a busy family farmhouse once stood.

The cul-de-sac that ended the road also made the driveway of the Basford place. A snug, center-chimnied Cape Cod cottage tied to a rambling barn by an ell stood on this rocky hillside lined with stone walls and cedar fences. The house and barn were painted earth tones and roofed with rugged, weathered cedar. "Meadowbrook Farm, 1789," announced a sign of old, cracked pine boards.

Chuck parked beneath the spreading sugar maple that dominated the dooryard. Fully six feet in diameter, the colossal shade tree must have been mature when a frontiersman, fresh from fighting Redcoats with Ethan Allen and Paul Revere, laid his flintlock and rucksack beneath its shade and set his broadax to the native white pine to clear his quarter-section and erect his farmstead.

Contentment. Peace. Permanence. These thoughts flooded Chuck's soul as he surveyed the rustic, two-centuries-old buildings and the maple, maybe a century older. He stepped out of the car, and the only sound that caught his ears was the *tit-tit-tit-tit-tit* of a chickadee, hidden deep in the aged maple's sturdy limbs. Far across the pastureland the rattle of a woodpecker answered. Chuck raised his head and tuned his ears. Other than the Regal's motor cooling, only the noises of nature invaded his hearing.

How long has it been since I've actually heard a hot engine cool? Chuck pondered. *Probably not since I left the North Carolina Piedmont hills—an eternity ago, or so it seems.*

Still, this peace, this quiet was not really permanent, Chuck realized. The ancient maple had been chained and bolted together to keep it from splitting down the middle and falling over on the house. Stan had threatened, "If not this year, next," to bring the giant behemoth down with his chain saw and split it into stove wood to heat the house. This simple old Cape Cod—the jewel of the New England housewright's craft—would one day crumble into dust.

The world itself will also, Chuck mused. Even the elements would "melt with fervent heat" in the Day of the Lord, God's Word warned. As a Southern hill-country pastor, Chuck had often preached that message from his pulpit. Now, here in northern New England in the peace and joy found in this, the Lord's respite from the busyness, the violence, the crassness that threatened to crush him, Chuck yearned for the day when Christ Himself would rule on David's throne. For the day when the FBI, the CIA, the Mossad, the KGB or SVR, even the world's armies would be dissolved. No more weapons of mass destruction—no threats of neutron bombs, of anthrax, of espionage and counterespionage.

Chuck was tired of it all. Nicki was dead. He wished only to pray, to read his Bible, to enjoy Jennifer's happy, lilting voice.

Chuck ambled into the barn. Turning, he slid aside the worn, wooden bolt that fastened the shed door. He crossed the old plank walk past the firewood pit and hurried toward the screen door into the kitchen. The inner door was open, blocked back by an antique sadiron. He strolled inside.

Chuck smiled as he read the note he found penciled on a pad left on the kitchen table: "Gone to Belfast. Back at one. Mae."

For whose eyes was the note intended, since it was necessary to walk inside in order to read it? Chuck laughed, considering. Here was a world where folks trusted one another, where crime— if it existed at all—consisted of picking apples without permission or taking more blueberries from your neighbor's wild patch than you needed to bake a pie.

Chuck gazed across the old-fashioned kitchen with its antique, black, iron-and-nickel wood range piped into an even older brick-hearth fireplace. Through the archway into the living room he spied a modern, Pentium-speed personal computer. Next to it sat a rack of CDs, and on a stand by itself, a laser printer. Grandpa Basford, Jennifer had written, had bought the computer— complete with Internet connections—partly for his own enjoyment, and partly for her use in preparing senior term papers for her college prep courses at Belfast Regional High School.

Chuck sighed. No. No computer today. He let himself relax in Mae's creaky old rocker beside the kitchen's back window and turned his attention to the fields, the forest, the birches, the pines, the alder-lined brook.

For some moments Chuck was lost in reverie, watching as a brown doe and twin fawns slipped from the alders to graze on a patch of clover, joining Stan's two sheep and milking Jersey. The fawns munched in perfect contentment, and the mother, though she grabbed a mouthful of grass now and then, stood alert, sniffing the breeze for enemies.

Suddenly the doe's white-lined tail shot up. She snorted and wheeled. The white-bellied fawn nearest her bounded into the bushes. The other paid no heed, until mother deer butted it with her head. Chuck laughed aloud at this antic.

Then the cause of the doe's alarm caught his ears: voices and footsteps in the woodshed. "Daddy's here!" cried Jennifer.

"That's not his car," protested her grandmother.

"Perhaps he's traded," rumbled a deep male voice.

"Daddy!" squealed Jennifer as she burst into the kitchen. "We've been worried sick about you!"

"I'm sorry. It hasn't been that long, has it?"

"But you didn't answer my letter or even call."

Chuck patted the envelope in his jacket pocket. Jennifer's letter had come while he was in Mexico, and he had read it, savoring her love, when he returned. It was just the usual chit-chat—nothing that needed to be "answered." But Chuck had learned that women often don't ask questions for information. Very often a letter or a phone call to the female of the human species is a social experience entirely apart from a male's notion of logic or a need to convey information. To a woman, it's give and take, love and be loved. Answer in the sense of respond. Warm noises rather than well-reasoned argument. "I've been away, darling. You'd rather have your daddy than a letter any day, I'll bet."

"Oh, Daddy!" Jennifer's soft, red-and-walnut ringlets tumbled past his cheek as she hugged him, her pale blue eyes beaming with joy. "I hope you've come to stay awhile—you have, haven't you?"

"I have some vacation time. Let's climb Mount Katahdin." To tell the truth, Chuck preferred rocking-chair rest to rock climbing just then. Maine's mile-high mountain, which sat at the northernmost reach of the Appalachian Trail, had several trails to the top. No particular mountaineering skills were required, but it was a long, dawn-to-dusk hike: half a day up and half a day back down.

"Oh, will you, Daddy?" Jenny squealed. "Can we camp out, too? Grandpa has a couple of pup tents!"

"You bet—if you don't mind the mosquitoes," Chuck laughed.

"We met this weird lady in Belfast," Jennifer said, growing serious.

"'Weird,'" Stan Basford echoed. "Maybe even dangerous."

Chuck knew that Maine communities were home to some crusty characters. But to hear Stan, who had spent most of his life here, describe her as "dangerous" gave Chuck concern.

"She just comes up to the table while we were eating lunch in Whitcomb's Café. She goes, 'You must be Jennifer Reynolds.'"

"I believe she followed us in there," Stan said with a worried tone.

Chuck recalled the couple who had tailed him to a motel in Costa Mesa, California. They were out there somewhere, trying to find him, surely. Were they now trying to get him through Jennifer?

"Show your dad what the lady gave you," Mae said.

Jennifer fished out a heavy silver necklace with a turquoise-studded cross dangling from it from beneath her T-shirt and pulled it off over her head. "She said I was to keep it out of sight. Not to show it to anyone but you."

Chuck examined the jeweled cross. He turned it over and held it up to the sunshine streaming in the window. There, etched plainly in the back, was a miniature winged bull.

"Excuse me." Chuck grabbed the rocking chair and sat down heavily.

"Daddy, you're white as a ghost!"

"Here—a drink." Mae drew a glass of water and passed it to him.

"Thanks." Chuck glanced again at the cross and its mystical symbol. He stared out the window, trying to make his mind focus on an illusion. *How could . . . ? No!* "Describe this woman for me, Jennifer."

"Oh Daddy, she was beautiful!"

"Sunglasses?"

"Yes, but she kept them pushed up. She was dark, like a good tan—olive, really. Black hair. Her hands had the most perfectly tapered fingers. And she had the neatest green eyes, like the sea."

"And she smiled a lot?" asked Chuck.

"Her smile could cause a thaw in February," observed Stan. "I didn't trust her."

"Oh, Stan!" Mae fretted.

Chuck held up his hands. "What did she say?"

"She said . . ." Jennifer frowned. "She said, 'Grasshopper, between five and seven, next two evenings.'"

"That's a hippie hangout," growled Stan.

"Oh, Grandpa, nobody says hippie today," Jennifer protested.

"I think," said Chuck, "I may have met this . . . this beautiful woman-of-mystery somewhere. My curiosity is about to get the best of me. I think I'll drive over to Belfast in a couple of hours." He shot a glance at the ticking mantel clock, which had just chimed one-thirty. "Want to come along, Jen?"

"Sure, Daddy!"

"Maybe you should take a cop in there with you," warned Stan.

"For the Grasshopper Sandwich Shoppe or for the woman with the black hair?" Chuck asked.

❰❰❰

Chuck and Jennifer took a corner seat in the Grasshopper at a quarter to five. Though he had eaten two bowls of Mae's clam chowder before leaving South Freedom, he ordered a Reuben sandwich to split between them and two cups of herbal tea. "In these places they think you're a dangerous part of the capitalistic, military-industrial complex if you order Coke," Chuck joked to Jennifer.

The waitress had no more than set their food before them when a dark figure in designer jeans and a green sweatshirt emblazoned with a bull moose moved from the shadows of the back hall toward them. Chuck studied the woman for a few seconds. It was the lady from first class on the flight from Cancun to Los Angeles.

Or was it? He had been fooled with a look-alike once before, and she had tried to kill him.

The lady pushed her sunglasses up, grinning.

"Nicki?" Chuck spoke softly, almost in awe.

"You're usually not nervous around me," Nicki said, laughing. "Something bothering you?"

"The last time I saw you . . ." Chuck didn't finish his sentence. *When was the last time I saw Nicki, anyway?*

"Yes?"

"You were wearing . . ."

"A navy blue business outfit," Nicki finished. "That denim Western shirt I bought in Tombstone was a mess after . . . after the murder."

"Daddy!" Jennifer was alarmed.

Chuck and Nicki each took one of Jennifer's hands. "Not to worry," Chuck said. "We haven't killed anyone."

"Your daddy wouldn't harm a kitten's whisker." Nicki did not make the same claim for herself.

"Where were you when . . . ?"

"When the gun went off? Asleep on the beach I had a little help, of course. I'm sure my angel arranged it. I got the details from the other hotel guests that evening. From a couple of witnesses, my clothes were really a mess."

"I really do believe God sends His angels to watch over us," said Jennifer.

"I'm sure He does," Nicki agreed. "How could I not believe it?"

"Then you weren't really . . . ? Was there a woman killed—of course there was." Chuck recalled his chat with Peron, the Quinta Roo police captain.

Nicki nodded. She dabbed her eyes with a tissue. "This time, at least, I had nothing to do with it. How could I have? I'd been shot like a zoo animal with enough dope to put a Bengal tiger to sleep. I'll give you the details when we can talk."

"I guess," worried Chuck, "there's a lady somewhere with a suit like yours."

"I'm sure there is," Nicki murmured. "It was really nothing but cheap imported Chinese polyester. They probably cut a thousand of them out of the same bolt of cloth. I change clothes more often than Imelda Marcos changes shoes, so it'd be an awful waste for me to buy expensive stuff."

"Even cheap goods look chic on the right . . . the right woman."

"What's that supposed to mean?" Nicki raised an eyebrow.

"Daddy meant 'the right figure,'" Jennifer giggled. "I'm easy to fit too."

They all laughed.

"Where are you staying, Nicki?" Chuck inquired.

"Bayside Inn, on U.S. Route One, across the harbor. For once, I'm registered in my own name. I even rented a car in my own name—drove here from L.A. You can take marvelous liberties with your identity once you are legally dead." Nicki chuckled at her own joke.

Jennifer looked worried, puzzled.

Chuck frowned. Having Nicki alive again presented a new difficulty. *It's my responsibility to turn her in to the FBI.* Chuck's stomach knotted as he remembered the Cancun murder and the Iraqis who had attacked him. Then, he knew, there were also the Russians.

Only hours ago, Chuck considered, he had left a document on Harry Thompkins's desk with information that would surely send Nicki to jail—once the FBI learned she was alive.

❰❰❰

Stan Basford loosened up when he realized that the gift of a necklace was Nicki's way of introducing herself to the daughter of a friend. Mae fixed a pitcher of Kool-Aid as Jennifer popped corn. The five of them sat on the Basford's screened back porch, listening to whippoorwills late into the evening.

"This must be the most beautiful place under heaven," Nicki said at last.

"There are some marvelous places of natural beauty in Vietnam," Chuck put in. "I saw a lot of countryside there during the war."

Nicki was silent about Vietnam. They returned to listening to the whippoorwills and the singing frogs in the pools along the brook that cut through the meadow.

"Mr. Basford," Nicki said finally, "I notice that you've got a computer. Do you have Internet access?"

"Sure do."

"May I use it to check my E-mail?"

"Be my guest. Jennifer will show you how to log on."

Moments later, Nicki had indeed found a message.

"That's just garbage," worried Jennifer, staring at the unreadable gibberish on the screen. "It looks like the stuff I got the time I tried to read a DOS file in Windows."

"Just about," Nicki agreed. She pulled a floppy disk from her purse and popped it into the drive slot. Then she hit Page Up, and the screen went black. Nicki hit Shift and a couple of F keys so fast that Jennifer could not follow her fingers. The laser printer sprang to life, spitting out hard copy.

Nicki hovered over the printer, capturing the single printed page as it came out. "Private mail," she said, though not unkindly. She logged out and shut the computer off. "Thanks."

◖◖◖

"Sir, Miss Towns did not come back last evening," the Bayside Inn's manager told Chuck on the phone early the next morning. "But she paid in advance, so we held the room open for her."

"Thanks." Chuck clapped the receiver down in disgust.

◖◖◖

"Mighty fine young lady you've found there, Chuck," Stan Basford said. He looked up from milking Molly, the Jersey milk cow.

Is Stan trying to be nice, or is he just fishing for my opinion on Nicki?

"Nicki's first-rate, I agree, Pop." He grabbed Molly's tail to keep her from switching flies while Stan finished milking her.

"You and she got something going?" The old man smiled wryly.

"No, sorry. Nicki's got a lot of things to work out before she can get . . . can get romantically involved with anyone." Though it had been more than fifteen years since the Lord had taken Shelly, Chuck still found it hard to chat about such things.

"Spiritual things?"

"Yeah. Other problems too. She and I are . . . are on opposite sides of a host of related matters."

"It's best to wait on the Lord's timing."

"You've got that right. For now, the lovely lady has vanished—again."

"I know the feeling." Stan chuckled. "I begin to panic when I lose Mae in one o' them big supermarkets in Belfast."

"May I use your computer a few moments, Pop, if I can catch Jennifer long enough to help me log on?"

"Sure. Jen's the expert."

"Jen, bring up all the directories in the PC's hard drive, one at a time, please," Chuck said moments later, as the computer booted up.

"Sure, Daddy. It's mostly school stuff."

"Letters to boys, I'll bet."

"Letters to *you*—lots of them!"

Chuck bent over the monitor, as Jennifer used the arrow keys to scroll down the menu. "It's a long shot. She probably deleted that E-mail transmission," he said. "Still, if you notice anything unusual, pause and retrieve it."

"Hniqi" was highlighted.

"Stop it there, Jen!" Chuck cried. "Print that out!"

Jennifer set the laser printer to printing at once.

"Now delete that file, please." Chuck lifted the single, terse printout:

> Hniqi, Please investigate. Pentagon has ordered 58,000 nickel-metal hydride dry cell auto batteries and 58,000 air-cooled truck motors with breaker-point distributors. Motors and distributors to be built by American Trucks Ltd., St. Louis.
>
> American Trucks has recently illegally shipped 58,000 vehicles with water-cooled engines to China via Russia, according to ABC's 20/20.

What do you make of this, Hniqi? Stay deep cover and advise us of your findings ASAP.

The transmission was signed, *CALF-HQ.*

"Somebody knows she's still alive," Chuck mused.

"Someday, Daddy, can you tell me what's going on?" Jennifer shook her head in dismay.

Chuck hugged his daughter. Then he held her away from him. "Jen, darling, a whole lot of people could get hurt unless I find Nicki right away."

From the recesses of his memory something began to jell in Chuck's thoughts, something about a terrible weapon that immobilized all military and civilian vehicles that had modern, electronic circuits in their ignition systems. But old-fashioned, breaker-point distributors were immune. And where would Nicki hurry off to to follow up on this frightening E-mail report? Chuck guessed it would be as close as possible to where such a weapon was likely to be developed and tested. Such a weapon would draw Nicki like an outdoor light draws moths in June, Chuck realized.

"There could even be a nasty international scene unless I take quick action, Jennifer," Chuck added. "That hike up Katahdin will have to be put on hold. I will be back, honey, and we *will* climb that mountain, just the two of us!"

Chuck hurried to his bedroom, where a private phone line was always kept open for his use during visits with his family. He dialed the Delta Air Lines desk at Logan International Airport, Boston. "When does the next flight leave for Roswell, New Mexico, please?"

10

The Bomb

*The Valley of Siddim was
full of asphalt pits.*

—Moses

Perro Prieta was a wide place in U.S. Highway 380 two hours
northwest of Roswell, New Mexico. Chuck found only one
public accommodation open that Thursday as he swung down off
the Albuquerque-bound Greyhound onto the boardwalk. Helen's
Beans and Burgers, he soon learned, was a haven where a chain-
smoking owner-waitress served local gossip along with stale
coffee.

"*Roswell Daily News*? Branch office is open only Monday and
Thursday, so you're in luck. Right across the street." Helen nodded
toward a hardware store, a stuccoed, two-story, tin-roofed building
with a tattered awning extended over the wooden sidewalk.
"Paper's upstairs. Cut through the store—or go around to the back
entrance, if you'd rather."

"Thanks." Though it was midafternoon, Chuck ordered pancakes and bacon while he considered his next move. To avoid leaving a trail, he had decided against renting a car at the airport in Roswell. Instead, he bought an anonymous round-trip bus ticket from Roswell to Albuquerque and paid cash. If anyone had actually traced him past Roswell, they'd be combing for him among Albuquerque's third of a million souls while he checked things out in this desert crossroads. Or so Chuck hoped.

Chuck considered uncomfortably that *Perro Prieta* means "dirty dog" in English. He watched two grimy loafers squatting on the curb in front of the hardware store while he waited for Helen to fix his pancakes, and he made a mental note to avoid the back entrance on his way to the news office. *No sense in letting them get me alone,* he decided.

"Motel around here?" Chuck asked as Helen passed him his plate.

"Several nice places in Ruidoso, near the horse racetrack."

"I'm on foot," he admitted, wishing at once that he'd kept that information to himself.

"Highway Haven." Helen smirked. "Half a mile up the road. They have six cabins—by the hour, night, or week. Fills up quick on weekends."

"Thanks."

"No problemo. Say Helen sent ya."

Chuck motioned toward a coffeemaker dripping and gurgling on the counter. "Could I have a refill—fresh cup?"

"Sure. I guess this pot's seen better days." Helen glanced ruefully at the muddy liquid in the decanter from which she'd poured his earlier cup. "This's left over from lunch," she chuckled. She hurried off to fetch a cup of hot brew.

"Thanks." Chuck smiled as she poured his java. Helen was beginning to loosen up, and except for a Mexican girl setting tables for dinner, he and she were alone. "Any excitement here in recent years? Since the flying saucers in '47, I mean."

"Now that's a story in itself. Air Force tried to cover it up. But best evidence is, they was using Jap prisoners as test pilots for experimental aircraft down at Holloman Air Force Base."

"Oh?" Chuck pretended to be surprised, though he had heard this version of the Roswell incident and the "Martian invaders" before.

"Mind if I sit down? Been goin' since five A.M. Dogs'r killing me."

"Be my guest!"

Helen sat and lit a fresh cigarette.

Chuck slid her the ash tray, smiling.

"This town could be famous, like Tombstone, Arizona."

"Hey, let's hear about it!"

"Billy the Kid shot three men one afternoon, right in front of the hardware store over there."

"Cool!" Chuck glanced again at the store. A plaque set into the stucco said, "Holmes Building, 1905." The notorious juvenile gun-slinger had himself been shot dead by a sheriff in 1881, Chuck knew, but he decided not to spoil Helen's story.

"Instead of a movie called *The Shootout at the OK Corral*, it'd be the *Hell-Banger Fight at Holmes Hardware*, if them Hollywood moviemakers could get it right."

"You sure can't trust Hollywood," Chuck agreed. This was not the story he was fishing for, but he'd learned long ago that you get more out of a storyteller by letting him tell his favorite tale first. "What else has happened? Anything recent?"

"Last week we had the FBI—came right into my restaurant." She lowered her voice.

"I didn't know those guys ever left Washington, D.C." Chuck laughed. "Just passing through, I suppose."

"Hardly! Serious business. Leastwise, Eddie Chisholm, who used t' write the local news, thought so."

"I thought the *Roswell Daily News*'s local reporter was Harrison," Chuck observed, remembering what he'd learned while reading the paper during the bus ride.

"Chisholm quit. Never came back after talking to them FBI fellers."

"Oh?"

Helen blew smoke rings, glancing at her helper. "Hey, Juanita. Turn them glasses upside down so's they don't look used!"

"Okay, señora."

"What scared Chisholm off, I wonder?" Chuck spoke quietly, suppressing his excitement.

Helen leaned across the table and narrowed her eyes. "It was the story about the girl, I'm sure. Them FBI agents got a federal judge to order the Roswell newspaper to destroy their whole press run. They even took the ones left in the box out front by the night paper truck. Then they marched right in and grabbed my copy!"

Chuck shook his head gravely. "Nobody likes to be treated like that."

Helen swore. "You're right. The girl's parents, they're scared too. That's why they ain't talking."

"Girl? What happened to her?"

"Her grandfather, Zeke Lewis, he said it looked like hives, shingles, and a bad sunburn, all at once. It was instantaneous. One minute she was talking about her horse. Next thing old man Lewis knew, she was dead."

"There must have been a medical report on the girl."

"Officially, it was sunstroke. Chisholm, he tried to interview the coroner. Doc wouldn't talk."

"Wow!" Chuck shook his head again. "Sounds like a woman I heard about who got herself cooked in a tanning bed that wouldn't shut off. Where'd it happen?"

"Out past the Bar L Ranch. L stands for Lewis, her family name. She was Marcie Lewis. Pretty little thing. She'd 'a been twelve this week."

"I'm very sorry. How's the grandfather doing?"

"Died two days later. Stroke—from grief, most likely."

Helen crushed her cigarette in the glass tray. "Them FBI fellers, they *still* didn't quit. They hired Mac Doogie, who runs the garage, to go back on the trail for Zeke's pickup truck. Mac brought it out on his hook and loaded it into a big U-Haul for them to cart it off."

"Sounds like they were trying to hide something, all right. Hey, thanks."

Chuck paid for his meal, $5.95 plus tax, with a five and three ones. "Keep the change."

Helen beamed. "Have a nice day."

"I will." He left, congratulating himself that he'd resisted passing Helen a twenty. Overtipping might make her suspicious, he decided, his old police savvy in full gear now. Instead of crossing the street to the news office, Chuck strode toward Doogie's Mobil, a pile of cement blocks and rusty sheet metal on the edge of town.

Mac Doogie was cursing at a corroded muffler on a car parked over his grease pit when Chuck strolled up. Doogie, a barrel-bellied brute with a tobacco-stained beard, was not the kind of guy to argue with, Chuck decided, bending for a quick glance. So he sauntered into the small office, stepped over a greasy engine block, squeezed past a pile of dusty used tires, and wormed his way to the Coke machine.

Chuck was on his second cold can in the afternoon heat, when Doogie's helper stepped in. "Can I help you with something, mister?"

"Did you see Mr. Lewis's truck when Mac towed it out here from the Bar L last week?"

"Yeah. Quite a mess." The skinny kid frowned suspiciously behind dirty glasses.

"Can you tell me about it?"

"Can't now. Doogie'll fire me if I don't get back to work."

Chuck tapped on the cracked glass that passed for a counter. An array of oil filters and spark plugs in faded boxes crowded in between dusty bags of salted peanuts and candy bars. "Mounds, with almonds, please."

"Ninety-nine cents," the kid grumbled, fishing out the candy.

Chuck produced the twenty he'd not given Helen.

Doogie's helper glared at the currency. "You want y' change in ones—or quarters?" Sarcasm was never so subtle.

"Give me the candy, please, and keep the nineteen dollars for yourself." Chuck grinned. "Then tell me all you can remember in the next two minutes about Mr. Lewis's truck."

Greedy eyes lit up. "It was the radiator, mostly."

"Burst?" Chuck guessed.

"Burst! Why, every single tube in all three rows—they was split lengthwise, like it had been full of liquid nitro. Water pump and thermostat housing was split, too."

"Battery?"

"Yeah. That was weird. Just the bottom of the case left, held down by its clamps. When that sucker popped, it peeled a piece of the hood open like a sardine can."

Mac's voice came from the garage. "Hal! Gimmie that welding torch if you're done with that customer. I gotta cut this crappy exhaust pipe off!"

"Thanks, Hal." Chuck strode out of the door, unwrapping his candy bar. As he glanced back, Hal slipped the entire twenty into his pocket without opening the register.

(((

The Highway Haven is at least clean, Chuck decided, sniffing at the Lysol aroma. *For $24.95 I guess I can't complain. Best hotel in town,* he chuckled to himself.

The scurry of a critter from the crawl space underneath as Chuck crossed the worn linoleum told him that someone shared his shade. He parted the venetian blind to see an old blue-tick coon hound lope toward the cottonwood by the drive.

Chuck turned the air conditioner on, then peeled off his shirt. "Phew! That hike left me sweaty." He opened his duffel bag and laid out a fresh shirt and underwear. *I need a quick shower, then I've gotta get to that news office before it closes,* he told himself.

Rental, Chuck thought half an hour later as he eyed the UPC bars etched into the vehicle's glass. The new, green, four-door, four-wheel-drive Jeep Cherokee hadn't been at the motel when he arrived. *They do get a few business people,* I guess. Heading toward the news office, he hurried past, pushing himself in the heat that threatened to rapidly undo the effect of a cool shower and clean clothes.

A worn set of stairs in the store led up from a corner behind shelves of nuts and bolts and kegs of nails. The plaster was gone, exposing laths in half a dozen places, and the dirty woodwork was done in 1950s beige. A paneled door bore a neat sign: *"Roswell Daily News*—Perro Prieta office. Walk In."* The only evidence of recent remodeling on this side of the door was a shiny brass dead-bolt lock.

"Mr. Chisholm?" Chuck quizzed, knowing better, as the young reporter turned from his work at the computer. The office, at least, had been painted recently, Chuck noted. What struck him most forcefully, though, was the computer: brand-new, with all the bells and whistles. A neat pile of Styrofoam packing material stood beneath the single window.

"Harrison," the man corrected. "Chisholm left last week."

"Breaking in some new equipment, eh? New lock too. Did one of the local stickyfingers come up and help himself?"

"Those loafers out front? Most of them couldn't fence a steer, much less a computer." Harrison grimaced. "Actually, it's a little more interesting than a simple burglary. FBI took it. Took our files too, so I've got to start over in this, uh, town without any background, unless I search the old clips in our news morgue in Roswell."

"Sounds like an extreme reaction for a story about a girl who died of sunstroke, don't you think?"

The reporter peered through oval, steel-rimmed glasses, rubbing his goatee with his knuckles.

Chuck returned the gaze.

"Whom do I have the pleasure of addressing? If you're government, I need to see some ID."

"I'll pass on that request." Instead, Chuck stepped over to the small office's single smoke detector and popped it open.

"Hey! What do you think you're doing?"

Chuck pulled out a tiny radio transmitter, which trailed a length of antenna wire. He snapped his penknife open and severed the antenna. "Know this was up there?"

"N—no! A . . . a bug?"

"You got it! J. Edgar Hoover would have loved it."

"You mean? How could you have known about it? Unless you're FBI." Harrison cursed.

"You're not that honored today." Chuck smiled wryly. "But if I'd given you my name, the FBI would be discussing us in Washington before I got downstairs. May I leave you with some free advice?"

Harrison shrugged. "Shoot, mystery man."

"Anything you send to the *Daily News* office in Roswell, unless you want the FBI downloading it and passing it around headquarters, needs to be hand delivered. Ditto for your phone. And if you have an Associated Press report that might get you in trouble, let your editor handle it."

"So you're saying my computer is bugged. My phone, too." Harrison picked up the receiver. "How do you find those things? The mouthpiece doesn't even unscrew on this phone."

Chuck grinned. "You've been watching too many James Bond movies. That's 1960s technology. This is century twenty-one. There's no way you can have secure transmission today without a coded scrambler."

"But the AP? When would I find a story in a town like this that would make national news?"

"I strongly suspect that's what got Eddie Chisholm in trouble. I have reason to believe the FBI is monitoring the Associated Press and instructing them to kill stories they don't like. National security interests, you know."

"I still don't know your name. Are you writing a book or something?"

"Or something. When I write my book, you'll get an autographed copy. Thanks." Chuck hurried down the stairs and across the store.

To his relief, the loafers had moved on. The green, late-model Jeep Cherokee sports utility vehicle that Chuck had seen at Highway Haven was now parked across the street. A dark, pretty woman in a straw hat and sunglasses peered at him from beneath the wheel. Then she grinned. The lady started the motor and made a fast U-turn.

Chuck made no attempt to flee.

The Cherokee stopped, and the power window on the passenger side slid down. "Hop in, Chuck!" Nicki said.

"Why am I not surprised to meet you here?" Chuck laughed.

"I'm driving down to Ruidoso for dinner. Want to ride along?"

"Sure. If you're coming back tonight."

"I hate to disappoint Helen, but there's a couple of good eateries by the racetrack."

"Helen keeps a giant-size squeeze bottle of ketchup on every table," Chuck protested.

Nicki snickered. "Like yourself, I've reserved a room at Highway Haven, so I've got to drive back here," she added.

❰❰❰

"Fantastic!" Chuck was impressed at the papers Nicki passed him as they waited to be served. The computer printout of the Associated Press story was datelined, "Perro Prieta, New Mexico."

"This one never ran." Nicki raised a pretty eyebrow.

"I guessed as much." Chuck read the tragic tale of an elderly rancher, Zeke Lewis, who had driven his old pickup truck through a hole in the fence at the U.S. Air Force's White Sands Missile Range to follow a stray horse. He soon found the horse, dead, where it had fallen into the shaft of a worked-out silver mine. When he climbed out, his granddaughter was dead too, bloated like she'd lain in the sun for days. Dead and bloated, also, were several dozen cows, all of which had been alive moments earlier. The cattle were hitched to spiral steel stakes, like those used to tether a dog.

Though the battery and radiator had both mysteriously exploded with the motor shut off, the old man finally managed to start his truck by coasting it in reverse. Rancher Lewis, the story said, died the day after the interview.

"That's terrible beyond belief," Chuck murmured, scanning the pages. "But how on earth did you get this?"

Nicki grimaced. "Hard work and good luck. That's my job—for CALF."

"Are you going to tell me, or not?"

"Might as well. We're in this together."

Chuck realized uneasily that Nicki was right

"Cat burglary last night. I climbed in the second-story window at the Perro Prieta office of the *Roswell Daily News*."

"But that's illegal!" That Nicki broke the law did not surprise Chuck in the least. But he cared for her, so he felt he needed to protest, all the same.

"Everything I do is illegal. I can't turn back, Chuck. They'll kill me sooner or later. Meanwhile I press on for Assyria in the new millennium. My daddy fought in a political war for America—and lost, thanks to news commentators and actresses like Jane Fonda, who encouraged the Vietcong. Feet of clay, again. America can't control its own press in time of war, even when national security demands it. But we Assyrians—we *shall* win our little fight." Nicki bit her lip.

Cute, thought Chuck. *Cute, yet dangerous.* "I was in that news office today myself, as you know. They have all new equipment. The FBI didn't stop with just grabbing their hard drives and disks. So the newspaper bolts a new lock on the door."

Nicki's emerald eyes lighted with glee. "Typical ineffective security there, too. The horse gets out, so you close the barn door. The FBI could use a professional, maybe. I've got an undergraduate degree in electrical engineering, as well as a Ph.D. in nuclear physics."

"I've seen your résumé."

"I keep forgetting. Actually, a lot of it was plain old Sherlock Holmes sleuthing for stuff the Feds missed."

"Such as?"

"Like a photocopied form tacked to the wall, a regular cheat sheet leading me through the maze to get into every department at the *News's* home office in Roswell. I even found Eddie Chisholm's computer password scribbled in pencil inside the desk drawer."

"So you used that data to retrieve this unpublished AP story from the paper's mainframe in Roswell? But why didn't the FBI drive out from their Albuquerque regional office today and grill Harrison? I'm sure you were being monitored."

"Oh, I'm sure somebody got grilled, all right. I drove into Albuquerque this morning, where I used the Internet connections at the University of New Mexico library to download this information. I was not surprised to see two very worried federal agents hurrying up the steps when I left." Nicki giggled. "I like meeting those guys like that. It helps me stay out of trouble, once I memorize a few faces. I know half the FBI staff east of the Mississippi on sight," she bragged. "Now I'm memorizing the ones in the Southwest too."

Chuck winced. "Eddie Chisholm, wherever he is, was picked up for questioning today, I'm sure." Chuck shook his head sadly.

"I'm driving out past the Bar L ranch tomorrow to do some snooping. Want to come along?"

"I'd love to." If what Eddie Chisholm had stumbled onto and CALF had passed on to Nicki to follow up on was as fantastic as it seemed, Chuck didn't want to miss the action.

"Good training. It'll be your initiation as a double agent." Nicki bit her lip again, grinning.

"Nicki, please. I can't get involved in CALF. I told you that in Maine."

☾☾☾

Chuck stared in disbelief next morning at the gap in the fence separating the White Sands Missile Range from the Bar L Ranch. "If this were Russia, this place would be crawling with guards lugging AK-47s!"

"Or Iraq," Nicki added.

"Most any place but the good ol' U.S. of A. I suppose the area is wired with motion detectors, though."

"Without a doubt. And they certainly are repairing the fence, but I wonder where the crew is this morning?" Nicki pointed to where workmen had recently poured a cement retaining wall to shore up a collapsed embankment. The arroyo had crumbled inward in a flash flood, letting the chain-link fence and barbed wire tumble over the day before rancher Lewis's colt had wandered through, the AP article had said. The only obvious deterrent at present was a dire sign advising, FEDERAL PROPERTY—TRESPASSERS WILL BE PROSECUTED—5 YEARS IMPRISONMENT & $20,000 FINE.

"Evidently they're still driving through." Chuck pointed to where a bulldozer had built an earthen ramp, apparently to let the repair crew come and go while working on the fence. The bulldozer was parked just beyond the gully, on federal land. "Civilian crew, I imagine. So it'll be done when it's done."

"This is just another example of what I mean by 'feet of clay,'" Nicki tartly pointed out. "We've become so used to people having this 'right' and that 'right' that the crew can just pick up and go off to work on another project. Who cares about national security anymore?" she scoffed.

"I do," Chuck protested. "They do have the place lighted for night surveillance." He pointed to several banks of floodlights on makeshift towers, wired to a generator.

"Let's go!" Nicki slammed the gearshift into *drive,* and the Cherokee shot ahead. But instead of making a quick U-turn, she steered for the gap and the dirt ramp.

Chuck grabbed for the key, then pulled back. *Too late to stop Nicki now. If I shut the motor off, the Cherokee will lose its power steering. We'd be upside down—inside a federal missile range. If we survive the wreck, we'll both be on our way to prison.*

Unless the Iraqis get Nicki first.

Up the other side of the gully they shot, just missing the parked bulldozer. "We'll be back on U.S. Highway 380 before they can get over here from Holloman Air Force Base," Nicki said confidently. "Check that out." She pointed toward the stump of a giant saguaro cactus.

"Holy cow!" Chuck stared. The plant, nearly three feet in diameter, had evidently exploded, leaving nothing but a shredded stump.

"Cacti are full of water," Nicki said. "If my theory is right . . ." She opened the door and hurried toward the stump.

"Hey! We're on federal property. This is a restricted zone."

"Come on, Chuck!"

"I should take your Jeep and leave you here to walk back," he protested again. But he hopped out and hurried over.

"That odor. I don't believe it's the cactus." Nicki wrinkled her nose.

"Carrion. Haven't they buried those cows, yet?"

"It's the horse!" Nicki plunged through dry sagebrush toward a pine that had been split as if struck by lightning.

Chuck hurried on her heels. The stench was so powerful once they got close enough to peer down the shaft of the old silver mine that neither he nor Nicki had any inclination to hang around.

She turned. Laughing, she ran toward the Cherokee.

"What's so funny?" Chuck slammed his door and buckled his seat belt for another wild ride.

"You, silly." Nicki fired up the motor. "You're such a wimp."

"Not a wimp. It's just that God has more important things for my life than rotting in a federal prison cell."

"We haven't hurt a thing. Can't argue with your values, though."

Once they left the White Sands Range, Nicki pushed the speedometer past eighty on a straight stretch of desert road. Dust rolled up behind, like from a crop duster's biplane. Even last week's sudden shower hadn't kept things damp for long. Chuck was no doubt right about an electronic detection system, Nicki realized, so she didn't plan to be around when the guards rolled up in a Humvee to investigate.

POP-POP-POP-POP-POP-POP-POP-POP! Tiny, smoke-trailing objects spattered on the road ahead, gravel and sand flying onto the windshield, chipping the glass.

Nicki screamed something in Vietnamese.

"Tracer bullets!" Chuck yelled. "They're shooting at us!"

Nicki hit the brakes. The Cherokee fishtailed. She let it coast, bringing the vehicle under control as the speedometer fell to fifty.

Another line of bullets spattered just ahead. Then they were caught full in the face by a blinding beam of light: three flashes; a pause; three more bright flashes. The universal signal for "Stop and surrender."

The light stopped, and an F-16 Fighting Falcon shot out of the dust toward them, missing the roof by what seemed mere inches. "If I were your captain, lieutenant, I'd have your wings for that," Chuck growled.

"He can't land that fighter jet in this desert." Nicki gritted her teeth. They were back up to sixty, now, and they struck ruts, making it nearly impossible to control the car.

Chuck watched the F-16 arc away from them, several miles out, moving at maybe four hundred knots, he figured. The plane banked and wheeled back. "They can't follow behind us, either. Those things stall out under 160 knots. But Nicki, they *can* shoot us or blow us up with a rocket."

"There you go again," Nicki snapped. "The United States Air Force is not authorized to shoot civilians unless fired upon, even when fleeing a crime scene. As an ex-cop, you know that."

"True." This fact did little to assuage Chuck's fears as tracer bullets began to spatter the road ahead again.

Nicki drove on. "That hotshot in the F-16 is only trying to intimidate us. More feet of clay. Any other nation on earth could protect its military secrets," she scoffed, gritting her teeth. "So he will just circle and report our position until they can set up a roadblock. He *ought* to be allowed to kill us."

"We might as well give up now." Chuck didn't like the fireworks, and Nicki was getting irrational. But mostly, his conscience bothered him. He'd let Nicki drag him along and into a near-treasonous escapade. Now they were cornered like rats in a grain bin.

The jet roared past, too close again. "It's not over until it's over, buster," Nicki yelled, though she knew the overzealous pilot could not hear her.

Suddenly Chuck reached across Nicki's lap. She hadn't fastened her seat belt, and in the emergency he found himself feeling protective. He snapped the buckle, just as the Jeep began to skid.

Nicki fought the wheel. The sport utility vehicle's short wheelbase and high center of gravity made it behave more like a rodeo bronco than a car on the rutted road.

The SUV flipped, rolling twice.

"Nicki? All right?"

"Uh-huh." She unbuckled her seat belt and fell into his arms where the Cherokee lay on its passenger side, deep in the ditch. The airbags hadn't deployed since the vehicle hadn't struck head-on.

Through the crazily canted glass, Chuck watched the F-16 climb up, up, then disappear.

"Give me my shoulder bag—it's under you! Then let's get out of here!" Nicki was mad rather than hurt.

Chuck complied, then he dragged his duffel bag from the backseat. They found themselves in a deep ditch leading to a dry brook that crossed the road beneath a plank bridge. The sharp drop onto the bridge had sent the Jeep Cherokee spinning out of control. Nicki now scooted back toward the bridge, Chuck following. They crouched underneath as the F-16 thundered in again, this time without firing.

"Think he realizes we got out?" Nicki wondered.

"I doubt it. That ditch is overgrown with willows. He came in pretty close, but he was moving too fast for more than a glance."

Nicki pointed up the creek. "That's north, back toward the highway. I remember that Route 380 crosses a small bridge just before we turned off onto the drive past the Bar L. Arrowhead Creek—something like that. I'd guess this is it."

"I'm sure you're right. It's maybe two more miles. Take us an hour—just about time enough to walk into the arms of a dozen U.S.

Marshals and New Mexico State Police. We're trapped. Face it, Spidergirl, you can't climb out of this one."

"Do you have a better plan? That plane's going to circle until reinforcements come."

"Turn ourselves in. It'll go easier if we give up peaceably."

"For you. I'm facing life without parole."

"Or the Iraqis. Pretty grim," Chuck agreed.

"Chuck, will you pray?"

"Does God really answer prayer?" Chuck was serious, not taunting. He wanted Nicki to answer her own question.

"I prayed when we were first shot at—'Our Father who art in heaven.' That's the only prayer I know."

"I heard you say something in Vietnamese. I suppose I thought . . ."

"That I was swearing. I don't swear. I respect the God of my Christian parents, the God of my father's ancestors, too much for that. But I have prayed, really. I prayed in that hotel room in Nairobi."

"Dear Father, we ask You to direct and deliver us. In Jesus' name, amen," Chuck prayed.

"Thanks. We can walk up the creek now. But if they threaten your life, I'm giving myself up, Chuck. I dragged you into this, and I won't have you go to prison, even though the Iraqi agents will probably have me assassinated in my cell if I'm arrested."

"Let's go."

They trudged maybe two hundred yards while the F-16 made several more passes over the rolled Cherokee. It was evident that the pilot didn't realize that they had gotten out. Then the *LOP-LOP-LOP-LOP-LOP-LOP* of another aircraft caught their ears.

"Chopper!" Nicki said.

"Yeah," Chuck agreed. "Duck beneath that cottonwood. I'll shinny up for a better look." He dropped down a moment later. "It's a U.S. Army MH-60 Black Hawk. It set down next to our SUV. That sucker's got more firepower than a B-17 Flying Fortress: rapid-fire Gatling machine gun, laser-guided Hellfire missiles—the works."

"Are they coming after us?"

"You betcha. Soon as they see that we got out!"

"They'll catch us!"

"Maybe. But I'm not going to turn you in, Nicki. Like you said, the Feds can't protect you from Saddam's assassins. I'm with you as long as you want to run. If we can stay next to the creek bank, we'll be hard to spot. We can probably reach that clump of willows at the bend in the creek before that chopper takes off this way."

11

The Vanishing American

*David . . . departed from there
and escaped to the cave of Adullam.*

—Samuel

It happened so fast that Chuck saw everything move in slow motion. Later, he realized that God had put things where they were to show them both that He was in charge of their destinies. Chuck and Nicki had just dived under the willows as the roar of the U.S. Army Black Hawk helicopter came almost overhead.

A deer shot out the other side of their hiding place.

"I'm giving myself up!" Nicki leaped up the bank, waving her arms.

Chuck grabbed her hand-tooled Western belt, yanking her down, catching her in his arms.

WHUMPF! Hit by a rocket, the deer exploded. Blood and guts rained down through the willow branches.

"Nicki, they're shooting to kill!" Chuck hollered. "Whatever they were experimenting with over by that mine shaft, the military is willing to risk murder and court-martial to keep it covered up."

"Chuck, please—we're not dealing with the military! It's the Nuclear Research and Development Administration. The NRDA detonated a neutron bomb over there last week. With the clues I've seen, it couldn't be anything else," said Nicki. "It's an atomic weapon, and an above-ground test like this is a violation of our long-standing, test-ban treaty with the former Soviet Union," she added. "There—I've told you, and that makes us both enemies of the state, like the Rosenbergs. Eddie Chisholm had no idea. He thought he'd run onto another weird experiment, like the Roswell flying saucers in '47."

"And you're after the neutron bomb formula for CALF!" Chuck guessed.

"It's the final piece of our little project," Nicki insisted. "The Pentagon intends to use a neutron wartip on the Vanguard Missile, which is to be fired from a new, top-secret nuclear submarine. Your company is helping them build it, as you very well know. But if CALF has the missile and the neutron wartip too, the United States won't have to worry about Saddam anymore. We will deal with Saddam ourselves. He's got to be destroyed before Assyria can rise!"

"Right now, you and I have got both the U.S. Army and the U.S. Air Force to worry about," Chuck said evenly, trying to take charge. "There's a good cover of sagebrush spreading west from here, back toward the missile range. If we can crawl under that while the Black Hawk searches the ditch, we may get to where we can follow the fence north to the highway." He wiped the deer blood from his face with the back of his hand. "They may even conclude they finished us off, once they see this mess. Let's go!" he said, as the big whirlybird's rotor noise got closer.

Half an hour's crawling and scrambling brought Chuck and Nicki to the shade of a boulder, where an old cottonwood had fallen over to form a brushy lean-to. "My police experience tells me that if they don't get us by high-tech before dark, they'll turn to good old tried and true low-tech after dark," Chuck remarked. "K-9s—bloodhounds or German Shepherds." He mopped Nicki's blood-splattered face with his handkerchief. "We've got to be the dirtiest desperadoes in history." He forced a smile.

"Let's hope they don't find any easily identifiable parts of that poor deer. Maybe they'll think it's us," Nicki said grimly. "Something just occurred to me, Chuck. I've got just what we need in my bag to get us out of this trap!"

Chuck stared. "Like maybe a personal jet propulsion system?"

"Remember, I went to Albuquerque yesterday, to the university library?"

"Yeah."

"Maps—old, detailed U.S. Geological Survey charts dated 1906, when this was still New Mexico Territory. White Sands Missile Range didn't exist then. Every mine shaft, every entrance, every ditch in Socorro County is on them. I made photocopies!"

"You mean there's a mine shaft tunneled through the San Andres Mountains? If you believe it's still there, you're a dreamer."

"Chuck, we've *been* there!"

"You mean *inside* the missile range, where that dead horse fell? They'll be all over us if we go back in there, Nicki. Shoot to kill on sight. After this, I'm sure of it."

"Chuck, they'll know our position only for the few seconds it takes us to run through the motion detectors along the fence."

"I told you—bloodhounds."

"The hounds will be trying to follow a *human* scent from the upholstery of the Cherokee. We smell like deer. Once we get past that rotting horse . . ."

"I'll go through snow, sleet, mud, fire, hail, even a manure pit for you. But a dead horse? Is any woman worth that much?" Chuck grinned, feeling silly.

Nicki fished the maps from her shoulder bag, along with a bottle of water and a package of tissues. She dampened several, then passed the water and tissues to Chuck. "Clean your face and hands while I study these maps. I suppose the mess on our clothes will have to stay. Like you say, it may throw the hounds off. Please go easy on the water. It's all we have until who knows when."

"Even if the mine shaft is still open through the mountain, it'll be plugged on the other end, I'm sure."

"Of course," Nicki agreed. "If the Air Force has kept the tunnel open, it'll be sealed with a steel gate and padlocked on the inside. And there'll be an alarm system."

"I see your point. It'll be fixed to keep intruders out. But we're already inside—or will be, if we can get back through that gap after dark." Chuck sighed. "It's a long shot."

"It's our only shot, Chuck. The alarm system will be a piece of cake. And see here, Chuck," Nicki said. She fished a battery-operated gadget resembling an engraving tool from her purse. "Electronic lock pick. It'll open Fort Knox."

"You don't surprise me anymore," Chuck laughed. "I'll bet one of those pens is a gun." He pointed to a row of writing implements in a series of small pockets.

"Oh, I think I could surprise you." Nicki grinned. She slipped out a pen and pressed a button. Out popped a steel rod, like a blackboard pointer.

Puzzled, Chuck frowned.

"Bug detector. This will find any radio transmitter made."

"We could have used that in Mexico. It would have saved us a lot of trouble."

"Chuck, neither of us had a clue. But I used it during the two days I spent as a nurse's aide in the Tucson hospital. I checked your clothing. No bugs. Who would have believed that they'd planted one behind your armpit like you were a pet goat? In the game of espionage, you lose a hand now and then."

"Well, like they say, 'It takes a thief to know a thief.'" Chuck laughed.

"Meaning what?" Nicki smiled, displaying a perfect, double row of pearly teeth between grimy cheeks.

"Why do I think you're beautiful when you grin like that?"

"Sometimes," said Nicki, "I think it would be fun to just vanish, all except my smile, like Alice's Cheshire cat."

❰❰❰

"Something funny's going on," Chuck whispered. It was past midnight, and the construction area around the gap in the fence guarding the White Sands Missile Range was lighted with powerful floodlights. He and Nicki could hear several men and a woman talking and laughing.

"I'll find out." Nicki began to squirm toward the fence.

"Wait." Chuck grabbed her ankle as she slithered past. His masculine protectiveness rose to the surface whenever he believed Nicki to be in danger.

"Can't hang around here." Nicki nodded toward the distant baying of the K-9s behind them. "'Course, if you're right, they'll never find us, 'cause we smell like deer." Nicki wrinkled her nose cutely, then pinched it to shut out the odor of dried deer blood and guts.

"Those guys may shoot to kill. Be careful."

"I've been shot at before!" Nicki crawled off.

Chuck waited and prayed.

Nicki was back ten minutes later. "Three men and a woman. They've dragged the seat from the bulldozer underneath a light, and they're using it for a card table. They have shotguns and bullhorns."

"Shotguns . . . like prison guards?"

"Exactly. You're not going to believe this—they're the crew bosses."

"So where's the crew? Bosses carry clipboards and tape measures, not guns."

"And bullhorns." Nicki grinned. "I heard them talking about having an easy night of it because the prisoners were sent back to the penitentiary. No prisoners, 'cause we are running loose. No prisoners, no fence building tonight."

"There's something missing in this picture. Prisoners, instead of civilian construction laborers—more like Red China. And working at night?"

"Don't you see it, Chuck? Of course you don't, since you don't really believe what I've told you about the neutron bomb being tested in there. They're building the fence after dark, so the crew can't look past their own lighted work area. And prisoners don't hold press conferences."

"Or write articles for the Associated Press. But neutron bomb?"

"Cut it out, Chuck," Nicki warned. "Now, let's slip inside the fence and scramble down that mine shaft."

"But . . . the lights."

"They're busy with their card game, behind the 'dozer. We can sneak right past," Nicki said confidently. "If there are any motion detectors, they'd be set up to send a radio signal back to the air base. We'll be long gone by the time they get those guards on the phone."

"Like a minefield in Vietnam." Chuck remembered his days as an Army chaplain in Vietnam as he followed Nicki onto the missile range. He had gone with the soldiers into territory just vacated by the enemy. They had walked single file, each man stepping in the others' footsteps, hoping to avoid land mines.

Nicki was the expert at sneaking around, so he let her lead. The faintest snap of a twig, they both knew, could send the card players after their guns.

They found the mine shaft easily enough. The stench of the dead horse was potent as they lay on their stomachs, peering into the black void. Nicki fished a powerful, palm-sized flashlight from her shoulder bag and pointed its intense beam downward. She outlined the rotting, brown-and-white horse. Then, playing the light past the dead beast, Nicki illuminated the horizontal shaft beneath the mountain.

"Let's surrender," Chuck said, gagging. "They can shoot me instead of this."

"You're kidding," Nicki whispered. She aimed her light at the iron rungs.

"Yes, of course I'm kidding."

"Ladies first." Nicki slipped over the edge and began to descend.

Chuck watched in disgust as Nicki reached the bottom, then slid over the filthy creature and disappeared into the tunnel under the mountain. A moment later her light appeared again, illuminating the horse cadaver. "C'mon. Hurry."

Chuck swung his duffel bag over his shoulder and started down. His head was still above ground when the card party abruptly broke up. The players grabbed their guns and raced to the gap in the fence. Two flop-eared, baying hounds followed by two German Shepherds shot from the darkness near where Chuck and Nicki had earlier hidden. The dogs circled, sniffing the ground, obviously confused.

A deputy sheriff and a uniformed state trooper hurried from the underbrush. "It's y'all's lunch that's attracting them," snarled the deputy. "See anyone come past here?"

"All quiet on the Western front," chuckled one of the poker-playing guards. Clearly he did not work for the sheriff.

"They're heading back to Route 380 by following this fence due north, likely," said the cop.

Chuck held his breath. The military had called in two civilian law-enforcement units to make use of their dogs, apparently. Things had quickly gotten desperate for pursuer as well as pursued, he grimly realized.

"Go get it, boy!" The lady guard tossed a half-eaten sandwich directly at Chuck. It landed in the brush only a couple of yards from the mine shaft.

Chuck kicked off the iron ladder and let himself drop into the blackness below. *Boomp!* He struck the bloated horse sitting down, slid off the putrid slimy mess, and scrambled into the shaft.

"Horsehide's tough, even if the horse is dead." Nicki doubled over, giggling.

Chuck tore the flashlight from her fingers. Grabbing her wrist, he led them at a trot deeper beneath the mountain. Finally rounding a bend, the couple stopped for breath. "What on earth were you laughing your silly head off for back there?" Chuck demanded.

"I guess you found a way to overcome your disdain for dead horses." Nicki broke into giggles again.

"Nicki, I . . . one of the dogs."

"I heard them barking. But that horse scent . . . I'm sure it held them off. Besides, if the Air Force personnel knew about the shaft, they'd have covered it as soon as they found the broken planks."

"I'm sure they know about it," Chuck snapped.

"Oh, they *know* about it, all right. I'm sure they have the same maps as I have. But staff changes after a few years, and details like old silver mines get forgotten. Let's just hope they don't rediscover it for a couple of days. There's sagebrush enough so it can't be seen from the work area. Now let's look at our maps."

((((

Dawn had begun to redden the sky toward Roswell when Nicki and Chuck reached a steel gate on the mountainside high above U.S. Highway 380. As they figured, a heavy old padlock held the gate from the inside.

"Probably no alarm system," Chuck asserted. "Like you said, it's been years since anyone's been back here. Maybe not since World War II, more than fifty years ago."

"I hope you're right. But alarm switches can be placed on the outside too—and at a later date, if there's concern about someone getting into White Sands through this mine tunnel. Let's wait until daylight before we tackle this gate."

Chuck sighed. Patience was not his forte.

"Look, Chuck!" Nicki pointed to the highway, more than a mile away. Red and blue flashing lights showed a military roadblock in the direction of Roswell.

Chuck pressed against the rock wall and craned his neck for a peek in the other direction. He could see the village lights of Perro Prieta. Right in the middle of the village he saw more flashing lights. "Somebody wants us pretty bad," Chuck said.

❰❰❰

"Wake up, big feller." It was broad daylight when Nicki tossed a pebble at Chuck's cheek. He had been sleeping on the opposite side of the mine shaft, his duffel bag as his pillow.

"Don't you ever sleep?" Chuck rubbed his eyes.

"Sure I do. But I don't have to sound like a chain saw when I'm asleep. If anyone even got near the other end of this mine shaft, they'd have heard you snoring."

"That's a couple of miles," Chuck protested.

"That's the point, exactly," Nicki teased. "Now let's get this gate open. I don't like us being trapped like rats in a sewer."

Chuck ran his arm through the bars and felt the edge of the gate on the outside. "You were right," he exclaimed. "There's an alarm circuit. Here's the switch." He pressed his face to the bars and peered upward. "The wire runs through a steel conduit tube, so I can't get to it. Wait. There's a plate at the bend, held by a couple of screws."

"You could use a screwdriver, maybe?"

Chuck grinned. He fished his jackknife out and opened the screwdriver blade. "Universal male tool of the trade," he chuckled. The screws easily came out, and he pulled the looped alarm wires out. "If I had something to clamp them with, I'd scrape the insulation off and squeeze the wires together, so the circuit wouldn't break when we open this gate."

Nicki fished a safety pin from her bag. She opened it, straightening it. "Universal female tool." She grinned, passing the pin to Chuck.

"Clever." Chuck poked the pin through both dangling wires to keep the circuit closed when they opened the gate, triggering the switch.

Nicki had popped open the padlock with her electronic lock pick by the time Chuck finished with the wires. She lifted the lock off, and they slipped outside with their bags. She closed the gate and relocked it. After removing the pin, Chuck screwed the conduit plate back in place. "Nothing like security at a federal military test site," he chortled.

Far below them the military roadblocks were still in place, so Chuck led the way toward a thicket of scrubby cedars crowding a damp hollow. The hollow held a mountainside spring watering the cedars. Here they found fresh water to drink and to clean up with. Chuck even managed to shave in cold water, using Nicki's makeup mirror to see his face.

Nicki had half a dozen granola bars in her bag. They each had one for breakfast. "Now," said Nicki, "I really can sleep." She propped her head on her leather shoulder bag and fell fast asleep.

It was late afternoon when Nicki awoke. She found Chuck watching Highway 380 and the village from the edge of the clump of cedars. "What's happening?"

"Sheriff took the dogs away in his truck hours ago, so they've given up searching the countryside for us," Chuck said. "Roadblock's still on, though." He pointed to where New Mexico state troopers were searching a Greyhound bus as Air Force MPs stood watching. It was parked in front of Helen's Beans and Burgers. "I figure one more night—maybe sooner—they'll give up the hunt."

"Maybe," Nicki said hopefully. "We can be patient."

"I think it's time you told me why whatever is going on inside White Sands is big enough to cause the Armed Services to use lethal force against us," Chuck said. "It's bad enough being a fugitive, without knowing what for."

"They tested another flying saucer." Nicki grinned impishly.

"Nicki, I've been honest with you," Chuck pleaded. "We've risked our lives for each other."

"I've already told you what I know, Chuck, and it may cost you your life if you repeat it to anyone."

"I'm beginning to believe it."

"Chuck, since it was tested above ground, that neutron bomb is a violation of the nuclear arms treaty with Russia. Besides that, this is apparently a more powerful neutron bomb than any ever tested before—the girl and the cows died instantly. In all neutron bombs tested up until now, the victims lingered for nearly a week before dying," Nicki explained.

"But how could you possibly know that's what happened? Marcie Lewis and all those cows—you mean?"

"It's the nature of the beast. Our people . . ."

"You mean CALF?"

"Right. We have information sources inside the Pentagon."

"I can see why you didn't want to talk about it. Are you trying to get me to turn you in—to put an end to CALF's espionage operations?"

"Is it really espionage when you're not a foreign nation with a government?"

"By my definition . . . go ahead, I'm listening." Chuck knew he was in a serious quandary. He had been busy protecting Nicki, while she protected him from unknown but very real enemies. Then she had died before his eyes, only to turn up alive in Maine.

Now they were both on the run again. Did the military operators of White Sands even know whom they were chasing? They had seized and examined Nicki's rented Cherokee by now for sure. They had certainly traced it back to Nicki—or to whatever alias she had used to rent it. "I'll keep my mouth shut and listen to what you have to say," Chuck said at last. If she were willing to talk, he could perhaps better understand how to deal with his conundrum. "But remember whom you're talking to. You can never persuade me to join CALF."

"I think I may surprise you." Nicki spoke with a mixture of elation and profound concern, as if nothing were more important in all the world. "Do you recall that scrambled E-mail message that I pulled off Stan Basford's computer in South Freedom, Maine?"

"You burned it in Mae's kitchen range as soon as you translated it. Yes, I remember." Chuck had found the message after Nicki carelessly left it undeleted on Stan's hard drive after being translated by her decoding disk. It seemed screwy even in translation, and he didn't want to admit to Nicki that he'd read it.

"One of our operatives in the Pentagon sent it to me. Something about air-cooled engines."

"Plus old-style breaker-point distributors and nickel-metal hydride dry cell batteries."

"Where did you get that information?" Nicki was shocked.

"You left it on Stan's hard drive. As you know, I traced you here easily enough, since you used your own name to buy a ticket from Boston to Roswell. I know just enough of the theory behind the neutron bomb to guess you'd head for White Sands. Go on with your story."

"The Pentagon has ordered 58,000 specially designed air-cooled motors from American Trucks, Ltd., in St Louis—equipped with old-fashioned breaker-point distributors," Nicki noted.

"And they have ordered an equal number of nickel-metal, hydride, dry-cell, twelve-volt batteries from Century Twenty-One Electronics in Chicago." Chuck grunted. "Those babies are expensive—$1,500 apiece. Harry could use an order like that."

"That comes to $87 million. Not a bad piece of change for a small manufacturer."

"I always knew you were good at mental arithmetic," Chuck said. "Now all this is supposed to prove that the Pentagon is also testing a neutron bomb?"

"By a little simple triangulation of what we already knew, plus using a couple of facts you and I have learned since coming to New Mexico, yes. It all points the same direction."

"Well, it's been known for many years that *any* atomic blast creates a powerful EMP, an electromagnetic pulse that will fry transistors and computer chips like bacon. This will destroy the electrical systems in all modern automobiles—including military trucks and tanks," Chuck said. "So I suppose the old style distributors, with breaker-point ignition, aren't affected by an atomic blast. But neither are diesel engines."

"Diesels run hot—they require water cooling." Nicki grinned. "I'm sorry to be so far ahead of you in this, but it's my field. And there's another factor," Nicki added. "The electronic ignition systems in modern military equipment can of course be shielded against the effects of EMPs. But I'm guessing that the Pentagon doesn't want it to leak out that our equipment—or an enemy's—could be exposed to electromagnetic pulses under battle conditions. Why would the Pentagon brass want the world to know that our military has the capability to destroy the ignition systems and radio equipment of an advancing army at the touch of a button?"

"Hey, I haven't told you what I learned about Zeke Lewis's truck—the '72 Ford." Chuck had begun to see how the pieces fit together.

"Let's hear it."

"Of course it was manufactured three years before electronic ignition appeared. There's your antique distributor."

"Which explains why he was able to drive it away from the blast site," Nicki agreed.

"The battery had exploded."

"I'm sure the radiator also exploded," said Nicki. "When a neutron bomb goes off, it extracts all the hydrogen within reach by a thermonuclear process. Water is mostly hydrogen, and sulfuric acid—battery acid—contains a lot of hydrogen also. The bomb will kill all life within several hundred yards because life contains water. That's animals, plants, people, even bacteria. But buildings, machinery, and hard goods will be untouched, except for their water-operated systems or high-tech electronics," Nicki explained. "We've just seen what one will do—right here, just a few miles from where the Manhattan Project set off the world's first atomic blast, July 16, 1945." Nicki could hardly contain her elation. "CALF can use this weapon on the Babylonians!"

Chuck shivered. "That does explain the air-cooled engines and dry cell batteries. But . . ." His jaw dropped. "Your E-mail said that American Trucks, Ltd., in St. Louis is building the engines. Nicki, I . . . I've heard a news report that American Trucks has sold thousands of heavy vehicles to Russia for military use. Wasn't it ABC News's *20/20* that did an exposé showing that the Russian government is reselling these same trucks to China in violation of our trade agreements with Russia?"

"Something like 58,000 trucks, maybe? And the *20/20* report leads to an interesting possibility that brings it all together," Nicki said. "CALF believes that the Pentagon is testing the neutron bomb in violation of international treaties to prepare for Armageddon," she added. "Some of our people think China's one-child policy could result in 200 million unmarried Chinese men. We believe they might draft those into a huge army, then they could march them through the Himalayas, cross the Euphrates River, and attack Israel—using *American* equipment."

"You mean the army of horsemen mentioned in Revelation, after the sixth angel sounds his trumpet and empties his bowl? Your CALF organization thinks that our American military believes that army to be Chinese? You're not serious!?"

"I *am* serious, Chuck. They'd have to cross land that once was Assyrian territory on their way to attack Israel. CALF believes that the Pentagon expects to stop this Chinese invasion with their new neutron warhead. We're talking about the warhead to be mounted on the Vanguard Missile System, which your people at Salem Electronics have been scurrying like squirrels to finish. The U.S. military could then seize all this American-built equipment and retrofit it with neutron-proof motors and batteries for their own use. Doesn't this go to show, that we can no longer trust our elected officials—the president and Congress?" Nicki wondered, elated at her rush of prophetic wisdom.

"Whoa!" Chuck cautioned. "In the first place, a lot of prophetic interpretation tends to be based on wishful thinking applied to current events. As recently as 100 years ago evangelical scholars taught that Revelation 9 and 16 had already been fulfilled by Mohammed, believed to be the Anti-Christ, who conquered the Holy Roman Empire with his army of Moors. My own parents were taught that Benito Mussolini, the Italian dictator who supported Hitler, would soon become the Anti-Christ. Then just a dozen years ago, during the Gulf War against Iraq, a lot of Bible teachers suddenly revised their teaching about the city of Babylon mentioned in Revelation. I strongly believe that those 200 million horsemen are a horde of fallen angels turned loose during the Tribulation to torment unbelievers."

"But Chuck," Nicki protested, "our CALF operatives know what the Pentagon's current theories are."

"'Current' is one key." He frowned. "Also, is this the majority opinion of the American military brass, or only the boiler-room scuttlebutt of a few officers?"

"What do you mean?"

"Just look at the vacillation in American military policy in recent years, through Presidents Reagan, Bush, Clinton, and today. This does make your 'feet of clay' concept almost believable," Chuck pointed out. "Some of our presidents read the Bible and made military decisions based on their spiritual advisor's interpretation of it. Others reversed their predecessor's policies. Several presidents over the past fifty or so years have warned of the Battle of Armageddon."

"President Johnson and his famous TV ad of a child being annihilated in a nuclear holocaust?" Nicki shuddered.

"Perhaps we're both being a little harsh on the president and Congress," Chuck cautioned. "On the one hand, they may not know all that's going on in the Pentagon. Then there are those members of Congress who've stated that it's time the old treaties were scrapped, anyway. You, of all people, know how technology has changed since we signed those treaties with the old Soviet Union. Then again, the Soviet Union collapsed in 1991, and some powerful senators feel that Russia can hardly expect us to honor a treaty made with a nation that no longer exists," he concluded.

"There is the possibility that the Pentagon is testing the neutron bomb, in violation of international treaties, actually in preparation for Armageddon," Chuck said. "I've seen a report that China plans to bring a vast army into Israel, using *American* equipment.

Some folks take Daniel 11:44, and the terrible message of the sixth angel of the Apocalypse to mean this."

"You got it, Chuck. And they'd have to cross land that once was Assyria on their way to attack Israel. The Pentagon expects to stop this Chinese invasion with their new neutron warhead. We're talking about the warhead that is to be mounted on the Vanguard Missile System, which your people at Salem Electronics have been scurrying like squirrels to finish. The U.S. military will then seize all this American-built equipment and retrofit it with neutron-proof motors and batteries for our own use. Doesn't this go to show that we can no longer trust our elected officials—the president and Congress?" Nicki wondered.

"I think you're being a little harsh on the president and Congress," Chuck observed. "On one hand, they may not know what's going on. Then there are those members of Congress who've stated that it's time the old treaties were scrapped, anyway. You, of all people, know how technology has changed since we signed those treaties with the Soviet Union. Then again, the Soviet Union collapsed in 1991, and some powerful senators feel that Russia can hardly expect us to honor a treaty made with a nation that no longer exists," he concluded.

❰❰❰

The Army lifted its roadblocks at midnight. Chuck and Nicki made the long hike into Perro Prieta at once. Near dawn, Nicki waited in an abandoned car behind Helen's Beans and Burgers, while Chuck bought a morning newspaper from a box in front of the restaurant. Helen's was also the local Greyhound stop, and already a lone passenger was seated on the bench in front.

"Going to Roswell?" Chuck asked. He unfolded the *Roswell Daily News* underneath a street lamp.

"Nope."

"West, then?"

"Albuquerque."

"Guess I'm a little early for the Roswell bus. What time does it come through?"

"Dunno. Later. Helen'll tell y'."

Chuck checked his watch. 5:25. The eatery, he knew, opened for breakfast at 5:30. Since he already had half a round-trip ticket, Roswell to Albuquerque and return, he needed only to buy a single, one-way ticket from Helen for Nicki's use. He returned his attention to the paper. Then he froze.

At the bottom of page one was Nicki's photo. A brief article, written by reporter Harrison, said that the FBI was seeking Ms. Nicki Towns and an "unknown male accomplice for trespassing in the White Sands Missile Range." Papers "found in the glove compartment of Towns's rented sports utility vehicle" tied the crime to her, Harrison wrote.

The article stated also that Nicki was "suspected of espionage activities in various plants holding military contracts." Chuck whistled. He ignored the stare of the young man on the bench and strode inside, where Helen was whipping up pancake batter as Juanita set tables. Chuck ordered a double stack of pancakes and extra eggs, toast, and bacon. He took a couple of sips of coffee while waiting for the food, then with the newspaper under his arm, he strode for the men's room behind the kitchen. He banged the restroom door loudly, then quietly slipped out the back entrance.

Nicki was sleeping peacefully on the backseat of an old Cadillac limousine with expired plates. Chuck passed her the paper. "I'm getting you a ticket to Roswell and a doggie bag for my leftovers. Stay out of sight until bus time—6:15."

"Yes, master." Nicki grinned and took the paper.

◖◖◖

The desert heat was already creating mirages on the hot asphalt as the big Greyhound droned eastward early that morning. Chuck and Nicki sat in the back, out of earshot of the other riders in the half-filled bus. "I was stupid to have used my own name to buy a plane ticket from Boston," Nicki spat out. "And that rental car!"

"That does seem a bit reckless," Chuck agreed.

Nicki shrugged. "There are half a dozen Nicki Townses in the Boston phone directory. But I also identified myself to the *News*'s managing editor in Roswell before driving out here."

"What did you learn from him?"

"Enough for a lead. Oh, he was plenty evasive. Said that writing about White Sands had just cost his most promising young reporter his career."

"Eddie Chisholm?" Chuck guessed. "So you came to Perro Prieta looking for Chisholm's files?"

"Right you are."

"I guess it's confession time," said Chuck. "Before I left Salem Electronics for Maine, I gave the Old Man a written report of my activities since I left for Tucson. It included a report on your supposed murder."

"'Alleged' murder—that's the official term for it," Nicki joked. "You did the right thing, Chuck. The FBI would have learned that I'm still alive and well, once they got the fingerprints from that body in Mexico. But until now, I've never been investigated by the FBI, so they haven't worried me. It's been the Iraqis. I expect that Saddam is glowering at a faxed copy of that *Daily News* article in his Baghdad office right now."

Chuck was silent for several miles. "Nicki, I've got to know—did you set that poor woman up to be killed in Cancun so you could disappear?"

"Chuck, you know me better than that!"

"Well?"

"She drugged me with a stun gun, like they use on wild animals—I've told you that already. She left me on the beach next to the breakwater with nothing but my bathing suit. She even took my room key."

"That explains why you had to climb into my room at the Ponce de Leon to get your things back. But . . . but people just let you lie there for hours?"

"To people on the beach, I was just another girl sunbathing. Girls go to sleep in the sun all the time. I got one wicked burn!"

"I'll bet! But who would pull a stunt like that? That gal packed a 9-millimeter Glock automatic pistol—a police weapon."

"Anna Malenkov was her name." Nicki smiled wryly. "When she took my clothes, she left her things in a locker in the hotel pool dressing room. I hung around until the pool closed, then helped myself to the unclaimed contents of the only basket left locked. Everybody at the hotel was talking about the murder, so I needed only to ask a few lead questions to get the whole story."

"Locks don't seem to slow you down, Ms. Houdini, and I guess you wore that poor woman's clothes. But who was Ms. Malenkov?"

"A Russian espionage agent, obviously. She was unlucky enough to put herself in the way of that Iraqi assassin when he came over the breakwater looking for me—or so you told me in Maine. She wanted my purse, apparently. I carry a lot of stuff with ties to CALF. Nothing she could have used, but she didn't know that. The Russians are still trying to figure out what CALF is. The Babylonians—Iraqis—they already know, and they fear us. We've infiltrated their organization, though they don't realize it yet."

"But she didn't really believe I'd think she was you?"

"I expect that was a last-minute innovation. With me sleeping on the beach, once she learned that we are the same size, she tried to have a little fun with you. Maybe shake you up."

"And all this because I had a satellite bug beneath my skin?"

"Sort of. The Iraqis followed you to get me. Malenkov apparently tailed the Iraqis. I don't suppose she figured that Iraqi killer would try to do me in until after dark."

"Wow! But Iraq has no satellites."

"The Peoples Republic of China has put several up there—with stolen American technology. Since China buys oil from Iraq, go figure!"

"American feet, made of clay again. Nicki, your analogy about the U.S. being Daniel's feet of clay seems so eerily correct it's frightening."

"This whole neutron bomb thing—Manhattan II, if you please. Like the first Manhattan, it's not under the control of our elected officials, the people who must deal with other nations—the president and his State Department. The Nuclear Research and Development Administration seems to make its own rules as it goes along. And the Pentagon doesn't trust either the president or Congress. It's a bomb waiting to explode, Chuck!"

"Nicki, that's conjecture, built on appearances. You know that."

"Would the president or Congress order the U.S. Army to fire a rocket at us from a helicopter? Our Constitution requires a trial. And the CIA—they've been involved in illegal covert killings in Guatemala. Yet when we do catch a mole selling secrets to Russia, a man such as Aldrich Ames, who caused the death of more than a dozen of our own people, our American courts don't have the guts to put him to death. We have become so weak we can't deal with traitors in the Pentagon or the CIA, or even with murderers in our inner cities, Chuck."

"I can't argue with that. Ames has to be our worst traitor since Benedict Arnold. He was busy for years fingering American agents in Moscow," Chuck noted. "One by one Mikhail Gorbachev, with the help of his pal, Yevgeny Primakov, was simply ordering American CIA agents to be taken off and shot in the back of the head."

"Do you want to continue to work for a nation that lacks the courage to put a man like Ames to death—a man who was sending his own coworkers to their deaths for Russian rubles, Chuck?"

"If your theory about our Vanguard Missile System being designed to carry an illegally tested neutron warhead is right, Nicki, maybe I'm in deeper than I realized," Chuck sighed. "The legal route, and I think the morally correct one, would be to serve notice on Russia that we will no longer abide by the old treaties. A new treaty might be in order, though," he said.

❰❰❰

"All flights to Boston are cancelled for the rest of the day, sir. Logan is socked in with fog, and it's expected to remain that way until the weather changes, late tonight, most likely." Nicki had given Chuck a roll of cash from her CALF funds to buy them both tickets back to Boston. She, meanwhile, was quietly waiting in an airport restaurant, hiding from FBI agents behind sunglasses and a newspaper. She planned to board using an alias and a fake ID, and both she and Chuck agreed it would be unwise for her to be seen buying plane tickets.

"So, the next flight will be . . . ?"

"Seven-twenty A.M. tomorrow—flight 307. We have several seats remaining in business class. None together, though."

"I'll take two." Chuck slid the cash across the counter.

❰❰❰

Holiday Inn, a mile from the airport, had a shuttle bus and a restaurant. Chuck and Nicki boarded the bus separately, and they made a point of not being in the lobby together when they paid for separate rooms.

"You're walking in to certain arrest when you return to your cousin's place in Somerville, Massachusetts, Nicki," Chuck worried. They were together for dinner at the motel restaurant that evening. "If the Feds don't nab you right here as you try to board the plane, that is."

"I . . . I hope you're wrong," Nicki said. "Oh, I'll get on the plane, all right." She giggled. "Who should I be this time? Blonde? Redhead?"

"Nicki, this is serious business!"

"You're right, Chuck. And you know what—if Art Towns is home when I go to the house, I'm sure he'll call the FBI himself."

"So, why are you going back?" Chuck was dismayed. On the one hand, Nicki had to be stopped from telling CALF about the top-secret neutron bomb test. If she were not arrested when she stepped off the plane in Boston, he knew he had no choice but to turn her in to the FBI himself. On the other hand, he was certain that she'd be thrown into a jail cell where an Iraqi assassin would worm his or her way into the prison system to kill her.

"I . . . I've got to have another look at that old manuscript."

"The prophecy in the clay jar—the one written by your well-connected Hebrew-Assyrian ancestor, Princess Hniqi?"

"Exactly. I translated the Hebrew text into English when I was an evening student at Harvard Divinity School. I need to read it once again. The old parchment is in my safe-deposit box at Old Bay National Bank in Boston. But my English translation is in my room at home. The translation of the parchment has some gaps, since my Hebrew back then was imperfect."

"Home? Eighty-eight Highland Avenue, Somerville?"

"It's the only home I've had since leaving Vietnam after Mother died."

"How did she die?" Chuck understood losing a loved one in death, and he spoke tenderly.

"Mother was beaten to death by thugs in Saigon for harboring a 'Yankee half-breed bastard.' I was that 'half-breed,' and I spent the next several years living as a street brat, until I was seventeen. I did manage to keep Mother's English Bible. It had my birth certificate tucked inside, along with a letter to my father from his cousin, Rachel Towns."

"So you got a job on a freighter bound for Boston when you were seventeen, to claim your American citizenship? You told me bits and pieces of this in Mexico."

"I traveled as a boy," Nicki giggled. "Disguises come easy for me. These eyes, for example. In Vietnam, kids with American fathers are called 'round eyes.' But in the U.S., I still looked Asian to most people. So I saved my money from a job flipping hamburgers until I could pay a surgeon to take a subtle tuck in the corners." She pushed the corners of her eyes up, grinning.

"What do you intend to do with the old document—and your translation?"

"Read it once again. I've got to go back to my roots before I die."

"Back to Vietnam?" Chuck did not like the sound of this.

"Jerusalem—the Temple Mount, the site of David's palace near the Old City. And to Nineveh to see the palace of Ashurbanipal, who along with David was my ancestor. I'd like to find the harem quarters where Hniqi lived."

"'The great and noble Asnappar,' Ashurbanipal is called in Ezra 4:10. Perhaps Hniqi carved her initials on a post," Chuck joked.

"Or her son did."

"I thought you told me her child by her second marriage was a girl? That Hniqi's girl married Ashurbanipal's grandson by a concubine?"

"Hniqi also had a son by Ashurbanipal. She named him Daniye'l—a Hebrew name, for he was the great-grandson of Hezekiah, king of Judah."

"The Bible does seem to imply that Daniel the prophet was descended from Hezekiah. That was part of Isaiah's warning to Hezekiah after he unwisely gave the Babylonian diplomats a tour of his kingdom," Chuck mused. "Though a great man before God, Daniel was also a slave in Nebuchadnezzar's palace."

"You catch on fast."

"But Nineveh? The ruins of ancient Nineveh are in Iraq. The Iraqis are looking for you!"

"So?!"

"You're talking like a teenager now. I can guess what you're thinking."

Nicki grinned merrily. "I like to live dangerously. You know that by now, Chuck."

And die suddenly. Chuck shivered. He declined to answer.

❰❰❰

"Ms. Sanchez doesn't answer her room phone, sir."

"I'm sure she's on her way down, then." *She skipped out on me,* Chuck decided angrily as he strode back to Holiday Inn's Breakfast Nook. He had wrestled all night with turning Nicki in, and he had finally decided to do so. Now his anguished decision had again been thwarted. "Forgive me, Lord," he prayed half aloud. This was God's intervention, Chuck knew, and he felt as though a great load had been lifted.

But "Ms. Sanchez" was waiting for him at the door to the restaurant. "Sorry, Chuck," she said quietly. "Let's find a quiet table."

"You've been crying, Nicki," Chuck observed as soon as they were seated. He frowned, his concern for her again wrestling with his conscience. *Is the Lord playing a game with me?*

Without answering, Nicki slid several color photocopies from her shoulder bag. The top photo was the body of a preteen girl laid out on an examining table. The child's flesh was mottled with red welts, and the torso and limbs were bloated horribly. The photo was labeled, "Marcie Lewis."

Chuck turned the photo over quickly in shock. He searched Nicki's face.

"Chuck, I can't go on," she said at last. "This is the most horrible thing I've ever seen. To do that to a little girl!"

"I'm ashamed to realize that my government would create something as monstrous as this." Chuck was appalled. "Yet I've been in Vietnam, and I do understand atrocities. Sometimes when you're pushed far enough—these things cut both ways." Glad that he had turned the photo over, Chuck shot a glance at the waitress. "Coffee, black. Toast. One egg."

"Ma'am?"

Nicki did not answer.

"The lady will have the same."

"Thanks, Chuck." Nicki slid the photos back into her bag.

"I . . . I've got to take a vacation from my work with CALF. I can't just go ahead and procure a weapon for them that would do this."

"I've no doubt you could get it." *She'll get a vacation, all right—in federal prison,* Chuck mused. "Taking human life is an awesome responsibility," he said aloud, remembering the two men who had killed themselves trying to kill him.

"And when it's innocent life. She was so young. Probably beautiful too."

"We are all beautiful to God—created in His image, which is why murder is wrong. Beautiful and precious, so that His Son died to pay for our most horrible sins."

"Jesus died—and He rose. I do believe that. But why did He die? I'm still working on that one."

"And I'm praying that God is working on you." Chuck sipped his coffee. "How on earth did you get those color photocopies, Nicki? Not that I really want to know," he added sadly.

"The day I drove to Albuquerque, I stopped in Socorro, the seat of Socorro County."

"Perro Prieta is in Socorro County. Go on."

"I called on the county coroner. I asked him about Marcie Lewis. He was evasive, and he got angry. Said if I wanted a copy of his report I'd have to get a court order. Then he let it slip that he sent her body over to the Roswell coroner's office, where their autopsy team has better equipment."

"So, last night, you . . . ?"

"Yup. I let myself into the Roswell city coroner's office by my usual, uh, route—rappelling rope and hooks. I avoid the security cameras and guards that way."

"But they'll miss these photos."

"Hardly. I pulled them out of their computer. If they even have hard copies, I didn't look for them. Chuck, these photos upset me so much it took me ten minutes to stop shaking so I could climb back down and hail a cab to ride back out here."

Chuck peered at Nicki. *Nerves of steel,* he thought. *But she gets upset over a kid getting killed, so I know she's got a heart.*

❮❮❮

"Chuck, it's ten minutes before they'll be calling us to board. I'm stepping into the ladies' room."

Chuck shot a worried glance at Nicki as she grabbed her bag and hurried off. He had been careful to procure nonconsecutive seats for them. But still, it worried him when she was not in sight. "OK, Ms. Sanchez," he sighed.

Half an hour out of Roswell, Chuck strolled back to seat 46-B, where he expected to find Nicki, a.k.a. Ms. Sanchez, sitting. But the seat was occupied by a balding, paunchy man in a rumpled green suit. "Sir, I expected to find a lady sitting here."

"Blonde in sunglasses and a pink dress."

"Blonde?" Chuck caught his breath at this revelation. "Tell me about her."

"She sold me her boarding pass at the last minute for a hundred bucks. I bet on too many horses at Ruidoso Downs, over near White Sands." The man chuckled in self-congratulation. "I says to myself, 'Mickey O'Toole, try the airport anyway. Maybe you'll just get lucky and find a standby ticket for y' last hundred bucks.' Was she a friend of yours?"

"I was trying to make friends with her," Chuck admitted.

"Hey, can't blame you for trying!"

That lady knows more vanishing tricks than David Copperfield, Chuck told himself as he returned to his seat.

❮❮❮

Two FBI agents seized and handcuffed the passenger from seat 46-B the minute he stepped off the plane in Boston. *I guess they won't take more than $470 worth of aggravation out of Mickey O'Toole's hide,* Chuck told himself, considering the price of the one-way tickets. He hurried off to catch the train to Marblehead Municipal Airport where he had left his old Corvette before driving to Maine in a rented Buick.

12

Terror in Baghdad

Do with me as You will, Lord.

—Nicki Towns

F BI, Boston office," the voice on the phone answered.

Chuck pushed the receiver hard against his ear in the noisy Logan International Airport. It was a quarter to five, and he needed to make an appointment before he hopped a train to Marblehead to retrieve his Corvette.

"This is Chuck Reynolds, security chief at Salem Electronics. We've got a problem involving a federal military contract that I need to discuss with your bureau chief, Edgar Hollis."

"One moment, please."

"Ed Hollis here."

"Mr. Hollis—Chuck Reynolds."

"Chuck who?"

"Reynolds. Head of security at Salem Electronics."

"Reynolds." Hollis paused. "Oh, yeah. You're the guy who disappeared on his way to Tucson. Ran off with that young engineer." Hollis virtually drooled with sarcasm.

"There's more to it than that. But yes, I did drop out of sight for a while. Mr. Hollis, I need to see you tomorrow morning, if possible. It's urgent."

"Let's see. Ten-thirty. I can squeeze it in, I think. Fifteen minutes, max."

"Thanks." Chuck hung up the phone. "Rather curt," he said to no one in particular.

◖◖◖

Chuck got off the Cape Ann train in Salem and walked out to Cappy's Chowder House for supper. He half hoped to find Harry Thompkins there and fill him in on as much of the Roswell episode as he dared. But Harry was not to be found.

After supper Chuck took a taxi to Marblehead Municipal Airport. He had had a remote starter installed in the Corvette after moving to Massachusetts from North Carolina that spring. New England mornings could be chilly. Too, business errands often took Chuck into the city, and he felt more secure in Boston's underground parking lots when he could start and unlock his car from a distance.

It was getting dark as Chuck strolled toward the little airport's long-term lot. He spotted his 'Vette on the far side. Chuck slipped the remote from his pocket and aimed it. He punched the start button with his thumb.

The Corvette exploded in a ball of flame, raining debris over several nearby vehicles.

Shaken, Chuck hurried into the air terminal and called another cab. *No point in letting whomever might wish to do me in see me walk off,* Chuck decided.

))(

"You did not get my report, Mr. Hollis? I left it with our CEO, Harry Thompkins, to pass on to you before I went on vacation!"

"Sorry. Maybe your CEO didn't like your version of what happened in Tucson. Why don't you print out another copy and fax it to me?"

"Do you know Jack Arnold and Larry Contradini?"

"Never had the pleasure of meeting those boys."

"They represented themselves as FBI agents to my boss and his secretary last week."

"That's a federal offense." Hollis cursed. "Let's see." He pulled a thick directory marked "Confidential" from a locked file drawer and flipped it open. "No Arnold in the national office in Washington. No Contradini, either. Maybe the secretary screwed up."

"Molly does not make that kind of mistake, sir." Without bothering Chief Edgar Hollis about his exploding Corvette, Chuck hurried out. *I'll just let the air terminal file a report with the Massachusetts State Police*, Chuck decided.

))(

"I'm a man without a country." Chuck's troubled mind ran on a book of the same title. The wide-bodied Sabena 767 climbed out of LaGuardia toward Brussels as Chuck, sick of heart, ruminated on this horrid thought.

The plane banked, and Chuck peered at Miss Liberty in her gown of copper far, far below. Her upraised torch seemed just now like a giant hand waving good-bye.

And the plane. Chuck felt like a traitor for purchasing a ticket from a Belgian airline. *Nicki might be right*, he considered. Uncle Sam, she believed, had become a feeble old man with clay feet, unable to fend for himself against terrorists beyond a few rheumatic whacks with a walking stick; more concerned with chasing rabbits out of the gardens of enemies halfway around the world than in dealing with the inner-city crime right in his own backyard. Now, like many Americans who make frequent trips overseas, Chuck had bought a ticket on a foreign airliner. Conventional wisdom held that foreign planes were safer from hijackings than those based in the good ol' U.S. of A.

Chuck was miserable.

And to his misery was added fear. His car had been bombed, perhaps by the same team of assassins who had tried to do him in in California more than a week ago. The two FBI agents turned out to be frauds. The report he had left with Harry to pass on to the FBI had vanished, and it contained enough damning evidence to send Nicki to prison for life. *Maybe me too,* he considered. *Unless the Iraqis get us both before the FBI does.*

And a U.S. Army helicopter pilot had deliberately fired a rocket at Chuck and Nicki—the same American military that seemed to have no remorse over roasting a child of eleven like a pig on a barbecue spit.

Nicki's offer to make him a double agent for CALF finally began to make sense. *But I can never, like the Rosenbergs, sell secrets to an enemy government; or, like Aldrich Ames or Benedict Arnold, hand my countrymen over to be shot or hanged. Nicki has a cause, a pure, just, noble cause—a cause that makes her a well-oiled cog in the wheels ushering in the return of the Lord. At least it seems that way.*

Yet Chuck knew that Nicki, however morally upright she might be, had never found saving faith in Christ as Lord of her life.

So Chuck was wallowing in misery.

He rehearsed again the events of the day. After angrily leaving the Boston FBI office, he had not dared return to his apartment. He was not actually being shadowed, he believed, but who could tell what booby traps might await him at any place he was known to visit? *My Jennifer. Will they find her too?*

So he had rented a car and had driven to Hartford. There, he took the train into New York City. After buying a small suitcase and stocking it with new underwear, toilet articles, and a pair of new shoes, he hired a cab to ride to LaGuardia International Airport on Long Island. Chuck patted his pocket, thankful that the Lord had given him presence of mind to grab his passport from his desk drawer when he'd reported back to Harry about Tucson, Mexico, and Nicki.

And Nicki? Chuck's daddy, long ago in the North Carolina hills, had a name for a trip like this: "A wild goose chase."

Nicki. She once saved my life. Yet I have saved hers—several times. Is she the cause of my present distress? Maybe Arnold and Contradini, whom Chuck now realized were impersonating FBI agents, were really CALF operatives, out to frighten him out of his wits until he came over to her side. The car bombing? Arnold and Contradini may have set it up, certainly. Or they could have had no knowledge of it. Perhaps it was the same assassins who tried to do him in a week ago. *Anyone with interest enough in me to want so badly to kill me would surely know how to find my car. What a fool I've been!*

"Not a fool, son. Just a sheep needing My tender care. When my child follows Me, he is no fool. Trust Me." *Where did that thought come from?* Chuck mused. "Be anxious about nothing." The words of Jesus broke into Chuck's troubled soul. He pushed the seat back and slept.

The cabin lights and the flight attendant's voice on the intercom woke Chuck before daylight. "We will be landing within the hour, and our attendants are now serving breakfast. Please lower the tray on the back of the seat in front of you."

Chuck checked his watch: 2:30. What a time to serve breakfast! He peered out the window to see that the sun was beginning to redden the countryside of Europe. The plane had crossed five time zones while he slept.

Chuck hurried to the Israeli El Al ticket line as soon as he disembarked from the Belgian Sabena 767. He had not bought a through ticket in New York. *If I'm being followed, why make it easy for them?* he reasoned.

❲❲❲

When the El Al 757 touched down in Tel Aviv that afternoon, Chuck had no more clue what to do next than when he had left the Boston FBI director's office a day earlier. When Chuck had been a North Carolina State Police detective, he had been a hunter often enough. Now he found himself the hunted as well as the hunter. Unlike the crooks he had chased, however, Chuck had only a vague notion of who wished to find him, of who wanted him dead. But he guessed that if he could find Nicki and turn her over to the CIA, his own danger might disappear

But will the hounds actually be called off if I turn Nicki in? And I can't turn her over to be tried as a spy; she'll probably be assassinated before being brought to trial. We've gone through too much together for that.

I'll just keep on and trust the Lord to help me work through this. Right now, though, I'm chasing a white cat across a snow-covered field— in a blizzard. Where would she go?

Where would she go, believing as she does that she's a princess in David's line, a distant cousin to Daniel the prophet? The general direction of his search, at least, at once became obvious. As soon as Chuck cleared customs, he boarded a bus going up to Jerusalem.

❲❲❲

The old Wall of Tears is carved of massive, carefully fitted stone blocks. Erected more than a dozen years before the birth of Christ, the Wailing Wall, as it is also called, was the foundation of the temple as it was rebuilt by the Edomite usurper, King Herod the Great, to refurbish Israel's ancient temple. The glorious First Temple of King Solomon once stood here, as did its restoration, built by Zerubbabel after the Babylonian captivity.

Mount Moriah, Chuck thought. He strolled eastward along the Street of David, gazing up at the massive, golden Dome of the Rock. This magnificent Muslim mosque, which dominates the Old

City, shelters the very rock where Abraham raised his sacrificial knife to slay the promised son, Isaac, four millenniums ago.

Chuck pondered the significance of this great, 1,400-year-old Arab house of worship. It stood on the site where Solomon's temple and its successors had stood for a thousand years, until destroyed by the Roman Legions in A.D. 70. Chuck had read in his Bible that one day this mosque would be replaced by a new Jewish temple, built after a pattern revealed by Yahweh to His prophet Ezekiel. It occurred to Chuck that this gilded mosque actually symbolized the struggle that Nicki had plunged herself into: the struggle between God's revelation and human invention.

Yet is Nicki fighting this war on God's terms? Chuck pondered. Though Chuck found that Nicki's struggle sometimes enticed him, Paul's words now echoed in his heart: "The weapons of our warfare are not carnal, but mighty through God. . . . bringing into captivity every thought to the obedience of Christ." He considered his own job in a military plant, realizing that national security was necessary. But sometimes the tension between the daily elements of the world and the values of eternity were more than Chuck could bear.

Chuck broke his stride and turned toward the Old City's northern wall. Just outside a gate in that old wall Mount Calvary stood yet. Two thousand years ago a man hung naked, writhing, dying, nailed to a rough stake with a rugged cross-member. *That man was Christ—God in the flesh, Creator and Savior, paying for my sin*, Chuck considered.

And Nicki? She had received the historical facts and prophecies of the Bible to the letter. But the spiritual truth behind these facts— that man is a sinner and can be saved only by the shed blood of the crucified Messiah, who was spat upon and cursed by the religious Jews, and flogged and nailed to a crude cross by the cruel Romans— had not reached Nicki's blind heart. Chuck felt hot tears on his dusty cheeks—tears of joy for Christ's death on his behalf; tears of sorrow for Nicki's blindness, for her self-righteous goodness.

Chuck approached the Temple Mount. He stood respectfully on the paving stones, watching faithful Jews, devout Christians and even a few Muslims pray, chant, or press their prayers scribbled on paper into the cracks between the massive marble blocks of religious orthodoxy.

Several Hasidic Jews caught Chuck's eye. They wore black suits, white shirts with no ties, and black felt hats, or prayer shawls of blue and white. Some also wore small boxes strapped to their foreheads with cloth bands. These phylacteries, he had heard, held scraps of paper with verses from the Law of Moses written on them. The words of Deuteronomy 6:8, Chuck knew, were supposed to be the basis for this revered practice: "You shall bind (God's words) as a sign   between your eyes." But did these devout ones really catch the spiritual meaning of Moses' words: that God expects us to bind the spiritual meaning of His Word before the eyes of our heart at all times? Again, Nicki's dilemma troubled Chuck.

Chuck's gaze went to a group of women shrouded in Jewish prayer shawls that looked for all the world like flags of Israel. They chanted, bowed, and prayed, wailing in sorrowful, heartrending tones. Then, murmuring to one another in Hebrew, the ladies strolled away.

One woman went off by herself, however, moving back toward the city center. Half a block away, she paused and removed her shawl. Replacing it with sunglasses, she slipped the shawl into a handbag of hand-tooled leather.

The lady was blonde. This did not surprise Chuck. Jewish women from northern Europe often had light hair. The woman was slender, athletic, and she walked with the grace of a gazelle. Something familiar about this lithe lady attracted Chuck. *I've come halfway around the world to find a woman, and even at the risk of being thought a stalker, I'm not about to let this little lady get away,* he decided. He fell in to follow her, careful to stay out of sight.

Jerusalem streets go up steps and meander down narrow, deeply shaded lanes. They turn abruptly under archways, spiral up hillsides. More than once Chuck found himself squeezed by a baggage-laden donkey, so that he had to step into a niche to let the time-honored beast of burden trot past.

After thirty minutes' zigzagging through centuries-old alleys, Chuck lost sight of his feminine vision. *On top of all this, I'm lost,* he realized. Panting, he set down his duffel bag and sat on it, ignoring the stares of several Palestinian children curious about this strange American. *Here I am in a strange, old city. It's late in the day, and I haven't eaten since an early lunch in Tel Aviv. I don't even know where I want to go next, and I haven't found a hotel room. My resources consist of a money card—if I can even find an ATM machine, and oh, yes.* He patted his pocket that held a thousand shekels of Israeli money, worth about $350 U.S.

Then he saw it: Hotel St. Constantine. Constantine, Chuck remembered from his reading, was the Roman emperor who had made Jerusalem a Christian city until the Muslim Turks under Caliph Omar conquered it for Allah and Islam. The hotel was an aging, ramshackle, stuccoed, tile-roofed affair, which he guessed dated from early British Mandate. Chuck would not have been surprised to see an Arab-robed Lawrence of Arabia descend the steps and race off on a motorcycle.

Well, I've got to have a room, haven't I? Chuck stepped into the street, which was wider than most. He then realized he was back at the Street of David. He mounted the steps to the lobby. The desk stood just to the left of the main entrance, and stairs to a second-floor balcony climbed up beyond the front desk. A small restaurant opened directly across the lobby, and a yellowed sign announced in English, Hebrew, and Arabic that breakfast was served at six.

Then he spotted her. The blonde was on the stairs, nearly to the top. She unlocked the door to room 237 and slipped inside.

"May I help you, sir?" The clerk, who spoke British-accented English, was a sleepy Palestinian in a red felt Muslim fez.

"Yes, sir!" Chuck approached the counter. "Room for one for tonight—second floor, if possible."

"All we have left is a room with no bath. The men's room is at the end of the balcony," the clerk said.

"I'll take it." Chuck set his bag down and reached for his wallet.

"Ninety shekels, please."

"That's an old unit of money," Chuck observed, counting out the currency.

"Indeed, sir. God considered the shekel so important that he weighed King Belshazzar by it the night Babylon fell."

"I . . . I guess you know your Bible."

"The people of Allah read the Bible as well as the Koran," the clerk answered smoothly.

You're pretty sharp. Chuck didn't say this aloud. But the man's Bible knowledge startled him. "Who is the lady who just entered room 237?" Chuck asked, instead.

"We respect the privacy of our guests, sir."

"I understand. I just thought she looked like an old friend." Chuck slipped a two-hundred-shekel note over the counter.

"Thank you, sir. One moment." He consulted a bound guest register. "The lady is Yvette LaRochelle, from Montreal, Canada. But I doubt that an American would, uh, know her. She speaks only French and a bit of Hebrew."

"Thanks." Chuck grabbed his bag and hurried for the stairs. He told himself silently that he would be in the restaurant when it opened at six o'clock, and stay until Mlle. LaRochelle came in without her sunglasses.

Two o'clock. Chuck stared at his watch's luminous dial. In his haste to leave the U.S., he hadn't had time to shop for more clothes than he could cram into a small bag, so his wardrobe did not include a bathrobe or slippers. But he had to go. He sighed and grabbed his pants from the chair.

The men's room was next to the ladies' room, off the balcony. It was an unpainted hole in the wall, and cockroaches scurried for the cracks when Chuck pulled the light chain.

Moments later he stepped out onto the balcony overlooking the lobby and padded toward his room, two doors past 237. A slender, dark-haired figure slipped from the doorway and melded into human form in the dim light. Chuck stopped and caught his breath.

"Oh! You startled me!" the woman squealed in English.

"Mademoiselle LaRochelle, *oui?*"

"*Non.* Marie dePomerleau!" The voice was hard, defensive.

"Or Ngo Thieu. Besides French, you speak English, Hebrew, and Vietnamese."

The lady tripped Chuck and shoved him.

He spun and rolled on the floor, avoiding her vicious barefoot kick. "Nicki, please! You'll break your toes!"

"Chuck! Why didn't . . . ?"

"I was certain you'd recognize my voice, Nicki."

"I did. But my reflexes work faster than my brain. Chuck, what room are you in?"

"239."

"Wait there. I'll be right back." Nicki hurried off to the ladies' room.

"What's going on, Nicki? Not that I'm surprised at your haste," Chuck asked moments later when she appeared at his door.

"May I come in?"

"Under the circumstances, yes." He stepped aside.

"How did you find me, Chuck?"

"Persistence. Luck. The Lord. You do make a cute blonde." Chuck grinned.

"You followed me here from the Wailing Wall? But I was a blonde before I left Roswell, New Mexico. I walked right past you on my way to the Northeast Airlines flight to Montreal. Didn't you see the FBI agents looking for me?"

"I'd like to see two FBI agents—Arnold and Contradini!"

"Not the same. But I've heard of Jack Arnold and Larry Contradini. Arnold's an American Iraqi sympathizer, and Contradini is Iraqi by birth claiming Italian parentage, which he imagines may give him an inside with the Mafia. His real name is Elias el-Haaj. Those two sometimes pose as FBI agents, and they're dangerous. Have you met these guys?"

Chuck told Nicki about how his report on her to Agent Hollis of the Boston FBI office was evidently intercepted by Arnold and Contradini. Then he mentioned his bombed 'Vette.

"The Iraqis, no doubt about it. Probably Arnold and Contradini. Our CALF agents have been watching those guys. Of course it could have been one of our friends from Arizona or California, but they'd be out of their territory."

"But what do the Iraqis want with me? I don't get it." Chuck shook his head.

"I imagine they think you've uncovered part of the Russians' espionage operation. When you flew to Tucson to meet with Falcon's security people, you got their attention. They keep tabs on the Russian operatives, since Iraq buys most of its military hardware from Russia."

"Or from China," Chuck added. "Please, Nicki, why are we talking shop in the middle of the night?"

"I'm leaving this hotel and getting out of Israel, since I've seen Jerusalem. Three days, and I've worn out my welcome, I'm afraid. I thought you might like to tag along, Chuck. I must see the ruins of Nineveh, in Iraq." Nicki grew serious. "Ashurbanipal and Hniqi, like Hezekiah, were also my ancestors. I need to see where they once walked this earth before I'm taken from it. I've got a week or two to live, at most."

"Nicki!" Chuck was shocked.

"I'm scared, Chuck . . . dear. I want to love you—to know that I'm loved by you." Nicki wrapped her arms around his waist and buried her head against his chest.

She had not said "make love." Chuck caught his breath, happy that Nicki had not resorted to seduction. He kissed the top of her head. Then he lifted her chin. "I understand. I'll follow you at a distance, always watching for danger. But you've got to go now. We can leave together."

"No. Meet me at the airport in Amman, Jordan, at noon tomorrow. I'll be that French Canadian blonde again. *Parlez vous français?*"

"*Non, mademoiselle.* But I do speak pretty good Canadian, eh?" They laughed together.

"I'm leaving Nicki Towns here in Israel. And I sure hope you remembered to get your Israeli visa stamp on a paper separate from your passport. They won't let you into Jordan or Iraq, you know, if your passport has an Israeli stamp."

"I did. I'm ahead of you." Chuck chuckled. "Do you usually carry Nicki in your purse? Let me guess—you entered Israel on a Canadian passport?"

"I entered Israel with *two* passports," Nicki laughed. "I simply made a U-turn and went through a second customs line." Nicki fished in her shoulder bag and extracted a business-sized envelope addressed to Mary Sanford, Chicago, Illinois. "Please mail this for me." She smiled broadly. "It's Nicki Towns's passport. Mary Sanford is another of my alternate *noms des guerre*."

Chuck shook his head. "So while the U.S. State Department is having the Israelis hunt for you, and Iraqi agents disguised as Palestinians are trying to find you in Israel also, you will be in Iraq as Yvette LaRochelle visiting the ruins of ancient Nineveh!"

"I seem to remember three Jewish boys with Babylonian names who found the hottest place in Iraq to be the safest place on earth." Nicki bit her lip and grinned.

"Shadrach, Meshach, and Abednego, plus the Son of God, in Nebuchadnezzar's furnace," Chuck finished. "I guess the Son is still greater than earthly rulers."

Nicki slipped out without answering.

Chuck put his light out and pulled his chair to the window. Five minutes later he watched a nymph in black jeans and leather jacket slither on a cord to the ground behind the hotel.

(((

The next morning Chuck hired a cab to drive him to the Ben-Gurion Hilton in the New City of Jerusalem. He ate a breakfast of Peter's Fish, caught fresh in Galilee, with barley loaves topped with goat milk curds. He strolled into the lobby and approached the desk clerk. "I'm looking for a Ms. Nicki Towns, an American. I'm supposed to meet her today."

"She hasn't registered, sir," the clerk replied without bothering to check the register. "Did you check the restaurant?"

"I'll do that right now." Chuck strolled into the restaurant and crossed to the serving counter in front of the kitchen. Ducking past two startled waiters, he entered the kitchen and hurried through, leaving by a side entrance. He crossed the street and waited beneath an awning.

Chuck checked his watch. Two minutes passed. Seventeen seconds more. Suddenly a police van screeched to a halt in front of the Hotel Ben-Gurion. Eight soldiers armed with cocked automatic Uzis raced up the steps. "America could use a little more steel like that and a little less clay," Chuck muttered. "Nicki's name got their attention big time." He patted the envelope in his pocket as he hurried toward an Israeli Post Office mailbox just down the street.

《《《

Chuck doffed his cap, a promotional number with, "Holy Land Tours—Been There, Seen That" stenciled across it. "Mlle. Yvette LaRochelle, *le belle du Montreal, non?*" he chortled, sweeping the dust of Amman's International Air Terminal with his new headgear. "Chucky's Bodyguard Service at your command!"

"Oh, cut it out!" the blonde giggled.

"Can you guess what happened when I used your, uh, usual moniker at the Ben-Gurion Hilton this morning?"

"Well, the U.S. State Department has an A.P.B. out for a certain raven-tressed lady, I'm sure." Nicki gazed over her shoulder. "I've said enough. You never know when you've got eavesdroppers with a parabolic mike. Let's eat lunch." Nicki nodded toward an airport concession McDonald's restaurant. "Not the Hilton, but the food is American."

She picked a table directly beneath a tinny speaker blaring American rock music. "Somebody ought to tell the manager that his speaker is cracked," she complained. She fished a camera lens from her purse and passed it to Chuck. "I'm going to nose around Baghdad for a day or two, then take the train to Mosul. The

Nineveh excavations are right across the Tigris River from Mosul. I'll want at least a day there, maybe two."

"Won't you need this lens?" Chuck was puzzled.

"I don't carry a camera. God blessed me with a memory for detail. Besides, pointing a camera in the wrong direction in Iraq can get you a long stay in the Baghdad jail. Shot, maybe."

"But what . . . ?"

"Look closer, Chuck. It *will* work on a camera, of course. But your camera was stolen on the bus, remember?"

"Well, OK." Chuck didn't remember, but he turned the lens over. "Hey, this little jewel's got its own battery pack! And it looks as though it might work as a telescope, without a camera."

"That's a night-vision monocular," Nicki whispered. "It's one of the pieces of special equipment CALF has furnished me. It increases the light up to twenty-thousand times, so that a few fireflies will give you virtual daylight through that thing. It could be handy for following a lady down an unlighted street." Nicki giggled nervously.

"It'll take some getting used to, but I'll manage." Chuck dropped the monocular into his own bag.

◖◖◖

The customs inspectors in Baghdad were unusually thorough, Chuck thought. Nicki, as Mlle. LaRochelle, passed inspection easily enough, he noticed. *Probably the Canadian passport,* Chuck guessed, as Nicki strolled off toward the lobby after being photographed for Iraqi internal records.

"Camera lens, sir?" the inspector asked in British-accented English. He held up the night-vision monocular. "Where is your camera?"

"I left it home," Chuck answered truthfully. He frowned, worried.

The inspector stamped Chuck's passport, then handed it to another official. "This way, please," the man said. Chuck was photographed from the front and from both sides, and a photocopy was made of each page of his passport. "Enjoy your stay in Iraq—and remember to take cover when you hear an air-raid siren." The guy grinned as if he had said something terribly funny.

"I'll remember that. Thanks."

Chuck found Nicki waiting near a street door. Once she saw him, Nicki quickly exited without showing recognition and walked directly to a Mercedes limousine marked "Baghdad Hilton."

Chuck waited until the limo drove off, then he stepped up to a cab at the curb. "Baghdad Hilton, please," he told the driver.

Chuck arrived at the Hilton in time to see Nicki disappear through the main entrance. He strolled inside and found a posh leather chair where he could watch the elevator.

Nicki checked in. Then she managed to board an empty elevator. It stopped at the seventh floor. Chuck waited. Moments later it returned to the lobby, and several passengers got off. Good. Chuck walked to the desk. "Room for one tonight. Seventh floor, please, if there's one available."

"Your lucky number, eh?" The man passed Chuck a form to fill out.

Chuck registered in his own name. Later, in his room, he began to consider his predicament—he had agreed to shadow a very frightened woman during her stay in Iraq, and he had never before seen Nicki scared. *What does she expect me to do?* he angrily asked himself.

I'm scared too, Chuck admitted to himself. *Lord, I am scared out of my mind,* he prayed silently. He considered his plight for a moment—and Nicki's. She expected to be killed within a week or two, yet she pressed on, gathering data for her heart's cause: CALF—the Contemporary Assyrian Liberation Front. *Is she afraid to die, not knowing that she would wake up in heaven with Jesus? She has sublimated her fears to serving her cause,* Chuck decided.

And what if an assassin were to appear? Could I hope to intervene? I would die trying, but she would also surely die.

Are we safer in Iraq as anonymous tourists than in America, where espionage agents and law officers are searching for us? Chuck found momentary amusement in the fact that Nicki's legal American passport was even now being flown to a post office box in Chicago, while she—in Baghdad—was believed by the Iraqis to be in Israel.

And soon my money will run out.

Chuck fished in his jacket for the slender pocket Bible he always carried. The Lord directed him to Psalm 91, and he began to read:

> He who dwells in the secret place of the Most High
> Shall abide under the shadow of the Almighty
> . . . .
> Surely He shall deliver you from the snare of the fowler
> . . . .
> He shall cover you with His feathers.

Chuck recalled his boyhood in North Carolina, when one of his grandmother's red hens had hatched a brood of baby chicks. A weasel slipped through a crack in his mother's old log poultry house one night. Chuck heard the commotion and grabbed his shotgun and ran out the back door. In the moonlight he shot the weasel as it struggled to drag the Rhode Island Red hen out under the henhouse door. The mother hen had given her life for the life of her brood. The chicks, unharmed, were quietly huddled in a corner.

"Heavenly Father," Chuck prayed, "I've failed to trust You. Protect me and Nicki, as You have always done in the past. And turn her blind heart to follow You.

"In Jesus' name, amen."

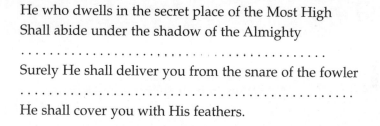

Chuck woke after midnight to the noise of a scuffle in the hall. Cautiously, he opened his door a crack. Four cursing Iraqi soldiers hurried Nicki, her hands cuffed behind her back, toward the elevator. Her blonde wig was gone, and her black hair drooped in tangles over her shoulders.

"Female American Satan!" snarled one soldier. "You will soon learn how Iraq deals with murderers!" The door slid shut, and they were gone.

Chuck dressed quickly. He slipped down the hall until he found a door ajar, the lights on. He peered inside. The blanket had been torn off, and the nightstand lay on its side. Nicki had evidently put up a short fight. *No doubt she'd have killed a couple of them if they hadn't found her asleep,* he grimly decided.

The arresting officers had taken Nicki's bag, toilet articles, and clothing. Chuck looked under the unused extra bed because the nightstand had tipped in that direction. There lay Nicki's Bible, slid just beneath the hanging bedspread. *The last time I saw this—let's see—the Ponce de Leon in Cancun. She had just gotten her head blown off by a double-barrelled shotgun, then she turned up alive and well four days later in Belfast, Maine,* he remembered.

Chuck noticed that the Bible held a pen. Apparently it had flopped shut when the nightstand tipped, trapping the pen where Nicki had just been reading.

Chuck opened to the passage: Psalm 91. Nicki had bracketed verses one through four. In the margin she had written: "This day I surrender my life and heart to Jesus Christ as my personal Savior. Do with me as you will, Lord." She had dated this notation and signed it, "Nicki Towns—Ngo Thieu."

((((

"I am being tried for the murder of General Rahman," Nicki told Chuck through the bars at the Baghdad jail.

"That happened in Nairobi—in East Africa," Chuck reminded her. "They can't try you here for an alleged crime on foreign soil. It's a violation of international law."

"They feel they must make an example of me. To them I represent the Great Satan, America."

"What about . . . ?"

"CALF? This cell is equipped with a microphone and a TV camera." Nicki pointed to the monitoring equipment, in plain view. "But it's OK to talk about CALF. Saddam's people have known all along that I work for CALF. To Iraq, we Assyrians are like the Kurds—we simply do not exist as a people. Any protest against Saddam Hussein's Ba'athist regime is treason. CALF is an American tool, according to them."

"Ba'athist," Chuck recalled. "That's the party of Iraqi nationalism."

"The trial is tomorrow," interrupted the jailer, who came to tell Chuck his visiting time was up. "The execution will be next week— exactly one week after the sentence is pronounced at the end of the trial." Smirking, the man pointed Chuck toward the hallway.

"Oh?" Chuck tried to remain composed as he walked ahead of the jailer toward the office. "What will they do—hang her?"

"Hanging is for ordinary criminals," the man explained. "In Iraq we shoot with a firing squad those guilty of crimes against the state. It's an honorable death, and we wish the world to know that we are fair and just."

"But I understand that she is being tried for murder."

"She killed a general. It is a crime against the government."

Chuck decided that it was pointless to argue with the jailer. He hurried back to his hotel, where he faxed a one-page letter with the details of Nicki's arrest and upcoming trial to the U.S. State Department in Washington. He also sent copies of his urgent plea to the head of the CIA, the director of the FBI, and the White House. *And to General Armstrong MacAdams, my old friend?* A still, small voice warned Chuck not to fax any messages to General MacAdams.

Chuck did not expect an answer to any of his faxed pleas. He was not surprised that official America was silent.

13

The Trial

I am the resurrection and the life.
He who believes in Me, though he may die,
he shall live.

—Jesus

W e have an American observer in our court today,"
announced Masoud el-Ahmed, chief judge of the Iraqi
People's Court. "We sincerely wish that he would return to the
United States with the report that Iraqi courts are both fair and
just." El-Ahmed grimaced at Chuck, then he began shuffling
papers with the other two judges sitting with him at a long table
down in front.

Chuck ignored the official greeting as he hunkered uncomfortably on a plank bench at the back of the tiny courtroom, which
he judged to be maybe fifteen feet square. He had spent most of the
past twenty-four hours alternately praying and scribbling hand-
written fax letters to Washington officials. Washington, however,
was silent. If the three obtuse, bearded, black-suited men behind

the long table in front had heard anything from American officials, it was evidently not about to delay Nicki's trial.

Trial? These men had no more right to try Nicki for an alleged act in a foreign city than did the *Baghdad Republican News*. Early that morning Chuck had given a newsboy an American dollar for a copy of the English-language edition. The boy's black eyes had shone in delight at the sight of the currency, knowing its value in black-market trade. "Going to read about the female American murderer, mister?" The boy beamed happily. "She's right on page two."

The child was right, of course. Chuck scanned the article, with its innuendoes and allegations, its bombastic venom at Iraq's having captured the "shameless killer" who had "brazenly entered Iraq with forged papers and a Canadian passport." The story was a mixture of truth and error, not unlike what one often reads in American newspapers. Chuck found this irony disheartening.

"The people of the Republic of Iraq versus the American, Nicki Towns, murderer," intoned Judge el-Ahmed. "Praise be to Allah. Bring forth the prisoner and let the trial begin!" El-Ahmed pounded his gavel.

A steel door opened at the far side of the courtroom, and Nicki stepped through. Chuck noticed at once that she was not handcuffed and she wore no makeup, though her hair had been brushed until it glistened. She wore the same navy blue suit she had had on on the flight from Cancun to Los Angeles. It had been freshly laundered and pressed, as had her white blouse. Instead of the walking shoes Nicki wore in Israel, she was now shod uncomfortably in new, black-patent pumps.

Four male guards in military camouflage fatigues, split-leather boots, and billed caps trod on Nicki's heels. One of them poked her ribs with the flash suppressor on the muzzle of his Russian AK-47 assault rifle. He muttered something in Arabic and pointed to a meter-high, three-sided frame of white-painted iron bars, topped with a steel rail with peeling paint. "Stand there, prisoner," he muttered.

Nicki stepped forward and grasped the rail to steady herself on the unaccustomed, ill-fitting high heels, evidently given to her for the trial.

The guard poked her again with his rifle. "Hands at side!" he ordered.

Chuck winced.

Nicki did not. She stepped back, giving the guard a look of pity.

Nicki faced Chuck and smiled. "Praise Jesus, Chuck."

Chuck smiled back. "I love you," he mouthed.

"The prisoner will speak only when spoken to," el-Ahmed warned.

The prosecutor was an Iraqi woman of about Nicki's age. Judge el-Ahmed nodded to her, and she stepped to the end of the judges' table and read the charge of premeditated murder in the first degree. Nicki, the prosecutor said, had been picked up as "a common street whore" by General Rahman's chauffeur, Ghupta, for "an evening of pleasure." Ghupta, for his part in the "conspiracy," had already been hanged, the prosecutor droned on.

What conspiracy? Chuck wondered. He found the proceedings intriguing as well as terrifying; the charges were contradictory and confusing. It occurred to Chuck that prostitutes are not usually involved in conspiracies.

"Ms. Towns," the prosecutor charged, "took the general's fee for her services, then she murdered him in cold blood with a syringe of asp venom before she escaped out a window."

"Do you understand the charges against you, Ms. Towns?" el-Ahmed asked. Chuck noticed that the judge spoke with the detachment of a car salesman asking a customer, "Do you understand the contract?" Though el-Ahmed had been almost emotional when he spoke to Chuck about Iraq's "fair and just" trials, he seemed now to be trying to distance himself from the proceedings. *Something is not right here*, Chuck thought.

The prosecutor called the state's first witness. Alif bar-Zani was a slender, hot-eyed youth of perhaps twenty-two. Bar-Zani stated his name and occupation: file clerk in the Iraqi Ministry of Customs and Immigration. Yes, he told the court, he recognized a photo of the Canadian tourist, Yvette LaRochelle, as the same woman he had seen with General Rahman two years earlier.

"And what were you doing on an August evening two years ago?" the prosecutor inquired.

"I was acting as evening desk clerk at the Ivory Towers Hotel in Nairobi, Kenya, East Africa."

"How did you happen to be in Africa?"

"I went there on orders of His Excellency, President Saddam Hussein," bar-Zani answered. "It was during a week-long convention of the African/Pan-Arabian Convention of Armed Forces. My task was to report any suspicious persons who might cause trouble for our military personnel or their attachés."

"What did you observe that evening in Nairobi, Mr. bar-Zani?"

"Ms. Towns, here, came in with General Rahman. She was clinging to his arm and looking on his face with messages of"—bar-Zani's voice now dripped with disgust—"of love. The general nodded to me as they went together into the elevator."

"Does the prisoner have any questions?" Judge el-Ahmed turned to Nicki. He motioned for bar-Zani, who had begun to return to his seat, to step back to the table.

"Yes, your honor!" She faced her accuser. "Mr. bar-Zani, isn't it true that General Rahman entered the Ivory Towers Hotel alone, except for his chauffeur, on the night you were on duty?"

"It is as I said, Ms. Towns. Otherwise I could not have recognized your photo," bar-Zani scoffed.

"Of course I was in the Ivory Towers that night," Nicki snapped. "I entered by the same alley door used by the maids and desk clerks."

Bar-Zani glared.

His Honor, el-Ahmed, stifled a chuckle.

"Mr. bar-Zani," Nicki pressed, "isn't it true that you received money from General Rahman's chauffeur to let me and the general use a hotel computer?"

"You lie!" bar-Zani screamed.

"Just a moment," cried the judge sitting closest to bar-Zani. He was an elderly man, who until now had not spoken a word. "A witness does not lose his temper unless a nerve has been touched. Tell us about the computer, Mr. bar-Zani."

"Well, I . . ." The youth became unhinged. His legs trembled uncontrollably.

An old Babylonian custom, Chuck mused sardonically. He just then remembered that only a few miles from Baghdad, Belshazzar's knees had also knocked when he read Yahweh's writing on the wall.

"Go on," the judge urged.

"I have no idea what was on the floppy disk—the one the general gave Ms. Towns to copy," bar-Zani whispered.

"How do you know all this?" asked the judge.

"The hotel's security system—I . . . I watched her on TV."

"What did you do with the fifty American dollars Commander Rahman's chauffeur paid you to let us use the computer, Mr. bar-Zani?" Nicki repeated. Though her voice was clear and without a tinge of anger, she now pressed home the opportunity to make her accuser account for his own culpability.

Bar-Zani fainted and collapsed on the floor.

El-Ahmed banged his gavel. "Guards! Put him in a cell. We will question him at length later."

"Ms. Towns, what was on that disk?" Judge el-Ahmed pressed.

"General Rahman died with that secret. So shall I." Nicki's voice was barely audible, but the words were enunciated crisply.

El-Ahmed glared, but he said nothing.

"The court wishes to know this," protested the judge who had interrupted bar-Zani.

Judge el-Ahmed cleared his throat. "The matter before the court at the moment is the murder of General Rahman. We can explore other issues at a later date. Next witness." He nodded to the prosecutor.

Colonel Salim Mohammed modestly identified himself to the court as his nation's leading authority in forensic medicine. He gravely displayed a plastic envelope containing a long, black hair.

"Where was the hair discovered, Colonel?" asked the prosecutor.

"In the backseat of the general's rented Rolls Royce limousine," he explained. "Our people examined the car after the murder."

Chuck wondered if the Kenyan police knew that the Iraqi military, guests in their country, had absconded with a critical piece of evidence needed to prosecute an alleged murder committed beneath a Nairobi moon.

"And what can you tell the court about the hair, Colonel?"

"We ran a DNA test on it at once. After Ms. Towns's arrest," he nodded toward Nicki, "she gave us a blood sample. The DNA is a perfect match."

"May we infer that the prisoner, Nicki Towns, was in the limousine with General Rahman, Colonel?" asked the prosecutor.

Mohammed shrugged. "We may certainly infer that Ms. Towns was in the automobile in Nairobi. Whether she and the general were there at the same time is a matter for the courts to decide."

"Thank you, Colonel. What else do you have for the court?"

Colonel Mohammed displayed a second envelope. It held an empty hypodermic syringe. "This syringe contained traces of the venom of African asps. This poison was also found in General Rahman's blood. Asp venom causes death within seconds," he explained.

"Where was the syringe found, Colonel?"

"It was thrust into General Rahman's bicep. I have seen such syringes several times in the arms of dead heroin addicts who overdosed."

"Your honors, may it please the court," the prosecutor remarked, "it is the state's contention that while the general and Ms. Towns were in the passion of lovemaking, Ms. Towns evilly and maliciously stabbed, poisoned, and killed our nation's great military leader. Such an act of treachery, your esteemed honors, deserves death. The state rests its case."

"Ms. Towns, do you have any final words?" Judge el-Ahmed asked.

Chuck felt as though she were being given a chance to make a dying statement just before the firing squad squeezed their triggers.

"May I question Colonel Mohammed, your honor?"

"Of course." The judge motioned for the colonel to return.

"Colonel, whose fingerprints were on the syringe?" Nicki asked.

"No one's."

"Not mine? Not the general's?"

"No one's," he repeated.

"How was the general dressed?"

"He was fully clothed."

"Fully clothed?" asked Nicki, fighting to keep her composure. "Fully clothed—for sex?"

"Well, he had removed his shoes and jacket. Oh yes, one sleeve was rolled up."

"Which arm, Colonel?"

"Left—the arm in which the needle was found."

"What does that suggest, Colonel Mohammed?"

"As I told the court once before, such conclusions are the task of the court."

"Thank you, Colonel. Thank you, your honors." Nicki nodded to the judges. She stood waiting, motionless in the primitive docket.

The judges conferred in a flurry of whispers. Finally, Judge el-Ahmed stood and rapped his gavel. "Prisoner Nicki Towns," he intoned, "it is the consensus of this court that you are guilty of murder in the first degree; and more heinous still, you have taken the life of a leader of the Republic of Iraq. So as God commanded through the great prophet, Moses, 'Whoever sheds man's blood, by man his blood shall be shed; for in the image of God, God created man,' so your vile blood shall stain the soil from which you came.

"It is decreed, therefore, that at sunrise one week from today you shall be shot through the heart. The execution shall take place at the state firing range at Al Khalis. Praise be to Allah!"

To Chuck's surprise, Nicki was directed to remain standing while an Iraqi news reporter, who had quietly been taking notes, snapped several photos.

They'll torture her until she tells what happened to her copy of Rahman's computer disk. Chuck paced the floor in his room in the Baghdad Hilton that afternoon after the trial. *No. They have Rahman's disk, of course. I imagine they have a pretty good idea where Nicki took the copy she made. Saddam would rather have the world know that he quickly executed Nicki for murder than have it leaked to the press that she walked off with the plans for his anthrax-warhead missiles. Embarrassment is not something Saddam easily deals with,* Chuck decided.

◖◖◖

The evening before the trial Chuck had laid on his bed, exhausted. Since visiting Nicki in jail, he had spent his time either composing faxes to try to get the U.S. State Department to intervene in praying and reading his Bible. He had read Psalm 91 through five times. This was the passage that he and Nicki—unknown to each other—had read just before her arrest.

"Nothing evil will happen to you" (v. 10) had been the Lord's promise. Yet Nicki had been arrested, surely to be tried, and convicted. *Isn't this "evil"?* Chuck had pondered, distressed. Further on, he had read, "He will tell His angels to protect you" (v. 11), and, "I will save him" (v. 16).

Yes, Chuck knew the song about being borne on angels' wings to the immortal home.

"But Nicki is innocent of murder!" Chuck protested to the Lord. "Does verse sixteen mean merely that You will watch over us as we die?" he asked in anguish.

Many had died horrible deaths, martyrs for the cause of Christ, Chuck remembered. "Dear Lord, Nicki is just a new Christian. This isn't martyrdom, Lord. She's about to be killed for getting caught up in a crackpot political scheme to restore Assyria as a nation."

How about Lady Jane Grey? Though a Christian girl of just seventeen, she was beheaded in the Tower of London for getting involved, like Nicki, in a political scheme. The thought made him frantic.

At this point in his wrestling with God, Chuck had scribbled out yet another fax, this one to Stan and Mae Basford, with a post-script to Jennifer. Someone had to tell Rachel and Art Towns what was going on. But Chuck had no phone or fax number for them, so he faxed the Basfords in Maine and asked them to relay the mes-sage to the Townses in Massachusetts. While he was waiting on the fax to Maine to go through, Chuck asked again about reply faxes from any of the departments he had contacted in Washington. None had arrived.

(((

As Chuck recalled yesterday's frantic activity of writing and sending faxes, and today's trial and sentencing, he remembered that in his grief he had forgotten to ask the desk clerk for fax trans-missions when he returned to his room after the trial. He hurried downstairs.

"We have three messages for you, Mr. Reynolds." The smirk-ing clerk held the papers to his chest, out of reach behind the counter. The guy could read English, of course. Hilton didn't hire clerks who could read only Arabic.

Chuck greased the clerk's greedy fingers with an American twenty. He grabbed the pages and fled for the elevator.

The first fax was no surprise. Chuck's written request for daily visits with Nicki was denied. Only next of kin were allowed to visit prisoners on death row. He was welcome to attend the exe-cution "as an American observer, however," Judge el-Ahmed wrote.

Chuck vowed right then that he would be there.

The second, faxed from Art Towns's auto dealership in Somerville, Massachusetts, stated tersely that the Iraqi government had denied him and cousin Rachel a visa, since relatives of criminals convicted of crimes against high officials are also unwelcome in Iraq. At any rate, Chuck had been nervous about the chance that Art and Rachel might come. Rachel, a naturalized American, had been born in Iraq in 1931. Would Saddam's government recognize her American citizenship? Chuck had worried. Too, he easily envisioned the irascible Art in a fistfight with President Saddam Hussein.

Chuck paused before unfolding the third message. Angrily, it occurred to him that there were those within the Pentagon who might imagine it a blessing to have Nicki shot through her heart in Iraq. She would thus carry the secret of the illegal neutron bomb test to her grave. A wave of guilt swept over Chuck for what he deemed at the moment to be his own treasonous thinking against America.

Fax number three had been typed lovingly by Jennifer. It began, "Dearest Daddy," and it was replete with smiley-faced kittens, which she had inked into every gap. Yes, she forgave him for postponing the hike up Mt. Katahdin. Jennifer promised to be "in constant prayer for Nicki's safety."

Then Stan had evidently dictated a paragraph. The Sheepscot Valley Community Church, where the Basfords and Jennifer worshiped, had given itself to a week-long prayer vigil on Nicki's behalf, Stan told.

Chuck wept.

Then he slept. He dreamed. And he dreamed some more. In his dream the U.S. Air Force lobbed a missile into Baghdad. It exploded near the jail, and the prison wall collapsed. The prisoners, all of them condemned to death for crimes they had not committed, were climbing out over the rubble, laughing and crying. A smiling Nicki clambered out and fell into Chuck's arms.

Chuck awoke. He went right back to sleep, happy, contented, trusting Jesus to work things out.

And he began to develop a plan.

Chuck arose to find the Middle Eastern sunshine streaming into his window. What had it been like for Daniel, 2,500 years ago but only a few miles from here? Chuck wondered. King Darius had decreed that any person who petitioned anyone but the king for a month would be thrown to the lions. But Daniel had petitioned the Lord. So had Chuck. And Chuck considered that his prayer was on behalf of Daniel's intrepid distant cousin, perhaps a hundred times removed. This cousin had already proven to Chuck that she had the bravado to attempt some pretty wild schemes. Until now, she had always pulled them off.

Now it was up to Chuck. And God.

They'll be watching me, Chuck told himself. Baghdad hotels were known for their bugs, and the Hilton was no exception, Chuck soon discovered. He found five radio transmitters hiding under furniture and behind fixtures. These he left in place. Saddam's people had been busy while Chuck was at Nicki's trial.

Then he went to work on his clothing. Trousers that he'd had the hotel service launder and press had been delivered to his room with a radio transmitter sewn into a cuff. He removed this, dropping it into a pocket before putting the pants on. Nicki's bug detector would have proved handy, he thought, as he examined his new extra pair of shoes. The heels, once held in place by small nails, had evidently been removed. They had been carefully reattached with new, slightly larger nails—the nail holes had no dirt in them. He considered simply prying the heels off to remove the transmitters. No. Better idea.

Chuck packed the shoes in a plastic hotel laundry bag instead. He had purchased the shoes in New York just before the flight to Brussels, and he had worn them only once. They hurt his feet, which had swelled cruelly during the all-night plane ride. Besides, for what he had in mind for the next several days, his scuffed, badly worn L. L. Bean forest ranger moccasins would prove more useful.

On the way to the lobby, Chuck stopped the elevator between floors. He quickly unscrewed an access panel in the ceiling and placed the bug from his pocket up there. *My Iraqi shadows will have an interesting time trying to figure out why I'm spending the day riding the elevator,* Chuck mused.

Chuck took a cab to the city market, and he soon lost himself in the crowd. Peddlers, selling everything from peppers to peacocks hawked their wares to passersby. Chuck soon found a stand selling dairy products, and he examined a display of cheeses made from sheep milk. "Five dollars American money for half a kilo," the vendor said, seeing Chuck's interest.

"Delicious cheeses," Chuck agreed. He smiled broadly, pointing to the display. He had eaten the Middle Eastern cheese sold in a market in Boston's Fanueil Hall, and he loved its tangy flavor. Chuck knew he could not eat in a restaurant for the next week, so he decided to practice the time-honored custom of carrying cheese for his journey.

"Excellent price, mister."

The price was outrageous for half a kilogram of homemade cheese—a little more than a pound—and Chuck knew it. Only tourists ever paid the asking price in these market stalls.

But instead of reaching for his wallet, Chuck opened the bag of shoes. "New shoes," he said. "One full kilo of cheese, exchange." Chuck tapped a cheese with his finger.

"Why you want sell shoes?" The vendor, a short, mustachioed middle-aged farmer, eyed Chuck suspiciously.

"Too small. They hurt my feet. But cheese, it makes me feel good." Chuck patted his belly.

The man laughed.

Chuck laughed.

The man looked at his own feet, shod with cheap, braided cloth sandals. His toes were dirty, the nails long and broken. "Try on?"

Chuck smiled. "Sure."

The vendor sat on a stool and put a shoe on. His feet were wide for his height, but much shorter than Chuck's. He put the other one on. Without tying them, the man took several stiff steps. Grinning, he turned to Chuck. "I buy." Proud of his trade, he passed Chuck a cheese.

Chuck immediately ducked between two vendors' tents. He zigzagged several times, working his way out of the market area,

looking over his shoulder until he was sure he was not being followed. Chuck circled until he came to the end of the narrow street
of shops. He peered down the lane, past the awnings. Two doors
from the cheese shop a young man sat on a motor scooter. He wore
an earphone with a wire to a radio on his belt, and he stared
intently at the cheese shop.

Chuck hurried off toward a clothing store catering primarily
to Iraqi nationals.

❰❰❰

"You are Lawrence of Arabia now, sir," laughed the shop-
keeper after Chuck had tried on clothes for an hour. He wore a tur-
ban and a striped robe of mixed camel's hair and goat's hair.

"If my friends could see me now!" Chuck tried his best to
keep up the merry banter as he parted with more than a hundred
dollars and silently prayed for Nicki—and for the Lord's direction.
"Say," he added, almost as an afterthought, "I've got a lady friend
who loves exotic clothes. What do you have in a traditional Muslim
lady's outfit?"

"One size fits all!" The merchant chuckled, displaying a gown
of hand-woven wool in unadorned black.

Chuck thought it looked like something between a blanket
and a monk's hooded shroud. "Do you have a veil?"

"Certainly." The clerk pulled a wide scarf of black silk from a
rack. He modeled it, wrapping it woman-fashion around his face.

Chuck laughed. "How much?"

"The dress and the scarf—two hundred dollars, American
money."

"It's good material," Chuck said. He shrugged. "One hundred
dollars."

"You have paid me well for your own clothes," the merchant
said. "So, agreed."

Lawrence of Arabia, a.k.a. Chuck Reynolds, was dressed like
a sheikh, and he carried a sack of traditional women's clothing

under his arm as he strode to the curb and hailed a cab. Chuck knew better than to rent a car in Baghdad. Rented cars required identification, and they left paper and electronic trails. "Where can I buy a good used pickup truck in Baghdad?" he asked the cab driver.

"Can't pick up a truck. Too heavy." The guy's English was about on a par with the cheese vendor's.

"Buy," Chuck said. "A truck—a light, uh, small truck."

"Oh? Trucks not for sale every day. Since the Americans bomb us, can't get parts. But I have friend who may sell truck. I take you there."

Before the morning was over, Chuck found himself the proprietor of a dilapidated, British-made FWD Land Rover. Though his beast, as he called it, definitely did not date from the Mandate era of T. E. Lawrence of Arabia, he decided that it probably predated Saddam by a couple of years. As he struggled with the left-hand gearshift in this right-hand-drive vehicle, Chuck remembered grimly that the camel-riding Lawrence met his death in a motor vehicle wreck.

Speaking of camels, Chuck thought, as he dodged his thousandth pothole in the road to Al Khalis. He swung wide and bore down on the gas, passing a camel lumbering beneath a load of sticks for firewood.

God is good, Chuck soon decided. He had not dared ask directions to the police target range. But a pair of wheel ruts across the desert led past several low, rock-strewn hills to an isolated compound on the edge of a dry wadi, which once had been a stream. It was a sheet-metal building surrounded by an ordinary chain-link fence. Deserted. No apparent security measures except a cheap padlock.

Nothing to steal, unless one wanted the galvanized iron roofing, Chuck decided. The back of the small building opened onto a row of wooden benches and armrests for shooting. The area beyond the benches had been bulldozed smooth, and a simple wooden frame held tattered paper targets.

Chuck found his eyes riveted to a thick stake about four feet tall standing near the back fence. The stake had an iron ring attached by a sturdy bolt that ran clear through. Several inches of sawdust around the stake bore dark red stains.

Chuck shuddered.

Next he eyed a small brick furnace with an iron door and a good-sized chimney a dozen yards from the stake. Near the furnace stood a fat tank of propane.

Chuck had to clamber down into the wadi to get behind the furnace. He picked his way across rocks and through scrubby brush until he found himself just opposite the furnace.

No need to climb up for a closer look. Chuck grimly kicked at the ashes from the furnace, dumped down the wadi's bank. Strewn clear to the bottom of this ravine, some eight feet deep, were ashes from years of disposal. Human teeth and bits of bone, bleached white in the Babylonian sunshine, were scattered clear down the bank.

14

Asshur Builded Nineveh

*Out of that land [of Shinar] went forth
Asshur, and builded Nineveh. . . .*
—Moses, Genesis 10:11, KJV

*From that land [of Shinar] he [Nimrod]
went to Assyria where he built Nineveh . . .*
—Moses, Genesis 10:11, NIV

He was trapped in a strange culture, trying desperately to rescue a condemned prisoner. Chuck felt like a neon giant
Gulliver among Lilliputians. He bumped out into the desert, away
from the village of Al Khalis, looking for a place to hide himself and
his vehicle until nightfall.

An excursion through several markets in Al Khalis had furnished Chuck with tools and supplies: a dozen unplaned boards
and a couple of good-sized posts, tall as his head; a hammer, nails,
and several small tools; a carpenter's saw; a hacksaw; pick and
shovel; crowbar; a skein of clothesline rope; a gasoline lantern; and
finally, a dozen three-liter plastic milk jugs of gasoline, besides half
a dozen jugs filled with boiled water. He surveyed his assorted
equipment and tried to make himself comfortable.

Chuck barely tasted the cheese, which he washed down with water, as he considered Nicki's plight and the herculean task he had laid out for the week of nights ahead. He dare not return to the Baghdad Hilton, though he had charged the next week's room fees to his Visa card. Chuck had purposely left a "Do Not Disturb" sign on the door. And he had left the TV on good and loud to entertain whoever was monitoring the transmitters in his room.

How much earth can I move each night with a spade? Chuck pondered. He was thankful, however, that the wadi had a wheel ramp left by the bulldozer.

Parked in the shade of a cliff of shale, Chuck tried to doze on the Land Rover's narrow seat. But trying to remain invisible, even with expanses of apparently empty desert and rocky hills in which to hide, was impossible. There were curious shepherds, giggling girls looking for firewood, camel drivers, hunters, the merely curious.

So instead, Chuck chose merely to remain anonymous and mysterious, managing at most three hours' sleep each day. He faked a British accent—which would have gotten him laughed out of London. Half a dozen times he practiced the few French phrases that he knew on the Arabic-speaking vendors in Al Khalis. He figured that if he used a language other than English, the locals might mistake him for a European rather than an American. Twice Chuck even tried Spanish phrases. Unshaven, doing his best to appear as unkempt as the dirtiest day laborer in Iraq, Chuck managed for a week to avoid being recognized.

And each night it was back to the target range to labor, to dig, to build until dawn. And to pray.

❰❰❰

Chuck lay on his stomach in the weeds behind the firing range studying the van that had just pulled up. With the night-vision monocular Nicki had left him, he carefully focused on the prisoner. Female, though wearing army fatigues like the guards. Hands cuffed behind her. Hair in a bun. Barefoot.

What if they rape her? It was nearly an hour yet before the scheduled sunrise execution, and the soldiers had plenty of time for cruel entertainment.

"Trust Me!"

Chuck started in fear. He turned to see who had touched his shoulder. No one was there.

"Because he has focused his love on me, I will rescue him." Chuck knew whose voice he heard this time, and he felt much calmer.

Nicki faces death. I also face death, he considered, as five soldiers armed with Russian-made assault rifles appeared at the rear of the building and sat down, smoking and chatting. *Will they shoot one round each or set their guns on full automatic and chew her body to pieces?* The devil was whispering in his other ear now.

He turned the monocular on Nicki again. She sat on a bench by herself, head bowed, appearing to pray. Chuck wished to see an angel in glowing white sitting beside her, but none appeared.

One of the soldiers casually strolled to the furnace, turned the gas on and lit it. The guard lighted his cigarette in the flame, smoking as he adjusted the flame. The door clanged shut. Chuck knew well enough that next time that door was opened the iron grate would be red hot. Nebuchadnezzar would have loved a gas furnace.

Chuck slid into the wadi and hunkered down next to his Land Rover. He pressed the button on his watch. Twenty minutes until sunrise. Above him the sky was beginning to redden.

I have forgotten something. He went cold in terror, and his stomach knotted. Engrossed in watching Nicki and her guards with the monocular, Chuck had missed one necessary step in his plan, a step that required the precious remaining moments of darkness to perform.

Chuck scurried along the gully, taking the long way around to stay out of sight since it was now getting light. He circled the metal building to the military van—a big, American-built GMC Suburban. Swiftly Chuck slit all four tires with his pocketknife, using the deft finesse he had once seen his grandmother use to dispatch a roasting chicken. He grabbed the vehicle's cell phone, ripped it loose and crushed it under his foot.

Chuck raced back, again taking the long way. Horrified, Chuck realized that Nicki, blindfolded, was already tied to the stake.

Chuck could not tell which occurred first: the crack of the rifles or his tug on the clothesline that he had tied to a loose brace. The execution stake and the earth around it collapsed in a shower of loose boards and small timbers into the pit next to the Land Rover—Chuck had built his booby trap carefully. From below, Chuck caught Nicki as she tumbled and hurled her onto the seat, the iron ring with its sawn off stool bolt still dangling from her handcuffs. Swatting the dirt and sawdust from his face, Chuck dove into the Land Rover after her.

Chuck heard the angry shouts of the soldiers as he started the motor. Two of them had already jumped into the pit where he had caught Nicki. Chuck lighted the fuse on a Coke bottle of gasoline, then arced his arm over the roof and threw his Molotov cocktail. Chuck popped the clutch and floored the gas.

The Land Rover stalled.

Two burning, screaming Iraqi soldiers scrambled back to the shooting range out of the pool of burning gasoline that the pit had suddenly become, as three-liter plastic bottles of gasoline, heated by the Molotov cocktail, popped open. A third man opened fire, cutting his burning comrade nearly in half in a hail of lead.

Chuck turned the key. The motor fired, caught, then sprang to life. He went easy on the clutch pedal this time, and the vehicle shot up the bank to high ground.

Chuck flattened out over Nicki, who lay half in the passenger seat, half on the floor. Bullets sprayed Chuck with glass shards. Holes appeared in the cab around him. By the time Chuck straightened up, the Land Rover had shot past the building, crossed the dirt jeep trail leading back to Al Khalis, and vehicle and passengers were tearing across the Iraqi desert.

Chuck circled wide, arcing back toward the wheel ruts out of sight of the soldiers. A hill now lay between the couple in the Land

Rover and their would-be executioners, and Chuck wheeled beneath an overhanging ledge and hit the brakes. He killed the motor and leaped out.

Nicki was sprawled beneath the dash on her shoulder, feet draped across the seat. Chuck dragged her upright and yanked her blindfold off.

"You didn't have to play so rough. My neck's going to be stiff for weeks."

"You're lucky even to have a neck, you know." Chuck had no time for humor. "Let's see your wrists."

"They're still at the end of my arms—I think."

Chuck fished out his pocketknife and opened a tiny screwdriver blade. The cuffs popped right off. He eyed the ill-fitting camouflage suit. "Get some women's clothes on while I climb this rock." He crammed into Nicki's hands the parcel containing the garb worn by wives in the strictest sects of Muslim fundamentalism. "Be quick about it. If they're coming this way, I'm coming down, dressed or not!"

"Yes, O great sultan!" Nicki bowed facetiously to his desperate orders and took the bundle.

Chuck climbed the rock. Half a mile back the target range's metal building glistened in the rising sun. One soldier was trying to tend the wounds of one of the men who had jumped into the burning gasoline. One guy, Chuck guessed, was dead already. The other writhed in pain, his pants burned off.

The big Suburban, Chuck could see, had been driven perhaps a hundred yards on its flat tires before the vehicle chase was abandoned. Two soldiers, still a long way off, were trotting up the road toward them.

Directly below the rock lay the rutted road into Al Khalis. Chuck realized that if he followed these wheel ruts it would put them in view of the two running guards, but far enough away that only a very lucky shot could touch them.

"Oh sheikh, come check out your harem!"

Chuck clambered down. A bowing, barefoot Arab woman in black met his gaze, modestly awaiting her master.

"I ought to have let them shoot you," Chuck laughed.

Nicki lost it and began to sob.

Chuck hugged her close. "I'm sorry. Rescuing damsels from death grates on my nerves."

"You've never done that before, Chuck," said the veiled woman.

"Done what?"

"Hugged me."

"Nicki!" Chuck forgot his feelings. "Get hold of yourself. Saddam's Republican Guard will come charging over that hill any minute now! We will be shot on sight anywhere in Iraq."

"Chuck," Nicki laughed, "*you* get hold of *your*self." She dove into the Land Rover. "Let's get out of here!"

Chuck eased the vehicle out from under the rock and into the ruts. He floored the gas.

Pop-pop-pop-pop! The Iraqis were shooting again. Chuck and Nicki held their heads low as the Land Rover bounced over a rise. They were out of danger—for now.

Al Khalis was a substantial village of low, mud-brick, tin-roofed houses, with a new quarter of modern homes. The town had no road bypass, so Chuck found it necessary to drive straight into downtown to reach the northwest highway across the Tigris River toward Samarra. He guessed that an Arab and his wife in a beat-up Land Rover wouldn't attract much attention in a country where camels, donkeys, bicycles, and trucks mixed it up on the asphalt with late-model Swedish Volvo station wagons and German Mercedes diesel sedans.

The bridge over the Tigris River arced upward, and Chuck maintained ninety kilometers as he pointed the old jeep toward the span. The Land Rover coughed, sputtered, and died just before they reached the crest of the narrow bridge.

Chuck leaped out and raced for the hood.

"I smell gasoline." Nicki pointed to the rear of the vehicle.

Chuck circled and scooted underneath. A neat hole, nearly at the bottom, was dripping gas. He grabbed the three remaining three-liter jugs of petrol. He could pour them into the leaking tank and hope that the leak was slow enough that the fuel would last for another half an hour. But the tank had been full half an hour earlier.

Or . . . ? As a teen, Chuck had once rigged an old car to run from a can under the hood. But that required a length of gasoline hose, and he had no hose.

Nicki slid in beside him. "Your pen?"

Chuck reached inside his robe and yanked his ballpoint pen from his shirt pocket. He passed it to Nicki.

She tore a strip of cloth from her scarf and wrapped the pen. "Try this."

Chuck rammed the cloth-wound ballpoint firmly into the bullet hole. It was a snug fit, and it might hold for thirty minutes—that was all they needed. Nicki was already pouring the gas.

The blast of an air horn and the howl of air brakes arrested Chuck. He froze, waiting the impact. He scrambled out, tangling both feet in his bedouin robe, then rolled, then managed to stand.

A huge Italian-built Fiat tractor-trailer tanker truck hauling gasoline had stopped inches from the back of the Land Rover. The driver, a tall, powerful, turbanned Pakistani, swung down. "Out of petrol?" he asked politely in British-accented English.

Chuck had expected threats and cursing. "We've got it licked," he said, affecting a British accent of his own. "Looks like you've got plenty of petrol, though."

"Forty thousand liters on board, sir. And I've got to cross this bridge with my lorry."

"We're ready, Chuck." Nicki tossed the empty jugs in the back.

Chuck slid under the wheel and fired up. They were off.

"Chuck! That truck! Stop!"

Just beyond the bridge Chuck pulled up. The heavy tanker truck had followed them onto the bridge. The tank trailer full of gasoline had broken through, and the big rig was settling into the bridge decking, the planking splintering beneath its bulk. It had hung up, and now it teetered on a steel girder beneath. It looked as though the semi was going clear through, taking the driver to his death in the river. Chuck made a U-turn and roared back.

The Pakistani driver jumped clear and landed running, just as his semi tore loose and plunged into the muddy Tigris. The big tanker ruptured on a boulder, and its volatile contents gushed like Niagara.

Nicki folded her seat down and let the man squeeze in back amongst Chuck's gear and tools. "That's one of Saddam's bridges that the army won't cross for a few days," he panted.

"Look back there!" Nicki screamed.

The men turned. A truckload of soldiers had just braked to a stop short of the gaping hole left by the gasoline tanker. A soldier, oblivious to the greater danger, tossed a cigarette through the hole in the river. The tanker went up in a ball of flame, the fire spreading from bank to bank as the burning gasoline drifted downstream toward Baghdad. The terrified soldiers took off, leaping over one another to jump from their truck. They raced back toward Al Khalis on foot.

"I wonder who they were after this time?" The Pakistani laughed dryly, angrily.

"You never know in Iraq," Chuck muttered. He mashed the throttle wide open. He had his own gasoline problem to deal with as they roared northward. In minutes, Chuck knew also, he and Nicki would need to hide or find new transportation, and he had no idea what to do next.

"They executed a woman this morning," yelled the Pakistani over the roar of the wind and the motor. "An American. I heard it on my lorry's radio. It's all over the news."

"What had she done, sir?" Nicki asked.

"She did one of Saddam's favorite generals in—Rahman. The blighter was a famous womanizer."

"Head of the Republican Guard, wasn't he?" Chuck wondered.

"Yes. Say, this old jeep looks like its been through a war. You're a lucky chap, though. With the UN embargo on, a lot of vehicles aren't even running. Can't get foreign parts, you know."

"Isn't the whole country a war zone?" Chuck joked.

"You're right. It is. Say, there's one of my company's lorries." They had reached a bend in the highway, where the main road into Samarra crossed a railroad track. The lights flashed red, though there were no gates at the crossing. A freight train was shifting on a siding, coupling and uncoupling cars. Only a few vehicles waited, since it was still early morning.

Chuck pulled up beside the semi.

"Thanks, man." The Pakistani scrambled out.

Nicki hauled Chuck's bag from the storage area behind the seat. She grabbed his last jug of water. "See if you can get between that farm truck and the train without hitting either." Without waiting for Chuck to stop, Nicki stepped onto the jeep's running board then climbed onto its hood-mounted spare tire.

"Nicki!"

She grinned through the shattered windshield and pointed. An open freight car was slowly moving up.

Chuck drove crosswise to the road, squeezing between the farm truck and the train. The driver leaned on his horn. Chuck ignored him, watching Nicki. She threw Chuck's stuff ahead of her. Black robe flying, she leaped aboard.

Chuck dived through the broken windshield—too late!

The farmer in the truck honked and cursed in Arabic.

Chuck studied the train. Five cars rolled past, picking up speed. Six. Seven. The eighth had the door open. Chuck leaped inside.

The train was gaining speed now, and Chuck found himself alone in a boxcar half filled with baled cotton. He slid the door nearly shut, leaving a crack for light. These sliding steel doors latched themselves from the outside when slammed, and he had no desire to be trapped like a caged rodent.

Nicki. Eight cars up. *Why couldn't she have waited for me? We'd have got on together,* he thought angrily. She had his clothes. And the water. He'd also stuffed several tools into his bag after rigging the execution stake to collapse into his hidden pit. What use he might make of them Chuck didn't know. But they were *tools*, extra hands to a man.

But Nicki has them—that woman!

Then Chuck laughed. And he prayed. *God permits such things to teach us about ourselves.* How often he had tried to tell Jennifer that! His mind ran back to when Shelly was alive, and it occurred to him that he'd been eaten up with anger and bitterness at her more than once until he confessed his sin to Jesus and let the Lord deal with his wounded male pride.

Slow, methodical Chuck. Impetuous Shelly. And Nicki? Nicki waited for nobody.

Chuck slid the door open enough to get his head and shoulders out. He began counting mileposts and timing them with his watch. The train was zipping past two per minute now. One hundred twenty miles per hour! Then it dawned on him. *These are kilometer posts. That's, let's see, seventy-five miles per hour. Still, a good clip.*

The track arced left, and Chuck noticed that three locomotives were pulling approximately two hundred cars. He could see Nicki's car now. Suddenly Nicki swung out, rappelling hand-over-hand on an invisible rope. She had tied Chuck's bag and the three-liter bottle of water to her waist, he could see.

She was on top of the boxcar now, coming his way.

Chuck held his breath.

Nicki leaped from car to car like a squirrel on a power line. She landed on his car and disappeared from view.

Chuck pulled the door open wider.

Nicki swung in, monkey fashion, landing on bare feet. "Were you expecting company?" she laughed.

"How on earth?!"

"Cotton bales, like this car. They're tied with hemp twine." Nicki snapped a cord to make her point.

"So you made yourself a climbing rope?" He pointed to the cord coiled around her waist.

"Yep. Weighted it with a wrench I found in your bag, so I could toss it over the boxcar. It caught and held."

"You're too clever!"

"Not as clever as the guy who rigged that trap door of loose boards beneath the stake."

"You're very observant for a girl being executed." Chuck's tone was somber.

"Chuck, I have more important things than death to think about now."

"Do you?"

"Chuck, I . . . I trusted Christ in that hotel room. I . . . I felt His hands on mine during that execution. He died for me, and He wants me to live for Him from now on."

❰❰❰

"We're not out of trouble yet," Chuck remarked after they had traveled for several hours. "I guess the Republican Guard will halt this train and search it soon."

"The official report is, I'm dead and cremated. You heard that truck driver."

"Unofficially, you're still alive. You saw that truckload of soldiers at the bridge."

"What else do you have in your bag, Chuck?"

"Your Bible."

Nicki dug into Chuck's bag at once and fished out her Bible. "For years I've used the Bible as a road map to revolution. God wanted the spiritual light of His Word to shine through my armor of self-righteous idealism, but I wouldn't let it. Yet I've read the Bible clear through several times."

"Your note next to Psalm 91. You said you are trusting Jesus as your Lord and Savior. That's an unusual passage to convict one of sin and salvation."

Nicki beamed. "'In Him will I trust,'" she said, quoting the last clause of verse two. "Remember that I told you once that I really believed that Jesus died, was buried, and rose again? Those are the elements of the gospel, the good news. But I would always tell myself that His death and resurrection, though miraculous, held nothing for me personally. I believed that God wanted me to work hard to bring in His kingdom with the rebuilding of Israel and the restoration of Assyria, while America crumbled into moral clay, top-heavy with egalitarian democratic excesses.

"But the Lord's message—'Unless you . . . become as little children'—that escaped me for years. Then that night in the Baghdad Hilton I realized that I could never escape God." She shrugged. "Oh, I knew I might give the *Iraqis* the slip again. But sooner or later I would die—with or without the Iraqis' help—and meet God. What could I tell Him? That I'd 'Done many wonderful works' in His name? That verse in Psalm 91 caught me, Chuck: 'In him will I trust.' Only by faith can I ever hope to see God. I trusted God then. *And God is real to me now!*"

❰❰❰

"I only wish I knew where this train is heading," Chuck worried.

"Mosul is the next city up the line. We should be there by sundown. It's right across the Tigris from the ruins of ancient Nineveh," Nicki explained.

"Here we go again," Chuck groaned. "I'm sure you'll want to see Nineveh."

"That's why I came to Iraq in the first place. Besides, there's more in Nineveh than just an ancient ruin—a lot more. And say, it's only a few miles from Mosul into Syria. I'm sure this carload of cotton is headed for a seaport there, and you could easily slip out in the dock area."

"No. I'm in for the duration, Nicki. I'd like to see Nineveh myself, but we are being chased like rabbits. The hounds are still baying behind us." He sighed. "Do you expect Nineveh to become the capital of this new Assyria you envision in the millennial reign of Christ, sort of like Jerusalem?"

"The prophet Nahum made it plain that Nineveh the city will never rise from the dust," Nicki said. "Some Bible commentators apply Nahum's message to all of Assyria, but to be consistent with Isaiah 19:23–25, which predicts the restoration of Assyria the nation, I take the narrower view."

"So . . . doesn't Genesis say that Asshur, the father of Assyria, founded Nineveh?" Chuck wondered.

"Translations differ. The old King James Bible says that Asshur built Nineveh. Later Bibles say that Nimrod, the founder of Babylon, built Nineveh. The trouble is not so much the Hebrew text as it is a reading of the context. One clue is that the Hebrew text uses the same word for 'Asshur' as for 'Assyria,' the nation he founded," Nicki explained.

"So what does all this mean to the modern student of Bible prophecy?" Chuck surprised himself. He, a former pastor and a Christian for many years, was asking Nicki, a believer for only a week, about the last days before Christ's return. But Nicki knew her Bible.

"Nineveh is a Bible type of religious apostasy."

"Granted." Chuck knew that already.

"But Asshur was a son of Shem—Noah's son—and brother of Arphaxad, ancestor of Abraham. Asshur, some scholars write, was a believer in Yahweh, a monotheist who became disgusted with Nimrod's idolatry. It was Nimrod's religion, rather than Asshur, that made Nineveh a wicked city. Who actually founded the city is not really important."

"But Asshur was worshiped as a god by the Assyrians," Chuck protested.

"By the *later* Assyrians," Nicki stressed. "Americans do not worship George Washington."

"Some of them certainly worship the city of Washington," Chuck said.

"Good point, Chuck. You see the progression. Nimrod, a pagan, may have been history's first polytheist. Even the ancient Greeks were monotheistic, though it's commonly believed other-wise. Their pantheon of gods and goddesses came about as their culture declined into sexual immorality and state worship," said

Nicki. "Man-made religion is like the Second Law of Thermodynamics. First there's the simple order and beauty of the worship of the Creator; then there's the disorder and chaos of idolatry," she continued. "I had read all of this over the years, but it made no sense to me until I found my center in the Jesus Christ of the Bible, just a few days ago."

Chuck was amazed. "Sounds like America in century twenty-one."

"You've got it, Chuck. Our nation's clay has begun to crumble, just as Nineveh, built of sun-dried clay bricks, crumbled and dissolved into the Tigris River in 612 B.C. Nahum predicted that precisely years earlier: chapter two, verse six. Like you said, Chuck, a lot of Americans worship Washington as the source of all good. For others, it's the stock market, Hollywood, sex, the school system, medical science, computers and technology, sports, canonized saints, consumer goods—the list goes on."

"And like Nineveh, America's gods will one day crumble and dissolve." Chuck shook his head.

⟨⟨⟨

Nicki and Chuck made themselves beds on opposite sides of the boxcar and slept on cotton bales as the train roared northeasterly across Iraq. When Chuck finally peered out, it was night in a city freight yard. They were apparently in Mosul. Soldiers carrying flashlights and Russian AK-47s were already working, car-by-car toward the middle, from each end of the long train. "Nicki, we're trapped!" he whispered.

"Don't you have a screwdriver with the tools you saved?" Nicki was already unwinding her homemade rappelling rope.

Chuck grabbed the screwdriver. He quickly found that he could open the latch to the opposite door. No soldiers over there. Good. "Let's run for it, Nicki!"

"Bad idea, unless you can outrun bullets." She twirled Chuck's wrench on her rope, then threw it backhanded, arcing it across the car's steel roof.

Chuck caught the wrench as it flew in from the other side. He wedged it against a door roller as Nicki pulled her cord taut. He held his breath, as Nicki, his bag and water jug in tow, climbed hand-over-hand onto the roof. "You're the expert at these things, I guess," he muttered, following her as her feet disappeared from sight. Once up, he helped Nicki quickly coil up her rope.

"They'll search the town, too, Chuck," Nicki whispered as they lay head-to-head on the roof. "We've got to hide here until they're done. They'll ask every hotel keeper in Mosul if they've seen an American couple."

"Nicki, you told me last night that there's more to Nineveh than an old ruin," Chuck whispered after the soldiers passed.

"Chuck, that computer disk I got from General Rahman— CALF set a computer hacker to work on it. They hired that guy who broke into the Pentagon's computer system—the one who's out on parole now. If what he decoded is true, Saddam has the beginnings of World War III underway in Nineveh. He's using an old Assyrian aqueduct as an underground munitions factory. So I didn't come here for a vacation."

"So it seems."

〉〉〉

Dawn had begun to redden the sky when a robed, turbanned Arab, his Muslim wife following two respectful paces behind, slipped out of the freight yards. "How will we ever convince a hotel keeper that we're Arabs, Yildah?"

"Mosul is close enough to Syria that I'm sure they get a few French-speaking tourists, Abdul. I'll do the talking," Yildah said.

"I'll speak first—in Spanish," said Abdul. "That'll throw 'em for a loop."

"It should establish who's boss," chuckled Yildah. They both laughed.

The Terminus was a mud-brick motel, plastered with cow dung and whitewashed. "He can't stand my snoring," Yildah explained as she ordered two rooms. She need not have made an excuse. Arab men, many of whom practice polygamy, often do not sleep in the same room as their wives, so the hotel keeper was not suspicious. Yildah paid the fee, seven dollars a room, with the universal currency of black market trade: American money, from Chuck's dwindling supply.

❮❮❮

"If Nineveh and Babylon were once rival imperial capitals, I guess the rift has been healed," Abdul said next morning as they sat on separate, facing park benches waiting for the tour bus to the Nineveh archaeological dig and museum. He nodded toward the Babylonian Tours Ltd. bus pulling up to the Holiday Inn, where they had walked to board, a dozen blocks from the Terminus.

"There are other rifts and rivalries, Abdul." Yildah slipped on sunglasses she had purchased in the Holiday Inn's gift shop after noticing that other Arab women wore them, even those with veils. She cast a worried glance at the sky as two American F-16 jets streaked overhead. "Mosul is north of the thirty-sixth parallel, so we're in the no-fly zone," she said.

"So we're safe." Abdul chuckled hoarsely.

❮❮❮

Yildah became Nicki, then Hniqi, as she gazed at the relief sculpture on the walls of Ashurbanipal's ruined palace in Nineveh. A bearded horseman, dressed in a rich, kingly embroidered gown, rammed a spear down the throat of a leaping lion as his horse reared. It was King Ashurbanipal himself. Despite the coarse, hand-woven woolen cloth of her warm Muslim dress, Nicki felt her skin turn to goose bumps. Ashurbanipal, she believed—along with the Jewish kings David and Hezekiah—was her distant ancestor.

Princess Hniqi of Judah had become Queen Hniqi of Assyria, later to be deposed and banished to the harem by Sardanapalus, Ashurbanipal's eldest son. Years later, living in exile in the valley beneath Mt. Ararat in Turkey, Hniqi had remarried. Her daughter by this marriage had wed the grandson of Ashurbanipal, whom Hniqi and her son by Ashurbanipal, Daniye'l, had rescued from the flooded, burning harem.

And Daniye'l? Had he indeed become Daniel the prophet?

Nicki trembled with excitement at the possibilities.

She now turned her gaze on a frieze depicting another of Ashurbanipal's violent exploits, the sack of the Egyptian city of Thebes on the upper Nile in 661 B.C., as recorded in Nahum 3:8. Ashurbanipal the learned scholar and library builder, husband in his later years to the beautiful young Princess Hniqi, had been Ashurbanipal the youthful, ruthless warrior-general then. Nicki trembled at the unspeakable cruelties depicted on this relief frieze, atrocities that he had wrought without mercy on his Egyptian captives. Did she really wish to claim kinship to such an inhumane despot?

Nicki grasped Chuck's arm. "I've seen enough, Abdul. Let's cut through the museum to the restaurant."

Middle Eastern coffee is so black and thick you could dissolve a railroad spike in it and not notice the spike. Chuck smiled wryly, remembering this old adage as he watched the thin goat's milk from the creamer disappear into the inky beverage.

Nicki, who also had ordered coffee, was lost in thought. *Just as well*, Chuck decided. Muslim men, he had noticed, seldom speak to their wives in public. *No point in making anybody curious.*

Four men sat down in the booth across the aisle. The two younger appeared to be wealthy Iraqis. They wore well-cut jeans, Italian shoes, expensive watches.

The other two were elderly Europeans, also obviously well-to-do. They were square-jawed old fellows, stockily built, with physiques that showed that they once might have been athletic— before they developed their beer bellies and arthritis. *Russians?* Chuck puzzled on it. Military advisers, perhaps. Odd, though. These guys are well past retirement age—early eighties, probably.

One of the older men was speaking loudly enough that Chuck heard his words: hard-edged, clipped speech. Not a Latin-based language, he decided.

Nicki was listening also. She raised her veil so Chuck could see her lips. *"Das ist Deutsche,"* she mouthed. "German."

"Understand it?"

She shook her head.

"How can you gentlemen help us smuggle our missile into the United States?" one of the younger men asked in English.

"Achtung!" answered the taller of the other two, a bald grandfather-type with soft blue eyes. He continued with an angry sentence in German.

"Sorry." The youth shrugged. "I don't speak German."

"Then we'll *parlaz en francais,"* the old man growled in French. "Too many Iraqis understand English." He launched into a detailed, serious discourse in the French language. Both young men hung on to every word.

Beneath her veil, so did Yildah as she sipped her coffee.

Abdul pretended not to be interested.

When the old man rose to leave, Chuck got a glimpse of his forearm. He wore a swastika tattoo and a serial number. The Nazi elite SS Corps had worn such serial numbers to show their allegiance to Hitler, Chuck knew.

"What was that about?" Chuck asked as soon as the four conspirators had paid for their lunches and left.

"We are sitting on top of one of Saddam's munitions factories. It was all on General Rahman's disk. I planned to nose around a bit tonight."

"Like at White Sands?" Chuck was alarmed.

She smiled. "This has been handed us by the Lord. I don't need to nose around now."

"That . . . that's certainly good news," said Chuck. "But right under Nineveh?"

"Exactly. It's inside an old underground stone water line that has not been used since Nebuchadnezzar's Medes and Babylonians destroyed the city."

"It's 2,600 years old!?" Chuck whistled. "And it must be a big pipe."

"Not that unusual. City water systems in ancient times didn't have pressure pumps, so it took a much larger aqueduct to supply the necessary volume. Remember that Babylon, for instance, was defeated three-quarters of a century after Nineveh fell when the Persian army actually marched through Babylon's water pipe to break up Belshazzar's famous party."

"Incredible to modern minds, but believable to anyone who knows the history of Bible times," Chuck agreed.

"According to our friends"—Nicki nodded toward the four, who were studying the displays in the museum outside the glass-walled restaurant—"right beneath where we sit, missiles are being built and outfitted with anthrax-dispensing warheads. Each one, CALF learned from Rahman's disk, is designed to take out a major city. They are putting together compact weapons designed to hide in the back of a large pickup truck, a full-size van, or a tandem-axle trailer that could be towed by a big car or a heavy SUV."

Chuck caught his breath. "The most popular vehicles in America today. Why, they could attack every major city across our nation—and in complete disguise and total surprise. 'Tora! Tora! Tora!' Pearl Harbor all over again, but immeasurably worse!!"

"There's more." Nicki lowered her voice to a whisper. "The young men plan a test run next week. They will destroy CALF, along with a hundred thousand or more American Assyrians, by wiping out every living human being in greater Chicago, Chuck!"

Chuck had never felt so helpless in his life.

"Chuck, I'm giving you the details this morning. This afternoon I'll head for Baghdad and create a distraction for Saddam's Republican Guard while you slip back into Israel and use your American passport to catch a flight to Washington." She patted his hand. "I'm offering my life."

"No one would believe me alone, Nicki."

"General Armstrong MacAdams. Listen carefully, Chuck. MacAdams has been selling military secrets to Russia for years, to pay his gambling debts. He's getting desperate. CALF has been watching him. He knows about the Iraqi infiltration of the Russian espionage system, so he would believe this. MacAdams has friends in the Pentagon, the CIA, and Congress. I believe he'd expose himself before he let these terrorists turn this anthrax missile loose on Chicago. He's our only chance."

"Armstrong MacAdams is my friend. I can't say I haven't suspected that he was behind the attack on me in Tucson, though."

"MacAdams wanted to throw you off track, maybe scare you. That's all."

"But the attempt on my life?"

"An Iraqi, MacAdams passed to the Russians that you were onto an espionage attempt, and the Iraqis assumed you were interfering with Russian espionage. They wanted you out of the way, permanently."

Chuck sighed. "And when we factor in those fake FBI agents, Jack Arnold and Larry Contradini, I expect we'll find we've just touched the tip of the iceberg. But I can't leave you in Iraq, Nicki. Besides, I'll need you to lead me through the maze of conspiracy in the U.S."

"Then I'll go with you, Chuck." She squeezed his hand. "But let me give you the rest of the details, in case one of us doesn't make it."

"Shoot."

"Chuck, this is the most sinister plot since Haman tried to use the Persian despot Xerxes to annihilate the Jews, in the book of Esther! There's a World War II connection here."

"What . . . that's impossible! You mean those old Germans?"

"Those two former Nazis are wealthy dealers in Turkish marijuana, Chuck. They're collaborating with Saddam's agents to finish something their former boss, Hitler, began more than sixty years ago."

"What do you mean?"

"For background, the first successful nuclear reaction was created in Chicago in December 1942, less than a week before Pearl Harbor. The scientists who built it, Enrico Fermi, Leo Szilard, and

Hans Bethe, were Jewish immigrants who knew that Hitler's scientists had already split the atom in Berlin in 1938."

Chuck shook his head. "Revenge—get even with Chicago for getting the bomb ahead of Berlin—that sort of thing?"

"That's about it. Hitler's scientists were forced to flee to America because they were Jews. Szilard got Albert Einstein to write President Franklin Roosevelt to warn him about what was going on," Nicki said.

"So now, in a load of marijuana?"

"Exactly. We're less than an hour by train from Turkey. Their modus operandi is to anchor a freighter load of baled marijuana in the Bay of Fundy. It's off-loaded onto Maine fishing vessels or yachts and docked in the port city of Bois Bay. They have the Bois Bay city cops, the Samoset County Sheriff Department, and the Maine State Police in that area in their pocket. Those ex-Nazis deal with a contact in Bois Bay who resells to drug lords in cities east of the Mississippi. He's known to them as Golden Boy."

"How does the hash leave Bois Bay?"

"Potato haulers, loads of Christmas trees, truck loads of blueberries or farm produce, semis loaded with new shoes from Maine factories, furniture trucks full of antiques, rental moving vans—they haul it all over the East Coast and as far west as Detroit and Chicago. Split it up in city warehouses. Parcel it out to dealers."

Chuck turned cold. "You heard all that, Nicki?" There was too much detail for Nicki to be making this up. But this was incredible.

"Bois Bay, Maine, is halfway around the world, Chuck. What I heard was basically a couple of angry, bitter, old men bent on settling an international score more than half a century old. They had no reason to believe they were being overheard."

As a former law officer, Chuck was keenly aware that hundreds of tons of foreign marijuana enter the United States each year. He knew that some of the trailer trucks on American expressways regularly carried baled marijuana hidden behind legitimate freight. He sighed again. "Feet of clay once more. America's borders have more holes than my grandmother's old meal sieve."

He recalled the handmade tin sieve his North Carolina hill-country grandma had once used to sift stone-ground corn meal for bread.

"You said it, Chuck. And you know what else? If I get out of this alive, I'm going to spend the rest of my life putting iron back into those feet of clay by means other than military espionage."

"By what means, Nicki?"

"America *can* change! But our nation must be led to revival, one soul at a time by people determined to follow in the steps of Jesus. Something else, too."

Chuck waited, amazed at the insight of this young Christian.

"I'm not afraid to die anymore."

"Don't let your new disdain for death cause you to do anything foolish. You're needed alive."

"Who needs me?"

The restaurant patrons probably had never seen an Arab grin at his wife before.

◖◖◖

Two days later an El Al 757 lifted off from Tel Aviv bound for Montreal. Yvette LaRochelle, on a duplicate passport issued by the Canadian consulate, was seated next to Chuck Reynolds, American.

In Reston, Virginia, the director of the CIA pinned a fax of a recent article from the *Baghdad Republican News* onto his bulletin board, right next to a fax from Mexico's Quinta Roo Provincial Police Department two weeks earlier. "Looks like I'll need to reassign you, Mr. Dowe."

"I expect so." CIA Agent Phil Dowe grimaced, studying the news report.

"She got her head blown off in Cancun last month. Last week she got her heart blasted out in Baghdad. Not much left of her to track down, eh?"

15

The Lion Lurks

Samson went down . . . and . . .
to his surprise, a young lion . . .

—Samuel

There's a lion behind every tree, it seems like, Nicki." Chuck frowned at Nicki across a restaurant table at the Montreal International Airport.

"Behind every branch, I'm sure." Nicki peered through the plate glass into a cluster of majestic northern black spruces just outside the terminal. She readily imagined a Canadian lynx—a lionlike cat of the northern forest—hidden among the limbs, lurking for its prey. "My ancestor, Ashurbanipal, was a lion hunter," Nicki mused. "I wonder—when he went after lions, do you suppose he imagined himself actually fighting Nebuchadnezzar and his Babylonians?"

"*Un biere? Cafe? Tea?*" interrupted the waitress, sidetracking the couple's dead-serious dialogue.

"Cafe, s'il vous plait," Nicki responded. She smiled at the waitress, then returned Chuck's frown.

"M'sieu?"

"Coffee, please," Chuck said in English. "I think we're ready to order—Nicki?"

"Oui, uh, yes."

"The Belgian waffle with fresh strawberries is very good this morning," the waitress suggested, without a trace of French accent.

"Sounds great," Nicki agreed. "And a side order of Canadian bacon, please."

"The same," said Chuck. "Say, why did you speak to us in French the first time around?" Chuck had visited French Canada often enough to know that bilingual waitpersons usually recognize him as an *anglais* American even before he opens his mouth.

"The lady—she is . . ." the waitress laughed and shrugged, "she is international."

Nicki laughed.

Chuck grinned. "That's a compliment." As soon as the waitress left, he added, "We've got to find a country for you to belong to."

"I'm looking for that country 'whose builder and maker is God,' now that I believe." Nicki laughed happily. Then she sighed. "My papers say that I'm *Mlle.* Yvette LaRochelle, 837 Rue de Ste. Laurent, Montreal, Quebec, Canada. However, when we enter the United States, there's that question the customs inspectors always ask."

"Where were you born?" Chuck finished for her.

"Exactly! Now that I'm a new creation in Christ, I can't lie anymore. I'll have to say I was born in Saigon, Vietnam, and then they'll ask to see my driver's license to prove my American residency."

"Who are you, really?" Chuck's pale blue eyes bored into Nicki's green ones.

"Ngo Thieu. And Nicki Towns. I was Ngo Thieu until I was in graduate school at MIT. When I entered college, my status as a third-world Asian-American opened doors like magic."

"Politically correct, I'm sure," Chuck agreed.

"For sure. I had never even been to school in Vietnam. My mother taught me to read English from her Bible, as well as Vietnamese by using magazines. I can't recall when I could not read. Also, Mother needed glasses, which she couldn't afford. So when I was small, I used to read labels on cans in the market for her."

"Did you always pick what *she* wanted to buy?"

Nicki smiled sadly, remembering. "No. Once in a while I would lie to her. One time she bought shrimp when she thought we were getting canned tuna, since Vietnamese labels sometimes don't have pictures. She thought the price had gone up."

"Until she opened the can?" Chuck ventured.

"She didn't get mad. She said, 'Oh, the fish cannery made a mistake.' She was funny, my mother. We were poor, but she spoiled me to pieces. I guess it's because I was all she had."

"Mothers can be like that."

"I used to read everything I could get my hands on," Nicki went on. "American magazines, books on history and science, novels—all the way from classics to trashy stuff—I read what I could find. After I applied to Harvard as a home-schooled student, I spent the summer in the Boston Public Library cramming for the college entrance exams, which included both the SAT and the ACT tests."

"One of the world's great public libraries," Chuck agreed. "But how on earth did you know what to study?"

"The reference librarian was a treasure. I explained my plight to her, and she helped me narrow my choices to a two-foot stack of books."

"Not The Harvard Classics' famous five-foot shelf of knowledge?"

"Not quite. I scored high on the reading sections of both the SAT and the ACT. I did well in literature, history, and science—the stuff that I'd read a lot of. But I flunked math."

"Uh-oh."

"They accepted me anyway—put me on probation and assigned me to a math tutor."

"So, later you transferred to MIT. By then you were a math whiz?" Chuck tried his best to follow this amazing, impromptu autobiography.

"Before I transferred I had begun to learn Hebrew. I badly wanted to translate the old parchment-in-a-jar that Daddy had left with Rachel—Hniqi's prophecy. In my spare time I mastered algebra, geometry, trigonometry, and calculus. After I began MIT, I continued at Harvard as a night school student to improve my Hebrew and keep busy."

"Wow." Chuck was impressed.

"So I *became* Hniqi—I changed the spelling to N-i-c-k-i. Rachel helped me petition a judge to legally change my name from Ngo Thieu to Nicki Towns. In retrospect, I ought to have taken Daddy's last name, but I was feeling very American, and I wished for an American name.

"Less than a year after I entered MIT I learned about CALF and about the abuse our Assyrian people have taken since the collapse of the Ottoman Turkish Empire nearly a century ago. For several years since my graduation I have poured all my energies into its cause."

"And in Canada you're Yvette LaRochelle, CALF operative incognito?"

"Yes. I'm Yvette here. I come to Canada whenever I need to vanish or to travel on a Canadian passport. Here I'm a French-Canadian girl—a Canuck. But now Yvette has to disappear for good, and fast!"

"You're right," Chuck worried. "You were Yvette when we left Tel Aviv, so Saddam's goons will be looking for you under that name. But I guess you can be Nicki again once we're in the U.S. The FBI, the CIA, the State Department—I'm sure they all believe you're dead—finally." Chuck sighed.

"That report in the *Jerusalem Post* about my execution in Iraq—I'm sure Saddam had it planted," Nicki mused. "He wanted the world to believe he can deal effectively with anyone who gets in his way."

"If it was published in Jerusalem and Baghdad, you can be sure that our overseas CIA operatives picked it up and faxed it to headquarters in Reston, Virginia, as well as the State Department," Chuck added.

"That still leaves the Iraqis," Nicki said. "Saddam's agents will scour Montreal for me once they figure out that I escaped his prison camp by way of Syria and Israel. I'll be a major embarrassment to them when I turn up alive. They'll watch all the places I'm known to visit in America too. I wouldn't dare go back to visit Rachel and Art Towns or return to my apartment in Salem. I'll have to start over. So I'll just be plain ol' Nicki, and trust the Lord to watch over me."

"You have this apartment here in Montreal . . ." Chuck's voice trailed off. "No. That's the first place they're going to look for you. We can't have you taking foolish chances, here or in the U.S."

"You're right, I suppose. But we *can* use my apartment for a mail drop."

"That would be too dangerous!" Chuck was alarmed.

"It beats a P.O. box, which they'll certainly be watching," Nicki objected. "Besides, I'm used to danger. The house at 837 Rue de Ste. Laurent is an old, three-story affair right on the river. My apartment has its own entrance, with a mail slot in the door."

"So, you could . . ."

"Climb up to a back window and retrieve our mail," Nicki finished Chuck's sentence. "Let's see, Chuck, you'll need a Canadian driver's license and transportation that can't be traced to your credit card. So you'll need to buy a used car. You can use my apartment's address long enough for the Quebec motor vehicles department to mail you your permanent driver's license and auto title papers. Then we'll leave town, and 837 Rue de Ste. Laurent will become a dead-end street for the Iraqis."

"I used up most of my cash on that Land Rover," Chuck worried.

"CALF will supply the money—neat bundles of Canadian and American currency that will slide through my mail slot." Nicki grinned mischievously.

"I thought you were done with CALF?"

"Yes and no. I work for Jesus now. But CALF will gladly contribute to our one final project. As I told you, there are thousands of Assyrians living in Chicago, and CALF's headquarters is there also. When I tell CALF what we learned in Nineveh, they'll raise the money and support systems faster than Donald Trump raises cash."

"*I've* got to get information about the Iraqi terrorists to the U.S. State Department, the Department of Defense, and the United States Attorney General's office," Chuck emphasized. "ASAP!"

"Tell NATO and the UN, while you're at it." Nicki's voice had a sarcastic, bitter edge.

"You don't think they'll take me seriously?" Chuck felt his stomach tighten. His report might seem so hideously ludicrous as to be totally unbelievable. Nicki, no doubt, was right. The CIA and the Pentagon would more likely believe a report about a moon-sized comet about to collide with the earth.

"The Feds are looking for you, you know, Chuck. The Alcohol, Tobacco, and Firearms boys—the ATF—no doubt they want to talk with you about a certain exploding Corvette, for starters, I'm sure. And probably the FBI is getting curious about your habit of vanishing every time their favorite female spy fades from view."

"Some of those guys do watch a lot of old James Bond reruns." It was Chuck's turn to be sarcastic. "Just the same, I've *got* to report what we've learned about those terrorists. I can fax letters anonymously from here in Canada. If I go in to the Boston FBI office, I may get detained until it's too late to stop Saddam's terrorists."

"Send a fax to the Associated Press. That'll get the FBI's attention. We already know that."

"True. I guess I might as well fax the *Washington Post*—personal to Bob Woodward—the *Washington Times*, the *New York Times*, and the *Chicago Tribune*. Maybe the national TV news desks and National Public Radio too. Once the authorities are forced to answer some questions from the media, someone's going to have to take some kind of action."

"Other than issuing disclaimers and trying to figure out who's sending crank faxes, don't count on it. They're going to figure that Y2K didn't stop the earth on its axis, so an Iraqi in a pickup truck won't destroy Chicago. Ho hum. What else is new? We've got to take some action on our own."

"Yeah," Chuck agreed. "Dear Father," he prayed, though it was more of a groan than a prayer, "You know what we've seen and heard. Help us to work through this awful responsibility. In Jesus' name, amen."

"Amen," Nicki agreed.

"Now let's begin by getting out of this airport, keeping as low a profile as possible," Chuck said. "We need to find a motel well out of town where we can formulate some plans. So, may I help you with your bags, lady?"

Nicki grinned. She grabbed a clutch purse, which Chuck had bought for her along with a new outfit of clothes and some makeup since the Iraqis had seized everything she owned. "I travel light."

((((

"Grand Manan Island is in Canadian waters off the Maine coast," Chuck explained a week later as he and Nicki rolled eastward on the Trans-Canada Highway toward New Brunswick in a three-year-old Dodge Intrepid. So far, at least, they were just a pair of tourists heading for the sea. "There's a ferry boat to Grand Manan from Blacks Harbour," he explained. "After I see you off, I'll drive the car to Machias, Maine, and wait for you at the Lobster Trap Motel, where we've already got our rooms rented."

"This is a bit elaborate, just to smuggle me across the border, don't you think?"

"Your job," Chuck explained, "is to pay a lobster fisherman to land you in Maine without going through customs. I want you to appraise just how easy, or difficult, it is to smuggle goods and people into the United States by way of the Maine coast, right under the noses of the U.S. Coast Guard. We need to know if those guys in the restaurant at Nineveh have a viable plan, or if they were just blowing smoke."

"My French is pretty good, Chuck. I'm sure I caught their intentions very clearly. Besides, I'm not exactly your typical smuggler," Nicki chuckled.

"I'm sure you're right. Some of these drug runners are certainly pretty sophisticated. Then again, plain, old-fashioned sneaking around is still pretty effective in some circumstances, apparently."

"Chuck, years ago on the ship I worked on traveling to America from Vietnam, I heard a couple of sailors talking. They told about a cocaine smuggling operation out of Thailand that used a high-speed, Australian-built fiberglass vessel equipped with the latest in radar. They deliver cocaine right into Seattle, apparently."

"I imagine the most effective strategy is simply not to draw attention to yourself," Chuck countered. "It seems to me that's the logic of using a lobster boat or a pleasure yacht."

"Oh, I agree. We do need a test run, and I won't take any chances. That's a promise. But if I can't get a Canadian lobsterman to take me to Maine, where are we supposed to meet?" Nicki asked.

"Back in Canada—Blacks Harbour, New Brunswick, at the Oceanside Holiday Inn, tomorrow evening. If you don't show up in Machias by noon tomorrow, I'll drive straight back to Canada."

〈〈〈

Chuck peered through pea-soup fog to watch a wiry fisherman huddle into his yellow rain slicker and navy blue knit cap as he slogged in rolled-down fishing boots uphill from the Machias wharves. The guy toted a small duffel bag as he hunkered over against the morning chill and mist. *Interesting characters, these waterfront rats,* Chuck observed. *Rough, but I imagine they make honest livings hauling lobster traps or as hands on a halibut boat.*

Chuck checked his watch. 5:45 A.M. Lobster boats had landed steadily since before daylight in this easternmost corner of the U.S. *I'd better get back to The Lobster Trap Motel, he decided. In this fog, I'll probably miss Nicki, given the way she slips in and out like a cat. She's eating breakfast there already and laughing at me, I'm sure.*

"Can y' gimmie a lift, buddy?" The young man in the rain slicker tapped on the glass. "This lowery weather's so wet I'm soaked right through my slicker."

"Ayuh! Just hop in the cah." Chuck chuckled and tried his best to affect a Down-East drawl as he opened the passenger side door of the gray Intrepid. "You fooled me," Chuck continued as the hitchhiker slid inside. "Did you fool that Canadian lobsterman who brought you into Machias?"

"I'd rather be a girl." Nicki sighed. "I enjoy being a girl, in fact. But I figure if the authorities get on that old guy's case about his boat passenger from Grand Manan, he can say he carried a man, without lying."

◖◖◖

"I'm not surprised that they're waiting for us here!" Chuck had parked the Dodge in a vacant lot where a one-room school once served the Fuller neighborhood in South Freedom.

"Let me look."

Chuck passed Nicki her night-vision monocular, and she sprawled across the hood of the Dodge Intrepid to steady the instrument, focusing it on a car parked opposite the Fuller Road, a quarter of a mile off in the darkness. "Two men," she whispered. "Massachusetts license XLT-3850. A rented Buick Park Avenue, so it's not the FBI."

"Saddam's thugs?" Chuck wondered. "They bombed my 'Vette, and they're still after me."

"Probably. Could be our old buddies, Jack and Larry. The guy on the passenger side is dark, smallish. Iraqi, maybe."

"'Jack and Larry' . . . ?"

"Jack Arnold and Larry Contradini," Nicki finished. "Your faux FBI agents from Boston."

"Oh? Contradini's the Iraqi posing as an Italian. Brags he has Mafia connections, I think you said?"

"Yes," Nicki agreed. "But that story has more baloney in it than an Italian meat market. His real name is Elias el-Haaj. And my CALF sources tell me that Saddam's network in North America is rather thin. Osama bin Laden, the Saudi terrorist who blew up American embassies in Kenya and Tanzania in 1998, seems to have had rather more success than Saddam in infiltrating the U.S., so bin Laden gets a lot more attention from the FBI. The Feds hardly seem aware that there's a dangerous Iraqi network in North America. Saddam's agents have to wear a lot of hats, though, because there are so few of them," Nicki added. "Since we already know that Arnold and Contradini are working here in New England, they'd be the logical ones to do a stakeout waiting for us."

"Well, they can't wait all night," Chuck observed, checking his watch. "It's 9:45. I'll drive you to the Basford farm once they've driven off."

"Chuck." Nicki's voice was tense.

"Yeah." Chuck reflected her fear.

"I can't put your in-laws and Jennifer in danger. You'll have to take me some other place."

"Nicki, it's me they're laying for!"

"Both of us, Chuck. They're using you to find me."

"Listen carefully, Nicki. *We have no choice! There is no 'other place' to hide you!* Now that we know they're watching the Fuller Road—and have no doubt tapped into the local phone circuit— we'll just take a few basic precautions and follow them. We can certainly find a way to hang a bell on these cats. Several million lives in Chicago depend on our going through with this, Nicki!"

"I'm listening." Nicki was upset. Her association with Chuck had put him and his family in danger beyond imagination. Yet they now had a chance to avert the worst terrorist tragedy in history.

"Once those guys drive off, I'll drive you to the house. Once you're there, stay indoors. Accept or send no phone calls and no E-mail. Not even scrambled messages. Got it?"

"I'm ahead of you, Chuck. If Saddam's assassins picked up a scrambled E-mail from the Basford farmhouse, they'd be onto us like Attila the Hun."

"After I drop you and our bags off, I'll drive over to Sheepscot Valley Community Church on the other side of the mountain—it's the Basfords' church. I'll park this car there and walk home through the woods. I know Pastor Jim Evans, and I'll let him know what's going on, even if I have to get him out of bed."

"But won't the car . . . ?"

"No. Folks around here are used to seeing out-of-state or Canadian plates parked at the church—their missions program is very active. A three-year-old Dodge with a Quebec license plate will appear to be just another itinerant missionary."

"How can I communicate with CALF? I've got to get us some special equipment from them—tracking devices, stuff like that," Nicki fretted.

"The church has a computer, a fax, and E-mail via internet connections. It's a different phone exchange from the Basfords', so it won't be bugged by our snooping friends there. CALF can make deliveries to the church by courier, or simply use UPS."

"They're driving off now, Chuck."

"Great. I'll drive you right over to the Basford's. Then I think I'll pay Jack and Larry a little visit."

"Chuck!"

"I'm not going to introduce myself. They're staying in one of Belfast's six motels, most likely. I can check them all and be back here by midnight. Now what was that license number again?"

❴❴❴

"Mass. XLT-3850" read the plate on the rented Buick in front of room 42 at the Ship's Wheel Motor Haven on Route One, near the Belfast city limits. Chuck focused Nicki's monocular for a better view. He scanned the parking lot. *Might as well learn all I can while I'm here,* he decided.

The door to room 42 opened. Chuck watched. A man stepped out into the chilly New England seaside evening. *What's this? More leads than I bargained for? This isn't one of the guys who was watching our road in South Freedom.*

The guy was tall, powerfully built, in tight jeans and cowboy boots. He wore a baseball cap over shoulder-length blond curls. Chuck focused the monocular on the guy's face as the man lit a cigarette. Sunglasses. Lines that showed premature aging.

Chuck lowered his view as the man reached to push his long leather coat back to slip his lighter into a jeans pocket. He wore only a T-shirt beneath the coat, and Chuck distinctly noted a holstered semiautomatic pistol under the man's well-muscled arm.

The guy strode casually to a new sports-model Cadillac backed into a space in a dark corner of the motel parking lot. He fired up and cruised to the street, quad exhausts rumbling menacingly to the tune of the 32-valve, 300-horsepower Northstar engine. The black machine was trimmed in gold, and ETC—for Eldorado Touring Coupe—was the fender insignia, Chuck noticed as the car passed beneath a light.

Chuck waited until the Caddy turned south on U.S. Route One. Then he followed, keeping his lights off until the street lights petered out a mile south of town.

"Bois Bay 19 miles," read a highway sign outside Belfast in the direction in which Chuck had seen the slick sports coupe vanish into the misty night. He checked his watch as he held the gas down: 11:45.

I promised Nicki I'd be in by midnight, Chuck reminded himself. A service station with a lighted phone booth loomed in the swirling fog. He braked, then stepped on the gas. *If they've tapped our phone lines,* Chuck decided, *chances are good they've also hidden a tape recorder in a waterproof box beneath a pile of leaves somewhere. No way I could call without tipping Jack and Larry off when they play it back tomorrow.*

He struggled with his conscience. *I promised her. And she'll worry. The whole family will worry.* Then Chuck recalled that six million greater-Chicago citizens slept tonight unsuspecting, yet they had awful cause to worry. The thought electrified him, pushed him onward, so that he forgot for some moments his promise and the fears that might consume them.

What will Stan Basford do if I'm more than an hour late? The thought put him in a cold sweat. His father-in-law, who had not fully been appraised of what was going on, would phone the Maine State Police and report Chuck missing—giving a description of his Dodge and its Quebec license plates. Arnold and el-Haaj would find that report on their tape in the morning. Chuck began seriously to look for a good place to turn around.

"Hey!" As the Dodge topped a rise in the winding coastal road, Chuck spotted a car following a semi up ahead. It was the Eldorado. Without increasing his speed, he eased up closer to the vehicle, keeping back a respectful distance.

Chuck flipped on his high beams for a glance at the Maine plate. He dimmed them at once. The vanity plate left him dumbfounded.

The truck topped the grade. The black touring coupe burned rubber to pass, forcing a northbound driver into a fog-bound parking lot at the bottom of the hill.

It was the Islesboro ferry terminal, and Chuck braked hard, hauling the Dodge off the highway. Tires squealing, he made a power turn in the parking lot and roared back onto northbound Route One, leaving the shaken driver of the car forced off by the Caddy still trembling behind his wheel.

DRG-DLR. That was the Caddy's vanity plate. Chuck had seen enough to realize that this flamboyant advertisement was no idle joke. He turned this over in his mind as he motored back toward South Freedom, but he could make no sense of it.

Chuck was at the Basford farm by 12:55. He gave Nicki, Stan, Mae, and Jennifer a hasty explanation, borrowed a flashlight, then drove off for the church. It was ten minutes' drive there, but more than an hour's hike over an old logging road to return, slipping past Stan's back pasture along an old stone wall and into the rear door of the barn. He could explain things to Pastor Jim Evans in the morning.

◖◖◖

"Chuck, I was worried sick when you didn't show up before midnight last night." Nicki and Chuck were hiking around Wild Youngman Mountain, toward Freedom Village and the tiny Sheepscot Valley Community Church, careful to stay out of eyeshot of neighbors' farmhouse windows. The morning dew had soaked through their shoes and socks, but they had needed an early start to deal with the day's ventures.

"Nicki, you have no right!"

"What's that supposed to mean, Chuck? We're in this together!"

"You've answered your own question!" Chuck strode on in silence, refusing for the next ten minutes to say more.

"How have I answered my own question?" Nicki demanded.

"You said, 'We're in this together!' Don't you see—like a business partnership. The comings and goings of the other person are not the other's business, so long as you get your job done. I could have been in Bois Bay—maybe found that Cadillac if I hadn't been afraid Stan would call the state cops. Now I've got to go back and search for it. You have no right to worry about me, Nicki." Chuck had cooled down now, and he spoke more softly.

"Chuck, I *care* about you!"

"Women are carers by nature. Probably I could easily find a dozen women, a hundred maybe, who'd say that."

"Chuck!"

"Nicki, I . . . I'm sorry." Chuck took her hand. "It was wrong for me to snap at you like that."

"Forgiven. We've both been under a lot of stress. Can we . . . can we ask the Lord to lessen the strain and help us both work through this thing?"

Chuck led in prayer. But when he had finished committing the matter to the Lord, he still pondered: "both work through this thing." Did Nicki mean the terrorist threat to Chicago? Or something more mundane, yet ultimately of greater consequence to both their lives than even the destruction of a great city?

☾☾☾

"Chuck, we do need to find out who was driving that Cadillac Eldorado you saw at the motel," Nicki said as they approached the church. "After you chat with Pastor Evans and tell him why we're parking your car here, why don't we drive down to Bois Bay?"

"It's a needle in a haystack. Let's start with the Maine Secretary of State's auto registration bureau."

"Good idea. Maybe we can narrow our haystack down to one bale, at the most."

☾☾☾

Chuck dropped the church phone in disgust. He was used to dealing with state officials in North Carolina, where he had been in law enforcement. Even in Massachusetts, his position as deputy sheriff, which allowed him to carry a gun and make arrests on the job, opened most doors in the state capital. "Stone-walled!"

"What'd they say, Chuck?" Nicki asked.

"Since I'm not an officer of the law, I've got to establish a 'need to know' before they'll give out the owner of that license plate," he explained. "So let's head for Bois Bay."

"Patience, Chuck. I need to use the phone line to fax CALF this morning to request some special equipment and some more cash to tide me over until we can hand this terrorist chase over to the FBI."

"It's all yours, partner." Chuck laughed, motioning toward the fax machine. "Better ask them for a bundle, unless our luck with the Feds improves."

❰❰❰

"I'm about out of cash myself," Chuck remarked. It was now late morning, and he pulled into a branch of Mid-Coastal National Bank on the edge of a Bois Bay shopping mall.

"I'll wait in the car," Nicki said.

"A thousand dollars please—five hundreds, and the rest in fifties." Chuck slid his Visa card and Quebec license to the teller.

The girl processed the request. She counted out twenty fifties. "Sorry, but we're out of hundreds, sir." She snickered. "Drug trade's got 'em all."

"No *kidding!*" Chuck was only mildly surprised at her remark. But he purposely tried to sound like a wild-eyed tourist. "Is it that bad? I saw a Caddy with 'Drug Dealer' as a vanity plate, but I figured it was just some rich dude showing off by thumbing his nose at the cops."

"Showing off, all right. But not kidding. That's Scotty MacKay, son of Donald MacKay. The Donald and Golden Boy. They own Bois Bay together—the old man owns the day, and the son owns the night. It's no secret around here."

"Marijuana, I suppose?" Chuck could barely contain his elation. Scotty MacKay was certainly the same Golden Boy the old Nazis at Nineveh had bragged about dealing with.

"By the ton." The teller smirked. "Once in a while the cops turn up a few bales of Turkish hash, but they never can seem to decide who owns it."

"That figures. Thanks." Chuck tapped his currency on the counter, folded it into his wallet, and strode out.

"MacKay Fisheries." Chuck stopped opposite the long wharf on Harbor Street and eyed the faded sign painted on the cavernous, ramshackle, cedar-shingled building that ran for a full block along the waterfront.

"I guess this would be Donald MacKay's place of business," Nicki ventured.

"Nice boat," Chuck observed. A modern, steel-hull fishing vessel was docked, and the crew busily off-loaded heavy plastic tubs of fish packed in ice. "Radar, too. I imagine a boat like this goes well out into the North Atlantic—to the Grand Banks, maybe."

"I think we're wasting our time here, Chuck. We already know that Donald MacKay has a reputation for running a legal operation."

"You're probably right. Wait." Chuck caught his breath. It was the Eldorado with the vanity plates. The car stopped just beyond the fish-packing plant's office entrance. The guy with the yellow curls stepped out and strolled toward the busy crew. "Golden Boy himself," Chuck muttered.

Chuck and Nicki watched as seven of the eight workers left the boat at once and gathered in a knot around Scotty "Golden Boy" MacKay. The forklift operator continued to haul tubs of fish into the plant however. The man who did not join the others sat on the rail smoking a cigarette and waiting.

"Chuck, he's offering those guys some night work! What else could it be?" Nicki said.

"You've got it, I'm sure. I'll bet the pay is good."

"If I had that tracking device from CALF, I'd bug his Cadillac *right now!*"

"They're sending only one tracking device, remember? Besides, you might not get away with it." He nodded toward the new Eldorado sports coupe, which sat in full view of the crew. Chuck started the Dodge.

"Where are we going?"

"That parking lot up behind Main Street. We're tourists, you know. I think we should visit the Smiling Cow."

The Smiling Cow was a curio shop with a lunch counter on the seaward side of Bois Bay's Main Street. It had a balcony overlooking the harbor where tourists could sip drinks and eat sandwiches until the cold weather closed it for the season. Chuck and Nicki ordered hot Reuben sandwiches and hot tea. Though chilly, the balcony afforded a full view of MacKay's Wharf and the fish-packing plant.

"What time do you suppose those fishermen knock off work for the day?" Nicki wondered.

"Soon's they get the fish out of the hold."

"Don't they then have jobs inside the plant?"

"A fisherman is a private contractor, Nicki. Those guys work for a share of the profits, so they'll quit soon's the boat work is done. That forklift operator works by the hour, of course, as does the crew in the freezer plant inside that old building."

"What about that fisherman who didn't join the others, Chuck? Did you notice him?"

"Yeah. He's not in on the drug deal. They'll make it rough for him until he quits. Meanwhile, if he opens his mouth, the local sea rescue team will find him floating in the harbor."

"Those guys play rough," Nicki said. "Like the Iraqis."

"I've got an idea, though." Chuck pointed toward The Dead Man's Chest, a small eatery on its own wharf a block from MacKay Fisheries. He used the monocular for a better look. A chalked sign by the door said, "Catch of the Day—Flounder: $9.99." Lighted neon signs in several windows advertised various brands of beer. "That place is a tavern. Let's wait here a while and see if any of those fishermen go in there when they finish."

◖◖◖

A waitress carrying a pitcher of beer stepped up to where Chuck and Nicki had seated themselves at a corner table in The Chest. "Fill 'em up?" She reached toward the tall glasses already on the table.

"Coffee, please." Nicki pointed toward her cup. "I'll have the flounder," she added, without picking up the menu.

"Beer for you, sir?"

"No, thanks. Same's the lady." Chuck smiled at the waitress and glanced into her face. The girl had tried unsuccessfully to hide an injury with makeup. "Nice little town you have here."

"The tourists seem to like it. You from away?"

"Used to be. May move to Maine, though," Chuck said.

"Don't move to Bois Bay—worse'n hell."

"I'll keep that in mind."

Nicki shot a glance at the waitress as she hurried back toward the bar. "I didn't know they wore outfits like that until after dark," Nicki whispered.

"I guess maybe the cutoffs go with the black eye."

"I suppose things do get a little rough in here at night," Nicki said.

"Earlier than that." Chuck stirred his coffee and pretended to ignore the squeals from the waitress serving four of the men they had seen two hours earlier on MacKay's fishing boat.

◖◖◖

"Did you hear those guys tell me there's a job opening at The Dead Man's Chest when I came out of the rest room?" Nicki asked once she and Chuck were back in the Dodge.

"Sure did. Take it as a compliment, Nicki. I listened to them too. That's what we went in there for, remember?"

"I remember, Chuck. One of them said something about the old Captain Ashcroft Mansion. That's all I caught."

"That's all we need!" He started the motor. "Now if we can just figure out how Arnold and el-Haaj fit into this," Chuck said, pulling out into traffic. "Let's get back to South Freedom. We've got work to do."

"I imagine they'll be there. It will then become obvious."

◖◖◖

"Arnold and el-Haaj, alias Contradini, were parked over there watching the Fuller Road yesterday afternoon when we came back from Bois Bay. So at least we know that Scotty MacKay hasn't killed them in their motel." Chuck spoke grimly as he helped Nicki unwrap the express packages left at Sheepscot Church by the UPS truck the next morning.

"You understand that this may be putting my congregation in danger." Pastor Jim Evans stroked his red beard and frowned. Evans was lanky like an old farmer, easygoing and gregarious. He knew of Chuck's reputation as a security expert on military projects, so he had readily agreed to let Chuck and Nicki use a spare church office for what they called "The War Room." Convinced as he was that Chuck and Nicki had correctly assessed the danger of a terrorist anthrax missile attack on Chicago, Evans was still fearful.

"Believe me," Nicki said, "if we could do this any other way, we would."

"As I've told you, Pastor, we faxed the State Department and news media before we left Montreal," Chuck explained. "If we'd waited until we got here to Maine, the FBI would be busting into the church about now." Chuck pointed to a folded copy of the *Belfast Journal.* "FBI Hunts Anthrax Missile Hoaxers," read the headline on a two-paragraph Associated Press article in section two. The article told that several federal departments and news media had received "unconfirmed" reports of an "alleged" plot by Iraqi terrorists to destroy Chicago. The notion that a Third World nation could smuggle a high-tech weapon of mass destruction into the United States undetected had been dubbed "ridiculous" by an FBI spokesperson.

Right next to the anthrax missile plot piece, another article told how the Illinois State Police had stopped a heavily loaded semi rig northbound on Interstate 55 just outside of Chicago for nonfunctioning taillights. The truck, registered to a Dallas, Texas, produce hauler, had crossed into Texas from Mexico. The driver, a Colombian, had displayed official papers to Illinois police. These seemed to prove that U.S. customs officials had passed scrutiny on his load in El Paso, Texas, certifying it to be lettuce from Mexico.

The truck was equipped with a forty-eight-foot trailer and carried eighteen tons of Colombian marijuana. The driver, "apparently a regular drug courier," wrote the AP reporter, "seemed puzzled that the Illinois State Police had arrested him."

◖◖◖

"I *am* going with you, Chuck," Nicki insisted that evening as they experimented with the combination tiny, sensitive microphone and powerful compact radio transmitter in the Basford farmhouse kitchen. They also had set up the receiving unit with its tape recorder, a device the size of a palm-held radio. The battery-powered receiver would track a car equipped with the transmitter up to ten miles away.

"Those guys are killers, and we're not even armed, Nicki." Chuck was pleading now.

"We're business partners, remember?"

"Nicki, I . . ." Chuck closed his mouth. He knew he could certainly attach the listening, transmitting, and tracking device to the rented Buick by himself. Nicki's agility and her knowledge of sophisticated electronic circuitry would enable her to do the job faster and with far less danger, however.

But something else was eating him. "Nicki," he began again, "it bothers me to put you in danger."

"And . . . ?"

Chuck shot a glance toward the living room where Stan and Mae watched TV and Jennifer exchanged E-mail with friends on the computer. He watched his daughter for a moment, her deep red tresses streaming lightly across her soft shoulders as she pecked the keyboard.

"Nicki," Chuck said at last, "I do care about you . . . too—like you care about me."

Nicki smiled. She took his hand. "Then we'll fight together 'til this job is done!"

◖◖◖

Nicki quickly slipped back into the Dodge where Chuck waited for her in the far end of the motel parking lot. "It's all wired up, Chuck. We can hear everything that goes on in that Buick."

"Not a moment too soon!" Chuck nodded through the windshield toward the Buick in front of room 42 at the Ship's Wheel Motor Haven. Two men rushed out, and the short, dark one, whom Nicki had guessed to be el-Haaj, alias Larry Contradini, hopped in. The man they believed to be Jack Arnold, however, hurried to a new red, three-quarter-ton, extended-cab Ford pickup with a fancy, color-coordinated fiberglass topper over the bed. The truck, the largest pickup built by Ford, had four doors and dual wheels.

"I didn't expect we'd get to try out this equipment quite so soon." Nicki plugged the headphones into her ears and adjusted the volume. "Yuck," she complained. "This black grease paint I put on is messing up the earphones!" She yanked them out and wiped her ears with a tissue.

"You do look like something out of an old spy movie, wearing that junk," Chuck teased. "Maybe you should have waited until we got there to plaster that stuff on."

"Chuck, el-Haaj is heading for Bois Bay *right now!*" Nicki suddenly cried. "He's on his two-way radio with Arnold in the truck!"

"Then maybe we've got a busy night ahead of us. Could be their boat's come in." He fired up the motor, waiting as the Buick pulled out, the pickup right behind it.

《《《

"If I'd driven to Bois Bay the first night, I never would have found Scotty MacKay," Chuck said. "I wish we'd had time to check the Captain Ashcroft estate out in advance, though." He and Nicki followed the Buick and the big Ford pickup south from Bois Bay, down the peninsula toward Port Clyde Lighthouse.

"Chuck, el-Haaj just told Arnold to follow him to Turkey Cove."

"It's all coming together, Nicki. Turkey Cove is on the way to Port Clyde Lighthouse. I've been past there with Jennifer and the Basfords when we were picnicking. The head of the cove is the old Captain Ashcroft estate. It's usually rented out to wealthy folks, except during a couple of holidays when the Ashcroft family uses it for reunions," Chuck explained.

"So Scotty MacKay has rented the place. They'll land the drugs in the cove, along with the missile."

"Exactly. That's why Golden Boy MacKay was paying his respects to Arnold and el-Haaj in Belfast the other night. Tie up loose ends of the deal, no doubt," Chuck concluded.

The car and pickup turned into a side road, then both vehicles wheeled through a wrought-iron gate set into an imposing, vine-covered brick wall. The electric gate clicked shut as Chuck and Nicki rolled past. A sign warned, "PRIVATE—ASHCROFT LANE." A softly lighted Georgian mansion rose at the head of the drive, and a large, two-story boathouse stood on what appeared to be a saltwater lagoon.

The road dipped into a gully past the estate, crossing a stone bridge over the cove. "Stop the car, Chuck!" Nicki grabbed the night-vision monocular as he braked to a halt on the bridge. She jumped out and raced to the rail.

"We're right on time for the party." Nicki fought to contain her elation as moments later she slipped back into the car.

"I saw a boat too," Chuck acknowledged, "right beneath the lights. The overhead door is still open."

"It's the *Pirate Redbeard*, a yacht out of Yarmouth, Nova Scotia," Nicki said. "A small luxury liner, in fact! Now *get this car out of sight!*"

Chuck pressed the gas, and he managed to reach the cover of a bend in the road as a car drove up from behind and turned into Ashcroft Lane. Chuck drove on for a quarter of a mile until he was sure they were not being followed. He pulled over in front of a country store that had closed for the day. "How are we going to get inside that place? I'm sure that brick wall is buzzing with electronic sensors, and they've got armed guards. This is not your typical mom-and-pop operation."

"So we find their photoelectric motion detectors." Nicki grinned. "They're designed to interrupt ordinary intruders who aren't expecting electronic surveillance—local burglars, curious tourists wanting to snap pictures."

"Every Achilles has a heel," Chuck observed. "Unfortunately, we haven't had a chance to prepare. And we're unarmed."

"So we improvise. Surprise is our best strategy," Nicki observed. She passed Chuck the tube of grease paint. "We're going inside. So cover up, big guy."

"Yeecch!" Chuck painted his face. Nicki crammed the screwdriver and pliers she had brought along to connect the surveillance equipment to the Buick into her jeans pocket. She passed Chuck the flashlight and monocular. "Let's go!"

Chuck followed. They covered the quarter mile from the darkened store to the cove in minutes, twice diving into the ditch to avoid passing cars. "Here's where we start," Nicki said as they hurried onto the bridge over the channel from the sea. "It's the only way past security."

Chuck was about to dangle a leg over the rail as he peered toward the boathouse. The yacht was already inside the cavernous waterfront building, and light streamed under the door, reflecting across the salt tide.

"Stop!" Nicki hissed. She grabbed his wrist. "Motion sensors—beneath the rail, probably."

"The bridge is state property."

"Do you think Golden Boy cares?"

"I see why you're good at espionage."

"I wish we knew when the tide turns," Nicki fretted.

"We do. I read the tide report in the newspaper this morning." Chuck checked his luminous watch. "It's 11:17 right now. High tide is 12:10."

"So we've got about two hours, while the water is still deep enough to float that yacht back out to sea. That gives them time enough to unload and time enough for us to crash their party."

"How?"

"We can forget wading under the bridge," Nicki affirmed. "I imagine it's bristling with motion sensors. If we slide over the rail, we'll set off an alarm too."

"So that leaves . . . ?"

"The good old flying leap!" Nicki hopped onto the bridge's stone rail. She pushed off hard before Chuck could protest, jumping wide of any motion detector beam under the rail. She vanished into the black void.

Seconds later Chuck heard a splash. He scanned the water with the monocular. Nicki was swimming briskly toward shore in the icy fall saltwater. Chuck rammed the instrument into its waterproof case and screwed the lid into place.

I guess if it's deep enough for a boat that size . . . Chuck fought his terror and climbed numbly to the rail. He leaped out and held his breath in the dark.

16

The Lion Roars

The sword shall devour your young lions.
—The LORD of Hosts

Shine your light on these hinges. North Atlantic swimming in October is not my favorite sport," Nicki chattered. She struggled to fit her shaking screwdriver into a screw slot. They were at a side entrance to the long boathouse's upper story, out of sight from the Ashcroft mansion. The door was padlocked, and when Nicki tried to pop the lock open with a pin, she found it rusted from the salt air.

Chuck and Nicki soon found themselves in a storage and repair loft. Chuck checked one door. It led to a staircase.

Nicki opened the other door. "C'mere, Chuck," she whispered. Far below, half a dozen men used a noisy conveyor belt to unload plastic-wrapped bales of marijuana from the big yacht and stash them, under bright lights, into a waiting tractor-trailer truck.

Nicki watched long enough to realize that several were fishermen she had seen on MacKay's Wharf. Then she quietly closed the door.

Chuck and Nicki silently looked over the contents of the large loft using the narrow beam from their tiny high-intensity flashlight: several red plastic five-gallon cans of boat gasoline; coils of nylon boat rope; a bench with an assortment of tools. Nicki seized a small metal box and opened it. It held a propane torch and a cigarette lighter. She rammed the lighter into her hip pocket and slipped over to the door to the catwalk. Chuck followed. They knelt, watching the process on the main floor.

Together they surveyed the situation, then slipped back inside.

"Those rafters are . . . ?"

"Sixteen inches apart," Chuck finished Nicki's calculation.

"That truck is right under us," Nicki said.

"Six or seven feet below this loft—a little higher than my head." Chuck observed.

"The truck is about thirteen feet tall, so we're up twenty feet."

"How did you know that?" Chuck whispered hoarsely.

"Ever watch a semi roll under a fourteen-foot overpass?" Nicki grinned. She passed a coil of rope to Chuck. "Tie one end right above the back of the trailer. Slide the rope beneath the next eight rafters—that's just over ten feet—halfway to the floor. Tie a knot, then leave three feet past the knot and cut it off. Tie that end to rafter number eight, and use a slipknot so I can yank it loose with one hand later."

Chuck opened the door and glanced out again. He caught his breath. Were these guys really the ordinary Maine fishermen he'd seen just yesterday in Bois Bay?

The crew carried an assortment of weapons that could intimidate an army: shotguns, AK-47 assault rifles, Glock automatic pistols.

Arnold and el-Haaj sat on bales by themselves, quietly smoking.

On the yacht, a tall, swarthy goateed man in a pricey dark pinstripe suit and deck shoes leaned against the fo'c'sle, arms folded, watching the activity with impassive interest. He wore a heavy gold chain, and large loop earrings twinkled in the glare from both ears.

Powerful halogen lights lit the scene, leaving Chuck and Nicki in darkness, up beyond the glare. *Still, I'm an easy target.* Chuck held his breath and prayed. He slipped onto the bare rafters and began uncoiling the rope as Nicki had directed.

A grim, determined Nicki met Chuck when he stepped back into the supply loft. While he was busy, she had barred the door to the lower-level stairs with a bench. She now carried a five-gallon plastic can of gasoline with the spout and cap removed. Out of it protruded a gasoline-soaked rag. "Molotov cocktail, super-special," she giggled. Nicki toted a short board under her other arm. She scurried onto the rafters, placed the board next to where Chuck had tied the rope, set the gas on it, then scooted back onto the catwalk, quietly waiting.

Somebody's going to get killed, and we have no right, Chuck thought. *Too late to stop her now.*

Someone shut the conveyor off. Chuck froze, startled by the silence.

Nicki remained motionless.

"You wharf rats get on back to the house." It was Golden Boy MacKay, who slipped from behind the truck. The crew moved toward the lower level outside door at once. "Take Arnold and el-Haaj, alias Mr. Contradini, with you. Tie 'em up—I'll deal with them later."

Two Uzi submachine guns pointed, and the safeties clicked off.

Arnold and el-Haaj paled as two of MacKay's fishing crew patted them for weapons. Both were clean, and they were marched out, hands on their heads.

The Turk with the heavy gold jewelry came off the boat with two of his boatmen, hands on their guns. Chuck noticed faces in several portholes. Does Golden Boy see those guys?

Scotty MacKay stood with two guys who had just stepped from the shadows. One man was short, wiry, with cornrowed hair that ended in a row of dreadlocks at the nape of his neck. The other, taller, had a shaved head, and like MacKay, sunglasses. *Uh-oh*, thought Chuck. *Not your down-home Maine coastal fishermen types.*

Guns drawn, the three faced the three Turkish drug runners. "Were those guys friends of yours or something?" MacKay jerked his thumb toward the two being marched off in terror. "No!" he snorted. "You want to get paid, that's all. Show Mr. Alif the money, Squirrel."

The guy with the cornrows let his sawed-off automatic shotgun dangle from a strap. He reached into the truck and withdrew an attaché case. He placed it on the conveyor belt and popped it open. Neat bundles of crisp green photos of Ben Franklin fairly burst from the case.

The bald one stepped back, fingering the trigger on his Uzi.

"Pretty stuff, all that money," sneered Scotty, shaking his blond curls. "But you ain't going to get it, and here's why." He peeled his sunglasses off. His eyes bulged. His voice quaked.

This guy's just bitten off a mite more than he can chew, Chuck considered, watching MacKay.

"Mr. el-Haaj, alias Mr. Contradini, he runs off at the mouth and it smells like a bilge pump on a herring boat," MacKay continued. "He bragged to me in the motel in Belfast that you people have got another deal going. You've brought a missile from Iraq with enough anthrax germs to kill everybody in Chicago. No, I ain't got no friends in Chicago, but I ain't going to be no part of no terrorist plot neither. My old man, Donald MacKay, has been a good citizen all his life, and this town has awarded him with more plaques than anyone else in the history of Bois Bay. I don't have no plans to screw up the good family name—we're loyal, hardworking Americans, Mister Alif!" MacKay then uttered a string of obscenities to emphasize his point.

"Take a good look at this money, Mr. Alif, because that's as close to it as you're going to get tonight. I'll pay you for the next load of Turkish hash, as agreed, *if* you don't bring along no more of Saddam's dirty toys. Now get back onto that boat and buzz back out to your freighter in the Bay of Fundy for another load, or you and your greasy little men will be Turkish rugs in my living room tomorrow morning!"

Alif stroked his goatee.

For the next three minutes Chuck felt like war reporter Ernie Pyle during D-Day at Omaha Beach.

Golden Boy MacKay, Squirrel, the Bald One, and two of Donald MacKay's fishing crew lay dead behind the truck. One Turk toppled headfirst off the deck of the yacht. A red pool bubbled up where he splashed into the water.

Alif hurried toward the still-open attaché case of money.

Nicki had coolly lighted the gasoline-soaked rag in the plastic can during the shootout. She swung, with one hand clutching the rope, into the open door of the marijuana-loaded trailer. She grasped the five-gallon can of gas in the other hand as she flew.

Nicki swung back out, kicking the case of money across the boathouse floor with her bare feet on her backswing. Flames gnawed hungrily into the gas-soaked marijuana, and burning gasoline surged from the truck and across the floor, gobbling up bundles of hundred dollar bills in its wake.

Chuck heaved on the rope with all his might, and he quickly had Nicki back on the catwalk.

Alif ran in terror, leaping into his yacht. His crew had already started the motor, and the boat surged toward the open sea, taking the boathouse's fiberglass overhead door with it.

Three of the fishermen rushed in from the yard. They shot their automatic weapons at the boat through the fire and smoke until their clips were spent, then ran for their lives as the flames spread.

Chuck and Nicki, outside by now, watched from the shadows as Arnold and el-Haaj ran for their vehicles. Burning rubber with both the car and the truck, the pair tore off toward the highway. They ripped the gate to Ashcroft Lane off its hinges with the rented Buick.

"I'd have been grilled like a steak, Chuck, if we hadn't got soaked through with salt water before we went in." Nicki was panting as they dived into the Dodge minutes later.

Chuck, out of breath, only shook his head. A Bois Bay fire truck, lights and sirens going full blast, turned into Ashcroft Lane just then. Two Samoset County sheriff deputies raced behind. "This road . . . ," Chuck panted, "this road leads across the peninsula. Unless you want to stick around to watch the credits roll by, I vote we take the other shore and skip the rest of the show."

◖◖◖

"We've still got a job ahead of us, Chuck," Nicki said. The lights of the city of Bois Bay glowed ahead, and the first traffic light on the south side of town turned red. "I can hear el-Haaj screaming away in Arabic. I think he's talking to someone on that yacht."

"You never lose your focus, do you Nicki? That's what I like about you."

"Chuck, that missile is still on the yacht."

"I'd guess the U.S. Coast Guard will pick them up within the hour. The police have called them by now, I'm sure."

"And I'd guess that Alif, that Turkish marijuana shipper, has also figured that out. Besides, the yacht may have gotten out to sea without the sheriff seeing it. With that burning gasoline, it may be hours before the firemen find the bodies and realize that a crime has been committed. Alif will be safely in international waters and aboard his freighter in the Bay of Fundy by then."

"Let's hope they're not looking for an arsonist, as well. Whew!"

"Shhh! They've switched to English!" Nicki listened in silence for some moments as Chuck drove north, following the signal from the Buick. "Chuck! They're . . . they're putting the missile into a motorboat, along with two Iraqis they brought with it."

"I imagine that Turk fears Saddam as much as he does the U.S. Coast Guard. But he'll still be incriminated if the Coast Guard intercepts the motorboat with the missile."

"Smith Brothers Point, Chuck—el-Haaj has told the guys in the motorboat to meet him there. Where is that?"

"Just up the coast. It's another old, nineteenth-century estate. Deserted, except in the summer. Let's tip the state police off."

"In person?" Nicki examined her face in the mirror on the back of her sun visor. "They're looking for an arsonist, you know. As for phoning them, we know by now that we're considered a couple of paranoid nuts."

"Then let's head for Smith Point and see what we can figure out when we get there."

"And let's clean up." Nicki fished a can of baby wipes from the glove compartment. She began to work on Chuck's face with the tissues as he drove.

Chuck hit the brakes as blue lights flashed across the road ahead. "State Police. That receiver of yours got a police radio band?"

Nicki changed frequencies. "Maine State Police and Samoset County Sheriff talking . . . they've found the bodies in the Ashcroft boathouse . . . firemen saw three guys go over the back fence." Nicki dropped the radio and grabbed two shirts from Chuck's duffel bag in the backseat. "Don't look. I can't let the cops see me all wet!" She tossed one at Chuck. "Hide your wet shirt under your seat!"

In the excitement, Chuck had forgotten he was wet. He peeled his shirt off and changed, keeping an eye on the police.

Moments later, a uniformed officer peered out under his Smokey Bear hat, then lit the Dodge's backseat with his three-cell. "You folks seen any hitchhikers?" A second cop fingered the trigger of his automatic shotgun. A third stood by the passenger door with a drawn 9-millimeter Glock pistol.

"No, officer." *If I tell him about the missile, we'll be detained for questioning while the terrorists escape.* This thought haunted Chuck's mind.

"Pop your trunk, please."

Chuck opened the glove compartment and punched a button.

Two troopers quickly checked the trunk while the third remained by Nicki's door. "You travel light," remarked the cop with the flashlight, stepping back to the window.

"My bags were stolen," Nicki said truthfully, not troubling the policeman with the tale of how she had lost them to Saddam's military.

"Have a nice trip."

"Thanks." Chuck stepped on the gas.

"Chuck, we've lost them! They must've gone through before the police set up the roadblock."

"We'll catch them here." Chuck turned onto the road to Smith Brothers Point.

❰❰❰

Behind the deserted Smith Brothers mansion, Chuck and Nicki found a twenty-foot open aluminum boat with Nova Scotia registration painted on the bow. "Big enough for two guys and a small missile to come ashore from that yacht," Chuck observed. "Nicki?"

Nicki had scurried up onto the back porch, where she fiddled with the receiving set, trying to attach some wires hanging from the roof of the crumbling, four-story mansion.

Chuck peered upward, where moonlight glistened in the frost on an old TV antenna, tilted crazily from the ridge.

"I've got 'em, Chuck!" Nicki squealed. "They're heading for . . . for Bangor . . . returning the Buick . . . Avis."

"Bangor International Airport. That'd be the only Avis agency in Bangor," Chuck filled in.

"There's more," Nicki added. "Something about Vermont . . . crossing the lake at Burlington."

"There's a ferry across Lake Champlain. After a drive through Adirondack State Park, you can pick up the New York Thruway— it's Interstate 80 and 90, right into Chicago. Let's go!"

"This lady does not travel in wet clothes."

"But . . ."

"I left a small bag of laundry in the trunk. Dirty, but there's a pair of dry jeans." Nicki and Chuck raced for the car.

"I'll change out back." Chuck grabbed his duffel bag and bolted off.

❮❮❮

"We can take State Road 69 from Winterport and wait for them along Interstate 95 in Carmel. Catch them coming out of Bangor traveling west," Chuck explained. He had visited Maine many times since Mae and Stan moved north with Jennifer, and he knew his way around.

"Yeah? Without that tracking device, we'll lose them before we get into New Hampshire. Sight tailing is tough—impossible without being spotted after a few miles."

"But the transmitter is on the Buick. All four of them are going to Chicago in that supercab Ford pickup, you said." He shook his head. "All right, we'll drive to Bangor and grab that transmitter, if that's what you want." Chuck bore down on the gas.

Nicki braced herself as Chuck made the Dodge's tires weep on a fast corner. "Our pals up ahead—they're driving the speed limit. Not a bit over," Nicki observed.

"Like maybe I should slow down?"

"No, no. But since the guys we're tailing can't risk getting hauled over, we're sure to gain on them."

"I hope you're right." Chuck fought the wheel for another fast bend in U.S. 1-A, the river road to Bangor. "So we grab the transmitter before Avis finds it? Then what?"

"We gas up and head for Burlington, Vermont. We'll catch them waiting for the ferry. I can attach the transmitter on the boat. Then we'll have them."

"Suppose they beat us to Burlington?"

"It's our only chance. We have no way of finding them otherwise."

◖◖◖

"There they go!" Chuck clenched his teeth and squealed the tires as he wheeled the Dodge Intrepid into the rental car section of Bangor International Airport. He had spotted the big red Ford pickup exiting beneath a street light. Chuck fought the urge to make a U-turn.

"There's the Buick!" Nicki pointed to a new Park Avenue with a missing grille and a mangled fender in the untended, late-night Avis lot. "Give me a minute." She grabbed the pliers and screwdriver and flew out the door.

"Now let's gas up," she said seconds later. Nicki held up the transmitter-audio bug, grinning. "This little pup's gonna help us again!"

"There's an all-night truck stop on the west side—Dysart's."

"Great! You pump gas, and I'll pick up some snacks for breakfast."

"Granola bars again, I'm sure," Chuck grumbled.

"Nutritious and delicious." Nicki snickered.

"Nutritious, I'll grant. The stuff *tastes* like sweetened cattle feed and glue."

"Look!" It was moments later, and Chuck was turning into Dysart's. "There they are!" The red pickup stood at a gas island, empty of passengers. "What luck!" Nicki grabbed the tools and transmitter and opened the door.

"Whoa, kid!" Chuck grabbed Nicki's arm.

"Ouch!"

He hauled her back across the seat and wrapped his arms around her. "Don't try it, Nicki. They could come out any moment."

"You're right. I guess I'm overtired. You hurt my shoulder." Nicki winced, rubbing her muscles.

"I'm sorry."

"Not your fault. I pulled a muscle when I swung on that rope and slung that gas can into the truck. But you called me 'kid.'"

"Sorry. I didn't mean to put you down."

"I kinda like that." Nicki laughed. "Reminds me of *Casablanca*."

"'Here's looking at you, kid,'" Chuck growled. "I need a fedora," he laughed.

"You couldn't look like Harrison Ford, no matter how hard you tried."

"Sorry. I meant Humphrey Bogart. He wore a fedora too."

"There they go." Nicki nodded toward where four men climbed into the heavy pickup at the gas island.

"Our turn to buy gas." As Chuck drove to the pump, he shot a worried look at the Ford truck just disappearing onto the westbound expressway.

◖◖◖

"I can drive once we cross Lake Champlain," Nicki offered. She was pinning her long black hair into a bun as they waited for a light in Burlington. "We'll both get a nap during the crossing."

"Oh, sure," Chuck yawned. He imagined waking up to find himself staring down a gun barrel at Arnold or el-Haaj.

"I doubt they'll recognize us," Nicki continued. She snatched Chuck's baseball cap from his head and jammed it on hers, then reached for her sunglasses on the dash.

"Hey!"

"You don't need it. Sun's behind us. While we're on the ferry, you just lie on the seat and sleep, like I said."

"OK. But what if those guys stay in their vehicle?"

"All the better," Nicki concluded. "I'll be underneath, so there's less danger of surprise. They've been up all night too, remember?"

"You sound chipper enough."

"I've been napping since New Hampshire."

Chuck's heart sank as they rolled down the steep street toward the ferry dock. The ferry was full. Already cars had begun to line up for the next boat, which he could see in the distance. "There goes that," he said.

"At least we know where they are—far side of the boat on the right. Drive me right up to the boat ramp, Chuck!"

Chuck passed the line of cars and braked to a stop.

Nicki piled out. She hurried up the incline and confronted a boatman, about to raise the auto ramp. "Got room for a walk-on?" she asked pertly.

"Ticket, ma'am?"

Nicki waved a twenty-dollar bill at the man. "Can you hold the boat while I buy one?" She nodded toward the ticket booth.

"Get on board. I'll take your money and buy the ticket when we return." The man sounded exasperated.

"Thanks. Keep the change." Nicki crammed the cash into his hands and scurried onto the boat.

I may never see her alive again. Chuck had had this thought several times before. But today, as he watched Nicki disappear among the cars and crowd on the cross-lake ferry, he realized that something far more powerful than merely his masculine protectiveness had kicked into gear. *I need that little lady,* his heart cried out. *I cannot live without her.*

Chuck put the headphones on and turned the radio to the transmitter's frequency as the ferry moved out toward New York State. He could hear heavy breathing, then Nicki's whispers. "Access plug here . . . good . . . poke this thing inside . . . got it . . . now seal the hole with some goop."

Nicki's voice faded, and the snoring of four tired terrorists replaced her whispered soliloquy.

Chuck prayed. He had not prayed more fervently since his Shelly had lain in the pallor of near-death, gasping her final breaths as he watched God take her to himself.

Finally Chuck fell asleep. Half an hour later he awakened with a start as the driver behind honked for him to drive aboard the next ferry crossing Lake Champlain.

❰❰❰

Chuck munched an apple and listened to Moody Radio's "Night Sounds" to stay awake as he jockeyed with eighteen-wheelers on the Ohio Turnpike. The knot in his stomach increased with each milepost as the Dodge ate up the distance westward to Chicago. He was thankful, though, that he had found Nicki grinning and waiting on the New York side of the lake.

"Chuck, they're talking again." Nicki stirred from her slumber. Though she had the headphones on, he'd let her sleep undisturbed. By two A.M., he knew, no amount of apples and peanuts could keep his eyes open. "Chuck?"

"Yeah?"

"Here—you listen." Nicki pressed a headphone to Chuck's ear. "Something about Michigan." She frowned.

Chuck held up a hand. "Shhhh! Good deal!" Chuck exclaimed after a moment. "I know that place!"

"You do? Where is it?"

"Hoffmann State Park, in Sacajawea County. Shelly and I went there for our honeymoon, more than twenty years ago. Actually, we spent most of it at Maranatha Bible Conference next door."

"But I distinctly heard them say 'Garfield City.'"

"Garfield City is the county seat, and it includes most of the county. Hoffmann Park's mailing address is Garfield City. It's one of those rural enclaves left natural in an urban area. I'm sure the park closes during fall and winter, so the place will virtually be deserted. Best beach in America, outside of California."

"From there it's . . ."

"A little more than a hundred miles to Chicago, as the crow flies."

"Chuck, they'll have a straight shot for their missile southeast—right across the lake. Those poor people!"

Chuck took the headset and pressed it harder to his ear. Realizing that the transmission was fading, he added 5 mph to his speed and reset the cruise control. "I'm hearing them better, now," he said after awhile.

"What are they saying?"

"Chit-chat, mostly. Guy talk. Wait . . ." He held up a hand. "Tomorrow night . . . midnight. Arnold is bragging that he's checked things out and found a service road where they can get the pickup onto the beach at night without being bothered by park rangers."

"We'll be there for the party." Nicki sat up. "Chuck, can we buy guns? Try a citizen's arrest, maybe?"

"I don't know any back-alley, black-market dealers in Garfield City, Nicki. With my Canadian driver's license, and you with no American identification either, nobody's going to sell us guns legally."

"Then we'll fight 'em with our fists!" Nicki, the resourceful, had run out of tricks.

"Yeah, right. We stroll right up and say, 'Nice night, guys. We were just wondering—you aren't going to fire that nasty ol' missile at Chicago, are you, you naughty boys?'"

"Chuck!"

"Nicki, I'm sorry. I guess right now is not a good time for my lame jokes. Say, I haven't seen that cell phone you got from CALF since you unwrapped it."

"It's here." She opened the glove compartment and pulled out the phone.

"Please punch in (703)-555-2397."

"Sure." Nicki dialed. "Who am I waking up?"

"General MacAdams."

"I told you I thought he'd help. It may take some arm twisting, though."

"You do realize this blows our cover?" Chuck noted, waiting for Armstrong MacAdams to answer.

"We may die. But we'll save Chicago in the process," Nicki spat out.

"General MacAdams. Chuck Reynolds here."

The general was as affable and garrulous as usual.

Chuck pled his case. He listened for a moment, then punched the off button. "MacAdams says it's all a hoax. That we've been misinformed, and that we're in the middle of a U.S. Air Force test of national security."

"Liar!" Nicki grabbed the phone and punched the redial button.

"MacAdams," grumbled the general.

"Nicki Towns calling."

"Towns. I've heard of you from somewhere."

"You bet your moth-eaten hide you have. Listen carefully, General, because if you don't, sir, the FBI will be ringing your doorbell before you can get your slippers on! My CALF operatives have more on you than J. Edgar Hoover had on the Rosenbergs."

Nicki listened for a moment. "Chicago can go where?" she asked. "You're looking at the rest of your natural life in a military prison, sir!"

She listened some more. "Excuse me, sir, that neutron bomb test at White Sands. August 17, two-fifteen in the afternoon. The Russians got their information from you—we know that, because we monitor your faxes, and we've broken your code—we have the best computer hacker in the country working for us! Want to hear more?"

Nicki listened a bit longer. "He's promised to phone the Pentagon right now, Chuck," she said quietly, hanging up.

"Does he think they'll believe him?"

"With the data you already gave him, he can make a pretty convincing case. I'm sure the Pentagon doesn't think *he's* a nutcase."

❴❴❴

"C'mon, Chuck. It's 9:30." Nicki rapped on Chuck's door at Sacajawea Holiday Inn, which fronted Lake Michigan in downtown Garfield City. "We've got to get out to Hoffmann State Park."

"Coming. Do you have the black grease paint?"

"I've got it. I hope you can find this Motorcycle Hill, over-looking Hoffmann Beach."

"We found it in the daylight all right. I'm sure it hasn't moved." Chuck knew they'd have no trouble locating the big sand dune where they planned to watch the terrorists set up their rocket. But he was less certain how things might turn out. No one in any official capacity seemed willing to believe his report about the anthrax-tipped missile about to be shot at Chicago.

❧ ❧ ❧

Half an hour later Chuck and Nicki were unpacking their small bag of surveillance tools on top of Motorcycle Hill, a sand dune used for trail bike races several times each summer. Chuck and Nicki had agreed that their last, best recourse was to use their cell phone. They would make as many phone calls to law enforcement agencies as possible, using whatever ruse might send the police, National Guard, FBI—whoever—out to storm the beach.

FBI. Chuck groaned inwardly at the shoddy treatment he'd received from the federal government's premier law-enforcement agency. He recalled his days as head of the North Carolina Bureau of Investigation, when relations with the Raleigh office of the FBI had been on a friendly, first-name basis.

"Charlie Yeaton," Chuck said aloud. "Nicki, when I was head of the North Carolina State Bureau of Investigation, I used to work with the Raleigh FBI district office. Their chief was a guy named Yeaton. I think I remember his home phone number." Chuck snatched up the cell phone and began dialing. "Charlie, it's Chuck—Chuck Reynolds," he said seconds later.

"How y'all doin'? Ain't heard from you since y' moved to Yankee-land." Charlie, a Piedmont hill-country farm boy like Chuck, was known in the Bureau for his Southern bias.

"I haven't forgotten my roots, Charlie." Chuck fought his fears, trying to be warm and cordial until he got Charlie's attention.

"Right now I'm watching three Iraqis and an American get ready to bomb Chicago with an anthrax-tipped guided missile."

"I reckon we could do without Chicago. Washington too. Don't tell my boss that, though," Charlie laughed.

"Charlie, this is serious stuff!" Chuck had become insistent, impatient.

"Say, Chuck, we had a funny one happen here'n Raleigh last week."

"Yes?" Chuck glanced at his watch, then peered at the terrorists through the monocular. *I'll let Charlie tell his yarn. Then maybe he'll shut up and listen.*

"Two reporters from the Winston-Salem *Journal*—you use t' live in Winston, didn't y'?"

"Yes. Go on."

"They come t' Raleigh to visit the legislature, and they ate at Big John's Roadhouse, out on U.S. Highway One. Ordered the $6.95 fish platter. Couldn't eat it all. But the menu had this $10.95 fish platter too. So when they paid, they ast Big John, 'What's the difference?' Ol' John says with a straight face, 'They're both the same, boys. The $10.95 one is for rich Yankee tourists headin' for Florida, who don't know no better.' Ain't that a gas?"

Chuck chuckled. "Charlie, we've got a *serious* problem, and I'm having trouble getting help from the FBI. I'm sitting on top of Motorcycle Hill, a big sand dune in Sacajawea County, Michigan. And I'm watching a terrorist attack about to occur against an American city—it could cost millions of lives." Chuck continued with a summary of what he and Nicki had seen and heard over the past three weeks.

"So *you* sent those anonymous crank faxes from Montreal? Hey, buddy, right now the Bureau is looking for you—though not with the kind of help you've requested. My advice: stay off the phone and find a shrink. My wife and I are watching the old King Kong movie on AMC tonight. They've just got to the part where the big gorilla tries to use the Empire State Building for a pogo stick. Bye."

"So much for that." Chuck raised his arm as if to throw the phone toward the party on the beach. Then he changed his mind and punched 9-1-1.

"Chuck, they've got company!"

Chuck hit the off button. In the moonlight he could see that two figures had joined the terrorists. One of the terrorists was bent over, petting a small dog.

"Girls," said Nicki. "Not over fifteen—I can see their faces." She passed Chuck the monocular.

"Two of them. Younger than Jennifer. Came from that campfire, probably. Ran off from their boyfriends." He jerked his thumb toward a flickering glow about a mile south toward Grand Haven.

"Chuck, they're going to kill them!" Nicki leaped up. "One guy's got his gun out!"

Chuck turned the monocular on a man holding an assault rifle. The guy yanked the clip out, then racked the bolt back. "He's unloading the gun, Nicki."

"He's handed it to one of the girls!" Nicki exclaimed.

The girls passed the deadly weapon back and forth, pretending to shoot each other and the terrorists with it. The Iraqis seemed to be laughing.

"Chuck, they'll . . ."

"Rape them? No. Those guys have something bigger on their minds: murder. Not the girls, though," he quickly added, pointing toward the glow of the Chicago night lights from the southwest.

The girls passed the gun back and pulled their hooded sweatshirts up against the biting October chill off the lake. They took their dog and began to stroll in the direction of the campfire.

The Iraqi with the assault rifle snapped the long banana clip back into place. He jacked a cartridge into the chamber and aimed at the retreating teens.

"Chuck!" Nicki hid her face in Chuck's jacket.

Chuck held his breath. Then he spoke. "That guy won't risk the noise."

The Iraqi stood the gun against the truck, unfired. He lit a cigarette as his companions doubled over, shaking in merriment.

"Guys are the same the world over," Chuck observed.

"And so are girls," Nicki noticed.

"I wonder where their parents are?" Chuck said. He redialed
9-1-1.

"Central dispatch. You're on a cell phone, so identify yourself,
please."

"This is Chuck Reynolds."

"Address and phone number?"

"I'm standing on top of Motorcycle Hill Climb, just outside
Hoffmann State Park."

"Sir, we've got to have a location if we're going to send aid."

"Ma'am, you have it. We're at Motorcycle Hill watching four
armed and very dangerous men on Hoffmann Beach. They're getting ready to . . ."

"How are they dressed? Approximate ages? Black? White?
Hispanic?"

"Iraqis. They have a guided missile."

"Sir, there's a five-thousand-dollar fine and a two-year jail
term for filing a false police report." Chuck punched the off button.

"Chuck, I'm going down there."

"No. I'm sure you could get as close as those teens. Maybe
even kill one or two of them before the others made a pincushion
out of you. I won't allow you to go. Besides . . . here, give General
MacAdams another shot. He seemed to listen to you."

Nicki took the phone and dialed the general. They talked for
some moments. This time Nicki made no threats. "Chuck," she said
at last, "MacAdams says he's got the Pentagon brass to listen to
him. Admiral Keefhawver—some such name . . ." Nicki stopped
midsentence and stared at the big lake that stretched before them.
Beyond this water, the horizon glowed with city lights all along
southern Lake Michigan, and the lights stretched northward along
the western shore to directly opposite where they stood. One of the
world's great megalopolises was spread along this vast waterway

from Indiana and Illinois far into Wisconsin. "Do you suppose the Navy . . . ?"

"I don't suppose anything." Chuck shook his head and dialed directory assistance. "I've got the direct line to the Sacajawea County Sheriff Department," he said moments later. "Sheriff?"

"This is an emergency line."

"This is an emergency, sir."

"Shoot."

"Four men with guns are on Hoffmann Beach with a pickup truck. They've got some sort of big rocket. Looks like they're getting ready to fire it across the lake."

"What kind of guns?"

"Long guns."

"Hunting in Hoffmann is illegal, day or night. But that's the responsibility of the Department of Natural Resources. I'll give you the DNR's number."

"Sheriff, these guys are *not* 'coon hunters with shotguns. They're carrying assault rifles. They have a rocket mounted in the back of their truck. Looks like the mother of all illegal fireworks." Chuck restrained himself from saying "international terrorists with a guided missile."

"Teens?"

"Adults. White males. They have a Ford pickup on the beach."

"Can't get a vehicle out onto that beach, far's I know."

"Sheriff, they used the service road behind the Hoffmann Nature Center—cut the chain off."

"Where are you that you know all this?"

"I'm on top of Motorcycle Hill with a cell phone."

"I know you're calling on a cell phone!" the sheriff snapped. "We'll send a car out to investigate."

"Thank you," Chuck said to a dead phone.

"They're getting ready, Chuck." Nicki pointed to the Ford pickup. Its topper, on hinges, had been folded open, and two Iraqis were busily raising the missile, angling it to arc across the lake toward Chicago.

"Lord," Chuck prayed aloud, "there are more than fifty right-eous in that city. I know I'm not Abraham, but Chicago is not Sodom." He turned to Nicki. "Please scan the police frequencies on your receiver. See if the sheriff's department is sending a car this way." Chuck fought to control his trembling voice.

Nicki began at once to listen in on local police chatter. "They're on their way, Chuck. Wait. I just heard a deputy dialing on a cell phone. He was mumbling the numbers as he dialed."

"Incredible—his radio mike was still on? Let's have it."

"785-9257."

From atop the big sand dune, Chuck watched traffic on Lake Michigan Drive. A brown Sacajawea County Sheriff Patrol car stopped at the Hoffmann Park's locked gate. Chuck turned the monocular on the vehicle: car number 57. He punched 785-9257 on his cell phone's keypad. *Worth a try.* Chuck fought his panic.

"Car 57. Buursma here."

"Deputy Buursma, the service entrance next to the Hoffmann Nature Center is open. Road goes to the beach. Four men with a red Ford pickup. Out-of-state plates. They are carrying assault rifles."

"Who is this?!"

"Never mind. Just do it! They will shoot to kill!" Chuck punched the off button.

"Chuck, they're going to fire the missile!" Nicki had the monocular now, trained on the rocket. She passed it back to Chuck.

The terrorists had scattered into the dunes behind the beach. "I imagine that sucker'll put out a lot of flame when it blasts off. They must have set a timer," Chuck said.

"More likely they have a remote control," said Nicki, calm now.

They both turned their attention to the sheriff patrol. The car had turned into the service road, and it tore off toward the beach with the headlights on and light bar flashing red-and-blue. "They're driving right into an ambush!" Chuck cried.

Flashes of submachine gunfire burst from the sand dunes. Two deputies rolled into opposite ditches from the moving patrol car. One returned fire.

"Are you getting any police transmission on that radio, Nicki?"

"Buursma is calling for backup. Says he's pinned down by automatic weapon fire."

"They'll believe him, at least—too late!"

"'Too late.' You're right, Chuck," Nicki echoed.

Both stared in horror as the anthrax-warhead missile rose from its launching pad on the pickup truck bed. It carried enough deadly payload to sicken—perhaps even to kill—every man, woman, and child in Chicago, Wheaton, Schaumburg, Des Plaines, Cicero, Oak Park, Skokie, and Highland Park. Six million human beings—Assyrians, Jews, Poles, Italians, African Americans, Hispanics, Irish, Anglo-Saxon, Dutch, Swedes, Germans—could be wiped out by an infectious disease in far less time than it had taken Hitler's holocaust.

There was nothing they or anybody else could do. Trailing flame, the missile bore southwest beneath a red October moon, racing toward the vast complex of cities along the big lake.

Chuck and Nicki lay facedown, covering their faces with their arms from the heat and flash of the takeoff blast from the pickup truck just below Motorcycle Hill. The searing wave passed, and they sat up.

Nicki suddenly grabbed Chuck. "Chuck!" She pointed to a bolt of fire breaking the watery surface far out on the lake. Trailing foam into the clear night, this second rocket, a SAM/Surface to Air Missile, streaked away in pursuit of the first.

The sky lit so brilliantly as the SAM destroyed Saddam's missile that, even though the explosion was miles out over the lake, Chuck and Nicki could clearly see the markings on the conning tower of the sleek, nuclear-powered attack submarine as it surfaced a mile or more off shore. It was the U.S.S. *Centurion*, SSN-27. The great, gray torpedo shape rose only enough so that Chuck and Nicki saw the sea monster's massive length silhouetted against the horizon. Then it dived and was gone.

Now that their eyes had refocused from the second blinding glare, they plainly saw a mushroom cloud miles above Lake

Michigan. It climbed up, up, up in the moonlight, spreading broadly before it began to drift apart.

"I'm sure that atomic blast cooked the anthrax," Chuck observed, gathering his wits. "But what will the atomic fallout do to Garfield City?"

"My guess is, it was another neutron blast, Chuck. Deadly close up but relatively harmless at that distance."

"And the *Centurion*—that big shark is not due out of dry dock in Groton, Connecticut, until 2005!" Chuck shuddered, recalling the merciless brainwashing Zeke Lewis had endured in 1947 for learning too much too soon about the so-called Roswell flying saucer.

Gunfire erupted again on the service road leading to the beach as two brown sheriff patrol cars squealed to a stop beside the first.

"We've got company, Chuck." Nicki pointed to a blue Michigan State Police cruiser, with flashers going, next to Chuck's Dodge Intrepid at the base of Motorcycle Hill. One trooper focused binoculars on the disintegrating atomic mushroom as the other peered into the Dodge with a flashlight. "Time to turn ourselves in." Nicki rose and began to stroll toward the stairs leading down the dune to the parking lot.

Chuck grabbed her arm. "Get down before you're seen! The Lord has something better for you than going to jail for helping save Chicago. Slip down to the beach." He glanced toward the Ford pickup. Three deputies had two terrorists in handcuffs. The other two, apparently, were dead, as well as one deputy. "As soon as it's clear, walk north. In under a mile you'll find yourself on the beach at Maranatha Bible Conference Center. According to the morning edition of the Garfield City *Chronicle*, they're having a week-long ladies' fall conference with some of the nation's top speakers on the platform."

"So I'll just sack out in a pew until breakfast, then register as a delegate."

"You got it! From Sheepscot Valley Community Church, Freedom, Maine," Chuck said. "I'll pick you up there—if I get out before you," he added ominously.

"What's the theme of the conference?"

"How to treat a husband." Chuck knelt, peering into her soft eyes.

Nicki grabbed Chuck's face and kissed him squarely on the mouth. Then she crawled into the underbrush and began to scurry toward the expanse of sand, where white-capped breakers rolled in and a fresh breeze lifted her spirits.

17

The Eagle Soars

The eagle mount[s] up . . .
And make[s] its nest on . . . the rock . . .
From there it spies out the prey; . . .
Its young ones suck up blood. . . .

—The LORD

Evening, officers." Chuck stood at the base of Motorcycle Hill, his hands away from his body, palms outward.

"Stay where you are," shouted a Michigan state trooper, who, with his partner, leaned across the hood of his car. Both cops had their 9-millimeter semiautomatic Glocks aimed at Chuck. "Put your hands behind your head. Lie facedown. *DO IT NOW!*"

Chuck obeyed.

Heavy footsteps crunched toward him, then stopped. "Careful, Jack," one cop said. "Some of these loonies carry grenades. They'll blow themselves up just to kill an American. Happened in Beirut when I was in the Marines."

"I *am* an American. I've been in the army, in Vietnam," Chuck protested.

The officers looked him over in the beams of their three-cell flashlights for some moments. The crunching footsteps began again. Chuck felt a searing pain in his left hip. "Roll over, cop-killer!"

Chuck rolled over, only to have sand kicked into his face. The officer drew back his foot for a third kick.

"Don't do it, Jack!" warned the older state trooper. "If you leave bruises, he'll find an ACLU lawyer. The Department will hang you out to dry, and you'll be looking at the next thirty years doing a minimum-wage security guard job."

"Maybe if this gun were to accidentally . . ." Chuck felt the cold muzzle of a pistol at the back of his head.

"That's enough, Jack!" The senior officer snapped his cuffs on Chuck.

"Deputy MacIntyre didn't even get a warning when these thugs shot him, Joe." Trooper Jack cursed.

"I'm a cop too," Chuck protested. "I didn't shoot anybody. I'm the guy who called you people."

"Got any ID?" Joe's voice softened.

"I've got a driver's license. My deputy ID is in my desk drawer," Chuck said truthfully. As chief of security for Salem Electronics, Chuck had been given deputy status for legal purposes by the Essex County, Massachusetts, Sheriff's Department.

Joe fished Chuck's wallet out. He briefly examined the contents. "Says here your residence is Montreal, Canada. I suppose you'll say you're a member of the Royal Canadian Mounted Police, and that's your horse." Joe's voice had its edge again. He briefly spotted the plate on Chuck's Dodge. "Quebec plates on y' car, Mr. Charles Robert Reynolds. Whatta y' gotta say t' that?"

"Let's go to the station," Chuck said calmly.

Sgt. Jack and Lt. Joe grabbed Chuck's arms and yanked him to his feet. Jack reached out to frisk Chuck's bulging pockets.

"Careful, Jack," Joe advised.

"No grenades," said Chuck.

"Shut up!" Jack snarled.

"Let him talk, Jack. What's in your pockets, Reynolds?"

"Cell phone, right hip; night vision monocular, pocketknife, nail clipper, comb, left front; small radio, right front."

Jack stood back while Joe played the light over Chuck's pockets. "No grenades," he concluded with a tone that said, "Too bad. I'd like to see this guy blow himself up."

Jack laid the contents of Chuck's pockets on the hood of the highway patrol cruiser. "This here's a police-band scanner." Jack brandished the receiver with which Chuck and Nicki had followed the terrorists from Maine to Michigan. Chuck knew of course that it would also pick up police-band radio. "This all adds up to one thing," Sgt. Jack concluded. "You're the spotter for that bunch of killers on the beach!"

Lt. Joe read Chuck his Miranda rights. Joe then held the door while young, muscular Sgt. Jack tossed Chuck face-first into the backseat of the big Ford Crown Victoria highway patrol cruiser.

⟨⟨⟨

"Quite a catalog of crimes you boys are being charged with." Sheriff Mike Veenstra glowered at Chuck and the two young Iraqis. The three were chained to the wall of the holding room. Chuck had figured out by then that Jack Arnold and Elias el-Haaj, alias Larry Contradini, had been killed in the shoot-out in the Hoffmann dunes. "When the prosecutor gets done examining the evidence in the morning, there'll be more charges, I imagine," Veenstra continued.

"Can we hear your list, Sheriff?" Chuck asked.

"Might as well. We've given a copy to the press. 'Capital murder of a law-enforcement officer.' You guys are going to get to test Michigan's new cop-killer death penalty—you'll be the first," Veenstra sneered. "'Detonation of an illegal explosive'—quite a bang, lit up the whole county; 'contamination of a public waterway; illegal trespassing on restricted property; attempted murder of law-enforcement officers; illegal discharge of firearms in a public place;

possession of automatic weapons without a permit; illegal possession of weapons by an alien; illegal entry to the United States; grand theft, auto.' And except for you, Reynolds, 'fleeing and resisting arrest.'"

"That's nice of you not to include me in that charge," said Chuck. "As I'm sure you know, I'm the guy who called in the report about these Iraqis." He nodded toward the other two.

"Iraqis—Saddam's boys, eh? How would you know, Reynolds?"

One of "Saddam's boys" began to squirm and grimace, chattering excitedly.

"Translate for us, Reynolds."

"I don't speak Arabic." *These guys can also speak French,* Chuck told himself. *If the sheriff knew that, he probably could find an interpreter easily enough. I guess I'd be smart not to let on where I've seen these guys before.* "That's universal language," Chuck said aloud. "He needs to use the bathroom."

Veenstra laughed. So did the young deputy at the desk. "Take him potty," chortled Veenstra, nodding at the deputy, "or you'll have to clean him up later."

〢〢〢

The Iraqis both carried American Social Security Cards, and drivers' licenses with New York addresses and Anglo-Saxon sounding names. But it was apparent to savvy Sheriff Veenstra that, except for the photos, the ID papers didn't go with the persons.

Chuck had several more reasons than the sheriff not to trust "Saddam's boys," though he decided to keep his reasons to himself. He propped himself up on his bunk in the Sacajawea County Jail, resting his head against the bare, cheap sponge pillow his jailers had provided. One of Saddam's boys was asleep. The other was busy unraveling threads from his heavy, hand-woven, camel's-hair-and-wool shirt. Chuck guessed he was braiding a cord. *Probably I'll need to keep him from hanging himself,* Chuck considered. *I doubt if his pal cares right now.*

Chuck dozed off. He awoke and froze, motionless. A dark presence stood before him. He opened his eyes a slit in the half-lighted cell.

It was the wiry young Iraqi who had been unravelling the shirt, and he held a cord looped into a noose.

Chuck silently waited. *I hope this guy's an amateur,* he thought. Chuck had heard that some of Saddam's Republican Guard were highly skilled professional assassins.

The Iraqi with the loop stretched out his arms and leaned toward Chuck. Chuck could see the guy's muscles tense in preparation for a garroting motion.

Chuck still waited.

The man moved in for the kill.

Chuck clasped his hands as if in prayer. He swung up hard, using both fists. He caught his assassin squarely beneath the jaw. Chuck felt sick as the Iraqi's jawbones snapped and the young man collapsed in a heap on the floor.

"He tried to strangle me." Chuck pointed to the braided cord that the Iraqi had dropped as two guards rushed in, guns drawn.

"You do this with your bare hands? You got a deadly weapons permit for those meat-paws of yours, mister?" screamed the guard, a tall, big-boned female of about thirty.

"Self-defense," said Chuck.

"Turn around!"

Chuck did as he was told.

She cuffed him and marched him back to the holding room, chaining him to the wall. "You spend the rest of the night here. No bathroom privileges."

Chuck decided he'd prefer peeing his pants to being locked up with the other Iraqi.

((((

"You get five minutes in the bathroom and a bowl of Cheerios. Arraignment's at nine o'clock." Sheriff Veenstra sat on the edge of the desk in the holding room, buzzing at his beard with an electric shaver. "Because of you guys, I didn't get much sleep last night," he complained. "Then you broke that guy's jaw, so he can't even answer his charges."

"No problem," said Chuck. "He doesn't understand English, so it won't make any difference."

"We got a translator, though. Missions teacher from the Baptist college in Grand Rapids. She speaks Arabic." Veenstra shook his head. "I guess I just don't understand missionaries. If people want to worship Mohammed, let 'em worship Mohammed."

"Would it surprise you to learn that Muslims do not worship Mohammed?"

"No-o-o-o-o-o?!"

Chuck decided this information was wasted on the sheriff.

"Who do you worship?"

"I worship Jesus Christ, who died for my sins."

"Thought you said you're a Muslim? Oh—you don't speak Arabic." Veenstra shrugged. "Right now we've got more important matters—the media!"

"Media?"

"Five TV sound trucks and at least a hundred reporters out there. Something about those Iraqis having a nuclear warhead that exploded over Lake Michigan."

Chuck smiled. Then he frowned. "The news media believe that?"

The sheriff suddenly found himself too busy to answer. Two men in black suits burst through the door, each displaying a leather folder with an ID card. "U.S. Marshals Dan Spearrin and Del Stratton," the first one spat out. "We have a warrant for federal custody of two Iraqi aliens in your jail, Sheriff."

"Now just you wait a minute."

The marshal unfolded the documents. He pointed to the signature of United States Attorney General Leigh Franks.

Sheriff Veenstra shrugged and reached for his keys. "What about this guy?"

"Name?"

"Chuck Reynolds." Chuck grinned.

"He's not on our list." The marshals hurried after Veenstra back toward the county jail's cell block.

◖◖◖

"Since you're a Canadian alien, we're deporting you, Reynolds," the sheriff told Chuck an hour later.

"Really? Didn't you get a positive ID on the prints you took from me last night?"

"Michigan State Police Lab in Lansing is backlogged. Could take a couple of days. If you still want to claim Massachusetts residence, I can let you bunk in the drunk tank until they come through," Veenstra chuckled. "Or we can go with your Quebec papers, and we'll drive you across the border to Canada this morning."

"Is that legal without a court order? I think I deserve an explanation." Glad as he was to get out of jail, Chuck decided to at least pretend to be indignant.

"The prosecutor says that without the Iraqis, we don't need you as a witness."

"Witness? Last night you were charging me along with the others."

"The charges have been dropped."

"So I'm free to go?" he asked hopefully.

"You get a free ride to Canada—straight to Ontario."

"What about my car?"

"The Dodge? It's in impound. Prosecutor wants us to hold it until it's been checked for evidence. Never know what the Feds might want."

Chuck decided to lick his wounds and not argue with Veenstra about his inconsistency.

"Your stuff is in that box." Sheriff Veenstra pointed to an old shoe box on the desk. He unsnapped Chuck's handcuffs, then the leg irons. "Clean up in that washroom."

"Then do I get those Cheerios?"

"Too late. Deputies you're riding with haven't eaten either. They'll stop at Bob Evans on the way out of town. That's on us."

"Thanks," Chuck said flatly. He took stock of the contents of his wallet: his Visa card, Province of Quebec driver's license, a Canadian hundred dollar bill, two loonies—dollar coins. "There was more than five hundred dollars in American currency in my wallet last night," he complained.

"Don't know anything about any American money. You're a Canadian, aren't you?"

Chuck declined to argue.

❰❰❰

"I'm at the Maple Leaf Motel, Sarnia, Ontario," Chuck told Nicki on the phone that evening. "I had a rough night last night, so I'm going to rest here quietly and see if I can get some sleep. Tell you about it later."

"You're stranded in Canada?" Nicki worried.

"Not really stranded," Chuck laughed. "I've already phoned Stan Basford. He's taking my Massachusetts driver's license and Social Security card to Bangor to get it on the Federal Express jet tonight. I'll have it by 10:30 A.M. tomorrow."

"You phoned the Basfords first?" Nicki pouted.

"I tried to reach you first. You were in a workshop," they said. "They couldn't find you."

"Actually, I was in the lobby of Maranatha watching the news. Sam Donaldson on ABC was reporting live from the Sacajawea County Courthouse steps, right here in Garfield City. Can you believe it?"

"What's the news?"

"Sam Donaldson says radiation tests prove that a low-grade atomic weapon exploded in midair over Lake Michigan about midnight last night. And get this"—Nicki was excited—"Donaldson said that the level of radiation was so low over Garfield City that it poses no immediate threat."

"That's good, I guess. What does it mean?"

"Don't interrupt me until I'm finished with the story, please, Chuck."

"Go on."

"Informed nuclear scientists speculate that Lake Michigan created an updraft in the fall night air, that pushed the radiation cloud into the upper atmosphere where it may settle later to wreak havoc elsewhere on earth." Nicki did a deadpan imitation of Donaldson's dead-serious manner.

"Sounds logical. I guess you don't agree, Doctor Nicki Towns?" Chuck had great respect for Nicki's Ph.D. in nuclear physics, even though he sometimes teased her about it.

"No, Chuck, I don't. Our military may have let a loose-cannon general violate a possibly outdated international treaty at White Sands Missile Range. If Donaldson is right, this is beyond irresponsible, of course." Nicki, somehow, did not sound concerned—only excited.

"But Chicago and the anthrax? The Navy may just have seen an atomic blast as the lesser evil," Chuck worried. "A conventional wartip might not have killed the anthrax bacteria and left it polluting the lake—at what cost? I guess that leaves . . ."

"A SAM with a neutron wartip. A neutron blast would totally destroy bacteria by enhanced, short-range radiation and absorption of hydrogen from the living matter, the same as it did to those cows and Marcie Lewis. But it would pose no long-term radiation threat to human populations. Those missiles were probably fifty miles from shore when they collided and exploded. So no one has anything to worry about."

"I don't know." Chuck was not fully convinced.

"Neutron radiation has a very short life, Chuck," Nicki went on. "It is dangerous only for about a quarter of a mile. So Donaldson is simply mistaken," Nicki affirmed. "Donaldson was repeating the usual, politically-correct wisdom about Hiroshima-type atomic bombs. But America's atomic scientists were authorized to experiment with neutron explosions in underground tests by President Jimmy Carter a quarter of a century ago. This is its first open use. I'm sure of it," Nicki stated confidently.

Chuck whistled. "So Donaldson said nothing at all about the anthrax either, I'd guess? And nothing about the U.S. Navy's secret *Centurion* SSN submarine?"

"Not a word. They claim the atomic warhead weapon was timed to explode over Lake Michigan just to scare the American people. Donaldson also said that 'informed sources' say that the nuclear weapon was built right here in Michigan, perhaps by a couple of University of Michigan engineering students who have ties with the extreme right-wing Minuteman Militia movement."

"So, what's the Iraqi tie-in?" Chuck laughed out loud.

"The militia extremists supposedly needed some Iraqis as a cover. The Iraqis were carrying valid New York driver's licenses, so the Pentagon is saying that the Iraqis have been in the United States for some time. They were supposedly paid by the Minutemen to stage a nuclear test."

"Can't they accept the fact that these guys came in with a load of Turkish marijuana two days ago, along with the missile? That'd be too simple for the media to believe, I'm sure. And I suppose it's not politically correct for our government to admit how vulnerable our borders really are," Chuck mused. "My grandmother's meal sieve really will hold water."

"The Pentagon can't hide behind the thin veil of political correctness very long this time. If General Armstrong MacAdams told the Department of Defense even half what we told him, someone's going to be looking under rocks in Iraq within a day or so," Nicki hypothesized.

❰❰❰

"Ni-i-i-i-i-ce pooches. There, there. Good boys. Enjoy your midnight snack." Nicki slid her wrist through the space between the chain-link fence and the gate to the auto-impound lot, petting the hungry Doberman pinschers. The dogs lapped up the five pounds of hamburger meat as if they hadn't been fed for weeks.

"Gotta go, guys!" She skittered across the street and crouched in the doorway of a derelict appliance store. This wasn't Garfield City's nicest neighborhood, but by 2 A.M. the panhandlers and muggers had crawled into their culverts and abandoned cars.

A Sacajawea County Sheriff patrol car pulled up to the gate. As Nicki watched, the deputy pointed his spotlight at the two guard dogs. They slept peacefully on the office steps of Al's Towing and Recovery Service. One Doberman raised its head and woofed weakly. "Al feeds his dogs too well," observed the deputy.

Seconds later, Nicki disabled the lot's alarm system. She opened the padlocked gate with a hairpin and slid it wide open. She taped an envelope with a brief note to the glass of the office door: "Dear Al, Here's a hundred dollars to cover the cost of towing our car from Motorcycle Hill, plus storage. Thanks."

Stepping across the dogs enjoying their diphenhydramine-induced doze, she hurried to the gray Dodge with Quebec plates. "Chuck's spare key. Good. Right where he left it," Nicki said to no one in particular as she fished the tiny magnetic box from under a fender. She started the motor and pulled quickly into the street without turning the headlights on, then stopped and rolled the gate shut. Hopping back in, she punched the gas down hard, pointing the car toward eastbound Interstate 96.

❰❰❰

"Wake-up call, Chuck!" Nicki squealed.

"Where are you?" Chuck fumbled with the motel room phone.

"Lakeside Breakfast & Dining, Port Huron, Michigan. Right across the river from your motel. I can see the Maple Leaf Motel sign from the parking lot on the American side. I've got your car."

"The sheriff let you have it?"

"Sure. In exchange for feeding the impound lot's Dobermans at 2 A.M."

"You . . . just took it?"

"I paid the fees. Besides, it's your car. Am I a thief?"

"N . . . no. But Nicki, that's criminal trespassing!"

"I know." Nicki sighed. "Old habits die hard. I'm sorry."

"You've put us both in the soup. Do you realize that?"

"Police bulletin on the car, that sort of thing? It'll be a couple of hours, yet. You can drive your car into Canada by then."

"No, Nicki. There'll be an APB out on that car by nine o'clock, latest. I can't cross the bridge from Canada until ten thirty, when my American ID comes in that Fed Ex package." Chuck groaned.

Nicki was silent.

"Tell you what. It's just after seven in the morning. Most Fed Ex offices open at eight. I'll grab a cab, get my package over the counter, and head straight for the Blue Water Bridge into the U.S. Wait for me at the restaurant, and *park that car out of sight from the street!*"

"Yes, master!" Nicki slammed the receiver down. "This began as such a perfect day." Her newly created conscience, however, had just reminded her that she had indeed broken the law.

◖◖◖

"What will you do with the car in Canada, Chuck?" It was 8:45, and he waited in the Lakeside Breakfast & Dining parking lot as a City of Port Huron patrol car cruised past.

"Sell it. First used car dealer with five hundred dollars gets it."

"Chuck! It's worth more than that!"

He grinned. "I know. And I'll get more. But right now I'd take five hundred dollars not to get caught with it here in Michigan."

"I'll wait for you over there." Nicki indicated the Best Western across the street.

"Wait in their restaurant. I'll be back by noon in a cab. Then we can catch the Greyhound to the Detroit International Airport."

"Chuck."

"Yes?"

"Be careful. I need you back with me. I'm sorry I gave you a scare."

"Forgiven. I need you too."

◖◖◖

"They're B-52s, aren't they, Chuck?" Nicki pointed to a row of seven huge bombers with soaring bald eagles painted on their noses.

"Fully modern B-52Hs, actually. Stratofortresses."

Chuck and Nicki eyed the behemoth, eight-engine super-bombers parked on the runway at Bangor International Airport in Maine.

"This airport used to be Dow Field, a USAF base. It had the longest military runways in North America until it was decommissioned a few years ago," Chuck explained. He eyed the huge bombers, possibly the first official military use of these vast, decaying runways in more than a quarter of a century. "Those big birds can travel halfway around the world at just under the speed of sound without refueling," Chuck said. "Each of those bruisers carries, let's see . . . more than thirty-five tons of bombs."

"Awful," said Nicki.

"Awful and awesome," Chuck agreed.

"Those are Raptors," Nicki said. She pointed toward rows of bombs nestled beneath one titanic fowl's charcoal-gray wings. The other six were likewise equipped with huge bombs.

"Raptors? I thought I knew my ordnance," Chuck said. "But what's a Raptor?"

"A Raptor is a one-thousand-pound LGB—a laser-guided bomb that can be guided by the B-52H's bombing crew with such accuracy that they can be fired down a factory chimney from several miles up," Nicki explained. "I learned that while doing background research for my job with CALF."

"Former job, I hope. 'Raptor,'" Chuck repeated. "Pertaining to a bird of prey—like an eagle."

"The American Eagle still soars apparently, Chuck."

"Hey! Did you realize that Bangor International Airport is the closest airport in the United States to Iraq. It's only ten hours! I suppose the Air Force figures that just this once in an emergency they can get away with fueling a fully loaded bomber group at a civilian base. This way they can make a round trip without refueling. Who'd look for one here, anyway?" Chuck mused.

"I think," said Nicki, "we've seen enough to know that someone, somehow, finally got through to the Pentagon that Saddam has an anthrax factory in Iraq right under the ruins of ancient Nineveh."

❰❰❰

"To most of us, Nineveh is the mythical Bible city of Jonah and the whale. Last night, Nineveh, its palatial ruins on the Tigris River, its museum honoring the noble warrior-scholar Ashurbanipal— and its modern factory of death—took a place in modern history along with Berlin and Stalingrad. Seven American B-52H bombers, flown nonstop from Bangor, Maine's, old Korean War-era military runway, turned Nineveh into a gigantic crater. These magnificent American eagles and their crews are already nearly home. This is Forrest Sawyer for ABC News, reporting live from Mosul, Iraq, in the northern no-fly zone."

"'There is no healing of thy injury.'" Mae Basford smiled wryly, quoting the Bible as she punched the red button on the remote control to shut the TV off and signal the family that breakfast was ready.

"That's from Nahum's prophecy about the final destruction of Nineveh—chapter three, verse nineteen," affirmed Nicki. Tears rolled down her face. "My old city is gone forever—at last. I am free to seek a greater city now."

A maple that still clung to its golden leaves glowed grandly in the fall morning splendor as the sun rose over the Basford homestead, sending warm rays reaching into Nicki's ebony hair and highlighting the oriental beauty of her olive complexion. Chuck gazed, speechless, for he was not used to seeing Nicki cry. Yet he realized that Nicki wept with a sorrow he could not fathom, a loss he could never appreciate.

Or can I? he wondered. There had been Shelly. *Oh, how my heart ached when I lost her.* This morning something moved Chuck to want to fill Nicki's loss, moved his heart with such potency that he knew he must act to meet her need—or leave her forever.

Nicki had taken a leap of faith just before her date with death in Iraq. Chuck had seen her grow as a Christian. He had seen that growth in her willingness to give up chasing CALF's golden hope of nationhood to follow Christ.

Together he and Nicki had done more for their country in a few days than some who had been heralded in ticker-tape parades down New York's Wall Street. Though heroes, he and Nicki were unsung. Nicki quietly accepted this. The real rewards of life aren't given out on earth, both knew.

Now she had heard the news about her ancestor's great city, its final vestige wiped for all time from the face of the earth. "I'm glad I got to see Ashurbanipal's palace before it was finally destroyed," she said, smiling and drying her tears. "Assyria will rise as Isaiah predicted, of course, but Nineveh will never again be its capital," she added.

"Breakfast, Daddy." Jennifer's grinning freckled face appeared in the archway from the antique farmhouse kitchen.

"In a moment, Jen."

Jen ducked back with her grandparents.

Chuck took Nicki's elbow as she stood from her seat in the rocker by the window. He slid his other arm about her lithe waist. Pale blue met emerald green—smile kissed smile. "I . . . I love you. W-will you marry me?" he stammered. Chuck's ears burned red as he realized he had said those same words to Jennifer's mom nearly twenty years ago. He had been embarrassed at his own vulnerability then too.

"Yes," she laughed. "If you're nice to me." Nicki's face lighted with the glory of heaven. She grabbed Chuck suddenly and planted a quick, warm kiss on his lips. "Chuck." Nicki caught her breath. "I've wondered for weeks when you'd ask. And there's a secret I've been aching to share with you."

"You? A secret?" His eyes danced with merriment.

"Everything I am is in love with you," Nicki breathed. "My heart, my soul, my body, my spirit."

"I love you too," Chuck reiterated. "But I've got another lady to deal with first," he laughed. "Then I'll try to be nice to you."

Nicki's eyes opened wide. "Who?"

Chuck turned toward the kitchen just as Jennifer popped back into the living room.

"Daddy??!"

Chuck grinned at his daughter of sixteen summers.

Jennifer disappeared.

"That lady. I've promised her a camp-out on Mt. Katahdin."

"I think you should leave tomorrow. I'll shop for a wedding dress while you're gone. Now let's eat breakfast."

◖◖◖

"Daddy, you're not going to carry that *thing* up Mt. Katahdin?" Jennifer wrinkled her cute freckled pug nose at the willow-wicker backpack Chuck tossed that evening into Grandpa Basford's old pickup.

"You got a better idea?" Chuck laughed.

"This!" Jennifer displayed a nylon backpack with an aluminum frame.

Chuck picked one up in each hand, hefting both. "The wicker one's larger, but they're about the same weight, considering size. What's wrong with it?"

"It looks . . ."

"Dorky." Chuck laughed as he finished his daughter's sentence. "I can just see a teenage moose calf rolling its big brown eyes and saying, 'When did that nerd leave the '50s?' Or bear cubs rolling in the fall leaves, giggling their woolly heads off at my old-style wicker backpack," he laughed.

"Cut it out, Dad!"

"The point is, there really is life outside the hallowed halls of Belfast Regional High School."

"I know, Daddy."

Chuck hugged Jennifer and kissed her forehead. "I would never deliberately embarrass you in public."

"Promise?"

"Promise."

"Well, I guess the bears and the bobcats and the jays and the chickadees won't tease us," Jennifer sighed.

"How far are you guys carrying that stuff, anyway?" Nicki frowned, surveying the pile of camping gear Chuck and Jennifer had piled into the truck for the trip to Baxter State Park.

"From the parking lot to Chimney Pond," Chuck explained. "It's just over three miles. We'll camp there tomorrow night."

"Well, that's not so bad," Nicki decided. "You'll need only water and a lunch to carry to the summit of Katahdin, then?"

"Chimney Pond is a rise of 1,400 feet from the parking area," said Jennifer, who had been reading a brochure about Baxter State Park. "It will be a pretty good climb."

"Whew," whistled Stan Basford. He set a Coleman gasoline stove in the truck and stared at the pile in his pickup bed. "How on earth . . . ?"

"We're stopping in Millinocket to rent a packhorse." Chuck winked at Stan.

"Stop it, Daddy! You know you said we'd make up our minds about what stuff to carry and what to leave in the truck after we get to Baxter."

"That's right," Chuck agreed. "Actually, I loaded stuff myself that I wasn't sure we'd use. I've been going around like a windmill for several weeks, and I haven't had time to plan this trip."

"Well, you won't need that, and you won't need that, and you won't need . . ." Stan's old guide sense was working full speed now, and he would have quickly reduced the load to bare essentials. But Chuck lifted the tailgate and dropped the door of the topper. "Let's eat supper," he chuckled.

◖◖◖

"Let's eat breakfast, Daddy!" Chuck and Jennifer had traveled two hours on only hot chocolate since they left the Basford farm in South Freedom at 6 A.M.. "Katahdin Shadows Campground," read the sign beside Quakish Lake, outside Millinocket.

"Great idea." Chuck pulled into the campground just as the rising sun blazed through the branches of the paper birches and sugar maples, gold and crimson in their autumn gowns. "Long-john weather," he observed. The morning chill hit his face as he stepped from the truck cab, and while frost still decorated the cedar-shingled roof of the roadside picnic shelter. "I'm still not used to northern Maine falls—colder here than either North Carolina or Massachusetts."

"Wimp!" laughed Jennifer. "Maine is my home."

"What's that, then?" Chuck pointed to the waffled, lace-trimmed sleeve of a lady's river-driver shirt that showed beneath her plaid flannel shirt.

"Oh, I'm wearing my long johns too," she giggled.

Chuck set up the gasoline stove and pumped up the pressure while Jennifer got out blueberry pancake batter she had prepared the evening before and carried along in a Tupperware jar. "The early pioneers had to cut firewood before they could cook. Are you sure this gas stove is roughing it enough to suit you?" he chuckled.

"Daddy." Jennifer's blue eyes darkened. "I did *not* come here to compete with you like you were another kid! I came here to *be* with you."

"We haven't seen much of each other lately," Chuck answered slowly. "Grandpa Basford has been your daddy since you were small, pretty much. I might have kept you with me, but then it would have been a series of baby-sitters. I decided you needed a mother as well."

"Grandma has been a wonderful mom." Jennifer paused to turn a pancake. "But I . . . I need *you*, Daddy, more than you can imagine."

"What would you say if I told you I asked Nicki to marry me yesterday morning while you were trying to get us to come to breakfast?"

"Did she say yes?"

"Yes."

"Nicki is the coolest person I have ever met. I *majorly* want you guys to get married."

"Is next week too soon?"

"Oh!" Jennifer dropped her spatula. "That'd be wonderful!" Then she added, "I guess I've just contradicted myself, haven't I? I need you. You and Nicki need each other, and I think it's neat you guys want to get married right away. But she's too young to be my mother. So maybe I'll just go on living with Grandma and Grandpa Basford," she sighed.

"Life is full of contradictions when you're a teen, Jennifer," Chuck observed. "Sometimes for adults too."

"What do I need, really?" Jennifer was thoughtful.

"A very wise person once said that the most important relationship in a girl's life is with her father, at least after she becomes a teen."

"That's cool." Jennifer paused. "Nicki never knew her daddy, did she?" she added.

"Only by her mother's reflections. She tried very hard to respect his memory because she knew he would have loved her as he loved her mother. That's why she has kept herself pure, when a lot of young women living alone were throwing themselves at men."

"That's heavy," Jennifer said. "Will . . . will you and Nicki live in Massachusetts, in your apartment?"

"I . . . I don't know. We're still dealing with the fact that Saddam's assassins want to kill her—worse than ever since we helped stop the anthrax attack on Chicago, I imagine." Chuck began to butter a slice of toast he had browned over the gas flame.

"Daddy, look?" Jennifer pointed to the north. "Katahdin!" Maine's highest mountain had caught the rising sun across distant

Millinocket Lake. Mt. Katahdin loomed tall and glorious on the horizon. "How far off is that?"

"Twenty miles. We'd have missed this view if we hadn't got up so early."

"Daddy, this trip is majorly cool!"

❰❰❰

"Man is born to die; his works are short lived.
But Mt. Katahdin in all of its glory will forever
remain the mountain of the people of Maine.

Percival Baxter, Governor of Maine, 1921–1923."

Jennifer read the sign aloud. She and Chuck had loaded their backpacks with cooking utensils, food, and two pup tents. Each carried a sleeping bag as they left the pickup truck at the parking lot beside Roaring Brook Campground and the Chimney Pond Trail up Mt. Katahdin.

"Daddy, my Katahdin trail guide says that the mountain is 5,267 feet high, but on the map it says 5,268 feet. You'd think they'd get their act together and agree on how high the mountain is."

"Let's see . . ." Chuck thought for a moment. "When I was in the eighth grade in North Carolina, I had to memorize the height of the tallest peak in each state along the Atlantic coast for a geography lesson. I learned that Mt. Mitchell in North Carolina is 6,684 feet. Mt. Katahdin was then 5,273 feet, seven feet short of a mile. So now it's only 5,267 feet. Looks like it shrank six feet."

"Maybe people are carrying rocks off the peak for souvenirs?" Jennifer wondered.

"Hardly. In fact, I've heard that a big pile of rocks has been built by park rangers up on the peak to bring the mountaintop to a mile in height. They add a few stones to it every few years."

"I guess maybe Governor Baxter was mistaken." Jennifer was thoughtful, and they trudged in silence for some time. "Mt.

Katahdin in its glory will *not* remain forever, because the Bible says that the earth will be dissolved some day. It's shrinking right now, apparently."

"Like all of creation, Katahdin is subject to the Second Law of Thermodynamics," said Chuck. "Order becomes chaos. Beauty decays. Like our bodies, it is crumbling measurably. Katahdin has lost six feet since I was a kid in school."

"David said in Psalm 121: 'I will lift up my eyes unto the hills, from where my help comes,'" Jennifer said. "Was he comparing God to a mountain?"

"Contrasting rather than comparing," said Chuck. "In verse two David added: 'My help comes from the LORD, who made heaven and earth.' Verse one in the old King James Bible has the punctuation wrong."

"Didn't pagans in Bible times believe that their gods lived in the hills, like the ancient Greeks and their Mt. Olympus?" Jennifer ventured.

"Exactly, Jen. David's point was that since our God created the hills, He's greater than the hills."

"We have a wonderful God, don't we, Dad? Y'know, I read somewhere that kids tend to view God the way they view their fathers, and I think that's right. I learned to love God from you, Daddy."

"That's a big responsibility." It was Chuck's turn to be silent for a while as they trudged uphill.

"Whew!" Jennifer sat down on a rock.

"Tired already?" Chuck teased. He plunked down beside his daughter, tossing a bundle of firewood at his feet.

"Daddy, why are you lugging all that firewood? We're camping in the *woods*. Besides, we've got the gasoline stove."

"Well, when Abraham and his son, Isaac, hiked up Mt. Moriah . . ."

"Cut it out, Dad! I know that story. Anyway, Abraham did *not* use Isaac for a burnt offering. God supplied a ram."

"That's true," Chuck agreed. "As for our firewood, we're not permitted to cut wood in a state park. I expect we'll wake up with frost on our tent flaps at Chimney Pond before we climb to the peak tomorrow morning, so a fire at breakfast time will seem good."

"You think of everything, Daddy."

"Not really. We do what we can with what the Lord gives us. But God is constantly sending signals our way to remind us He's really in charge, if we listen and study His Word."

"You're right, as usual," Jennifer chuckled. She paused as they watched a man and a woman, both laden with enormous packs, round a bend in the trail below them and march steadily upward as though their packs were filled with helium.

"Appalachian Trail hikers," Chuck observed. "They've been walking north from Georgia since July, probably, and I imagine they'll watch the sunset from the mountaintop tonight. Probably roll into their sleeping bags and watch the sun come up from there too." The couple wore shorts, though it was a chilly October morning in Maine. Both were deeply tanned from months of dawn-to-dusk outdoor activity. They seemed to walk as effortlessly as if on level ground.

"I saw something about the Appalachian Trail on our map," Jennifer said. "I thought it was just another Baxter Park trail."

Chuck laughed. "The Appalachian Trail follows the Appalachian Mountain Range from its southern end, in Georgia, to the top of Maine's Katahdin, the northernmost peak of the range. When I was your age, Jennifer, I hiked the North Carolina segment of the Appalachian Trail, and I dreamed of one day hiking its entire length. But in God's direction, my life has never had the three months to spare, and now I doubt that I'll ever do it."

"'Build thee more stately mansions, O my soul.'" Jennifer smiled, quoting lines from Holmes. "I learned 'The Chambered Nautilus' this year in our Great Authors lit class. I think it means that as God moves us from one stage to the next, our life's tasks become greater. Maybe God has greater things for you than hiking the Appalachian Trail, Daddy."

"I'm supposed to be advising you, my sixteen-year-old super-achiever." Chuck patted Jennifer's shoulder. "Let's go! Onward and upward!"

◖◖◖

"Daddy, why did you call me a 'superachiever' back there on the trail?" Jennifer gave a plastic tent stake another whack with the heel of her hatchet and peered into her father's warm eyes from where she sat. "I know—I get straight A's and I'm head of the cheerleading squad and all that stuff. But I'm just doin' what I do best."

"I wonder . . ." Chuck searched for more words. "Maybe I've been wrong to tease you about being a superachiever. But . . ."

"What?" Jennifer eyed her father suspiciously.

"But I noticed the calendar on your desk when I went into your room last night to carry your stuff to the truck. 'October 21'?"

"Yeah." Jennifer was silent a moment. "I crossed that off."

"Why?"

"If I'm gonna make National Honor Society, I've gotta study. I can't waste time at the teen harvest party."

"What do your friends do on Saturday night?"

"A lot of girls at Belfast High are regular party animals. I hear them bragging about it at school all the time." Jennifer wrinkled her nose in disgust.

"The harvest party is sponsored by Sheepscot Valley Community Church, right?"

Jennifer frowned. "I guess I ought to go. Most of the kids at church are going."

"One more observation, Jennifer."

Jennifer cast Chuck a worried frown.

"You are now old enough to be responsible for your own choices in life. Jesus, at twelve, was considered adult enough to be 'about [His] Father's business,' for example."

"So why wouldn't you let me drive Grandpa's truck on the way here this morning?" Jennifer's eyes were full of mischief.

"I don't get to drive a classic Chevy step-side pickup very often. You can drive home, though." He passed his daughter the keys.

"Does this mean no more fatherly lectures?" Jennifer kissed his cheek.

❰❰❰

"I can't imagine that the Garden of Eden was as beautiful as this!" Jennifer scanned the five peaks of the Brothers Mountains from Katahdin's summit, watching as a bald eagle soared toward the far-off hills. She put her binoculars down to view the panorama of sugar and red maples closer in, interrupted here and there with a yellow-leafed birch or basswood. "What are those, Daddy?" She pointed to a stand of trees highlighted against green pines and deeper green spruces. The leaves had turned nearly white in their fall foliage.

"Let's see the binoculars." Chuck focused on the leaves for a moment. They were oval, pointed on the end. "Grey as your grandma's hair," he said at last. "There's only one tree that turns that color in the fall."

"What's that, Dad?"

"White ash. The wood is so white that one time I fooled my grandpa by putting a chip of it on his plate on Thanksgiving Day. He thought it was turkey white meat until he tried to stab it with his fork."

They laughed together.

❰❰❰

"What will you and Nicki do after you're married if Saddam's killers come after her again?" Jennifer was driving her grandfather's antique Chevy truck as they rolled through the fall countryside on their way back to South Freedom.

"There's also the possibility that the U.S. Justice Department will wish to prosecute her once it's learned that she didn't die in Iraq." Chuck sighed. "But we'll continue to do what we've done right along. Pray, and trust God to work out the details. Now that

Nicki is done with CALF, I imagine that things will gradually improve."

"Daddy, there's this boy, Aaron, in our church—he's my age—his dad is a surgeon, a medical missionary at a hospital in Niger, West Africa. Aaron lives with his grandparents so he can finish his high school education while his parents serve the Lord as missionaries." Jennifer wiped her tears with her flannel shirt sleeve.

"Do you need me to drive?" Chuck wondered why his daughter was crying.

"I'm all right." Jennifer smiled. "If you and Nicki need to leave the country for protection for a few years . . ."

Chuck did not answer.

18

The Flight into Egypt

Flee into Egypt, and stay there until I bring you word.
—An angel

"I never should have gotten you into this, Chuck." Nicki peered earnestly at her fiancé.

Chuck returned her gaze for a moment. Without answering, he turned in his chair to stare out across the whitecaps of troubled Bois Bay through the plateglass of Shoreside Diner. It was a windy autumn day, and beyond the breakwater of great granite slabs, the schooner *Heritage* was furling its sails, no doubt for the final time this tourist season. Sailing vessels nowadays used their diesel donkey engines to get into difficult harbors when the wind was up, he considered.

Chuck and Nicki had driven to Bois Bay that morning because Chuck had a job interview at Coastal Resources, a consulting firm specializing in security for the many small industries springing up in coastal Maine. He had realized finally that he could never go back to his old job at Salem Electronics North. Maine would be their home from now on, he and Nicki had decided together. Vacation trips north to visit Jennifer and her grandparents had given him an intimate knowledge of the Pine Tree State and a love for its forests, its hills, its seacoast, its people.

"Chuck, you're whistling." Nicki knew that Chuck often whistled when he was deep in thought, always on key, usually an old hymn. "What hymn is that?"

"That line is, 'No turning back, no turning back.' It's from 'I Have Decided to Follow Jesus'." Chuck grinned. Then he frowned.

Nicki patted his arm. "I love you very much," she said, "I do want to marry you. Yet . . ."

"I understand." Chuck waved his hand. "Many years ago, as a teen in a little mountain church in North Carolina, while that song was played on an old piano I made a decision that there would be 'no turning back' for me as I followed the Lord. He's led me to marry you—I'm certain of it. I shall not turn back on you."

"Perhaps we should wait."

"I didn't buy that new fall suit yesterday to wear to your funeral!" Chuck returned to watching the sailing ship. "Something just occurred to me," he said at last, "something I read in *Down East* magazine several years ago. Where this restaurant now sits, a church once stood. Its pastor watched a sea rescue from right here, from this very spot."

"And he wrote a hymn?" Nicki grinned, guessing.

"'Throw out the lifeline across the dark wave,/There is a brother whom someone should save.' But on this stormy day the wind kept flipping the lifeline and life preserver back to the crew in the rescue boat. So a young sailor pulled off his boots, grabbed the line, and jumped in to rescue the man in the capsized fishing boat. Then they were both in exactly the same predicament."

Nicki thought about this for a moment. "Except . . . ," she added, "except that they both now had a line to the rescue boat."

"That's just my point. I'm already in the storm with you. Nothing can change that—the Iraqis see me as linked with you, whether or not we marry. Saddam's goons will continue to try to get us both once the Iraqi dictator catches his breath over the bombing of Nineveh and the loss of four agents in the U.S. in one month. But Jesus is our break-proof lifeline."

"Saddam seems to have a better perception of who's helping whom than our own CIA and FBI." Nicki wrinkled her nose.

"Sometimes I find that your 'feet of clay' analogy has an eerie ring of truth." Chuck shrugged. "Sooner or later someone at some level of the federal government has got to lay aside professional pride and talk to amateurs like us. Eventually someone must get to the bottom of this maelstrom of espionage and terrorism." He shook his head. "If we try to turn General MacAdams in now, the people in the Pentagon covering for him will have both of us killed, and the CIA will just cover it up. For now, you and I have no choice but to lie low, wait for the right break, and pray!"

◖◖◖

"Look here, Chuck." Stan Basford spread the Belfast *Journal* on the coffee table. "That attack on Nineveh stirred up quite a hornets' nest."

Chuck scanned the newspaper. In one article a spokesperson for the National Geographic Society decried the bombing because the "Chaldean ruin of ancient Nineveh contained possibly the greatest treasure of Akkadian clay cuneiform documents known to historians." Amnesty International had worried to a reporter that the "civilian Iraqi personnel" who ran the tourist trade at the Nineveh archaeological dig were "nearly all Kurds, whom Saddam is also persecuting." Though the bombing occurred at night with little loss of life, "the means of livelihood for thousands of Kurdish people was entirely destroyed."

An editorial quote from the Russian Communist Party newspaper, *Pravda,* pontificated that "A surgical strike" by the U.S. Marines "could have avoided" such "senseless wholesale destruction" of the ancient ruin, a "treasure belonging to all humanity."

Furthermore, declared *Pravda*, the United States had produced no evidence that Saddam's laboratories beneath Nineveh had "ever produced any anthrax bacteria."

An unrelated article explored the nighttime explosion over Lake Michigan. A team of *Chicago Tribune* investigative reporters had gone door-to-door in waterfront neighborhoods in Garfield City, Michigan, and Milwaukee, Wisconsin, seeking eyewitnesses. The official Pentagon report declared that "a single rocket, built by a Michigan right-wing militia group, The Minutemen, had been shot from a Michigan state park" and had exploded in midair, scattering "minimal atomic radiation" into the atmosphere. U.S. Attorney General Leigh Franks was in the process of formulating charges against several members, who had yet to be arrested, the article stated.

The *Tribune* team, however, found five eyewitnesses in Garfield City and two across the lake in Milwaukee who claimed they had seen "two separate fiery streaks merge" above the big lake, producing the powerful explosion. A Garfield City teen girl was also being held in a Grand Rapids psychiatric ward for "recurring Hiroshima-syndrome nightmares," according to her psychiatrist, who refused to let the media use his name. The girl, whom the FBI had been unable to interview because of her mental illness, was alleged to have been on a state park beach when the rocket was fired.

"What do you make of this, Nicki?" Chuck pointed to a single sentence in the article about "widespread reports" of street lights blinking off and on, TV sets rapidly changing channels, electric garage doors popping open, and heart pacemakers acting erratically.

"It's called EMP—electromagnetic pulse, Chuck. Any type of atomic explosion will cause EMP. A neutron blast will create such a powerful EMP that had the neutron wartip exploded directly over Garfield City it would have shut the city down for months. For instance, the EMP would have ruined the computerized electronic circuits in automobiles in much of the city, as well as destroyed all personal, business, and industrial computers," Nicki explained.

But no atmospheric radiation from the blast had been found in the several major cities east of Garfield City where U.S. Environmental Protection Agency scientists were testing air samples, according to the Associated Press. Prevailing winds were theorized to have caused the supposed atomic cloud to drift eastward to blanket several metropolitan areas, including Detroit, Cleveland, Toronto, Buffalo, Syracuse, and Boston. But though the explosion seemed to have been an atomic reaction, scientists are baffled that only trace radiation had turned up in tests conducted with high-altitude balloons.

An epidemic of fatal, childhood leukemia, such as that believed to follow the atomic tests in Alamogordo, New Mexico, and later, in Nevada, after the A-Bomb tests of 1945 and 1951, was feared by environmentalists, the article went on. Yesterday the Canadian Premier issued a stern rebuke from Ottawa, warning the United States that all "atomic debris" drifting over Toronto would be analyzed for possible redress of grievances in the World Court. ACLU lawyers in several major American cities were gearing up for class-action suits on behalf of pregnant mothers and their unborn children. It was unclear, however, whom they planned to sue or what they would use for evidence. Several major environmentalist lawsuits against American industry, based almost entirely on anecdotal evidence, had been won in jury trials, Chuck sadly recalled as he read.

On an inside page, an official statement by the U.S. Joint Chiefs-of-Staff declared the "two-flash theory" to be "groundless conspiracy hysteria." The Pentagon claimed this theory to be on a level with the two-gunman theory of the Kennedy assassination in 1963. Credence had once been given to the Kennedy conspiracy by the private, 8-millimeter Zapruder movie film that supposedly showed a second shooter on a grassy knoll behind the presidential parade. A so-called "Zapruder II film," taken from a nighttime television security camera at the Garfield City public marina, showed only a single streak of fire over Lake Michigan, the Pentagon asserted.

When a *Chicago Tribune* reporter contacted the marina's head of security about the alleged Zapruder II videotape, he refused comment, except to say that the tape had been reused the following evening and therefore had been completely erased. It was not until two days later that FBI investigators seized the videotape, the marina security chief admitted. A *Tribune* editor speculated in an editorial column that FBI laboratory technicians, working in Washington's J. Edgar Hoover Building, may have had access to "highly classified counterspy enhancing devices" able to restore data erased from a video film.

Nowhere in any news article or editorial could Chuck find a suggestion that the B-52H bombing raid on Nineveh may have been triggered by reaction to the explosion over Lake Michigan. "I guess this will keep the Pentagon brass busy issuing press releases for a while," Chuck finally observed.

"Aren't you afraid they'll be looking for you and Nicki? Maybe want to question the two of you?" It was Mae Basford speaking. She and Stan had been told only that Chuck and Nicki were witnesses of the explosion, and that they had tipped off several officials in advance.

"We're concerned about it," Chuck admitted. "But if the FBI wanted us very badly, I'm sure they'd have been here before now."

"Today's young people find it hard to get involved," growled Stan, ordinarily sanguine about his son-in-law's business. "Didn't mean you, of course," he quickly added. Though Stan Basford had spent most of his life on a backwoods Maine farm, the citizens of South Freedom had once elected him to the office of selectman, an honored position of authority in a New England community.

"I do tend to duck when I see trouble coming," Chuck agreed. He chuckled nervously. As far as he knew, only he and Nicki knew about the U.S. Navy's top-secret USS *Centurion* nuclear submarine. Chuck theorized that the Navy's high-tech, advanced-art sub was kept hidden in Lake Michigan to keep its existence secret from the Russian Federation's vast navy, ever vigilant for new American submarine warfare capabilities. Chicago's Great Lakes Naval Station, Chuck decided, was probably the nuclear-powered super-sub's home port.

"Did you see the USS *Silversides* when you were in Garfield City, Chuck?" Stan asked. "Only submarine based in the Great Lakes, far's I know. The *Silversides* sent a lot o' Jap shipping to the bottom of the Pacific during the War," added Stan, who had missed being drafted in '42 because of flat feet. "'Course she's a museum piece now."

"Do you mean World War II?" Chuck, who had been a Vietnam War chaplain, sometimes gave in to the urge to remind Stan that more than one conflict had sent young Americans to fight on foreign soil during the twentieth century.

◖◖◖

"Of course you'll want your wedding announcement run in the Belfast *Journal?*" Mae Basford's offhand question at the supper table caught Chuck and Nicki by surprise.

"Well, I . . ." Chuck became painfully aware that this was the bride's decision, so he stopped midsentence.

"We're having studio portraits done in Belfast tomorrow," said Nicki. "And I have engaged a photographer to be here for the wedding."

Mae appeared puzzled.

"I see no point in publishing our wedding," Nicki continued. "Neither Chuck nor I are from around here. We'll send printed announcements to Chuck's old boss, Harry Thompkins, as well as Art and Rachel Towns in Massachusetts and to Chuck's North Carolina cousins," she added.

"Hey, I just got a neat idea!" cried Jennifer.

"Let's hear it, Jen." Chuck was happy to have the heat taken off him and Nicki. He realized he could not reveal to his family why he and Nicki didn't wish their faces displayed in newspaper pages.

"Pastor Evans wants to run an announcement in the church bulletin next Sunday, and he's asked me to be the reporter. So I'll just type it up on Grandpa's computer, two narrow columns wide, like a newspaper article. The church's photocopier will do a sharp job of reproducing your studio photo. We can say lots more about Daddy and Nicki than the social editor at the *Journal* would ever publish. That'd be just super!"

"I'm sure it would, dear." Grandma Basford gave Jennifer a tired glance.

"You're a lifesaver, Jen!" Nicki hugged her soon-to-be step-daughter.

"You're sure Pastor Evans won't mind?" Mae worried.

"Great idea, if you ask me!" declared Chuck, who had not been asked. *This should satisfy Mae's desire to advertise our wedding, without plastering us up as* 'Wanted, Dead or Alive' *for the general public and the Iraqis to see,* he decided.

"My, how times have changed." Mae chuckled as she hurried to the stove to check on her pie, baked from fresh, fall northern spy apples grown on the tree next to the old stone wall.

❰❰❰

"I'm a simple person, and I want a simple wedding," Nicki had told Chuck. She repeated this refrain more than once when Mae and Jennifer had urged more elaborate preparations. "Let's have the wedding on Sunday, October 22, right after church," Nicki suggested one day. "Can't we make it a harvest potluck? Country churches do stuff like that, don't they?"

"Well, yes," Mae agreed. She put on a fretful frown.

"When would we decorate?" worried Jennifer. "The teens have a party in the church fellowship hall on the night before."

"The church teens are decorating for their harvest party, aren't they?" Nicki grinned as though she had discovered a key to the whole problem.

"Yes, but they're not *wedding* decorations. They'll use leaves and cornstalks and pumpkins, stuff like that."

"Why would I wish spring flowers for a fall wedding?" Nicki grinned again. "The teens could just leave the decorations up after their party."

"Sure save a lot of headaches," Stan put in.

"But when would the actual wedding take place?" Mae was puzzled.

"Immediately after the benediction," said Chuck. "I performed a couple of weddings like that when I pastored in North Carolina. Saves the hassle of country menfolk having to dress up twice in one week." He chuckled, watching Stan try on a new pair of black, navy-last oxfords he'd bought for the wedding. Stan's usual dress-up outfit consisted of L. L. Bean gum boots worn with carefully creased green wool trousers and a neat plaid shirt—year-round. When Stan and Chuck had purchased identical charcoal-gray gabardine suits at Franklaynes Menswear in Belfast, Stan had advised Mae that, "Now you can lay to rest any more worries about what to lay me out in when the Lord calls me home."

☾☾☾

"Couldn't resist, I guess." Chuck nodded to Stan as they viewed the tin cans, shaving cream, and crepe paper plastered over the new Ford Explorer SUV Chuck had rented for the honeymoon. "I'd just as soon the whole town didn't know what we're driving off in," Chuck added in disgust.

"Ayuh! Should o' seen what they did for me and my first wife at our wedding in '44. I had an old Model A Roadster, and six guys jest picked it up and walked it sideways until they had it bumper-to-bumper 'tween a couple o' giant elms. Darned if I didn't think I was going to have to cut a tree down to get my car back."

"How did you get it out?" Chuck was nervously trying to appreciate Stan's tale.

"Jacked it up and slid planks under the wheels, crosswise. Greased 'em good. Got a neighbor with a pair of work hosses to haul it sideways with a logging chain."

"I guess tricks on the groom have been around since Laban and Leah," Chuck answered mildly as he and Stan hurried inside where Pastor Evans waited in his study for last-minute instructions.

❮❮❮

At the close of morning worship, Pastor Evans offered a "special invitation for those who wish to follow the Lord in holy matrimony." Chuck and Stan slipped down a side aisle to meet Jim Evans at the front. Jennifer, blushing in a fall orange formal bridesmaid's dress that complemented her red hair and freckles, marched alone down the center aisle as the organist, puzzled with the proceedings, continued to play "Jesus, I Come."

At this point Nicki appeared in her bridal glory at the rear, clinging to Art Towns's elbow.

Pastor Evans slipped to the organ. He pushed the sheet music to the "Lohengrin Wedding March" in front of the open hymnal. *Play this*, he mouthed.

Nicki had never forgotten the Mexican wedding in the ballroom of Arizona's famed Hotel Gadsen. A dazzling white silk gown, complete with a Spanish mantilla, tiara, and fan, set off her ebony tresses, olive complexion, and bright emerald eyes.

❮❮❮

Nicki tripped on the loose braided rug, and it sent her sprawling that morning at dawn on the kitchen floor of the rented honeymoon cabin above Snowshoe Lake in Maine's northern wilderness. For five glorious fall days the sun had shone brightly, illuminating the Maine wilderness so that she and Chuck could take marvelous hikes through the newfallen leaves, as well as canoe rides along the shoreline watching feeding moose, or just to pick brilliant bouquets of low-growing, red-leafed plants.

But Chuck and Nicki were keenly aware that they were not alone in the woods. It was deer hunting season, and almost daily citified hunters, looking silly in their new woolens, pounded on the door of the log cabin to explain that they were lost, cold, and hungry. Nicki and Chuck gave each hot coffee and a photocopied map from a stack thoughtfully left by the cabin's owner, then sent them on their way. Rifle shots echoing across the leafless woods from sunrise to sunset had kept the newlyweds nervous since their arrival.

Last evening the mercury thermometer on a pine post supporting the porch roof had registered twenty degrees Fahrenheit. Black clouds had billowed from the western hills, and Chuck remarked that even their rented Explorer's four-wheel-drive might not be equal to the frozen ruts if this turned into a nasty snowstorm.

So Nicki had wrapped herself in her bathrobe and struggled into the kitchen at daybreak to check on the weather.

"You all right, Nicki?" Chuck hurried out in his flannel pajamas when he heard her fall. "Good night! Stay DOWN!" He dropped to the floor and grabbed Nicki's ankle, dragging her away from the window. A neat hole had been drilled through the big old aluminum teakettle on the wood-fired heater against the back wall, and steam filled the room as boiling water poured onto the hot stove. Another hole penetrated the Thermopane window, though the glass had not shattered. "Dumb fool city hunters—shoot without looking for buildings behind their targets!" Chuck scurried on hands and knees to the door and scooted onto the porch.

Two men stood on a ridge in the growing daylight, several hundred yards distant.

Chuck stood up, waving his arms. "Get away from here, you idiots! This cabin is not a deer!"

One of the men answered, but his voice was carried off in the breeze. They waved, then slung their weapons across their shoulders and strolled out of sight over the crest of the hill as if nothing had occurred.

When Chuck returned, Nicki had removed the teakettle. She sat on the floor, their cell phone to her ear. "They were shooting at us, warden. Yes. We're in the Richardson cabin, south end of Snowshoe Lake."

"Warden's coming to take a statement?" Chuck wondered. "Those knuckleheads are out of here by now," he added. "You wasted a phone call."

"What should I have done? I only dialed 9-1-1." Nicki looked up crossly.

"You did the right thing. Weather's getting bad, and it's begun to snow. We'd better pack and head for South Freedom as soon as we're done talking with the law."

"Aw-w-w! It's only been five days. I'd hoped for a week," Nicki pouted.

"There's a nice hotel right in downtown Bangor," Chuck offered. "Good restaurants nearby. The *Nutcracker Ballet* starts tonight in the Queen City Opera House." He lifted the teakettle from the sink. "Only one hole?"

"Bullet's inside, lover. Five quarts of water will stop a lot of lead. We used water-filled jugs as targets on the shooting range when I practiced with CALF."

"You're right." Grimly, Chuck picked up the kettle. He poured out the remaining water and fished out the projectile. "Whew-wooo!" he whistled. "Bar the door, and stay away from the windows!" Chuck dived for the bedroom. "Ralph Richardson left an old twelve-gauge in the closet. I hope there's some ammo to go with it!"

Chuck found the double-barrelled shotgun and quickly loaded it. He began to dress.

"Will you please tell me what's going on!"

Chuck fished the missile from his pocket. "Twenty-two caliber or .223—that's not deer hunting ammo! If you hadn't tripped on that rug . . ."

"That bullet was intended for me, Chuck!" It suddenly dawned on Nicki that this was not a hunting accident. "It was a .22 bullet that John Hinckley used to shoot President Reagan!"

"This is from a varmint gun, illegal for hunting deer in Maine." Chuck held the bullet up so Nicki could appreciate it. "Possibly military—M-16 maybe, or a target rifle. The M-16 uses a .223 bullet with huge powder charge. They're popular with assassins."

"But Chuck, isn't it possible that a hunter could have been shooting at a coyote?" Nicki simply did not wish to believe that their honeymoon was being ruined like this.

"No. Coyotes aren't that common in Maine. Besides, only deer rifles and shotguns loaded for deer are permitted in the woods right now."

"The Iraqis again." Nicki turned cold.

Somebody rapped at the door. Chuck peeked out through the bedroom curtains at the green Maine Warden Service four-wheel-drive pickup parked behind his new, tan Explorer. "It's the warden."

"Ain't that little feller just too cute for words." As he examined the small-caliber bullet Chuck had handed him, Maine State Game Warden Ronnie Mason made no attempt to disguise his contempt for hunters from the city.

Chuck considered warning the warden that he believed the hunters were assassins. *No,* he decided, *they'll try to kill us if they think the warden believes their intent was homicide.*

"Let's have a chat with those boys," Ron Mason continued. "They're parked just over the hill. I saw their vehicle on my way up—out-of-state plates."

Chuck grabbed his coat. He turned to Nicki. *Stay out of sight,* he mouthed.

Nicki frowned.

The hunters had unloaded their guns by the time Chuck Reynolds and Ron Mason hiked up the ridge. At the warden's request, both displayed Maine hunting licenses and New York driver's licenses, with the same Manhattan apartment number as a home address. Both had American sounding names, though their English bore a heavy Middle Eastern accent.

One hunter carried a Browning pump-action shotgun. Warden Mason sniffed the barrel. It had not been fired. The other man indignantly handed over a brand-new Ruger semiautomatic .223-caliber varmint rifle. This gun had been fired minutes earlier,

Warden Mason's nose told him. "I shot at a deer!" the man said as he glared angrily.

"I'm sure you did, sir," Mason calmly agreed. "Your .223 caliber may be legal where you're from, but it's considered a woodchuck gun here in Maine."

Chuck stood back as Warden Mason quietly questioned the men. The warden, it seemed to Chuck, was only going to write a ticket for a misdemeanor, then require the hunter with the small-bore rifle to leave the woods. It was certainly possible that the hunter might merely have been blinded by the sun.

"Where's your clip, sir?" Warden Mason asked, almost as an afterthought.

The rifle owner scowled and dug into his hunting jacket's pocket.

Mason whistled as he took the clip. "They let you hunt with a fifty-round banana clip in New York State?"

"Sorry, Warden. I've never been hunting before."

"I'm writing you an appearance ticket for the district court in Bangor on this one," Mason said. "I've got to keep your rifle as evidence. It's only fair to warn you that if you fail to show, the judge will issue a bench warrant for your arrest, and we do extradite from New York State." Warden Mason nodded toward a new, mud-splattered sports utility vehicle half hidden behind a clump of balsam firs. "Smart thing for you to do, mister, is to get on home. Once you've seen the judge and paid your fine at the county courthouse in Bangor, your gun will be waiting for you at the Maine Warden Service station."

◖◖◖

"I guess you didn't tell Warden Mason who those guys probably are," Nicki remarked when Chuck strode back into the cabin. "Wise move."

"You're very perceptive," said Chuck. "If he'd believed they were killers, he'd have tried to arrest them on the spot for attempted murder."

"And they'd have used their pistols to kill both of you, Chuck."

"How do you know they're packing pistols?"

"Loose pant legs not tucked in, like hunters' breeches. They have pistols strapped to their boot tops, both of them; I guarantee it."

"I asked you to . . ."

"I did stay out of sight." Nicki grimaced. "Fortunately, their SUV was parked behind some firs. I threw their distributor cap in our stove."

"Good girl! It'll be a long hike back to Bangor for those guys." Chuck smiled grimly. He pointed toward the ridge, where the morning sun caught the glint of binoculars. "The warden took their only rifle, but left the other guy with his shotgun because he was legal. I expect they may be planning to drive off a ways and ambush us. But once they discover their vehicle won't start . . ." Chuck shook his head. Nicki's ingenuity always amazed him. "Right now, fortunately, we know where they are," he added.

"How did they find us here, Chuck? We didn't even use a return address when we sent my cousins in Massachusetts a wedding invitation."

"Tailed Art and Rachel Towns to the church here in Maine, most likely. Probably staked out their house in Somerville. They want you real bad." Chuck opened the door. "This cabin stands between us and those goons on the ridge, so they can't see us as we walk to the Explorer. Anyway, their pistols and the shotgun are little better than popguns at that distance."

"So . . . we just drive off. And when they jump on their horses to try and cut us off at the pass . . ." Nicki giggled and sniffed, smelling the burning plastic distributor cap in the heating stove.

"I'm glad you find it funny!"

"Not simply funny. So ludicrous it's hilarious."

Nicki drove. Chuck rode shotgun with the old double-barrelled 12-gauge loaded, both hammers cocked. It was downhill for the first quarter mile, and Nicki managed to bump over the frozen ruts at 30 mph, slush and mud flying.

"Hang on, Chuck!" Nicki hit the brakes and downshifted. The Iraqis' SUV shot down out of a pair of ruts leading uphill into a fir thicket. It tore across in front of them as the driver tried frantically to square away onto the graveled road leading from Snowshoe Lake. But with neither his power steering or power brakes operative in the coasting, dead-engine vehicle, he lost control. The swerving sports utility vehicle flipped over on the steep downgrade, then rolled onto its top in the ditch.

"Nicki, those guys are armed and dangerous!" Chuck yelled as Nicki braked the Explorer to a stop and began to back up.

"So are we. You're armed, and I'm dangerous."

Chuck leaped out and took charge of the situation as the hapless Iraqis struggled on their bellies through broken glass and twisted steel. "Hands on your heads! Stay down!"

The Iraqis obeyed.

Chuck checked their ankles. Both wore snub-nosed .38-caliber revolvers in leg holsters. He grabbed their guns, dumped their ammo into the wet snow, and tossed the pistols into the wrecked vehicle with the Iraqi's shotgun. "Now get up—into the road!"

Nicki walked up to the men.

"I don't think the lady likes you," Chuck growled.

"Jesus loves you," Nicki said, smiling. "Christ died for your sins."

One of the Iraqis immediately fell to his knees and began begging Nicki for his life.

"You said 'Died' Nicki. He thinks you asked me to kill him. I don't think his English is so hot."

"We'll let you live, sir," Nicki promised. "But we've still got to tie you guys up. Remove your boot laces—both of you!" she motioned, showing them what she wanted.

They obeyed.

Using two boot laces, Nicki tied their hands behind their backs. Then with the other pair of rawhide laces, she tied both Iraqis together in the snow to a white birch on the uphill side of the road.

"Nicki, we can't leave these guys here. They'll die of hypothermia, unless some deer hunters come along," Chuck worried.

"Then let's call help!" Nicki pulled out a book of matches and lit the entire pack. She flipped it next to the Iraqis' upturned SUV, which by then was oozing gasoline. The vehicle erupted in a ball of fire, sending a tall column of black smoke spiralling upward into the lightly falling snow. Pistol bullets popped like firecrackers as burning gasoline surged downhill away from the SUV. Louder explosions indicated that the shotgun ammunition was going off.

"You've told me many times that Maine has a very efficient fire lookout system, Chuck," Nicki observed. "Let's give the local fire warden something to report."

((((

"Well, they're onto us again," Nicki worried as they bounced toward the highway.

"Yeah." Chuck brooded, thinking. "But how? If they'd used a radio transmitter, like the one we chased those terrorists from Maine to Michigan with, they'd have been inside our cabin with us the very first night. Those things are good only for about a ten-mile radius, so they'd have had to stay close behind us."

"We're back on Saddam's satellite, Chuck. Anywhere this Explorer you rented in Portland goes, an Iraqi is tracking us from Baghdad and phoning directions to a killer here in Maine. Their cell phone is burning in the gasoline fire right now, of course."

"Why doesn't the U.S. Air Force just shoot Saddam's satellite out of the sky?" Chuck wondered. "Don't say it—'feet of clay,'" he quickly added. "Fortunately for us, those guys will spend the next several days in the Penobscot County Jail. That'll give us time to . . ."

"To what, Chuck?"

"I just don't know, Nicki." Chuck's euphoria over his marriage and new job had quickly been replaced by despair.

❰❰❰

Chuck lay on his back in the dark and snow beneath the big Ford Explorer parked that evening in the freight yard in Brownville Junction, Maine. At this remote, backwoods train switching yard, cars from Canada's mighty east-west Canadian Atlantic Railway recoupled day and night. Freight bound for cities in the States was coupled into Maine Central Railway trains for delivery to all points south, from Maine to Florida. This shortcut across the northern United States was Canada's Montreal-to-Moncton rail route to the Maritime Provinces and the Atlantic Ocean.

"Found it," cried Chuck at last. He aimed his flashlight past the transmission's transfer case and thrust his fingers in. The satellite tracking device, smaller than a pack of cigarettes, was fastened by its magnet to the SUV's floorboard.

"Can I trust you not to hop a freight car, like you did in Iraq?" Chuck grinned. He handed Nicki the device and pointed toward a Canadian Atlantic boxcar sitting on the westbound track toward Montreal.

"Just trust me!" Nicki trotted off. "That's pretty cool thinking, Chuck," she said, returning moments later. "Once they've followed that thing to Montreal, they'll look all over the city for me there, under my old alias, Yvette LaRochelle. If we're lucky, they'll follow that satellite transmitter clear to the Pacific Ocean. Are you still sure you don't want to join CALF, smarty?" she laughed.

"Trust me, I don't."

"Trust the Lord. And lighten up, sweetheart." Personal danger did not weigh nearly so heavily on Nicki as it did on Chuck.

❰❰❰

"We have, I'd guess, maybe a week to get out of the country to some place where they won't think of looking for us," Chuck said. "It should take Saddam about that long to get a new team of assassins onto our trail. Those 'deer hunters' will quickly be deported, I'm sure." He and Nicki were eating breakfast next morning in the posh dining room of Boston's downtown Hilton Hotel near the Common. "I can get cash for my shares in Salem Electronics, but it's going to take me a couple of days." He sighed, thinking. "We can take up to ten thousand apiece out of the country. Once that's gone, we'll need employment."

"There's that old manuscript," Nicki said quietly.

"The Hniqi parchment? I'm sure you'll want to take it along, and I don't blame you. But if you try to get into your safe-deposit box—if the Iraqis are watching it . . ."

"That's a mite paranoid, Chuck, though I can't say that I blame you. The Iraqis simply don't have enough agents to watch us all the time. I learned that much from CALF."

"Arnold and el-Haaj bugged my apartment and the restaurant where Harry and I used to eat. I'm certain now it wasn't the FBI."

"*Bugged* it," Nicki repeated. "If they had men enough to watch it, would they have bothered to bug it?"

"Good point. I guess Arnold and el-Haaj were Saddam's entire force in New England. And his most recent appointees are nursing their wounds in the Penobscot County Jail in Bangor right now."

"Do I detect a note of sarcasm?"

Chuck laughed. "OK, so I go back to Salem today and clean out my desk."

"Remember to say good-bye to Miss Molly," snickered Nicki.

Chuck rolled his eyes. "I'm sure she misses Arnold and el-Haaj more than me."

"Maybe if you had been nicer to her?"

"Next, I'll go over to my apartment and grab my papers." Chuck ignored Nicki's tease. "I'll let the landlord keep what I can't stuff into a suitcase. But what about your apartment?"

Nicki giggled. "It was just an address. CALF paid the rent. When I resigned, they cleaned it out, I'm sure. I do have a . . . a fairly major business transaction coming up, though. It should be worth a few dollars to us."

"Oh?"

"When I was a student at Harvard, the university library offered me fifty thousand dollars for the Hniqi parchment. They even ran a carbon-14 test to authenticate its age."

"Let's see—2,600 years old. That must make it about the oldest intact parchment in existence. Say—that's even older than the Dead Sea Scrolls!"

"I could put it up for public auction and maybe get twenty times that figure—a million or more, they advised me."

"Why don't you?" Chuck asked, though he knew the answer. With the publicity, Nicki could hardly expect to live through an auction.

"Oh, I could have sold the manuscript years ago, before I had the Iraqis on my back. But . . . I just couldn't let such a document disappear into some private collector's vault. It's too precious not to be passed on for public use. Harvard's rare documents curator will see that it's kept available for scholarly research."

"I imagine it's an archaeological treasure of interest to Bible scholars too. But how do the American Assyrians and CALF feel about all this?"

"They'd like to see it in the American Assyrian Ashurbanipal Library in Chicago, of course. One of them has even said he will match Harvard's price. But . . ." Nicki sighed.

"But?"

"This way it gets much wider exposure. The Ashurbanipal Library is little known, except to our own Assyrian people, who are a very narrow slice of the American population. Hniqi's story is for the entire Christian world to appreciate."

"So . . . ?"

"So when do I get the money? You're not greedy?"

"We do have a tight schedule, Nicki."

"I can't just walk into the library with the manuscript and expect them to cut me a check for fifty grand on the spot. There has to be current research, a committee meeting, that sort of thing. Their official offer to purchase expired years ago."

"Well." Chuck sighed.

"CALF owes me one," Nicki affirmed.

"I thought you weren't selling to the Assyrians." Chuck raised an eyebrow.

"I'm not. But they'll manage the sale and deposit the money in a secret account I've kept in a Swiss bank in Zurich for several years. The Ashurbanipal Library will get a facsimile inked onto genuine vellum, hand-copied in Hebrew by a rabbi, at Harvard University's expense, of course. That will be worth several thousand dollars, so they'll be rewarded also."

"A facsimile of the manuscript, not the check, I presume," Chuck laughed.

◖◖◖

Chuck returned to the hotel from a day of closing out accounts to find Nicki napping on the bed. "It really blows people's minds when you pay cash for airline tickets, Nicki," he laughed. "Would you believe that the ticket agent had to really scrounge around just to make change?"

The woman on the bed rolled over and sat up. She blinked, then gingerly touched her Chinese eyes. Where Nicki had had flowing, wavy, off-her-forehead locks, this woman had bangs and straight, waist-length hair.

"Who . . . ? What did you do with my wife?"

"I am Ngo Thieu," the lady teased in Vietnamese. She smiled, and her eyes glowed iridescent green in the afternoon sun streaming over Beacon Hill. "I went out to see a plastic surgeon this morning. When my stitches come out in a couple of days, I'll be ready to travel, Chuck." She pointed to tiny surgical stitches in the outer corners of each eye. "He didn't have to do much—just put my eyes back the way they were when I left Vietnam."

Chuck gaped.

Nicki giggled. "The Iraqis will be looking for Nicki Towns, Assyrian. Fortunately, they are watching for my face. It's a good thing they can't track me by my fingerprints or DNA."

"But . . . but your passport?" Chuck stammered.

"I had a new passport photo taken this afternoon after the operation, and I took it right over to the Boston office of the U.S. State Department, along with my Vietnamese birth certificate."

"Well . . . I . . . *did* purchase your ticket in the name of Ngo Thieu. But I never imagined. Did I really marry . . . ?"

"Kiss me, Chuck," Ngo sighed. "It's time you get used to kissing the face I was born with."

(((

Dearest Jennifer,

Chuck began on hotel stationery he found in the nightstand. He laid his pen down, for his eyes had filled with tears. He was leaving her, not for a week "on business" this time, but perhaps never to see her again. Chuck worried, too, that Jennifer might not merely worry and pray, but become bitter and rebel. Yet Jennifer had a close relationship with the Lord, two loving, supportive grandparents, and, at nearly seventeen, she was moving into adulthood at a rate Chuck found—well, terrifying.

My Darling Daughter,

He began again,

Please share this letter with Grandma and Grandpa Basford. As you can see by the postmark, Nicki and I had to cut our honeymoon short to settle our affairs in Boston, then we are leaving the country. This has been a crazy fall. Already I have been to Mexico, Israel, Iraq, and Canada. I hope I can tell you enough of our situation to help you understand, yet I realize you won't really understand. Nobody could, not knowing all the answers.

It is important that you remain strong, pray, read your Bible, obey your grandparents. Most important of all, trust God to work out the details of your life and ours. Do not defeat the Lord's purposes in your life as Esau did by being bitter (see Hebrews 12:1–3; 12–17). Instead, bless God with your praises daily, and He certainly will bless you.

When I met Nicki, she was involved in a movement to overthrow a foreign government, an enemy of the United States. Her father's family were exiles from that country, since her grandparents were among a number of Christians who were slaughtered by this enemy government. Their case was ignored by the League of Nations, and more recently by the United Nations.

Nicki believed she was helping fulfill a Bible prophecy (Isaiah 19:23–25). Though I do agree with her interpretation of the Bible, I cannot agree with the methods she was using, and Nicki has also come to see these methods as wrong. Jesus told Peter to put his sword away (Matthew 26:51–54). Like Peter, Nicki has turned her back on using violence to bring Christ's Kingdom to earth. She and I will of course fight to defend ourselves or our country.

I know this is heavy stuff, but it's necessary for you to know if you're going to make any sense out of why Nicki and I have to leave.

Nicki and I have both been shot at several times, and my car was bombed (that's why I no longer have my old Corvette). Two days ago at Snowshoe Lake while we were on our honeymoon, Nicki was fired at by two assassins, and they would have killed her if God hadn't caused her to trip and fall to the floor.

DO NOT DISCUSS THIS WITH THE WARDEN OR POLICE. THE PEOPLE WHO WANT TO KILL NICKI MAY TRY TO KILL YOU, MAE, & STAN IF THEY BELIEVE YOU ARE MAKING TROUBLE FOR THEM. EVEN IF THESE TWO ASSASSINS GET DEPORTED, MORE WILL COME IN THEIR PLACE—I'M SURE OF IT!

Nicki and I are not going into a court-sponsored witness-protection program, Jennifer. There are spies in our own government who would kill us if we were to try to get help through the courts. Sooner or later these things will come out, and we will be free to come home.

If you find what I have told you hard to believe, here's a little assignment: Go to your school library and look up magazine articles about Aldrich Ames in "Reader's Guide to Periodical Literature." Ames is a convicted spy serving a life sentence for espionage against the United States. He caused the deaths of at least a dozen American CIA agents working in Russia before he was caught. Nicki and I are in the same kind of danger as those murdered Americans Ames targeted in exchange for Russian money. There is this difference, Jennifer: we do know who our enemies are; they did not until it was too late.

The Ames case leads to another of Nicki's intriguing theories. She believes that the United States of America, if divided into ten regions, may become the "Feet of Clay" of Daniel's prophetic image vision of the last days before Jesus' return to set up His millennial Kingdom (Daniel 2:32–45). The clay (verses 42–43) is democracy corrupted by courts that have undermined our Constitution, Nicki believes. "In any nation but America, Ames would have been put to death for betraying his country," Nicki said to me one day. "Uncle Sam's hands are tied by public opinion. He is a weak giant, unable to defend himself," she said. I could not argue with Nicki. There was a time when traitors, such as the Rosenbergs (another assignment—this one's in your encyclopedia) were executed. God is just, as well as loving. I believe the time will come when evil men such as Ames and those who wish to kill Nicki will be dealt with in justice and righteousness.

Now for some lighter things. We are traveling to a sunny, happy land where business is booming, Americans are welcome, and there'll be lots of opportunity to serve the Lord. Probably when you see us again, you will have small brothers and sisters. We expect to eat well and live well. You cannot write to us, but Nicki and I will write you as soon as we make friends who can mail our letters to you from another country—that should be quite soon.

Love, Daddy

Dear Jennifer,

Here are my additions to your father's letter. We both love you very much. You can't imagine how happy I am to have Chuck Reynolds as my husband. I wish with all my heart that you could go with us as we fly into the sunset, but very soon, I believe, we'll return for a happy sunrise together. Oh, how I loved to watch the sun come up in South Freedom over Grandpa Stan's barn!

I have only this advice: Laugh a lot; cry a little; pray a lot. Read the Bible clear through each year. Trust Jesus—He'll see you through.

Love, Nicki

))) (((

As the Vietnamese Airlines 747 lifted into the night sky out of Osaka, Japan, to turn southwest over the East China Sea, Chuck Reynolds felt Ngo Thieu's grip tighten on his fingers until the circulation ceased. Chuck realized that the dread and wonder he felt at returning to the land he and his buddies had left just short of winning a war a quarter century earlier could scarcely match Ngo's fearful excitement at returning to the land of her nativity.

So fiercely had his wife, as Nicki, fought to preserve her legacy as an Assyrian that it seemed as if she must actually have become another person. Yet Nicki was not another person. Would the dichotomy between Nicki the Assyrian exile and Ngo the Vietnamese refugee tear her apart? Chuck wondered.

Tomorrow Nicki and I—or is it Ngo? he pondered, *will eat breakfast together in the city of two names—Ho Chi Minh City and Saigon— a city bound to its French colonial and communist past, yet one that is trying to rush into its modern future as a commercial and tourism center in Southeast Asia. Each name, too, has its own human tales of blood, of grief, of sorrow—and of hope and forgiveness.*

This was the continuation of their honeymoon trip, a trip that Chuck had begun with one woman and continued with another. Chuck and Ngo relaxed in their first-class seats, tilting back now to sleep, if sleep would come.

"Chuck?" The woman next to him snapped the light on, turning it into her own face.

"Yes?"

Nicki rounded her eyes with her fingertips and grinned. "Take a last look, darling. It may be a long, long time before you see me this way again."

"Good-night, Ngo." Chuck kissed his Asian bride and flipped the light off.

19

Shangri-La

Your sins are forgiven. . . .
Arise and walk.

—Jesus

I'm coming *home,* Richard."

Chuck tuned his ears to the soft voice of the pretty blonde who bent toward the guy in the next seat. The man, who sat next to Chuck, had laid aside an English Bible he had appeared to be trying to translate into spoken Vietnamese by speaking the words aloud. He now spoke to his wife in English.

Chuck had spent most of the flight from Osaka to Saigon trying to soften the expected cultural shock by absorbing all he could from the mostly Asian passengers in the Vietnam Airways 747. This friendly couple in the next two seats, however, had interested him only a little since they were Americans like himself.

Until now.

Chuck glanced at Penelope Hayward, then returned to pretending to read a travel magazine, listening to her tell her husband about her childhood in Vietnam.

"How old were you?" Richard asked.

"Six months when we left Indiana. I was eight when we flew out of here during the evacuation. Doctor Yoder and his wife gave me and my sister Amy their seats on the plane. They escaped later with the boat people."

Chuck knew this scenario. Desperate groups of refugees had been getting out of Saigon in '75. They included American and European missionaries; businesspeople, both Westerners and Chinese; families of government officials; and officers in the South Vietnamese army, with their families.

Chuck was there too, a young GI with seminary training, chaplain to a fighting unit that had seen its men chopped up like mincemeat by ambush after ambush. Though considered a noncombatant, Chuck had insisted on tramping through the booby-trapped rice paddies and mined palm groves on patrol with the soldiers. Once, when his unit's M-60 gunman had been cut down by a Vietcong ambush, Chuck, who had handled hunting guns since childhood, had grabbed the machine gun and laid down a line of hot lead while his boys found cover and the sergeant designated a replacement for the gunner.

But if fighting in the paddies was hades, the evacuation of Saigon, overrun by North Vietnam regulars and Vietcong, was the abyss of hell itself, Chuck remembered. He had grabbed his .45-caliber pistol, his only weapon through most of the war, and commandeered a boat carrying refugees to a freighter-cum-passenger liner in the harbor just to get things moving in the confusion. A Saigon city official's wife had brought her maid along, and the girl carried a baby wrapped in a cloth. She lugged a pig, as well, also wrapped in cloth, under her other arm. "No baggage," Chuck had yelled, seeing that the overloaded boat might easily swamp.

The shrieking maid had held up both bundles, protesting loudly in a torrent of Vietnamese.

"Choose one!" Angry at the woman's irrational behavior, Chuck had used sarcasm. He had then turned, using his pistol to hold off a desperate mob. The official's wife translated Chuck's English for her maid while the boatmen pushed their motor launch off.

When he turned back, the maid still clutched the pig. The drowned baby bobbed in the murky flow of the Saigon River. Chuck had spent his tour of duty among soldiers who cursed with every breath, yet he had not once resorted to profanity. This time, horrified by the nature of the murder, he swore at the deranged pig owner.

"She say she can get more baby. Not get more pig," the maid's mistress had explained.

❰❰❰

"Perhaps we can find your parents' graves," Richard suggested.

Chuck's thoughts returned to the present. He had learned during the plane ride that Richard Hayward was an English professor from a Christian college in the Midwest and his wife, Penelope, was a health education instructor as well as a part-time nurse. Having no children, they had taken a sabbatical from their jobs to teach English for the Hanoi government.

Like many other Americans, the Haywards would use the Bible as the basis for their English lessons. Vietnamese Communist officials, some of them with Christian beliefs themselves, often overlooked the Bible-as-textbook approach to evangelizing spiritually hungry Vietnamese, so long as no Christian literature was handed out and no attempt was made to organize converts into churches.

Now Chuck learned that Penelope Hayward had a deeper link than he to Vietnam. "Your parents died in Vietnam?" Chuck asked, intruding into the private conversation.

"Yes." She answered quietly, fearful almost.

Chuck and Nicki had already introduced themselves, and Penny and Rick knew that the Reynoldses, like themselves, were Christian believers. Chuck, they knew, had been an Army chaplain during the war. Now, they decided, he was probably an American entrepreneur, returning to help rebuild Vietnam in a new era of wide-open markets and free-wheeling capitalism, encouraged even by Communist officials.

"I lost my wife when our daughter was three," Chuck told this daughter of missionary parents. "It's not the same as losing parents," he quickly admitted.

Penelope pointed a finger at her head and sadly mouthed one horrid word: *Bang.*

Richard's jaw dropped at this shocking revelation. "You never told me this, Penny. I thought . . ."

"That they died of a fever. No. I've never told anyone about it until now. I watched my parents' execution. They shot them both, like in that old news photo of the Saigon Chief of Police killing a Vietcong suspect with his pistol. Just like that."

"I . . . may we trade seats, Chuck?" Nicki asked quickly.

"I'll trade with Chuck, if it's all right," Penny said, fighting tears. She rose from her window seat and began to squirm past her husband.

As Nicki hugged Penny and prayed with her, Chuck brooded silently in the window seat, watching the distant green line of the coastline of Southeast Asia crawl past to the west as the plane droned southward. Americans had given their lives on many fronts in Vietnam, Chuck knew. But here was a woman who had seen violence on a more personal level than he or Nicki had experienced, yet the Lord had brought her through. Chuck had believed only an hour earlier that the Haywards were hopeless idealists. Now his assessment of them shifted 180 degrees.

◖◖◖

"They're still here!" Nicki pointed to a row of ornate, leather-padded iron chairs on a low platform along one lobby wall of the

Hotel de Ville. The shoeblack stands, like the old French hotel, dated from the old days of French colonialism when Chinese businessmen seeking a bit of Western opulence could have their kangaroo-leather, high-topped dress shoes waxed to a mirror sheen by Vietnamese street boys for a few copper coins. "I was a shoe shine boy here for a couple of years after the war," Nicki explained.

"Boy?" Chuck raised an amused eyebrow.

"Yes. The work available for girls was not suited to the way my mother raised me. Also, I respected my father's memory."

"I understand. But how on earth did you get a job?"

"With my fists." Nicki laughed. "And I had to keep my job with my fists, too, at least once a week."

"You she-tiger!" he laughed. "Is this where you learned to fight?"

"There were always six or eight boys wanting to rent each chair. Whoever could beat the others in a fistfight got the job."

"So you just . . ."

"Dressed like a boy. Then I would pound the dickens out of the next guy in line."

Chuck shook his head and stepped to the counter. "Room for two. Top floor, please."

"Forty dollars plus tax. Fifty-two, total," the elderly Vietnamese clerk said in Asian-accented English.

Chuck turned to Nicki. The price was reasonable in an American economy, even in this aging hotel. But it was much more than a vendor down the street had told him the Hotel de Ville charged. "What do you think?"

Nicki spoke softly to the desk clerk in Vietnamese. She pointed at the shoe shine stand where several businessmen and a lady were getting their shoes polished.

The clerk shrugged, held up his palms, grinned.

"*Merci beaucoup*," Nicki responded, this time in French. She passed the man a twenty-dollar bill. "Two nights, in advance, please." Armed now with a door key, Nicki strode toward the elevator. "C'mon, Chuck!"

A porter grabbed their bags before Chuck realized what was happening.

As the porter plunked their bags on the antique, brass-trimmed open-cage elevator, Nicki tipped him with an American quarter. After the elevator operator let them off at the fifth floor and toted their bags to their room without being asked, Nicki paid him with a quarter also.

"You gave that guy only twenty dollars—for *two* days?" Chuck was amazed.

"Tax and all. It's the going rate—I was listening to that street vendor, too, while you were trying to figure out if she meant what she said! Some of the help—the porter and the elevator boy, for instance—pay the manager for the privilege of working here and collecting tips, unless things have changed in that department since I left."

"I'm surprised that the guy didn't get mad when you caught him trying to rip us off because we look like tourists." Chuck shook his head.

"Oh, I sweet-talked him a bit. Told him that I used to shine shoes here. That helped him save face by letting him imagine he was doing a favor for an old friend."

〈〈〈

"Where have you been today, Chuck?" It was the second day since their arrival in Vietnam, and Chuck had spent several hours as a cyclo—or pedicab—passenger exploring Australian hotels and resorts along the Saigon River in downtown Ho Chi Minh City.

"Job hunting."

"Did you find anything, Chuck?"

Nicki sounds a mite worried, Chuck thought. "We've only just arrived," he explained. "Our rent is ten dollars U.S. money a day, so we're not about to go broke for several months. But I've been looking around. No interviews yet. Just visiting a few places where I may apply later." Chuck's biggest concern at the moment was the security of the funds in cash he and Nicki had yesterday deposited in Saigon's new Honshu Bank of Japan, though he tried not to worry Nicki. The unstable condition of the Asian economy made him concerned that his and Nicki's financial status could nosedive before he found a satisfactory job.

"Chuck."

Chuck had heard this tone before—flat, emotionless, a warning. He cleared his mind for what Nicki might have on hers. "Yes?"

"This is our honeymoon, lover." To Chuck's surprise, Nicki's worry was not money.

"I . . . I know." To tell the truth, Chuck had nearly forgotten. Romance had all but evaporated with the assassination attempt at Snowshoe Lake. There had been the night trip to Boston after shipping the satellite tracking device to Montreal from Brownville Junction in a freight car, then switching auto rentals in Portland to ensure that they were traveling in a nonbugged vehicle. A whirlwind of legal and financial papers to deal with in Boston, changing hotels every day, always looking over their shoulders. Nicki's dramatic transformation from a slightly Asian Caucasian to very Asian Oriental. Separate airline ticket purchases in Boston and Los Angeles. Only in Osaka did they purchase tickets as husband and wife and take adjacent seats. The jet lag. The culture shock.

And the need for a job before their money ran out.

"Can we take a few weeks off?" Nicki asked. "Maybe go camping up north?"

"Y . . . yes. But camping in Vietnam?" Chuck had visions of man-eating jungle tigers and twenty-foot pythons.

"I know just the place." She grinned and held up a travel brochure. "We'll need some gear and a motorboat, of course. Ha Long Bay, near Hanoi. We'll buy our gear here in Saigon. Then we can take the train north to Hanoi, where we can pick up a boat at the Hanoi waterfront on the Song Coi River."

"Hanoi?" Chuck was alarmed. Hanoi was the Communist capital of Vietnam.

"It's safe," Nicki said confidently.

"But it's been a dozen years since you lived here."

"While you've been visiting Australian tourist resorts looking for work, I've been busy—making friends, asking questions, reading travel guides from the hotel lobby, and practicing my native language. Would you believe it's all coming back?"

"I'd believe . . . I don't know what I'd believe about you. . . ." Chuck found his wife's self-confidence to be breathtaking at times. His voice trailed off, and he turned his attention to adjusting the elderly air conditioner that struggled rheumatically against the stifling heat.

"It's not so warm up north this time of year," Nicki observed "The weather is dry and comfortable. We'll both wear native Vietnamese clothing and try to remain low-key."

"Which means that you've got to do all the talking." Chuck usually had no trouble dealing with street vendors, since most in Saigon could speak a bit of English. But near the capital city, where Westerners were seldom seen, English might make him an object of suspicion.

"You can speak to *me* anytime, Chuck. Where we're going, there's nobody else to talk to."

Both found that the romance was coming back.

🌙🌙🌙

"You didn't buy the train tickets?"

"No," Chuck answered softly. To avoid saying more for the moment, he stepped onto the balcony. In the twilight, the traffic along Dinh Phung Boulevard below was an unceasing flow of humanity. Businessmen, tourists, wrinkled old grannies were pushed along on bike wheels in cyclos—three-wheeled pedicabs once known as rickshas. Motorbikes and bicycles darted in and out. Pedestrians hurried along beneath broad, conical hats of woven rushes. Autos, trapped in the throng, moved at what surely seemed to the drivers the pace of oozing glue. Unlike Iraq, no donkeys, camels, or horses though. The only animals present in Ho Chi Minh City were dogs.

"Many shall run to and fro." Chuck smiled, remembering the closing words of the prophecy of Nicki's distant cousin, Daniel. "'Knowledge shall increase,'" Daniel had added to his inspired observation of life in the latter days as he peered two and a half millennia into the future. Daniel understood books, certainly; for though he had never seen a printing press, he had written a book. But electronic communications—the ability to transport bookfuls of knowledge at the speed of light to any corner of the earth—this would baffle Daniel.

For the moment it baffled Chuck, and it worried him. Just this morning he and Nicki had eaten a late breakfast in a curbside cafe overlooking the Saigon River. Freighters from around the world plied this muddy current, carrying computers, TVs, refrigerators, automobiles; leaving laden with rubber, rice, sugar, textiles, shoes. American freighters flying the Stars and Stripes, pleasure cruisers carrying tourists from Australia, boats bearing the red flag of the Peoples Republic of China or Japan's rising sun. And . . . ?

"Nicki!" Chuck had exclaimed. He pointed to a freighter bearing an eerily familiar Middle-Eastern national flag. The ship's name was painted on the bow in red, flamelike symbols, mysterious to the uninitiated.

"The Babylonia," translated Nicki, who had learned a few Arabic words during her incarceration in Baghdad. "That ship is from Iraq."

Though the tropical evening was warm, Chuck shuddered on the balcony now, remembering. Nicki had been right, of course. "We could introduce ourselves to that ship's captain and mingle with those Iraqi sailors. They wouldn't know us from Adam and Eve," she had laughed.

Chuck stared again at the moving throng below. One tap on a computer key halfway around the world, and he and Nicki would be running again, he realized. Being lost in the crowd was only a transient experience in an era of electronic communications.

He felt Nicki's arm around his waist, and she rumpled his hair. "Worried, darling?" Nicki kissed his neck and blew, warm and humid, into his ear. "I *do* understand why you couldn't bring yourself to buy those train tickets. There are several changes and a lot of checkpoints along the way, I'm sure."

Nicki did not now repeat her old argument: "There are thousands of Ngo Thieus in Vietnam," to which he had always countered, "But only one Charles Robert Reynolds." Instead she said, "*If we go to Saigon and Ha Long Bay we'll find a way that doesn't require that we show our ID every few hours.*"

"Thank you," Chuck said. *Thank You, Jesus,* he prayed.

"Close the shutters and come inside," Nicki murmured. "We'll worry about the trip later."

《《《

The *Empress of Beijing* plowed northward along the Vietnamese coast toward Hong Kong, its antique, coal-fired steam engines belching soot into the tropical night. Squirming uncomfortably inside a cabin cruiser lashed to the *Empress's* deck, Chuck had adjusted his folded canvas, which passed for a mattress, for what seemed like the hundredth time.

He was trying to sleep while lying across the ribs of their old, wooden, French-built cabin cruiser. Nicki had bought the boat several days ago for five hundred American dollars.

Chuck had had a new, Toyota-built V-6 installed for two thousand more. And for five hundred dollars, the *Empress's* captain had agreed to strap their small cabin cruiser to the ship's deck for the journey north.

An outlay of three hundred dollars more had bought them a tent, gasoline stove, aluminum cooking utensils, canned goods and baking goods, snorkeling gear, rock climbing equipment, and an air mattress.

Ah, that air mattress! It was supposed to keep the honeymooners comfortable for the week they would spend at Ha Long Bay. Chuck believed it might have that capability, but it required a flat surface on which to lay it. Inside this motor launch, riding on the Chinese vessel's deck for the journey of five days and five nights, not a flat surface could be found. Sleeping in the open air was out of the question because of the pitching sea.

Chuck now vowed to change things tomorrow—if he and Nicki could communicate with the Chinese sailors well enough to borrow a couple of wooden pallets and several loose boards from the *Empress's* hold, that is.

"I've asked the captain to put us and our boat off at Haiphong before he continues to Hong Kong," Nicki explained the next morning. She had spread open a tour map of Vietnam as they ate a breakfast of tea and crackers. "It will take about four hours with our boat to reach Ha Long Bay from there. Except for an occasional fishing boat, we should have an oceanside paradise to ourselves."

((((

But Ha Long (Ascending Dragon) Bay was anything but a deserted Eden, Chuck and Nicki discovered. As he steered among the three thousand tiny, towerlike islands, boat villages appeared around every bend. These were family-sized barges lashed together three or four dozen to a group to form neighborhoods where naked small children played and jumped from boat to boat, women cooked rice and fish over coal fires in steel-bucket or clay-pot stoves, and men mended fishing nets or repaired their boats. Instead of sails, on the barges there were clotheslines draped with brilliantly colored shirts, sarongs, scarves, and trousers.

Smaller boats putt-putted with outboard motors throughout these floating islands as traders took squid, crabs, and fish in exchange for fresh water, vegetables, textiles, gasoline, kerosene, and coal. Other vessels were there too, small fishing boats anchored to the barges. These were used dusk-to-dawn to furnish a livelihood for these sea people as the men went nightly to cast their nets, like Peter and the apostles on Galilee, to feed and support their families. Chuck and Nicki found that they had traveled from a world moving at the speed of light to a world little changed in two thousand years.

"There's *got* to be a place where we can be alone!" Nicki was dismayed as she unfolded a brochure titled *Natural Wonders of Vietnam*. These unique, rugged islands, according to the text, had "Once been on the bottom of an ancient sea bed."

Chuck pointed their boat's bow eastward, toward the open sea. "I guess we won't get stranded for lack of gas," he said, nodding toward where a trader passed twenty-liter plastic cans of gasoline to a fisherman on a barge.

"First time I've seen a floating service station," Nicki agreed.

❮❮❮

"This is our cave!" Nicki grinned, grabbing the bundles as Chuck heaved them from the boat. "I told you we'd find a spot by ourselves, Chuck. And the weather is great!"

"The weatherman certainly agrees with you." Chuck had been listening to English-language broadcasts on his short-wave radio, switching occasionally from Hong Kong to Singapore to Bangkok then back to Hong Kong, trying by triangulation to guess what the weather for the next five days would be in their protected corner of the South China Sea. "Except for morning fogs, it's supposed to be fair weather," he said.

❮❮❮

Splash!

"I think I've married Spiderwoman," Chuck laughed as, moments later, he dived in to join Nicki swimming in the tropical sea. Though the ocean was warm by American standards, it was cool enough in November so that sharks were seldom seen this far north. According to the natives, only "crazy Americans" found swimming fun this time of year. "How are you going to get back up there?" he asked. Nicki had rappelled to the top of a sheer, thirty-foot cliff above their private cave. She had left her climbing clothes on the ledge and jumped off.

"The same way I got up there the first time, smarty."

"You're the monkey!" Chuck was decidedly not a rock climber, and this was no Mt. Katahdin.

"Get our snorkeling masks from the boat, Chuck."

"Sure." He grabbed the ladder and swung aboard.

"This place is one vast aquarium." Nicki bobbed up after some moments of snorkeling and watching the endless profusion of tropical fish dart among the rocks in the sunlit sea. "Sure would be fun if we had air tanks," she laughed.

"We tried to rent them, remember?" he reminded her. Rented diving gear was feasible to use only for a day or two. Buying, Chuck had told Nicki, was out of the question until he found a job. Unlike their boat, there might not be a chance to sell the equipment for even close to what it cost once the honeymoon was over. "I've had enough of swimming for now," he added. "Why don't we rest awhile, then explore the cave. I'd like to see some of those stalactites in there close up."

◖◖◖

"Five million dong," the trader said, eyeing Chuck and Nicki's boat. "Best price I give you."

Chuck had already refused offers of boatloads of fish by the ton, a shipment of pots and pans, and cans of gasoline. One trader had offered him a load of Chinese-built TV sets which, he assured Chuck, would "Bring good price in Hanoi. Make big profit."

"He can make his *own* profit then!" Discouraged after two days of haggling, Chuck had snapped at Nicki. Now he was about to accept the Vietnamese currency, barely enough money to pay for the two airline tickets he and Nicki needed to fly from Hanoi to Saigon. Saigon was their home now, but this city of their choice lay nearly a thousand miles to the south.

"Let me," Nicki interrupted. She patted Chuck's arm, then began to dicker with the man in Vietnamese. A Chinese trader, he needed a boat he could trust to take him weekly through the

Kiungchow Straits, back and forth from Hong Kong. Nicki had seen the glint in the man's eyes when he examined the powerful, new Toyota V-6 engine below decks. An animated dialogue followed.

Chuck thought at times that Nicki and the Chinese merchant would come to blows, and he would have to defend her. The battle of words raged on, rising and falling.

Chuck was embarrassed.

Nobody else on the dock seemed to notice.

"I buy," the trader declared at last, switching to English to get Chuck's attention. He grinned as though he had won the battle and counted out the million-dong notes into Chuck's hand, fifteen of them.

Chuck passed the Chinese trader the boat keys. Then he immediately handed the money to Nicki. "In this corner of the world I guess women are expected to be trusted with only enough money to buy a chicken or a kilo of rice," he laughed.

(((

Chuck frowned as he sat in the lobby of Hanoi International Airport waiting for their flight to Ho Chi Minh City. The wall mural opposite him could not be misunderstood. though the words were Vietnamese. Two valiant North Vietnamese soldiers were shown finishing off a cowardly white-bearded Uncle Sam, dressed in a top hat and a red, white, and blue stars-and-stripes suit. They stabbed him with their bayonets as he begged for mercy. "What's the sign say?" Chuck asked Nicki.

"In honor of the glorious heroes of the American War," she translated.

Chuck watched the passengers come and go for a few moments. Most of these were young men and women, born since the war, or like Nicki, too young to remember. No one else even bothered to look at the mural with its peeling paint, he noticed. Several shaded lamps above it had bulbs missing.

"American?" inquired a Vietnamese man who stepped up just then. The guy stuck his hand out to Chuck, bowing slightly.

Chuck rose and shook the man's hand. He was short, slender, black-haired with no trace of gray, though wrinkled around the eyes. He wore a rumpled black suit with no tie, like an independent businessman. "Yes, I'm an American," Chuck said.

"I fight Americans." The man grinned.

Chuck frowned.

"That many years ago. Now we happy when Americans visit our fine land."

Chuck smiled. *Happy for our money, no doubt,* he thought. *But at least this man's friendly.*

"I find Jesus from Americans. Many Vietnamese know Jesus."

Nicki smiled. She spoke to the man softly in Vietnamese. They chatted for a while.

"Jesus, He bless you both," the man said in English. He hurried off.

"Tell me about that guy, Nicki," Chuck said as soon as the man was gone.

"He's a Christian—once a Buddhist, like many in Vietnam. He's Communist, though. Like a lot of them, he doesn't see any inconsistency."

"To many people, Communism is just another system of law and order, I guess," Chuck observed. Though Chuck hated the larger implications of Marxism, he tried to understand this Asian Christian's perspective.

"He explained that only a few Vietnamese still resent Americans. Even those who remember the war are not bitter, except the few hard-line Communists, many of whom run the government. Some of the people even still remember that it was the Americans who liberated them from Japanese imperialism after World War II— with the help of Ho Chi Minh, of course, that man said."

"Of course," Chuck agreed. "Now the Vietnamese play American music on Japanese radios." He nodded toward a Vietnamese teen girl who snapped her fingers in time to the rock tune on her CD player.

¢¢¢

"I am now a development agent for Australian Wallangong Resorts, Ltd., and you, darling, are my assistant and personal translator." Chuck made this happy announcement a week after he and Nicki had returned to Ho Chi Minh City's nineteenth-century Hotel de Ville. "We move into the Royal Wallangong Hotel tomorrow. It's a brand-new place, and they're giving us a five-room suite."

"Dare I ask how much?" Nicki caught her breath.

"Sixty thousand Australian dollars to start, plus expenses and perks. That's not quite forty grand, U.S. money. Hardly a king's fortune, but with housing furnished . . ."

"Oh, Chuck," Nicki cut him off. "In this city that's a lot of money. If we're careful, we can save."

"For a little farmstead in Maine," he laughed.

¢¢¢

"We look for American ex-GIs like you to work as front men for us, Chuck." Monty Andrews, vice-president of Australian Wallangong Resorts, Ltd., warmed to his subject as Chuck and Nicki listened and took notes. "We need college men, men with executive experience. And your lovely wife, Ngo Thieu, will open a lot of doors for you, I'm sure."

Nicki smiled appreciatively.

"I'd like to offer you a job, as well, Mrs. Reynolds."

"Thanks just the same." Nicki laughed. "But we're a team."

"Well, let me know if you change your mind," Andrews added.

"I've already gotten the impression that Americans are accepted quite well in Vietnam," Chuck said. He told Andrews about his encounter with the former North Vietnamese infantryman at the Hanoi airport. Chuck also mentioned the anti-American mural.

"There are some of those murals here in Ho Chi Minh City too." Andrews cursed, then chuckled. "They do get vandalized once in awhile, but six months' jail time usually gets the word out that the Communist government won't stand for being made fun of. Most Vietnamese are embarrassed by them, though. Especially here in the South, where there are still several hundred thousand veterans who once fought against Ho Chi Minh's regulars along-side American GIs to keep their democracy. Right now, though, most are happy enough to see the officials look the other way so that free enterprise can thrive. That's where we come in."

"You said *family* resorts?" Nicki queried. Neither she nor Chuck had visited Australia, but both assumed that the Western, nominally Christian pattern of family living prevailed in Monty Andrews's homeland as it did in North America and most of Europe. Nicki was aware, however, that businessmen, who usually travel alone, often forget family commitments when visiting a distant city.

"Yes, ma'am!" Andrews was emphatic. "Saigon and southern Vietnam are only a few hours by plane from Australia, and just a little farther from New Zealand. About the same from Japan and a short trip from Manila in the Philippines. We can also cut deals with the airlines to offer cheap airfare from Europe and North America." Andrews rubbed his hands together in pleasure.

"Families—with wives and children?" Chuck did not wish to misunderstand or to be misunderstood.

"Absolutely. Our prices range from the low end of Holiday Inn's scale to the high end of Hilton's poshest. Nothing higher or cheaper. Some rooms free for kids under eighteen, with their parents in tow."

"Sounds like you've been to the states, Mr. Andrews," Chuck observed.

"Yes. Europe, too. My job is to find out what people all over want, what they expect for services—and provide them for a reasonable price. And please call me Monty."

"So, Monty, my job is to find good tropical resort sites all over southern Vietnam, places with support services and other attractions, as well as local authorities friendly to the development of facilities such as golf courses. Then I'm to nail down ninety-nine-year leases on the real estate. Right?"

"You got it, Chuck. Good luck!"

◖◖◖

Chuck glanced with pleasure again at the sterling silver cup engraved with "Charles R. Reynolds—Royal Wallangong's Developer of the Year." He squeezed Nicki's hand, then returned his attention to the evening's entertainment. In only a year on the job, he had beaten two seasoned Americans, an Aussie, and a German in securing deals that, in coming months, would bring three new Royal Wallangong Family Resorts to Vietnam.

"You're not happy, Nicki," Chuck said at last. "Is it because Monty wants us to move into their new hotel in Nha Trang?"

"More than that. See those girls? Several aren't a day over fourteen."

Chuck glanced at the six pretty young dancers. They wore identical, traditional *ao dai* outfits in dazzling, demure white. Their flowing silk pants and loose gowns covered them from their throats to their ankles. The dances—swaying like palm trees as they sang old-time Vietnamese folk songs—were certainly more modest than the performances of cheerleaders at American high school games. "What do you mean?"

"Two of them were discussing tonight's performance in the ladies' room earlier. They said they were glad they get to wear clothes for a change."

"You mean some of them are entertainers in local bars?" Chuck was indignant, though not surprised. He'd already heard stories of teenagers used for salacious entertainment. This is Vietnam, not America with a tradition of Christian values and at least lip-service for chastity. Here, there was little protection for girls who voluntarily sold themselves, sometimes to finance drug addictions, he knew.

"Downstairs," said Nicki. "It's called the G-String Tavern, they said."

"I've never heard of it. You mean, in this hotel—the people we work for run it?"

"Exactly, Chuck. It's advertised only by word-of-mouth. I'm afraid I butted in when the girls were talking, and I asked a few questions. They seemed to think I was naive."

"That's hard to believe." He shook his head.

"Let's pay it a visit—tonight."

Two hours later Chuck and Nicki used their company ID cards to gain admittance to a room two levels underground. Ignoring the maître d's offer of a table, they hurried across the crowded, smoke-filled room to a group of men engrossed in the girls on stage.

"Monty?"

Monty Andrews turned.

"I can't accept this." Chuck passed Andrews the silver award cup. "Consider this my resignation." Chuck took Nicki's elbow and strode toward the door.

"Reynolds!?" It was Monty Andrews, reeking of rum. He grabbed Chuck's sleeve. "I wish you'd reconsider."

"I can't. *Family* entertainment? We'll vacate our suite by the end of the week."

"Those girls, Reynolds. They . . ."

Chuck and Nicki hurried toward the elevator. "Same girls?" Chuck asked Nicki as the elevator rose toward ground level.

"A couple of them were. I'd like to get my hands on their daddies!"

"Most women would blame the mothers, like the empty-heads on the TV talk shows," Chuck said.

"Ever notice, though? It's the girls without fathers, or with weak, abusive fathers, who cheapen themselves before men," Nicki observed.

❲❲❲

"In this land the world moves on motorbikes," Nicki laughed. Except for bicycles, these seemed to be the only vehicles on the narrow dirt road north of Ho Chi Minh City this morning. She and Chuck were comfortable in their new, air-conditioned Mazda sedan as they motored across the rice paddies of the interior plateau. Straw-hatted farm families, ankle-deep in water, bent over their task of transplanting rice in the patchwork of green fields that stretched toward the hills bordering Cambodia. Farther off, a farmer with a wooden plow followed a plodding water buffalo to prepare the soil for another crop.

"Look at that guy!" Chuck pulled the car over to let a farmer squeeze past, his motorbike dwarfed by the load on his homemade trailer, which teetered along behind on old motorcycle wheels. The trailer was stacked with perhaps a dozen pigs, each going to market in its own individual wicker cage. A live sow, trussed with thongs and bamboo canes, squealed with every bump. "God's been good to us," Chuck said. "We might have had to travel like that on motorbikes, but now this car is paid for. We couldn't have done it in a year on my salary if it hadn't been for free housing as part of the contract."

"I know." Nicki shot a worried glance back at the light trailer Chuck had hitched behind the Mazda. It carried all their possessions. "How could we ever accumulate so much stuff in just over a year in Vietnam?"

"Phu Rieng will not be Ho Chi Minh City," Chuck said. "Are you sure you want to move there? We'll be lucky to find a house with indoor plumbing, much less electricity. And I'm unemployed once again."

Going out like Abraham to follow God wherever He would lead was not a new experience to Chuck. Since meeting Nicki, though, his life had taken some crazy turns. Now Richard and Penelope Hayward had written asking Chuck and Nicki to join them in a "new, exciting ministry." Open foreign missionary work was illegal in Vietnam, Chuck knew. But the letter intrigued him. Since they were forced to leave their nice apartment in Ho Chi Minh City anyway, they decided to check things out in Phu Rieng.

Just a week before, Chuck had quit a promising job at Royal Wallangong, Ltd. The next day's mail had brought the letter from Rick and Penny, inviting Chuck and Nicki to "see what the Lord is doing here in Phu Rieng." The letter had gotten Chuck's attention, not only by its timing, but by the language. It was filled with phrases such as "praise the Lord" and "laboring in God's vineyard for a harvest of souls." Chuck was jolted back to the fact that beyond the tawdry, commercial secular world that had become so much a part of his soul there lay another reality. There was a spiritual reality—that heavenly kingdom that Christ advised his hearers to "seek first" in their lives.

"What do *you* want to do with it, Chuck?" Chuck had stared in surprise at a ten-thousand-dollar bonus check drawn on the Royal Bank of Sidney, Australia. It had come in the same mail with the Haywards' letter. He had returned the award to Monty Andrews without hesitation. Should he return the money also? To Chuck, the money seemed another symbol of the decadence of which he wished no part.

"I *earned* that money," Chuck said at last.

"Then put it in the bank." Nicki raised an eyebrow. "The devil's had it long enough. Now you can use it for God."

Chuck sighed. "If it's all right with you, I want to pay off our car. Unless you want to sell it and buy motorbikes, like the nationals."

"We'd take a loss. Since we can pay for it now, I think we'd be smart to keep our car until we know what the Lord has for us next," Nicki said.

"You sound like the Haywards—spiritualizing everything. Good point though. We bought that vehicle on half down, so I think this will just about cover the balance we owe after a year's payments." Chuck had slipped the check from his former employer into his checkbook, then grabbed his payment coupon book and hurried out the door.

"Did you notice that man?" Nicki asked now as they drove along the dirt road across the paddies.

"The guy we just passed on the bicycle, you mean?"

"Yes."

"I saw him," Chuck said. It was a farmer in his twenties on an old bicycle with no fenders and rusty spokes. He pedaled with one foot. He had tied his crutch to the other pedal, shoving it down with each revolution of the crank to make up for a missing leg. "I've seen lots like him since we came here. Many of them are too young to have been in the war."

"Old land mines left from two wars," said Nicki. "I wonder if the mine was French, North Vietnamese, or South Vietnamese?"

"Or American. Our army left thousands of them when they retreated. Those mines will be killing people for the next hundred years."

"It's inexcusable," Nicki said. "Mines can be made cheaply with biodegradable triggers that will neutralize themselves in a month or so, making them harmless to people who pass by after a war. That technology has been around for years."

❰❰❰

"This is a Jaipur Foot," Penny Hayward explained. She set a full-sized rubber leg on her kitchen table, then adjusted the wick in her kerosene lamp.

"Jaipur. Sounds like some place in India," Chuck pondered.

"Really," agreed Rick Hayward. "It is a city in India, near New Delhi."

"This foot was invented by a Hindu doctor in India," Penny explained. "We first saw it a couple of years ago when an American missionary from Bangladesh, Larry Golin, showed it around during a chapel service at our college."

"Bangladesh?" said Chuck. "Refresh my memory."

"The land was once part of British India," Dick told, "on the northeast side, south of the Himalayan Mountains."

"That puts it just over the hills from where we are here in Vietnam," said Chuck.

"Over a lot of hills," Nicki laughed. "Burma and Laos are in the way—not your weekend trip by packhorse."

"OK," said Chuck, "so this Larry Golin told you guys it costs about forty dollars to manufacture these feet in Bangladesh. And Vietnam not only has a serious amputee problem because of land mines, but it has a good supply of cheap native rubber."

"That's compared to $2,500 for an American-style prosthetic foot," Rick explained. "Besides being unaffordable to any but the rich in Vietnam, American-made artificial legs and feet are so cumbersome that Vietnamese farmers, the people who need them most, can't use them. They were designed for folks who wear shoes. Our farmers wear sandals or go barefoot."

"No kidding!" Chuck was appalled. "So we have a chance to put thousands of impaired Vietnamese back on their feet in Jesus' name. Is that what you're saying?"

"More than just that," Penny put in. "Mr. Golin explained that an amputee in Bangladesh is an outcast. Even though many can learn productive jobs that don't require walking or standing, businesses usually refuse to hire them. Such people are believed to be cursed, an evil omen. So they spend their lives as beggars."

"It's much the same here in Vietnam," Nicki said. "If you're different, you're shunned and ridiculed."

"We think we could start a factory to manufacture these feet at prices most legless Vietnamese can afford. Perhaps we could put an enterprising, responsible Vietnamese Christian to work managing the place so it would continue on when we have to go back to the States. We've already started a second year here as English teachers, longer than we had planned," said Rick. "We'll need to leave next year. Larry Golin, however, has agreed to give us three months of his time to train our nationals to manufacture the Jaipur Foot if we pay his expenses. It'll meet a serious need and soon become a self-sustaining business."

"Then what we need is start-up venture capital." Chuck was getting enthused, yet he was realistic.

"Fifty thousand dollars," said Penny. "We've done the numbers."

Nicki started to speak, then closed her mouth.

"Perhaps you could introduce us to one of the executives at Royal Wallangong, to whomever might be responsible—the department that puts money back into the local economy," Rick suggested.

"They *do* give quite a bit of money away—like to publicize it, in fact. However . . ." Chuck fished for words. "I quit rather suddenly," he finished.

"Sorry." Rick sounded embarrassed.

"What Chuck means is . . . shall I tell them, Chuck?"

"Go ahead, Nicki."

Nicki told how Chuck had returned his award when he learned that Wallangong, Ltd. was using young teens for lewd, exotic shows to entertain men in a hidden basement lounge. "The company puts millions into the United Nations Children's Fund," Nicki concluded. "Much of it is designated to buy contraceptives for teen girls in underdeveloped countries. I'm sure a lot of it is spent here in Vietnam."

"No way!" said Penny.

"Way," said Nicki.

Penny's blue eyes grew dark. "Hypocrisy knows no shame," she said.

"Chuck, you had no choice," Rick agreed.

"Fifty thousand dollars." Nicki repeated Penny's figure. "The Lord gave me exactly that much a few months ago from the sale of an ancient manuscript. I've had friends in America deposit the money in a Swiss bank for me. Once we work out the details—a written spending plan, that sort of thing—I can have it transferred from my bank in Zurich to a savings account at the Honshu Bank of Japan in Saigon. Then I'll ask the bank to cut a cashier's check for enough to get our factory underway."

《《《   ¦

"The water? Maybe something you ate?" Chuck steadied Nicki as she vomited into the toilet.

The day after they agreed with the Haywards to help start a prosthetics factory, Chuck and Nicki leased three rooms at the Hotel le Tigre, a century-old French establishment in downtown Phu Rieng. The apartment was on the fourth floor, and it included a gas hot plate—no oven or refrigerator—and electric lights on the hotel's diesel generator from dusk until midnight.

The bathroom was an ornate affair, with fire-glazed clay tiles in oriental shades of blue and yellow, a huge, zinc-lined wooden tub on carved marble dragon-claw legs, with heavily plated nickel-on-brass fixtures. The cold water faucets gave out a thin but steady yellow trickle. The hot water did not work. When Chuck asked the hotel manager about the hot water, he laughed and said that that was what the hot plate was for.

"I've puked almost every hour since 2 A.M.," Nicki moaned. "Blow that out." She indicated the stub of a candle sitting on the back of the toilet. It had served for light from midnight until dawn. Daybreak had begun to lighten the room.

"You are one sick girl! It's two hours to the nearest doctor, in Saigon."

"Not to worry. Penny's a licensed practical nurse. I'll ask her if she's got a . . ." Nicki bent over the bowl again.

"Got a what?"

"In her kit of supplies—if she's got . . ." Nicki retched again. "Get me a drink of water, *please!* Then I think I'll have a bowl of ice cream with a pickle." She forced a laugh, fighting the urge to throw up again. "Penny may have a PG test in her kit."

Chuck frowned. Then he grinned. "Gimmie five!"

"Not quints. You know I haven't been taking fertility drugs, silly!" Nicki slapped Chuck's outstretched palm.

"What are we going to do, Nicki?" Chuck returned to his worry mode.

"I'll just give birth, like every mother since Eve—like every mother in Vietnam. My mother had me in a dirty back room in Saigon, alone. I have you and Penny—and Jesus, and that's a whole lot more than she had."

"You don't know yet that you're pregnant."

"I can feel it in my soul—in my guts, I mean." Nicki bent over the bowl once again. "Oh, Chuck, I'm so happy," she moaned at last.

❰❰❰

"Hanoi is *not* one of my favorite cities." Chuck once again checked the sheath of papers in his briefcase as he, Nicki, and Quang Dat Li waited for the plane to Ho Chi Minh City, nearly a thousand miles to the south. They were all there—the official documents and permits stating that Quang Dat Li, a deacon in the Evangelical Church of Phu Rieng, could open a factory to manufacture prosthetic feet and legs in a vacant warehouse in the city of Phu Rieng.

Jaipur Foot of Vietnam, Ltd., the enterprise was to be called. It would have no official connection with the church, though Quang, the president, as well as all the trustees of the corporation, were members of the Evangelical Church. This was not mentioned in the official documents however.

"Consider it a learning experience." Nicki laughed. "Dealing with officials in this land gives new meaning to the term 'red tape.'"

"Red is a noble color in Vietnam." Quang joined the merriment, nodding toward a pair of elderly Buddhist monks in flowing crimson robes, begging from passengers in the airport lobby.

"God has blessed this venture from the start," Chuck said. He now tried to overcome his uneasiness as an American in Vietnam's capital by looking at the positive side of things. And things had certainly gone well. Aside from a brief incident when Chuck had turned up the wrong walkway outside the capitol building, only to be stopped by a surly guard who poked a loaded, cocked Chinese-made assault rifle into his ribs, the Communist officials had treated them courteously, sometimes even cordially. "We've accomplished in a few days what could have taken weeks, and we actually got all our papers signed."

"Maybe months," agreed Nicki.

"Perhaps years," Quang said. "Honorable lady, if it had not been for you . . ." Quang's voice dissolved into tears as he patted the Jaipur Foot on which he had learned to walk again in recent weeks. This leg and foot would be the model for the thousands his factory would turn out annually for shipment all over Vietnam, and perhaps for export into Cambodia and Laos.

"How are you doing, darling?" Chuck asked.

Nicki, who was six months pregnant, patted her belly. "Great! *Two* heartbeats—can you imagine?"

"It is *your* money," Chuck insisted. Nicki had not caught his meaning the first time. Money was to her something to use to help others. No big deal. Though Chuck was certainly interested in their babies, his immediate concern was that Nicki was using up her entire bank account, fifty thousand dollars, to underwrite this manufacturing venture.

As "investor," according to the documents, Nicki had permitted her Honshu Bank of Japan passbook to be photocopied, then she had signed her name as Ngo Thieu to legal papers until it seemed that her hand would cramp. Though Nicki Towns was an American citizen, she held dual citizenship. She had furnished a copy of her Saigon birth certificate to the Hanoi officials.

((((

"Look at this, Nicki!" It was months later, and after a shopping trip, Chuck and Nicki were eating lunch at an old French waterfront cafe in Ho Chi Minh City before driving home to Phu Rieng. He folded his copy of *USA Today* to the page he was reading and passed it to Nicki.

"They reap what they sow," Nicki observed. She quickly read the two-paragraph article. A retired U.S. Air Force general, Armstrong MacAdams, a veteran of the Vietnam War, had been arrested for selling American military secrets to Russian espionage agents. Some top-secret American technology had been found in Iraq, manufactured in Russia from American designs stolen by MacAdams. The second paragraph mentioned that "a network of Iraqi spies" was believed to be working behind the scenes across America, shadowing Russian agents.

Nicki read the second paragraph aloud to Chuck.

"Product control?" Then it hit him. "Those are Saddam's goons, the same guys trying to kill you! This could be our chance to go home."

"I . . . I just don't know. Where is home anyway, Chuck?" She peered at their twins, propped up in their portable car seats. Would this be her children's home—or would America?

❰❰❰

"That woman's composure at the funeral was incredible," Nicki said. As Chuck drove, she turned to check on three-month-old Carly and Nicholas as they slept in the backseat of the Mazda.

Chuck downshifted to pass a three-wheeled motor-scooter-truck loaded with market-bound vegetables before answering. "Gia Liu," he mused. "She's from Hong Kong—Chinese. Except for the folks in our church, she has nobody in all of Vietnam."

Days earlier, young Gia had been riding on the back of a motorbike behind her Vietnamese husband, with her baby, the same age as the twins, strapped to her back. The husband had dodged a flock of Muscovy ducks that had waddled into the road. The young family had skidded into a roadside canal, where Gia's husband and baby drowned.

The funeral for the father and baby was the day before Chuck and Nicki drove to Ho Chi Minh City for a trailer-load of supplies for the Jaipur Foot plant. Spools of nylon and cases of tools jounced along in a trailer behind their car as they discussed the tragedy.

"Gia really *wants* to get back to China," Nicki said. "She has a large family in Hong Kong." Nicki was thoughtful for a moment.

"Now that General MacAdams has been arrested, perhaps we should consider going back to America," she continued. "Quang is already running the plant most of the time without our help."

"I only wish I knew if the CIA is looking for you. Perhaps I could find out through the U.S. consulate here." Chuck sighed. "And say, speaking of Hong Kong—did you see the Chinese freighter anchored in the river just a couple of blocks from where we ate lunch?"

"The *Empress of Beijing?*" Nicki laughed. "That was some boat ride! Maybe we can try it again next time we need a vacation."

"Crazy woman!" Chuck grinned. "You know, though, I'd go anywhere for you."

"Maybe we could get Gia a ride to Hong Kong on the *Empress*, Chuck?"

"So soon after the funeral of her husband and baby? Does she really know her mind?"

〖〖〖

"I don't like the looks of this!" Chuck circled the block, then pulled the Mazda and trailer into an alley across the street from Jaipur Foot of Vietnam. A ponderous, black, Chinese-built limousine was parked in front of the factory's main entrance. Several national police in green-and-red uniforms and knee-length black boots were perched on heavy Honda motorcycles, fingering Chinese assault rifles. Each officer wore a bandolier of ammunition across his chest and a pair of grenades slung from his belt.

"They may just be checking to see if we've got too much American influence in this operation," Nicki said evenly, fighting her fears.

"*Christian* influence, you mean. It doesn't add up. Americans and Aussies are welcome in Vietnam so long as they're here to spend money or educate," Chuck said. Chuck and Nicki's main involvement in the Jaipur Foot factory was as business advisers, and now that the plant, with thirty employees, had operated for six months, they soon would no longer be needed.

"Well, since I'm Vietnamese, probably it would be smart if I go in ahead of you, at least until we know what's going on," Nicki said.

The senior officer spotted their car and motioned for two of his men to follow him toward the alley. Nicki hopped out and hurried to meet them.

The officer, who introduced himself as "Colonel Hung, police marshal of the Democratic Republic of Vietnam," strutted up to her and bowed. "Ngo Thieu?" he asked.

"Yes, I am." Nicki caught her breath

"I am arresting you in the name of the people of Vietnam for the crime of illegally fleeing justice." Hung unfolded a long document typed on thin rice paper and began to read it aloud in a torrent of Vietnamese words.

The other two cops grabbed Nicki and handcuffed her, even as their senior officer read the charges.

Chuck checked the sleeping babies, then strode into the street. By now the traffic had stopped and a curious crowd had begun to gather. Chuck lost track of the officer's rapid-fire charges after the first few words. He heard only that Nicki was under arrest. Then the marshal read a phrase that turned Chuck cold in the sweltering heat, nearly arresting his heart: "Republic of Iraq."

Quang Dat Li rushed into the street with Gia Liu on his heels. "Chuck, Chuck!" He waved his hand.

Gia rushed past them both. "I take care of babies."

"They've been here about an hour," Quang said. "I sent for Gia as soon as I spoke with Colonel Hung. I realized that you would need her."

Chuck was not so much as permitted to kiss Nicki before she was pushed into the backseat of the long, nine-passenger sedan between two policemen. He thought he saw a glimmer of compassion in Colonel Hung's eyes, however, when, through Quang, Chuck insisted on making copies of the official papers on the Jaipur Foot factory's office photocopier. "Leaving copies with others is strictly forbidden," Hung said. "But since he is the husband . . ." He nodded toward Chuck. "I, too, have a wife." He turned to his driver. "Wait outside," he said, following Quang Dat Li into the office to use the copier.

☾☾☾

"Ngo will be held in jail until she is extradited by Iraq," Quang explained, scanning the sheath of papers he had copied from Hung's official documents. "She is wanted in Baghdad for murder and escape. She has been condemned to die."

"The charge is false," Chuck said, without explanation. "But Saddam is evil. He will stop at nothing to kill her. Does it say where they will take her?"

"Hanoi. There is a jail there built by the Japanese occupation army in 1942 during World War II for Vietnamese war prisoners. The North Vietnamese military used it for French prisoners during their war with France, then later American prisoners were held there. It's still in use."

"The . . . the old 'Hanoi Hilton'!? I . . . I knew guys who spent time there," Chuck stammered. "Will they let me visit her?"

"Yes, once she's been processed, I'm sure. Usually not more than one visit in cases like this, I think. Brother, I'm terribly sorry."

Chuck shot a glance across the street where Gia Liu sat in the Mazda holding the twins. He was surprised to see that she was happily nursing one of them.

A plan began to take shape in Chuck's mind.

20

Why Sarah Laughed

Is anything too hard for the LORD?

—An angel

I need to use a computer with a fax. It was after eight in the evening, and Chuck tried to collect his wits as he stared blankly at the row of elevator doors in Ho Chi Minh City's downtown Royal Wallangong of Australia Hotel.

"We are in contact with Washington on a daily basis," the diplomatic attaché at the U.S. Embassy in Hanoi had told Chuck on the phone earlier. Chuck had phoned the American Embassy long distance from the Jaipur Foot factory's office in Phu Rieng as soon as he heard Quang Dat Li's translation of the charges against Nicki. "Matters like this ordinarily take several days to work out, you understand."

Chuck did not understand. "May I speak to the diplomat himself, please—to Mr. O'Connor?"

"That's impossible. Mr. O'Connor is in Tokyo at a convention until next week. As I said, we'll have an answer from Washington probably in about a week."

"In the meantime they'll put my wife on a plane to Baghdad to be shot!"

"That's a possibility, Mr. Reynolds." The young man paused.

Chuck's imagination ran on what he'd do to the guy if he had his hands on him; then his wrath turned back to despair. The phone line was still open, but he could think of nothing useful to say.

"In a few minutes, sir, I have a telephone conference with an official in Vietnam's government. We'll be talking about another American who has run afoul of their law here. I will mention Mrs. Nicki Reynolds to him. If it then seems urgent, I'll fax what I learn to Washington this evening so they'll have it when the State Department begins its day in a few hours. May I have Mrs. Reynolds's Vietnamese name?"

"Ngo Thieu." Chuck put the receiver down.

Washington is twelve hours from Ho Chi Minh City, the other side of the earth, Chuck considered as he stood now in the hotel's lobby. Already secretaries and junior department heads were sitting down to their day's work in the U.S. State Department. Chuck needed to get somebody's attention in a hurry, before the little people with giant egos who run America's capital were too busy to stop to have compassion for an innocent American woman about to be shipped off to face a latter-day Hitler.

"I will never leave you nor forsake you." Chuck knew his Greek New Testament. As this verse drifted now into his imagination, he remembered that the negatives are doubled in the original language. The Lord's message here uses the most emphatic language known to mankind, so intense that it is ungrammatical in English: *I won't never leave you!*

"God, help Nicki! In Jesus' name." Chuck's prayer ended there, for he truly did not know how to pray.

Then there were the twins, little Carly and Nicholas. Chuck had left them with Gia Liu. Gia was a Chinese widow, a bereaved mother, only nineteen. Chuck and Quang had tried by turns to make this girl understand enough to realize the gravity of the situation.

Gia, from Hong Kong, spoke Mandarin Chinese. She knew a little English, and she had learned a bit of Vietnamese in the year since her marriage.

Chuck spoke English and no Chinese. He had learned a little Vietnamese.

Quang was fluent both in English and his native Vietnamese. He knew only a few words of Chinese.

Had the circumstances not been so desperate, they would have been comical. Chuck, Quang, and Gia in Gia's tin-roofed, one-room hut. Two fussing infants. Chuck had tried to settle her fears, yet not say enough to alarm her. Quang, trying first English, then Vietnamese, attempted to translate Chuck's explanations.

Gia had bowed and smiled. She cuddled the twins like the heavenly gifts that they were, acting as if they were hers to keep. Though Gia was not fully aware of it, little Carly and Nicholas might really become hers to keep.

Chuck promised to pay all of Gia's living expenses in Vietnam until the babies could be reunited with Nicki. He then used his car to tote bundles of diapers, clothing, baby powder and lotions, laundry soap, canned orange juice, and safety pins to Gia's simple home. He grabbed whatever he could find that Gia might find useful for their care as he frantically searched through their apartment for baby things.

Then Chuck left for the two-hour drive to Ho Chi Minh City, not knowing when he might return, or even if he would return.

Chuck now prayed again in the hotel lobby. He checked his watch: 8:27 P.M. He hurried into an open elevator. Thankfully, his key to the private office floor still worked, and the door soon opened into the executive suite.

Give me wisdom, Lord, Chuck prayed. He was keenly aware that, no longer an employee of Royal Wallangong, he could be arrested for trespassing, perhaps spend the night in the Ho Chi Minh City jail.

But God had brought him here, Chuck believed. There simply was no public fax service available in Ho Chi Minh City this late in the evening.

Movement, and the glow of a computer screen in a glass-walled executive office beyond the rows of cubicles, caught Chuck's attention. He studied it for a moment. Monty Andrews's office, Chuck realized. The venetian blind was nearly closed, but a shadow passed across, then back.

Chuck strode purposefully toward Andrews's office. He rapped.

"Yes?" It was Annie Higgins, Andrews's Aussie assistant. "Woll, Mr. Reynolds! Welcome back!" Annie exclaimed as she opened the glass door. "I didn't blame you for leaving. Mr. Andrews talked for days about finding you and trying to hire you back, but he never could bring himself to do it. Shameful how they treat those girls, you know. And . . ."

Chuck waved his hand. "Annie, please! My wife's been arrested and taken to Hanoi."

"No!"

"Yes."

"I loved that girl. Most of them Vietnamese girls are, y'know, servile. But Nicki, she was special."

"Nicki is an American with a college education," Chuck said firmly. "It's 8:45 in the morning in Washington right now. I need to use a computer with a fax." Though the Jaipur Foot office had a computer, they had not yet added a fax since Internet connections were not available in Phu Rieng.

"Of course. Right over there. Take your time. It's going to take me a couple of hours to finish up."

Chuck's notes were brief and to the point: Nicki was a patriotic American with all the rights of a citizen. Her father died serving his country in Vietnam. She was the mother of his twins. Nicki was being falsely accused of murder by the government of Iraq. As an afterthought, Chuck added that Nicki had inside information valuable in the prosecution of General Armstrong MacAdams, recently arrested for espionage.

Chuck found himself incredibly lucid that evening. He remembered names, addresses, titles, and fax numbers of several top-level executives in the State Department, though he had used them only once before, when he had faxed warnings about the Iraqi anthrax missile from Montreal. He composed a letter to each one, and finally a letter to the new Secretary of State, Harold O. Cosgrove himself. "Urgent—Immediate Reply Requested," Chuck typed in bold capitals at the bottom of each fax.

Every single fax went through. Chuck printed out the confirmation slips and folded them together with the hard copy originals of the faxes.

"Annie, you're going to be around for a while?" Chuck stuck his head into her boss's office.

She checked the clock. "Another hour. Mr. Andrews needs this stuff in the morning. But you're welcome to stay as long as you need to."

"You're sure? I need to step out. You may be gone when I return."

"Say, didn't you say you're working here now?"

"No, Annie." Chuck held up his elevator key. "I'll slip this under Monty's door when I leave, OK?"

"I trust you." Annie chuckled and went back to work.

◖◖◖

The light was on in the captain's quarters in the fo'c'sle of the *Empress of Beijing* when Chuck drove out onto the dock with the Mazda. The plank was up, but a rope attached to a small bell dangled over the rail. Chuck jangled the bell and waited.

A barefoot sailor in shorts appeared moments later, pouring Chinese profanity onto Chuck down below.

"I need to see Captain Chan Ling, please, if he hasn't gone to bed. I'm on business."

Captain Ling remembered Chuck from the honeymoon trip. Yes, he said, he had an extra stateroom with two hammocks for adults and space enough for two babies and a couple of bags. Yes, he would gladly take them to Hong Kong. The *Empress* would sail at ten o'clock tomorrow night, on the high tide, less than twenty-four hours from now. Yes, Chuck could get off the freighter at Haiphong in northern Vietnam and catch a steamer upriver to Hanoi, if he preferred. "May-bee," said Captain Ling, "may-bee we sail to Hanoi, stay one day, take on freight, if not get a full load here in Ho Chi Minh City. You ride all way with us?"

That was exactly what Chuck's heart had been crying for—a backup plan in case Washington didn't come through.

Chuck hurried back to the Royal Wallangong. He took the elevator straight to the suite of offices, which overlooked the city. He peered out the massive expanse of plateglass over sleeping Ho Chi Minh City toward the waterfront. The *Empress of Beijing* slept in the moonlight with the rest of the city.

Chuck strolled toward the executive fax machine, taking his time. The more time he killed, the more likely he was to find a reply from Washington, he reasoned. Chuck could not bring himself to admit that it was his subconscious fear of finding no reply at all that made him drag his feet.

A single page had dropped into the basket in Chuck's absence. Common sense told him that it was probably a late-night report from a field man up north who wished Andrews to read his report with his morning coffee.

Chuck flipped on the light and picked up the page. "Department of State, United States of America," read the letterhead.

Dear Mr. Reynolds:

Re your request for action by the government of the United States on behalf of Ngo Thieu, alias Nicki Towns. No action can or will be taken on Ms. Thieu's behalf by this office. Our consulate in Hanoi indicates that she is a highly dangerous international terrorist wanted for espionage and murder in Iraq.

I have also been on the phone with the CIA. They confirmed the Hanoi Embassy's message, and further notified me that she is wanted as a spy in the United States also.

If I can be of further assistance, please let me know.
Very Truly Yours,
Harold O. Cosgrove
Secretary of State

"This is incredible and unbelievable," Chuck said half aloud. "This answer, and from Secretary Cosgrove himself! But why? I suppose he believes neither of us will ever . . ." Chuck sank into a chair and prayed.

Nearly a thousand miles away, Nicki stirred in her sleep during her first night in the old "Hanoi Hilton." She slept on a dirty concrete floor, chained by one ankle to the wall of her cell. "I will never leave you nor forsake you." These words ran through her mind just at that moment. She came awake, remembering these verses that she had once read in her mother's old Bible. There was more to that passage. "The LORD is my helper," Nicki's memory commenced again, "I will not fear. What can man do unto me?"

"Thank You, Jesus, for your promises." Nicki fell asleep. After the limo ride to Ho Chi Minh City there had been a plane ride to Hanoi. It had been a long day.

◖◖◖

"The babies are yours to keep in Hong Kong until I come for them," Chuck told Gia next day with Quang's help. "But we must leave at once for Ho Chi Minh City to catch the *Empress* before it sails."

"Yes! I go Hong Kong!" Gia grinned and bowed. But, "No, no, can't take babies."

"Why not?" Chuck's heart sank.

"Babies belong to mother, to Nick-ee."

"Please explain that Nicki is in prison in Hanoi. She may die soon. Unless Gia takes Carly and Nicholas to Hong Kong with her, they may never see their mother alive again," Chuck urged Quang. Chuck found himself amazed at his own composure. *The Lord is in this*, he decided.

"Don't understand," Gia protested.

Chuck smiled. "I don't understand either, Gia. But God understands. That's the way it is. You take my babies to Hong Kong. I'll go to Hanoi and get their mother, then we'll find you in Hong Kong. The twins and I must leave Vietnam. The authorities do not want us here."

❰❰❰

Gia had another spell of reluctance on board the *Empress of Beijing* that evening when she discovered that Chuck had paid for only one stateroom for two adults and two babies. He tried to explain that he had no intention of bunking in the room with her, even though there were two hammocks. "I sleep on deck with babies," she insisted.

"I father. You daughter," Chuck countered. "I sleep with sailors. You sleep with babies." He took a blanket and left, closing the door. The vessel was already steaming down the Saigon River toward the South China Sea, and there was simply no more to be said or done.

❰❰❰

"How are they treating you, Nicki?" Chuck peered into the holding cage where Nicki had been brought for them to talk in the presence of a guard.

"The rats haven't bothered me—yet." Nicki forced a smile. Then she fought tears. "My babies!"

"Gia Liu has them. Carly and Nicholas are going with her to Hong Kong." Chuck wondered if the guard understood English. He decided he'd given Nicki all the information he dared reveal. "I've brought you food—bread." He pulled a small loaf from his pocket and held it up for the guard's inspection.

Rope, Chuck mouthed as soon as the guard stepped away. *Inside. Tonight. Three o'clock. Northwest corner. Below guard tower.* "I'll pray for you," Chuck said aloud.

"Your time is up, sir," the guard said in English.

◖◖◖

Vietnamese prison clothes are ideal for sneaking out at night, Nicki told herself as she considered the gray garments she wore. It was ten minutes to three, and she had tied fifty feet of thin but rugged nylon cord to a bar of her window, lowering it into the exercise yard. Chuck had tucked the cord, wound tightly on a nail, inside the loaf. The bread, happily, was now inside Nicki.

The nail had done the rest. She had used it to pick the large, old-fashioned lock on her Japanese-occupation-era leg irons. Several hours of digging at the ancient lime mortar, and she loosened a brick enough to slide one bar out. It was enough to let her slender, wiry figure squeeze through.

Nicki had never rappelled without leather gloves before. Now she winced in pain as the cruel cord tore at her flesh, slicing into her slender, tapered fingers. *Never mind. There are guards in those towers with orders to shoot to kill,* she considered. The only place not in view of their vigilant eyes was right beneath the tower itself, and she had to get there fast.

Nicki found a hole beneath the tower and squirreled into it. She caught her breath as strong arms hauled her out the other side. She found herself swiftly wrapped like a market pig into a coarse hemp sack. Her assailant pulled the drawstring tight.

◖◖◖

The sun had begun to redden the sky downriver toward Haiphong and the sea as Captain Ling checked his watch. In another ten minutes the tide would reach its crest. He yanked a cord. A shrill blast of steam commanded his sailors to draw up the gangplank, hoist the anchor, open the throttle.

Ling gazed out at the activity below. A lone sailor, taller than the rest, dressed in loose breeches and hand-woven shirt like the others, hurried across the wharf, fearful of missing the boat. The man wore an American baseball cap pulled low and sunglasses over his eyes as he trotted through the shadows. He reached the gangplank just in time, and he struggled beneath a large gunny sack as he scurried up the gangplank. The man slipped on a loose cleat, nearly dropping the sack with its contents into the black water of Hanoi Harbor. He regained his balance, stepped onto the *Empress*'s plank deck, and disappeared below.

Chuck rapped on the door of the tiny stateroom Gia shared with Nicholas and Carly.

It opened a crack.

Chuck forced his way in without speaking. He swung the long sack into the hammock Gia had just left. He grabbed his pocketknife and ripped at the binding cords.

"Oh!" Gia squealed.

"Quiet, Gia. Help me get her loose."

Gia obeyed.

Chuck kissed the sack's contents, then stepped back. "You have an adult roommate now, Gia. No talking, ladies—the sailors could get suspicious. Help Nicki clean up, Gia. I'll be back in a couple of hours with bowls of rice and fresh water for each of you."

"Where are we going, Chuck?" Nicki gasped.

"Hong Kong. Then home—Maine." He slipped out and hurried toward the open deck.

❰❰❰

"Reverse engines." Captain Ling, on the bridge, grabbed a mike and yelled this angry command in Chinese.

Chuck sat on a capstan, peering into the dense fog ahead. *Why are we slowing?* he wondered. Then he saw it—the drawbridge over the Song Coi River had not been raised. He made ready to dive below decks to avoid being hurt.

The *Empress* shuddered, came to a stop, and began slowly to back up. But not before Chuck got a look. A long line of military vehicles roared across the bridge and disappeared into the fog beyond the river.

Finally the pulleys and steel cables began to squeal and groan. The old bridge rose up, up, up. The *Empress of Beijing* began to move again toward the open sea and Hong Kong, three days' sail to the north.

"We nearly hit the bridge this morning, Captain," Chuck said, hours later. "Does that happen very often?"

"Never, sir. I radio the bridge minute we leave dock. Always before they have open."

"Military takes precedence, I guess?"

Captain Ling cursed in Chinese. "I listen to police radio. Some prisoner escape from old Japanese military jail—a woman. Must be very, very important," Ling concluded.

"I'm sure she must be," Chuck agreed. *Does Captain Ling know that the woman who got on with me in Ho Chi Minh City in the dark is not Nicki?* Chuck wondered. *I guess I'd be smart not to let him find out.* He hurried below to check on his family.

◖◖◖

Four days later a China Eastern Airlines 767 circled Los Angeles International Airport, waiting for a runway. "That woman across the aisle—would you like my hair to look like hers again?" Nicki asked.

Chuck glanced at the black-haired Middle-Eastern beauty. She was about Nicki's size, and she sported wavy, off-the-forehead hair, nearly waist length. Chuck looked at Nicki's bangs and straight Asian hair, which she had kept straight with daily ironings since going to Vietnam. It had begun to curl a bit in the days since her arrest and flight. "You're beautiful just the way you are, darling."

"Well, *I'm* changing my hair back as soon as I can get a curling iron," Nicki said emphatically. "I'm leaving my eyes, though. My mother was Vietnamese, and I've come to appreciate that."

The plane dropped its flaps and landing wheels.

Chuck and Nicki tightened their seat belts nervously and hugged the infants closer.

"Chuck?"

"Yeah?"

"Will they be waiting for us?"

"The Iraqis? Not a chance. It will take them two or three days to figure out where we are."

"What about the FBI? Once they started that massive manhunt, I imagine the American embassy in Hanoi figured out you'd sprung me from jail."

"Like you said   " Chuck shrugged.

"Better an American prison than Baghdad," Nicki finished.

"And like I told you, the minute you're picked up, I'll start a national media blitz the like of which hasn't been seen since the Clinton affair." Chuck tapped the briefcase on his knees beneath little Nicholas. In this he had hoarded all the paper documentation of the attempts on their lives since Baghdad, as well as documents about the attack on Chicago.

"In fact, I think we should go straight to Washington and chat with Chet Wood," Chuck added. "I'm sure he'll be interested in putting you on Satellite Network News's prime time show, *Chet Wood's World*. You should be good for an hour, maybe two. Perhaps Chet could get the Secretary of Defense to answer questions about what we've learned."

"I'd love to see the Secretary face the nation," Nicki agreed. "But I *hate* publicity."

"Billy Graham was bashful too, I've heard." Chuck laughed.

The babies were sleeping, and Chuck and Nicki, who had all their belongings in underseat bags they had bought in Hong Kong, waited until the mob of business passengers and glad-to-be-home tourists pushed past. Then, struggling with bags and babies, they followed the crowd up the ramp into the terminal, lining up for customs with the others.

"Chuck—those guys are FBI!" Nicki nudged her husband right after they passed inspection, nodding toward where two men in dark suits and sunglasses held the pretty woman with the lovely black locks. They had already handcuffed her.

"You've got the wrong woman!" the lady protested.

"I'd identify myself to get her out of trouble—but our babies," Nicki worried. Little Carly began to cry lustily.

"They'll learn who she is soon enough," Chuck said. "You just keep your head down and keep on walking. I've gone through too much trouble getting you back to lose you so soon."

☾☾☾

"Orange County Airport—American Airlines terminal," Chuck told the cab driver. He passed the man a fifty, practically all the U.S. currency he had left after purchasing plane tickets at full price in Hong Kong. Chuck had cleaned out his bank account in Ho Chi Minh City before boarding the *Empress of Beijing* with Gia and the twins. Most of the funds, however, had been given him in Vietnamese dong or Australian dollars. Also, he had taken enough cash in Chinese yen to meet Gia's needs in Hong Kong for several months.

Chuck had hoped to sell the Mazda sedan, but there hadn't been time. Instead, he had passed Quang the keys at the freight wharf. "The car is for the Jaipur Foot work. The trailer too," Chuck had said.

"Pull off here, driver," Nicki now called. "That bank."

"Glad to, lady." The driver wheeled onto the expressway off-ramp.

"Bank of Los Angeles—California's Leading Financial Institution," the sign read. "We need American money, lover." Nicki indicated Chuck's briefcase. "I'll wait in the car with the babies."

"No hassle." Moments later Chuck grinned as he stepped back into the taxi. "They took the Aussie dollars. I'll swap the dong in D.C."

"Chuck, I passed through customs using my own American name," Nicki said, amazed, as they drove along.

"God's doing, darling," Chuck answered quietly. "I imagine those FBI agents figured you'd use an alias, so they depended on visual recognition. They sure weren't expecting you to be lugging a crying baby."

(((

"Well, they won't trace us through any flights out of L.A. International today." Chuck held up two standby boarding passes for the next Orange County to Washington, D.C., flight on American. "Our plane leaves in ten minutes—nonstop to Ronald Reagan Washington National Airport."

(((

"I don't like this," Nicki worried as the plane leveled off above the San Bernardino Mountains. "It's four hours to Washington. That gives the FBI time to check all the flights out of L.A. and Orange County. Long Beach too."

"We sure don't have parachutes." Chuck chuckled helplessly at his own flat joke. "It's my fault. I should have used my head and bought us tickets on a flight that touched down in Kansas City. We might have gotten off there and switched to Amtrak."

"I'm sure the Lord knew what He was doing when He made those standby tickets available." Nicki patted Chuck's hand. "Sorry, honey. We did get off without waiting, and it *is* going to take them several hours to check the flights."

(((

"Did you see them? *Don't* turn around!" Chuck grabbed Nicki's elbow and hurried her down the long corridor at the Washington National Airport in Arlington, Virginia.

"I saw." They were now two dozen steps past the security checkpoint gate. "Two guys in black suits. They flashed their cards—practically running. Five minutes sooner, and they'd have caught us!" Nicki gasped.

Chuck virtually rammed Nicki into the backseat of the first waiting cab. He dumped the twins into her lap and jumped in. "Quality Inn on Arlington Boulevard, please," Chuck ordered. "There's a nice tip for you if you can get us there in ten minutes."

❮❮❮

Nicki waited with the twins in the lobby of the Arlington Quality Inn as Chuck made several calls from a pay phone. "I've got us rooms in a Holiday Inn in Silver Spring, Maryland, and another room in a Ramada, about five miles away in College Park. I've called local cabs from both places to swing around the Beltway and pick us up. We'll each take one child."

"But," Nicki protested, "I've got to feed them both."

"No problem." Chuck forced a smile. "I'll grab another cab and run over."

❮❮❮

"Aren't you taking some rather elaborate precautions, Chuck?"

"We have no choice." Chuck's eyes fairly blazed with fury. "Someone wants us bad. They'll check the logs of every cab company that serviced the Washington National Airport this afternoon. You can bet that the FBI will have agents checking the Arlington Quality Inn looking for us before the chickens go to roost."

"You and your quaint sayings!" Nicki giggled, then returned to nursing Carly. After some moments, she looked up. "Chuck?"

"Yeah?"

"I'm not an 'international terrorist,' you know. But you're right. Somebody wants us both, but not on criminal charges."

"Am I supposed to feel relieved? They'll use criminal charges to hold us until they find a way to make us disappear. I can think of several reasons why they might want either of us, and they're all pretty grim. But let's hear yours."

"To begin with, MacAdams, your old buddy from Vietnam, has been squealing like a broken wheel bearing to save his own skin, I'm sure. Then there are a number of Pentagon brass who'll have their careers terminated if we can ever help the Justice Department put the pieces of this puzzle together."

"The State Department will be embarrassed too," Chuck said. "Once this fax from the Secretary of State is shown to the nation, more heads will roll."

"I was looking through your papers during the flight from Hong Kong," said Nicki. "Secretary Cosgrove's name was properly typed in, and it certainly was on official stationery. But the letter wasn't signed."

"No! But Nicki, you're right! I guess I was so out of it that night that I figured the signature just didn't copy."

"The Secretary's name was typed right below the closing. There wasn't even room for a signature. Congress would demand Cosgrove's resignation if he were to send you such a blatant fax without researching my background," Nicki said. "Even if he, personally, wants to get rid of me, the Secretary of State of the United States of America would never let Saddam do his dirty work for him, unless he could justify it to the public," she went on. "Think what fun the *Washington Post* would have with that one."

"Assuming I find a way to get that fax to the *Post* while I'm still alive, that is. Whoever composed it sure used overkill."

Nicki smiled. "It worked, lover. It scared you enough to rescue me from that jail in Hanoi. My cell smelled like the rhinoceros cage at the Boston Public Zoo!"

"That's the only reason you wanted out, I'm sure!"

((((

"Did you even get past the receptionist?" Chuck looked up from his task of trying to satisfy two babies at once with pacifiers.

He and Nicki had moved together to a room in Washington's Downtown Quality Hotel the day after they had flown from Hong Kong.

"I spoke with the great man himself."

"You're kidding!"

"Not kidding. I spent half an hour with one of his aides. He listened and I talked."

"Who wouldn't?" Chuck laughed. "You do have a way of holding a person's attention! But you said 'the man'? And the photocopies of our documents? Did you leave them with Chet Wood?"

Nicki's eyes danced with glee. "The papers were what did it. While I was being interviewed, a couple of researchers were studying them and making phone calls. Then they just cut the interview short—barged right in."

"You mean our documentation really grabbed them?"

"Sure did—your papers, plus the initial official confirmations Wood's people got from phone calls to the Pentagon and the State Department. Mr. Wood popped in with his research team. 'This is great stuff, Nicki,' he said. He wanted our phone number. Can you believe it?"

"And when you said we aren't staying two nights in a row in the same motel . . . ?"

"He wants me to phone him tomorrow at two."

"Then use a pay phone. Be sure it's several blocks from our motel." Chuck frowned. "If Chet Wood's aides make even half the phone calls they need to follow this up, the FBI is monitoring their lines already, trying to get leads to find us. Whoever has ordered us picked up will take this right down to the wire to keep us off the air."

21

More Iron Than Clay

The Spirit of God came upon Saul
when he heard this news,
and his anger was greatly aroused.

—Samuel

"Our guests tonight have an unusual story to tell," Chet Wood began. "Dr. Nicki Towns Reynolds was born Ngo Thieu in Vietnam, the daughter of an American veteran. Nicki believes she has information to give a new, troubling spin to the recent arrest of General Armstrong MacAdams, possibly amounting to a military conspiracy within our own Pentagon. The conspirators, she believes, have flaunted international treaties while creating weapons of mass destruction, all without authorization from the president or Congress. Yet these same people have covered up a spy ring selling plans for those weapons to the Russian Federation. All of this is being done in the name of keeping America the most powerful military machine on earth. Nicki is here with her husband, Chuck Reynolds."

◖◖◖

"Gramma! Grampa!" screeched Jennifer Reynolds. "It's Nicki! She's on TV."

Stan Basford dropped his *Belfast Journal* on the floor beside the kitchen rocker. Mae, her hands dripping from the dishpan, hurried after her husband. "Since we've had that cable hooked up, our granddaughter's been finding the oddest things on the tube," Stan grumbled.

"Why, it *is* Nicki, on *Chet Wood's World*," Mae said.

"And there's Daddy!" Jennifer squealed.

"Don't have time to write, and here they are on national television. Modern communications!" Mae sputtered.

◖◖◖

"There are several sinister twists to this tale," Chet continued. "These twists seem to involve espionage as well as repeated tries to assassinate the lovely young mother and her husband who are with me in this studio tonight."

Chet Wood was bearded and grandfatherly in an open, cable-knit cardigan sweater over a pastel shirt and suspenders. He paused for dramatic effect.

"Also," Chet went on, "waiting in a studio in Roswell, New Mexico, is Mrs. Alice Lewis, mother of twelve-year-old Marcie, who was killed two years ago during a top-secret but illegal U.S. Air Force military experiment at the White Sands Missile Range near Roswell. And by satellite from Bismarck, North Dakota, Eddie Chisholm, a young news reporter harassed and hounded by the FBI for years for trying to pass facts to the Associated Press about Marcie's strange death.

"Here with me in the studio as well is Senator Nate Greene, Chairman of the Senate Armed Services Committee. Senator Greene hails from North Carolina where, coincidentally, Mr.

Reynolds was also born. Senator Greene is named for his ancestor, General Nathaniel Greene, one of the great heroes of the American Revolution. There's an eerie twist here. More than two hundred years ago General Greene investigated espionage by the traitor General Benedict Arnold during the Revolution. This was our nation's first major case of espionage. Six generations later, General Greene's descendant, Senator Greene, is investigating espionage by another American general. And interestingly, Senator Greene and Chuck Reynolds both served their country in Vietnam under that man, General Armstrong MacAdams.

"My listeners are aware, of course, that MacAdams, a retired U.S. Air Force general, was arrested two weeks ago for selling American military secrets to the new regime in Russia. This story has unfolded as the most involved, most sensational case of espionage in half a century. Certainly nothing even close has surfaced since the Rosenberg spy scandal, fifty years ago.

"As most of my listeners also know," Chet added, "the Senate Armed Services Committee holds the purse strings to America's defense budget. As such, the Committee, as well as its chairman, Senator Greene, is keenly concerned that defense funds be spent only on projects authorized by Congress and the president. Senator Greene and his committee are in charge of investigating this case since it involves, directly or indirectly, serious misuse of defense funds. Would you start us off with a summary of that investigation, please, Senator?"

"Thank you, Chet. First, a new development. On orders of the Department of Defense, federal marshals this afternoon arrested a second Air Force general and two of his staff at the Pentagon. Simultaneously, at the J. Edgar Hoover Building in Washington, federal marshals, acting on orders from the Justice Department, picked up three high-ranking FBI officials. All six are being charged with high-level espionage. Some are charged with direct involvement, the others with cover-ups, including the attempted murder of Dr. Nicki Towns Reynolds. There is an irony to this story. As head of the Senate Armed Services Committee, I am ready this evening to unveil to the American public much of the very same information about top-secret military projects that was stolen by these internal spies. I do so with full cooperation of both the Secretary of Defense and the Chairman of the Joint Chiefs of Staff. Since our nation's enemies already know these facts, the only reason they are still kept under wraps is to enhance the vanity of a few men in high places in Washington."

"Wow!" Chet Wood said. "You're telling us that on my show you will pass out top-secret military information, like a circus clown tossing candy to kids?"

"That analogy is a bit extreme, though it may certainly seem that way to a few observers."

"Can you give us the names of those arrested this afternoon, Senator?"

"That's classified, for the time being."

"Are you playing games with us, Senator Greene?"

"Chet, we're giving you breaking news, so don't push for more than you're entitled to. Already you've scooped the *Washington Post* and the wire services," Greene snapped. "The Justice Department is withholding the names of the six arrested pending further investigation. I expect that the U.S. Attorney General will hold a news conference sometime tomorrow. Even the president doesn't yet know who they are."

"But you do?"

"Yes, Chet."

"All right, fit this into tonight's topic." Chet asked, "What does all this have to do with repeated attempts on the lives of Nicki and Chuck Reynolds, and with FBI attempts to arrest them? As recently as this morning, right here in Washington, they left their hotel only a dozen steps ahead of the FBI. When I heard about that one, I got the uncomfortable feeling that someone out there doesn't want my guests talking to the American people."

"Retired General Armstrong MacAdams was being fed top-secret information from inside the Pentagon," Greene went on. "The persons taken into custody today were part of this conspiracy.

MacAdams, in fact, was being bribed to keep his mouth shut about illegal atomic tests at the White Sands range in New Mexico, tests that violate international treaties signed in 1963 and 1968, including one dating back to the Kennedy Administration.

"Nicki Towns Reynolds, I have learned, was once part of an organization that had been gathering data on both the American military and on Saddam Hussein's operations in Iraq," Senator Greene told. "In the process, Nicki and her organization stumbled onto the MacAdams spy ring. Further, information originating with Nicki tipped off our Air Force two years ago," the senator continued. "Her observations, both in the U.S. and inside Iraq, were the basis of our strategic, B-52H strike against Saddam's Russian-built anthrax missile factory hidden beneath the ruins of Nineveh in northern Iraq."

"And the general who ordered that air strike? Is he the man you said was arrested today?" Chet quizzed.

"I can't answer that question." Senator Greene's face was impassive.

"I think it's time we introduced Nicki and Chuck Reynolds. Nicki, can you tell us about the bandages on your fingers? Hold them up to the camera."

"I'd like to unwrap one hand, Chet."

"Go ahead, if you don't mind."

Nicki displayed the fingers of her left hand. "I got these lacerations from a thin, nylon cord while rappelling four stories down from an infamous jail in Hanoi, Vietnam, last week. They've become infected because it was several days before I could get medical attention."

"That's terrible. What jail was that?"

"Vietnam veterans call it the 'Hanoi Hilton.' It's where North Vietnam kept American POWs during the war."

"Do I understand that you have some very intimate connections with Vietnam?"

"My husband, Chuck, is a veteran."

"Chuck, you were in the Army?"

"I was a chaplain, Chet."

"But there's more. After a station break and a word from our sponsors, we'll learn why Nicki was in prison in Hanoi. And why people in our own military have used both the FBI and the CIA to try to stop her. And there's a thread that goes all the way to Baghdad. Don't go away!"

◖◖◖

"Before our break, Nicki," said Chet, "you started to tell us about your ties with Vietnam?"

"Yes, Chet. I was born in former South Vietnam. My father was an American serviceman, an engineer responsible for building landing strips for the war effort. Before I was born he was killed by a Vietcong ambush, shortly after he married my Vietnamese mother in Saigon."

"During our break you told me that your father had an unusual heritage. Tell us about that."

"My dad was a naturalized American, born in Iraq."

"Iraq? A lot of Americans think that Iraqis are the bad guys."

"Like America, Chet, Iraq has a diversity of ethnic cultures. For instance, there are the Kurds . . ."

"We know about that. That's what the no-fly zone is all about, to keep Saddam from bombing the Kurds, right?"

"Right, Chet. There is also a substantial Jewish population in Baghdad. And there are Armenian Christians. My father's parents were Assyrians, displaced since Nebuchadnezzar overthrew Nineveh in 612 B.C. They have had a Christian heritage for some seventeen hundred years. My father watched his mother and sister cut to pieces by Iraqi machine-gun fire in an attack on their village in 1933."

"Thank you, Nicki. That's fascinating. We'll hear more from you later. Chuck, how did you and Nicki meet?"

"Well, Chet, I had just been brought in as chief of security at Salem Electronics North, a small electronics plant in Massachusetts, just outside Boston's so-called Silicon Beltway. We had a federal contract to manufacture several components for a top-secret missile project. It's cutting-edge military technology." Chuck shot a glance at Senator Greene.

"Just use good judgment, Chuck. Russia's Foreign Intelligence Service, the SVR, which replaced the old KGB, now knows all but the tiniest details about the Vanguard Missile at this point in time— thanks to General MacAdams and the people the United States Marshals' office arrested today."

"Here on my show! You guys are talking top military security like it was another game of golf," Chet chortled.

Senator Greene laughed nervously.

"Nicki is a nuclear physicist—she has a Ph.D. from MIT," Chuck continued. "My boss had just hired her, but we soon learned that she was walking off with our plans."

"Is that true, Nicki—you were stealing stuff?"

"Never did I take physical property. I stole ideas, memorized facts. Today I realize that stealing is stealing, period."

"We learned also that Nicki had held a series of jobs, all in plants with contracts to work on the same Vanguard Missile project. In a matter of months she had learned more about this missile system than our own engineers knew."

"That's unbelievable!"

"I disagree, Chet. It is very believable." Greene was now speaking. "Ethel Rosenberg's brother, with far less education than Nicki, in 1945 memorized the details of the atomic bomb being created during World War II at America's Manhattan Project in New Mexico. The Rosenbergs later passed this data on to the Russians. But I should tell you this . . ."

"What's that, Senator?" Chet cut in.

"The Vanguard Missile, which Nicki Reynolds was in the process of stealing when she had to flee for her life, was used two years ago by our Navy to shoot Saddam's anthrax missile out of the sky over Lake Michigan, thanks to a tip-off from Nicki and her husband. Six million men, women, and children in Chicago can probably thank Nicki and Chuck that they are alive today. Yet certain elements in our government wish to ship her to Baghdad to be executed."

"I can't believe you're telling this on national television, on my show, Senator. Go on. Why does Saddam want to kill Nicki? She looks like a nice lady to me. I wouldn't be afraid to have her as a neighbor, would you?"

"Saddam's official reason is that she supposedly murdered his top military adviser, General Rahman, former head of his Republican Guard. This allegedly took place about four years ago in Nairobi, Africa."

"That *would* make him mad," Chet chuckled. "But if the murder took place in Nairobi, why isn't the government of Kenya trying to prosecute her?"

"Good question. There's a question as to whether she ever killed the man. More importantly, Nicki's activities uncovered a web of Iraqi spies working here in the United States. That's why Saddam wants her dead, Chet."

"Now that the whole world knows, maybe you've defused things."

"That's part of my reason for agreeing to appear on this show— to stop this insane prosecution and persecution of loyal Americans. Several levels of American law enforcement have been used for more than two years in attempts to hand Nicki over to Saddam's executioners. Her husband, Chuck, has been a target, as well."

"But you said Nicki's a spy, and she's admitted to spying. Nicki, tell us how you became involved in espionage."

"First of all, Chet, neither I nor any member of my organization has ever passed any data we became privy to over to a foreign government. Second, most of what we know comes from legitimate sources. We learned of probable experiments with the neutron bomb, for instance, when the Pentagon ordered thousands of air-cooled truck engines with breaker-point distributors, as well as an equal number of very expensive dry-cell automotive batteries."

"Neutron bomb!" Chet rolled the term over his tongue and leaned toward the camera. He stroked his beard and appeared shocked. "Even I know that those things are supposed to fry the circuits in all electronic ignitions that have been used in cars and trucks for the past quarter century—American built, Japanese, European too. Ordering engines with antiquated ignition distributors for military use should have raised some eyebrows in the media."

Nicki grinned. "Even an ordinary consumer journal like *Popular Science* can publish stuff like that—and they do so regularly. Yet it's considered treason for someone inside the government to leak it out, stuff that's all over the Internet web sites—on *Yahoo!*, *America Online*—you name it."

"So what organization are we talking about here?" Chet quizzed. "Something like the Michigan Minutemen that the FBI is trying to blame for that attack on Chicago? It's my belief that if the Minutemen had done it, they'd have made some arrests two years ago. Even I can see that there's a smoke screen here thicker than the fog off of Lake Michigan!"

"CALF," said Nicki. "The acronym stands for Contemporary Assyrian Liberation Front. I was once their top operative, though I've since quit CALF. Without my help, it's little more than an Assyrian social club."

"CALF? As in baby bull, right? I've had my secretary confirm that you have one of those symbols tattooed over your heart. I guess it's pretty neat—an ancient Assyrian winged bull. So there are Assyrians living in America?"

"You bet there are, Chet! About a million of us. There's a large concentration in Chicago."

"Wow! No wonder Saddam chose Chicago to test his anthrax missile. Go on."

"CALF managed to get inside Saddam's American organization. Since our ancestry is Middle-Eastern and some of us speak Arabic, several of our members simply pretended to be Iraqi sympathizers."

"What did CALF learn?"

"That Saddam's agents are here to spy on Russia's SVR espionage agents in America. The Iraqis run sort of a product-control operation. Like stealing-to-order," Nicki explained.

"Car thieves do it all the time." Chet shrugged. "They line up a customer, who picks the make and model he wants right out of a dealer's showroom."

"CALF has learned that Iraq is one of Russia's prime customers for military designs—designs stolen directly from American industry. The Iraqis aren't well enough established in the United States to conduct their own espionage, so they use the Russians, who've been stealing American secrets for more than half a century. So Saddam's people simply try to keep tabs on the Russians," Nicki added.

"CALF is a small, underground Assyrian patriotic organization of only several hundred members. They are dedicated to overthrowing Saddam's government and reestablishing Assyria as a nation, possibly with the cooperation of the Kurds," she summed up. "CALF is pro-Israel. They believe fervently in Isaiah's prophecy that Assyria will one day rise as a pro-Israel nation. That's chapter nineteen, verses twenty-three through twenty-five."

"A Bible angle, eh?" said Chet. "Well, this brings us to the General Armstrong MacAdams connection. Can you fill us in on that, Senator?"

"Sure. MacAdams passed on to Russians, under the control of former Soviet KGB head Yevgeny Primakov, who was at that time Russian Foreign Minister and more recently Prime Minister, details about the *Centurion* nuclear submarine, our nation's stellar, and until today, top-secret defense weapon. It was Primakov, with the help of former Soviet Premier Mikhail Gorbachev, who caused the executions of a dozen American CIA agents after their names were given him by CIA spy Aldrich Ames, who is now serving life in prison.

"The U.S.S *Centurion* was completed several years ahead of schedule in the Groton, Connecticut, shipyards," Greene went on. "It was towed up the St. Lawrence River, through the Great Lakes, and into Lake Michigan while disguised as an older-model sub, bearing the name and serial number of a sub that had been scrapped. The *Centurion* was outfitted in a secret facility adjacent to the Great Lakes Naval Station north of Chicago," Senator Greene revealed.

"So it's no longer a secret. But why Lake Michigan?" Chet asked.

"Hiding the *Centurion* in the big lake was part of the strategy of keeping it out of sight of the Russians," Senator Greene explained. "Our submarine fleet has played cat and mouse with the Russian fleet on the world's oceans almost since the end of World War II. That game did not diminish with the collapse of the Soviet Union and the supposed end of the Cold War a decade ago. At least one of our submarines officially lost at sea may actually have been torpedoed in the Atlantic by a Soviet sub.

"The Russians learned of the *Centurion's* existence from General MacAdams about three years ago. The American public is learning of the *Centurion* even as I speak. If that sounds cryptic, recall that Russian dictator Stalin knew about the Manhattan Project and our first atomic test in March 1945 before President Truman learned of it in July. Two years ago, when the *Centurion's* neutron-tipped SAM— Surface to Air Missile—the Vanguard, was used to knock Saddam's missile down over Lake Michigan, the Navy continued to deny its existence. When the *Chicago Tribune* found witnesses who saw two rockets fired, the Pentagon cried 'conspiracy hysteria.'"

"How did the Pentagon learn of the planned attack on Chicago in time to counterattack?" Chet wondered.

"That's a story in itself." Greene waved a handful of fax documents in front of the TV camera. "Even I was not aware of these until you phoned my office a few days ago. A week before the attack, the Pentagon and the State Department received these fax letters, sent from Montreal by Chuck Reynolds, detailing a plan to bring an Iraqi missile into Maine in a load of smuggled marijuana from Turkey. Two elderly former Nazi SS officers who have gotten rich shipping drugs into the United States helped set this up. But the official Pentagon reaction was disbelief and denial.

"Though even the United States Coast Guard admits that America's coastlines are as porous as a sieve, our top military brass simply could not bring themselves to believe that Saddam would have the gall to use such a mundane means to import a powerful, deadly weapon of mass destruction," Senator Greene added. "The notion of attacking Chicago from the back of an oversized pickup truck seemed ludicrous to the Pentagon and the CIA. As a further attempt to rub American noses in the dirt, the missile was equipped with an American-built military surplus launching pad purchased from a warehouse in Bangor, Maine, it has since been learned."

"You've got to be kidding, Senator!" Chet paused. "Is there something in the fact that the bearer of bad tidings was a lowly civilian, and not an official source, like the CIA?"

"Nothing brings out the insecurity and egotism in a public official who's been at his job too long than helpful interference by the people he's sworn to serve. You're certainly right, Chet."

"So this evening the American people are learning a military secret that the Russians have known for three years. Is that correct, Senator Greene?"

"Yes, it is. It's pointless to hide from American taxpayers—my constituents in North Carolina—what Moscow and Baghdad know about already. Some of this rises to the level of arrogant professional elitism, an attitude that says, 'I'm better and more powerful than you common folks because I know stuff you don't.'"

"Sort of like the twelve-year-old who lords it over his nine-year-old kid brother because he knows the facts of life." Chet chuckled. "Maybe some of us really were found under a cabbage leaf in Mama's garden!"

"But to give the devil his due," said Greene, "when MacAdams learned from Chuck Reynolds about the attack on Chicago just before it occurred—or more specifically, when Nicki threatened to expose MacAdams—he became frightened and got on the phone and tipped the Pentagon off. They believed him, fortunately. They called the *Centurion's* captain and put him on alert. Then they followed up days later by bombing Saddam's anthrax plant."

"It would seem that the Pentagon finally got the message," Chet mused. "Nicki, you take the story from here."

"First, Chet, let me digress," said Nicki. "I think it's been implied that I oppose both the testing of the neutron bomb and the development of the U.S.S. *Centurion* as a water-based antiballistic missile launch pad. In fact, as a scientist and a Christian concerned about the security of her nation, I oppose neither."

"My apologies," Chet said. "I may have misstated the case when I introduced you. Please go on."

"My concerns are, first, that the neutron bomb test at White Sands was a violation of a nuclear test ban treaty signed by President Kennedy and Nikita Khrushchev, head of the old Soviet Union, right after the 1963 Cuban Missile Crisis. My own feeling is that we should void that outdated treaty by first telling the Russians what our intentions are. Then we could conduct responsible testing of this new, controlled-radiation weapon. A little girl was killed in the White Sands test two years ago because it was conducted hastily, illegally, and irresponsibly to keep Congress, the president, and even the Secretary of Defense in the dark."

"That's quite a revelation, Doctor Nicki Reynolds! Continue, please." Chet was amazed.

"Secondly," Nicki said, "the Vanguard Missile, as it is now deployed, using the *Centurion* as its underwater launching pad, is also illegal—it is a violation of the 1972 ABM—Anti-Ballistic Missile Treaty—signed by President Nixon and Soviet head Leonid Brezhnev. Again, I'm in favor of the Vanguard and the U.S.S. *Centurion*. But our president and Congress need to come clean. There is legal provision to void this old treaty by a unilateral, six-months' notice."

Nicki smiled. "Now back to your original question as to why I have been the subject of an international manhunt by the FBI and the CIA. Within weeks after Chuck and I tipped MacAdams off about the anthrax attack, Chet, I was shot at in Maine by an Iraqi assassin. So we fled to Vietnam, where we enjoyed nearly two years of peace and quiet. Then an official in Hanoi figured out—I'm

certain from official papers I signed as the investor in a small pros-
theses business there—that I was wanted in Iraq for an alleged
murder in Kenya. My husband faxed the U.S. State Department the
day I was taken to prison. Here is their reply." Nicki passed Chet
the fax.

"It's unsigned!"

"No kidding, Chet," Nicki chuckled.

"Let me see that!" Senator Greene took the document from
Chet Wood. He frowned, quickly reading the fax. "I can assure you
that Secretary of State Cosgrove knows nothing of this—it's not his
style. A reply such as this on the Secretary's stationery is a federal
offense. Whoever sent this fax was blatantly passing Nicki off to the
Iraqi executioners, not expecting that it would ever get back to
Washington," the Senator concluded.

"Chuck, you had phoned MacAdams once before, right after
you learned of Nicki's theft of sensitive data from your plant?"

"I had. I was attacked in Tucson right after my phone call to
MacAdams, whom I'd considered a friend since the days when I
served as his chaplain in Vietnam. It was not until later that I
learned he was involved in espionage."

"I can supply the details on that episode too," said Greene.
"When MacAdams learned from Chuck during an in-flight phone
conversation between Boston and Tucson that CALF's operatives,
through Nicki, had assembled all the plans to the Centurion's
guided missile system, MacAdams panicked. He tried to have
Chuck killed in the Tucson air terminal by using an Iraqi assailant.
When the assassination failed, he tried something else—by using
his Pentagon connections to pull strings in the FBI, MacAdams was
able to have a satellite transmitter sewn into Chuck's body. You see,
MacAdams was in a position to intimidate Pentagon brass by
threatening to use the media to expose their plans to detonate a
neutron bomb without authorization by Congress or the White
House."

"But Chuck and Nicki tell me they believe it was the Iraqis
who tried to bump them off." Chet was puzzled.

Chuck appeared shocked. Was Armstrong MacAdams another Aldrich Ames?

Nicki was aghast. The man her husband once trusted was more evil than she had imagined.

"They worked together," Senator Greene continued. "FBI agents—whom we now have in custody—used an unlicensed surgeon to get the bug into Mr. Reynolds's body. Then they passed this information over to MacAdams, who notified the Iraqis to take the dirty work from there.

"It seems that Iraq owns a satellite that it purchased from China. Spying on American citizens is apparently its primary use," Greene told. "There are an unknown number of Americans whose automobiles, purses, clothing, or even persons are right now infected with these bugs so that they can be tracked from Baghdad anywhere they may travel. Many of these folks infected with Saddam's electronic bugs are public officials—senators, top-level military leaders. Others are corporation CEOs. While our CIA has been busy in espionage operations throughout the world, on the home front we have developed feet of clay ready to crumble."

"Senator!" Chuck could scarcely contain his excitement. "That quote from the prophet Daniel—Nicki has used it often to explain America's military and moral predicament! I'd like to add something that I think is pertinent, Chet."

"Go ahead, Chuck."

"Since leaving CALF, Nicki has put feet to her newfound Christian faith. Her focus for the past several months has been establishing a factory in Vietnam to manufacture artificial feet, the Jaipur Foot. Thousands of Vietnamese farmers have lost both their health and their livelihoods by having body parts blown off by land mines planted by several armies twenty-five to forty years ago. She also invested fifty-thousand dollars of her own money in this project."

"And the government of Vietnam tried to turn her over to Saddam Hussein!" Chet shook his head. "We've got to take a station break now," he said. "When we come back, we shall bring on a couple of folks who became intimately, tragically involved in an illegal experiment conducted at the orders of one of our military leaders. Thankfully, the man responsible is now facing court-martial and criminal charges. Don't go away."

◖◖◖

"At this juncture," said Chet, "those of you who have young children watching may wish to send them to bed. What happened to Marcie Lewis could cause severe emotional trauma."

Chet now turned to the TV screen opposite him in the studio. "Alice Lewis is the mother of twelve-year-old Marcie, who died near her ranch home outside Roswell, New Mexico, two years ago. Tell us what you noticed about Marcie that terrible day when her grandfather carried her body into the ranch house, Mrs. Lewis."

"She was bloated, like she'd been dead for days, though she had been out of her grandfather's sight only a few minutes. And she had burns all over her body."

"Was her hair burned off?"

"No. That really scared me. Of course I was very upset. But to see my daughter's body mutilated in such a way. If she'd fallen into a fire, her hair would have been gone and her clothes would have been burned." Mrs. Lewis stopped to dry her tears.

"Even after two years I'm sure it's very painful." Chet paused. "Your family has seen strange deaths before, haven't they?"

"Zeke Lewis, my husband's father—he's the grandfather who brought Marcie home—he died two days later of a stroke, and I'm sure it was the stress of that experience that brought it on. Well, Zeke, he saw that famous UFO in 1947 immediately after it crashed near Roswell. He didn't talk about it much, Chet."

"But there came a time when he told you and your husband about what happened to him. Zeke had once told a local news reporter what he'd seen, something like that?"

"Zeke told a reporter that the flying saucer was an Army Air Force experimental plane. The pilot and copilot were Japanese. Prisoners, he believed."

"How did Zeke know they were Japanese?"

"Zeke spent several years in the Pacific during World War II. He had seen plenty of captured Japanese before."

"So Zeke would have recognized a Japanese pilot?"

"Oh yes, Chet."

"After the paper published Zeke's story, what happened to Zeke?"

"The Army Air Corps sent MPs to pick him up. He was held several days without sleep. Brainwashed and threatened. Told that they were curing him of a dreadful mental illness."

"Mrs. Lewis, did anything like this happen after Marcie's death?"

"It certainly did. We got letters and phone calls from government lawyers threatening to prosecute us for breaking a hole in the fence separating our ranch from the missile range, even though everybody knew it fell over in a gully washer. The IRS audited our books and nearly ruined my husband's cattle business. They demanded to see all our business receipts for the past seven years."

"Tell us about the day the coroner came to the house with Marcie's death certificate, Mrs. Lewis."

"Well, he brought two New Mexico state troopers with him. They drove into our yard with their lights flashing, like there was a crime in progress. My husband asked the cops what they wanted. They said they'd come along to protect the coroner, since we had threatened to shoot any public official on sight."

"Had you made any threats?"

"Of course not! The only thing my husband ever threatened was a coyote bothering the calves."

"So the coroner came in. And the cops. He showed you the death certificate and asked you to do what?"

"To sign. The certificate said that Marcie died of solar radiation and sunstroke. That girl was *not* sunburned, Chet. I saw her myself—we're talking about my daughter. She had been scorched and blistered in places where she was fully clothed. So I refused to sign. So did my husband."

"And?"

"They said there'd be an investigation."

"That sounds like a threat to me. Did you sign?"

"Yes. We had no choice. And something else was strange, Chet."

"What's that, Mrs. Lewis?"

"It was the Chaves County coroner that came to the house with the cops, not the Socorro County coroner who actually took Marcie's body away."

"Mrs. Lewis, I spoke with the New Mexico Department of Public Health on the phone this morning. They told me that there is no way a coroner would ask the next of kin to sign a death certificate. The coroner is supposed to sign, not a family member. And ordinarily he would simply mail it."

Chet faced the camera. "When we come back, a news reporter will tell his surprising account of what he learned at the Lewis ranch. Don't go away."

◖◖◖

"Eddie Chisholm was once the bureau chief for the Perro Prieta office of the *Roswell Daily News*. Perro Prieta is the village nearest the Lewis ranch," Chet began.

"Eddie was also a stringer for the Associated Press. Yet he has spent the last two years as a day laborer. Only a month ago did Eddie finally land another reporting job, at a small weekly in rural North Dakota. An editor there saw Eddie's potential and was willing to hire a young man with an employment record that included allegations of irresponsible work habits and manufactured stories sold as fact. Eddie, is it likely that the AP will ever buy a story from you again?"

"Not unless bananas grow in North Dakota, Chet."

"Why not, Eddie?"

"I'm a liar. That's what the Socorro County medical examiner and the FBI told my former editor at the *Roswell Daily News*."

"Wait a minute, Eddie. You said *Socorro* County medical examiner. But Mrs. Lewis said it was the Chaves County examiner, whose office is in Roswell, who furnished the official report on Marcie Lewis's cause of death."

"The section of White Sands Missile Range where Marcie Lewis died is in Socorro County, Chet. So her body was initially sent to that county's office for an autopsy. About the time I wrote my article for AP, Marcie's body was seized by the FBI and held in cold storage for a while. Somebody in authority was unhappy with the first autopsy, so her body was shipped to the Chaves County examiner. His office is in Roswell. Coincidentally, the FBI branch office for southeastern New Mexico is in the same building."

"How did Marcie Lewis die, according to the Socorro County examiner?"

"By a massive dose of atomic radiation, Chet."

"What else did you learn about the Lewis girl's death?"

"I spoke with her grandfather just before he died. He was hospitalized with a stroke and barely coherent. He said cows died and bloated instantly from the same cause that killed his granddaughter. They swelled up suddenly, like corn in a popper, he said. Zeke had climbed down into an old silver mine shaft. From there he saw the flash, so he was not burned."

"Go on. What else, Eddie?"

"Zeke Lewis drove his truck toward home until the motor seized up. Then he carried Marcie's body the rest of the way in the hot sun."

"But if this was a neutron bomb explosion, like we've heard today, it would have instantly fried the electronic circuits of a pickup truck and made it inoperable. Or so I've been led to believe."

"I saw the truck before the FBI confiscated it, Chet. It was a 1972 Ford, so it had the old-style ignition. Zeke Lewis was able to drive it for several miles until it died with an overheated motor."

"What caused it to overheat, Eddie?"

"The radiator. Every single tube was ruptured. I've never seen anything like it."

"Nicki, as a nuclear physicist, give me your take on this."

"Chet, everything Mrs. Lewis and Eddie Chisholm have described is consistent with a neutron blast. A neutron bomb will seek hydrogen as it explodes. Human bodies and cow bodies are mostly water, and radiator fluid is mostly water. Water is mostly hydrogen. Eddie's deduction about the '72 Ford's ignition is also correct. That explains why the U.S. Army is buying old-style ignition systems to retrofit its equipment. The military needs to protect itself against electromagnetic pulse, or EMP, from its own weapons. EMP is a side effect of all atomic explosions, of course.

"But there is another, sinister, side to all this," Nicki added. "CALF has learned that the air-cooled motors and dry-cell batteries the Pentagon has ordered will fit several thousand American-made trucks that we sold to Russia, but which the Russian military has resold to China."

"So we zap the Chinese with a neutron bomb, then grab our trucks back—speaking of cute tricks!" Chet chuckled. "But where does that leave our military in regard to several nuclear nonproliferation treaties signed by several of our presidents over the past forty years, which Nicki mentioned earlier in this show? Senator Greene, you get the last word tonight."

"This was done without the president's knowledge, or mine, Chet. The Secretary of Defense and the Chairman of the Joint Chiefs of Staff were also appalled at what has gone on behind their backs. The arrests of today, if they result in court-martials, will determine whether America shall be run as a government of the people or be governed by tyrants who wish to build an empire. It is very important, Chet, that we understand that there's a difference between keeping America's defenses strong, as with the U.S.S. *Centurion* submarine, which I support; and arbitrary violations of international treaties, which I do not support."

"Thank you, Senator. For Satellite News Network, this is Chet Wood. Good night."

((((

Faisal al-Pasha peered down the long row of two hundred computer screens that glowed in his bunker five floors below Baghdad's central square. Each tube bore a map of a state, a region, or a city in Israel, England, or North America. Crimson crescent moons stood out like bloody scimitars from each map.

Al-Pasha smiled, overseeing the task as his team tracked the Great Satan. As al-Pasha watched, one of his computer operators from time to time would tap a button to switch his screen to a map of another part of the globe or for a close-up of the region already on the screen.

Al-Pasha now grinned broadly, peering at his own screen. It was a hologram of the White House in Washington. A red crescent, labeled "#1" moved from behind a long desk shape in the Oval Office. A second red crescent, labeled "#4" moved to meet it. The moons seemed to touch, then crescent "#1" moved back behind the desk shape as crescent "#4" remained stationary.

Al-Pasha frowned, noting the time on his screen. It was after three A.M. in Washington. He picked up a royal blue telephone and waited. "I wish to speak with His Excellency, President Saddam Hussein," he said after some moments.

Al-Pasha scowled in rage, listening. He cursed profusely in Arabic. "And I have *my* orders. Get His Excellency on the phone!"

((((

Commander John H. Watson stood watching the radar screens in the missile control center of the U.S.S. *Centurion*. "What's the word from the Coast Guard?" he asked a radio operator.

"All clear, sir. The Coast Guard station in Garfield City reports that all boats within a hundred miles have left the area."

"Thanks."

"Washington on the line, sir."

"I'll take it!" Watson barked. The commander gazed for a moment at the radar screens. They were tracking a target drifting high in space in the night sky, some forty-five degrees above the northern horizon. "We're ready to do it, Mr. President," he said as he watched.

"Fire," the commander pronounced quietly while still on the phone with the Commander-in-Chief. He spoke the word without emotion, peering intently at the target on the screen as the president waited. Firing the first shot in what could turn into World War III was not an action Watson took lightly. As Commander Watson watched, the target simply disappeared from the screen.

"It's done, Mr. President." Watson paused. "Thank you, sir." He hung the phone up.

"Retract laser gun," Watson ordered.

Midway on the black, open deck of the U.S.S. *Centurion*, which now rode nearly submerged, a fat, conical, rocket-shaped device tipped with a pyramid of open stainless steel beams surrounding a large, concave mirror pointed skyward. This laser gun, which used deuterium, nitrogen trifluoride, helium, and hydrogen to produce a cascade of amplified photons, could—shooting at the speed of light—explode any satellite or spacecraft in the Western hemisphere. The touch of a button in the submarine's missile control center would wipe out enemy reconnaissance or an incoming ICBM—Intercontinental Ballistic Missile—in an instant without so much as a whimper of warfare being heard on earth. The big assembly now slid on its hydraulically operated brackets back into the bowels of the nuclear sub.

"Dive," said Commander Watson. "Back to home port."

"Aye, aye, sir!"

◖◖◖

Heinrich van Oosterhaus stepped onto his fourteenth-floor balcony at Garfield Towers Retirement Apartments to catch his breath. At after three in the morning he had been taken with a coughing fit, and though the autumn breeze off Lake Michigan was sharp, the fresh air made van Oosterhaus feel better. He grasped the railing and clutched his robe, peering through his bifocals at the distant glow of Milwaukee on the western horizon.

A thin, red line darted across the elderly man's vision on a diagonal. It seemed to leap from the black lake and terminate in a star, far to the northwest. The star twinkled once, and it was gone.

Van Oosterhaus shuffled inside and slid the glass door shut.

"You OK, Henry?" Martha van Oosterhaus stirred in bed when she heard the door latch click.

"Yeah." Heinrich coughed and cleared his throat. "But I'm seeing things."

"What?"

"A red line. I saw just one. It disappeared so quick, I'm not sure if I really even saw it."

Martha sat up and switched on the light. She picked up the bedside phone. "I'm calling Parkview Hospital for an ambulance. You're having a stroke, Henry."

◖◖◖

Faisal al-Pasha's knees turned to jelly and he was forced to steady himself on the back of a chair. He had never before seen His Excellency Saddam Hussein, except on a TV screen. But the stocky man with the bushy mustache and emotionless round face who stood next to al-Pasha now certainly *looked* like Saddam. Faisal al-Pasha right now wished for all the world that he had not had to make that phone call ten minutes earlier.

"The red moons—they are all gone, Your Excellency." Al-Pasha tapped the computer screen with a nervous finger. "The President of the United States was *right there* a moment ago, talking with his Secretary of State, Harold O. Cosgrove, and it is the middle of the night in the States. But now we seem to have lost our satellite, Your Excellency," al-Pasha moaned.

"Or else our Syrian dry cleaner in Washington forgot to mend the president's suit again." Saddam chuckled at his own dry joke.

He could see as well as al-Pasha that there were no red crescents on the other screens either.

The chatter of a fax machine caused both men to turn to the center of the room. An aide grabbed the fax as soon as it dropped out. He glanced at the English-language text, then passed it to Hussein. "Shall I translate it, Your Excellency?"

"I read English," Saddam growled.

The paper bore the Great Seal and signature of the President of the United States of America.

◖◖◖

The red-eye flight out of Washington's Ronald Reagan National Airport droned northeast toward Boston. Chuck, unable to sleep, slid a window shade open and peered eastward, where the stars twinkled in a cloudless sky above the sea.

"What do you see, honey?" Nicki crowded Chuck's shoulder for a better look.

"The moon." Chuck pointed to a deep orange crescent low in the east, rising over the night Atlantic's leaden sheen.

Nicki watched for a moment, remembering. "I saw a red moon once in Africa. Red dust, I'm sure. But all I could think about then was that something violent was about to occur."

"And it did."

"Yes. That's why we've been running from the Iraqis for three years."

"It's over now." Chuck squeezed Nicki, then plucked Carly's hand from its infant grasp of her mother's bosom and kissed the tiny fingers.

"Let's move across the aisle," Nicki suggested moments later. "Then we can tip back and sleep without bothering anyone."

Chuck surveyed the empty seats in the half-filled plane. A child, who had been squirming in a row by himself, had moved ahead with his mother. Two full rows were now empty. "Good deal!" Chuck whispered. He shouldered Nicholas, and Nicki slid out with Carly, then waited for her husband to take the window seat on the left.

"You're restless, Chuck," Nicki murmured some time later. "Must be something about this row of seats." She giggled quietly and nodded toward where the former occupant slumbered on his mother's lap.

"I *have* been asleep, I guess." Chuck shot a glance across the aisle, where he had left the shade up. The crescent moon had risen where he could no longer see it.

He slid open the shade next to his head, peering inland to the west. "There's a satellite," he muttered, more or less to relieve his nervous boredom.

"Somebody up there's watching us," Nicki laughed. She squeezed close to see.

"Very funny!" Chuck paused. Then his mouth fell open. "Holy cow!"

"That satellite—it simply exploded!" said Nicki. "Oh, Chuck, you don't suppose?"

"Yes, I do suppose," Chuck said, calmer now. "I had a chat with Senator Greene after the show. The U.S.S. *Centurion* is the only submarine built with the capability to knock a satellite out of its orbit in the sky. That new sub can, from Lake Michigan, easily eliminate any enemy satellite over the Western hemisphere with its cutting-edge laser gun, Nicki."

☾☾☾

"Let's find out what they're saying about us, Nicki." It was near dawn, and Chuck paused at an all-night newsstand near the entrance to a restaurant in Boston's Logan International Airport. A pile of early edition *Boston Globe* newspapers had caught his eye.

"Sure. Buy one," Nicki yawned. "If you can bring our bags, I'll tote the twins inside and find us a seat."

"Senator Greene got the limelight. You're not even mentioned." Chuck was plainly disappointed. "And here's an unusual article: 'The president called a surprise news conference at 4 A.M. Eastern time today to announce that the Navy's new laser weapon exploded Iraq's only satellite during the night. The president told media representatives that the Chinese-made satellite's only purpose was spying on the United States, Israel, and the United Kingdom. Radio transmitters linked to Iraq's spy satellite have already been discovered planted on the persons of numerous governmental officials. The Chief Executive refused to divulge names of public officials successfully bugged by Iraqi agents in the U.S., however,'" Chuck read aloud.

"What's that about treaties being voided?" Nicki asked, almost in awe.

"It says that the president will ask Congress to 'immediately renounce the 1972 Anti-Ballistic Missile Treaty, under provisions of the treaty's Article XV,'" Chuck read. "The writer calls the 1972 treaty 'antiquated' and 'a threat to American security' by 'casting a wet blanket over American engineers' aspirations to develop adequate SDI/strategic defense initiative systems in the face of growing worldwide dangers. The SDI concept was pushed by President Ronald Reagan, though ridiculed as science fiction "Star Wars" by Reagan's detractors,' this article says, Nicki. And look at this—the president wants to scrap the 1963 nuclear test ban treaty too. But he expressed 'cautious optimism' that 'a balance can be found that will permit America to defend itself against terrorists and rogue nations' without once again reverting to the Cold War arms race," Chuck reported.

"Chuck!" Nicki squealed so loudly in her surprise that a couple at the next table stopped eating to stare.

Chuck turned to the back page, then passed the paper to Nicki. "MacAdams Kills Self," read the headline. Two terse paragraphs told how U.S. Air Force General Armstrong MacAdams, a twice-decorated Vietnam War veteran, had hanged himself in his cell. MacAdams feared facing public humiliation at his upcoming trial for selling American military secrets to agents of the Russian Federation, the article said.

"He was once my friend," Chuck remarked.

"That's past tense," said Nicki. She was silent for some moments. "God vindicates His own," she added quietly. "And He does it in ways to show that He, not we, bear the glory."

((((

"You're not going to believe this, lover!" The turbo-prop flight from Boston to Belfast's Mid-Coastal Regional Airport had taken just under an hour. The rising sun outlined trees, houses, grazing Holsteins, automobiles, fishing boats riding at anchor, and people as the plane wheeled over the control tower, then banked to square away for the runway. Nicki shook Chuck awake. "Look!"

Chuck peered out. Stan Basford's old pickup was parked on the runway, next to the hangar and small ticket office. Two Waldo County Sheriff Patrol cars were also parked there, and the deputies had roped off the area.

Jennifer stood in the truck bed, waving and screaming and doing a cheerleading dance.

Crowded next to the fence was the band from Belfast Regional High School in its blue-and-white uniforms. Pastor Evans of the Community Church, lean and bearded, stood with the high school principal and several members of Evans' congregation from South Freedom.

Three TV sound trucks, cameras and reporters ready to pounce, stood to one side.

Chuck shook his head in disbelief.

Nicki clutched his arm.

The twins began to stir and fuss.

"The Iraqis would be easier to deal with than this, darling," Chuck laughed. He kissed Nicki as the plane touched down.

Nicki was crying as she hugged Chuck and the babies. Chuck found himself crying too.